P9-CFV-945

Praise for
STEPHEN HORN
and
LAW OF GRAVITY

"A riveting tale of suspense and intrigue. Stephen Horn has written another must-read. Find a comfortable chair and plan to stay up late."
Sheldon Siegel, author of *Criminal Intent*

"Memorable characters, a wonderfully labyrinthine plot, and a genuinely surprising ending."
Booklist (*Starred Review*)

"An incisive look at power and betrayal . . . Horn carefully inserts just enough about politics and the law to jump-start the plot so that he can concentrate on sculpting fully fleshed-out characters."
Ft. Lauderdale Sun-Sentinel

"A big picture Washington thriller juiced within an inch of its vastly entertaining life."
Kirkus Reviews

"Horn is a master of the small and telling twist."
Publishers Weekly

"Scratch a lawyer in Washington and you'll find a writer. It could take a lot of digging, however, to find another Stephen Horn."
Washington Times

And resounding praise for Stephen Horn's
sensational *New York Times* bestseller
IN HER DEFENSE

"A solid, winning debut . . . Stephen Horn has proven
that he can write courtroom intrigue with the best of
them. Cleverly conceived and executed, the story keeps
you firmly in its grip from start to finish."
Clive Cussler

"Dizzying . . . witty, hard-boiled writing and a twisted
little tornado of a plot . . . the kind of read from which
I could not be interrupted by man or beast."
Newsday

"Amazing . . . a legal thriller that easily keeps pace
with the works of Scott Turow and John Grisham."
Library Journal

"Horn does a terrific job . . . Pitch-perfect on the
pretrial courtroom action, trial scenes, and the thrill
of competition that drives so many legal eagles."
New York Post

"Crisp, intriguing . . . fresh and original . . . intelligent
storytelling . . . eminently satisfying."
Publishers Weekly (*Starred Review*)

"Great fun, a legal thriller with real surprises."
Phillip Margolin

Also by Stephen Horn

IN HER DEFENSE

STEPHEN HORN

LAW OF GRAVITY

HarperTorch
An Imprint of HarperCollinsPublishers

This is a work of fiction. Names, characters, places, and incidents are products of the author's imagination or are used fictitiously and are not to be construed as real. Any resemblance to actual events, locales, organizations, or persons, living or dead, is entirely coincidental.

HARPERTORCH
An Imprint of HarperCollins*Publishers*
10 East 53rd Street
New York, New York 10022-5299

First HarperTorch paperback printing: May 2003
First HarperCollins hardcover printing: July 2002

HarperCollins®, HarperTorch™, and ❦™ are trademarks of Harper-Collins Publishers Inc.

Printed in the United States of America

Visit HarperTorch on the World Wide Web at www.harpercollins.com

10 9 8 7 6 5 4 3 2 1

For Caitlin and Ben,
whose stories are only beginning

LAW
OF
GRAVITY

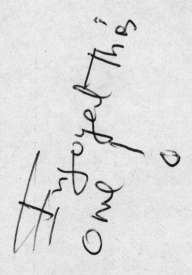

PROLOGUE

The Bronx, 1955:
The Start of the Investigation

A RADIO ON A WINDOWSILL was struck first, followed by a clothesline, which snagged a flower pot, then a mop from a fire escape. The heavier objects accelerated with her in gravity's pull, while sheets, towels, and underwear followed as if a tail on a plummeting kite, then a shroud.

A scout car arrived after daylight, and soon the street was closed and the curious were confined beyond the sawhorses across Morris Avenue. The patrolmen rendered their report to a sergeant. Police photographers captured the scene. The medical examiner peered under the sheet. The building's tenants watched the show from their windows, craning their necks left, right, up and down, silently engaged in a process of elimination.

A detective in a raincoat and fedora stared past the protruding heads toward the roof six stories above. The heads stared back. Then the medical examiner beckoned and the detective stuffed his notebook into his jacket and walked around the sheet, stepping over the red rivulets that flowed toward the drain in the concrete square. The detective's jaw was set. Sometimes he resented all the infringements on good order that were part and parcel of city life: graffitied walls, blaring horns, crushed citizens on the pavement.

The medical examiner crouched and pointed. "Look at that," he said, shaking his head. "I tell you, there's no justice."

1

Washington, Present Day

I HAD NOTHING TO DO with the disappearance of Martin Green.

I had nothing to do. I was passing the days. And the nights. One to the next. No agenda, no appointments, no to-dos. No interests, hobbies, or curiosity. No ambition. When I showed up at the Justice Department, colleagues got tunnel vision. Law books, computer screens, even blank walls became hypnotic. Those who couldn't dodge without being obvious just smiled and mumbled about the workload or the weather. My poor secretary tried to be supportive. She covered for my absences and sent greeting cards with inspirational messages. She even offered encouragement when she handed me the summons from Evans. He'd been supportive, too. It was, however, time to move on.

"Sit down, Philip," he said, his gaze fixed on the papers in front of him. A moment passed before he looked up to study me. "How are you feeling?" he asked. His expression said he wasn't expecting good news.

"I was thinking of taking some time off."

"Do you know Martin Green? You and he over-lapped on the Hill."

"No. A few weeks or so."

"He's missing. The story will be in the *Post* tomor-row. It's going—"

"No more than a month."

"—to hit the fan—" He stared at me, then leaned back and sighed. "You've *had* time off, a *lot* of it. It's time to get back to work."

"I don't think I'm ready."

"It's time to get back to work," he repeated. "There are policies, Philip, precedents."

"Alan—"

"Are you listening? He's *disappeared*."

"Lots of people disappear. We don't usually get in-volved."

"He's a Senate aide, a senior staffer for the Intelli-gence Committee—*Warren Young's* committee." He looked at me for a reaction; getting none, he continued. "Green had access to important secrets. The FBI is treat-ing it as a matter of national security."

"And?"

"And we want you to oversee the investigation."

"We?"

"The attorney general and I."

"I don't handle national security matters, Alan. I'm in the Appellate Section. I write briefs."

He frowned at me. "Yes, that's what you're *supposed* to do. The reality, as we both know, is quite different." He was making a valid point about my lack of produc-tivity.

"So, you're going to promote me to national security matters?"

He acknowledged the illogic with a shake of his head. "In all honesty, you ought to be fired, but there are the mitigating circumstances"—he made vague motions with his hands—"and what's more important, you're well qualified for this job."

"Why?"

"The vice president has read the writing on the wall. He'll never get the nomination to succeed Forsythe, which makes Warren Young the party's best chance to keep the White House. A spy right under his nose could end his candidacy before the first primary."

"We don't care about politics, Alan. We're the Justice Department."

Evans closed his eyes and took a deep breath, then exhaled slowly through his mouth. It was a relaxation technique he'd read about in an airline magazine and it seemed to work. When he spoke again his voice was very deliberate. "In case you've forgotten, Philip, Senator Young and the president, the boss of your boss and mine, are in the same party. That means people are going to question our objectivity. If we investigate and let Young off the hook, if we declare that Green isn't some goddamn spy, the opposition is going to cry 'whitewash.'"

"And that's where I come in."

He pushed himself up from his chair and went to the tall window that overlooked the courtyard. He clasped his hands behind his back and began speaking to the glass. "The AG is being realistic. You used to be a political animal. You worked for the other party in the White House and on the Hill. Why would *you* go into the tank to help Young?"

"Because my boss told me to?"

He shook his head. "Not you. You're the man who

puts truth ahead of politics and self-interest. Everyone knows that."

"And they'll never forget it, will they, Alan?"

He peered at my reflection and said, "What happened wasn't right but there's nothing to be done. For better or worse, politics is the fuel that drives decisions in this town. You know that—you knew it then. We have to take the world as we find it." He spread his arms to acknowledge the world outside the window, then returned to his chair. "Anyway, what's past is past. You know the terrain and we're confident you'll go wherever the evidence leads. Let me add that when you did do the criminal stuff your instincts were second to none. You, my friend, are ideal for the job."

"That's very good, Alan. You didn't even mention the most important reason."

He tried to meet my gaze but looked away. "We never discussed another reason," he said. He reached for the fountain pen he fondled when discomfited.

"I'm leaving Washington."

He stopped in midreach, eyebrows arched. "Leaving? To go where? Do what?"

"The Pacific Northwest. Oregon or Washington. Find some small town surrounded by mountains and hang out a shingle."

He sat back and regarded me for a long moment before he spoke. "Are you a member of the bar out there, Philip?"

"No."

"Do you have any connections out there, someone to help you get started?"

"No."

"If I may ask, do you have the resources to live on while you try to build a practice from scratch?"

"I suppose I don't."

There was a moment of awkward silence before he continued. "The days when people went into towns and hung out shingles are long gone, I'm afraid. You'd need a job right away, a way to make ends meet until you're up and running."

"I'll join a firm. Shuffle papers and write memos while I study for the bar. That's what new lawyers do." He was shaking his head before I even finished.

"I'm telling you this as a friend. You're going to have to fill out all kinds of questionnaires. What firm is going to be interested in a middle-aged guy with your"—he fumbled for the right word—"issues?"

A valid point. "I do have issues."

"You'll wind up on your own and without proper insurance. What happens if you have a . . . a relapse?"

"The term is 'nervous breakdown.' "

"Right. You've been in and out of the hospital—what?—three times? Forget for a moment that I'm trying to persuade you to take a job. I'm talking as a friend here. You've got to be practical."

"Practical," I repeated.

"Realistic." He seized the fountain pen and stroked it for a moment while he made up his mind. "Look, I'm going out on a limb but here's a proposition. Take the assignment. Do the kind of job we know you can do. When it's over—and that could be in as little as a week or two—I'll arrange a niche for you in the U.S. Attorney's Office in Portland. As long as your salary is in the department's budget they'll be glad to have the help. As a government lawyer you can make contacts, study for the exam, and when you're ready, make your move to whatever hamlet you choose. How about it?"

"And if I say no?"

"You're an unproductive lawyer on the public payroll. That's as plain as I can make it."

"How long before you need a decision?"

The answer to that was plain, too. He was looking through the doorway to the hall. "Your FBI agent is here. Afterward, I want you to tell me who she looks like." He stood up. "Come on in, Blair," he called, grinning from ear to ear.

I rose as Alan made the introductions. "Philip Barkley, Special Agent Blair Turner."

"Hello," I said.

"Hello," she replied. She barely acknowledged me before taking a chair and turning her attention to Evans.

"Blair is with the Counterintelligence Squad and is very highly regarded," he said. "Probably will head an office some day. Right, Blair?"

"A division," she replied, waiting a beat to smile. "Maybe the whole Bureau."

Evans nodded enthusiastically in agreement. "Philip here is an old hand. He's been around and he knows the Hill. His experience will prove useful."

"That's good to hear." She didn't sound convinced.

"Why don't you fill us in on what the investigation has uncovered so far?" he asked, still grinning like an idiot. He swiveled in his chair to give her his full attention.

The future director of the FBI began without preamble, speaking to Evans and ignoring me completely. Now he had me wondering: who *did* she look like? Brunette, gray eyes, extraordinary nose. A profile that could make being ignored almost painless.

"Martin Green has been on the Intelligence Committee staff for five years," she began. "He is—was—considered very diligent and reliable. He has clearance to receive sensitive information in compartments above top secret and has seen literally hundreds of sensitive documents pertaining to various programs and operations, and has had access to the contents of regular briefings of the committee by the intelligence agencies. According to his colleagues, he began acting peculiar about three weeks ago, very nervous and distracted. Something or someone was clearly worrying him, although he claimed that he was just overworked. He also began to act suspiciously. He was observed on two occasions in late August making calls from a public telephone at Union Station."

"Phone booths," Evans muttered. "Sounds like a bad movie."

"It gets worse. During the week of August 6 he was on leave for five days, supposedly to attend to family matters in New Jersey. It was a sham. His father says that he hasn't been home in months. We think he was in the New York area, though, and we're still trying to piece together why he went and what he did."

"Maybe he has domestic problems," offered Evans. "That's what it usually is around here when people disappear on us." He glanced at me and frowned when he realized his faux pas.

"Possibly. He's been living with a woman named Diana Morris, a membership director of some software industry association. They've been together for three years. We've only talked to her briefly but she claims to have no idea where he's gone."

"Why elevate this to a national security problem?" I asked. "Maybe he owes money to bookmakers whom he calls from phone booths. Maybe it was *a lot* of money and now he's lying in an alley somewhere waiting to be found."

"He took a suitcase and clothes," she replied. "His car is missing and he cleaned out his checking and savings accounts the day before he left. If he gambles, no one has seen any evidence of it, and that wouldn't explain his trip to New York."

Evans and I digested the summary for a moment before he spoke. "Any idea where he's gone?"

"No. As a precaution we've checked the trains, planes, buses, and boats, and we've put out a bulletin to state and local police across the eastern half of the country."

"Is there a warrant for his arrest?" I asked.

"No, as far as the rest of the world is concerned this is a missing persons case."

"Maybe that's all it is," I said. "We can't prove it's more than that."

Evans looked glum. "Is there more?" he asked.

"That's essentially it." She closed her notebook. "We're looking for him. And we're working with other agencies to assess the potential damage."

The assistant attorney general removed his glasses and pinched the bridge of his nose. He was almost apologetic when he said, "Philip here will be directly overseeing the investigation."

"I see," she said tonelessly. Apparently, someone had put a word in for me at the Bureau.

Evans tried to mollify her. "Naturally, we'll be relying heavily on your judgment and those of your colleagues as to the proper course of action. Philip has had some useful experience in criminal work and on the Hill, and I'm sure you two will make a good team."

"I'm sure," she replied.

Evans looked over at me. "I'm sure, too," I said.

"Good. The AG wants to be kept advised on your progress so let me hear from you frequently."

"When would you like to get started, Agent Turner?" I asked.

She stood up and slung her bag over her shoulder. "There's no time like the present. Your office?"

A few moments later we were down at the "office" they'd found for me when I returned to work. It was doubling as a storage room and the space required for cabinets and file boxes left just enough area for a desk placed sideways to the door. Blair had to wait while I went searching for another chair, and after an awkward minute involving the chair, the door, and some storage boxes, she was sitting alongside the desk. I had to keep my own legs in the kneehole to make room for hers. Any remaining questions regarding my stature in the department were now resolved.

"We have an appointment with Senator Young tomorrow morning at eleven," she began. "I think he wants to offer his support."

"That must be it," I said.

"Do you realize that we're probably meeting the next president of the United States?"

"That's very possible."

She looked around, considering her next words. "I want to ask you something."

"Sure."

"How do you feel about this assignment?"

I shrugged. "It's an assignment, I guess."

"I think it's an opportunity."

I nodded, but said nothing.

"Persistence and determination alone are omnipotent, but knowing the right people can't hurt."

"That sounds like a quote."

"Calvin Coolidge."

"Coolidge said that?"

"All but the last part. I'd say we've got an opportunity to impress the next president with our professionalism, don't you?" Before I could answer, she added, "Look, I make no secret about my ambition, Philip. I intend to go farther than any woman has gone in the Bureau."

"Ambition is good," I said. I tried to lean back in my swivel chair but it struck the wall.

"Don't patronize me, please. I want to know how you're going to approach this job."

"I think our professionalism will be more appreciated if the senator likes our conclusions."

She smiled. It was a nice smile. "Do you believe Green is a spy?"

"I don't know. It's still a little early for me."

"Have you dealt with espionage before?"

"No."

"I think we're going to find that he had a fight with his girlfriend, or got caught in the wrong bar on Capitol Hill and is terrified about being outed. If it's not one of those, then it's probably an early midlife crisis."

"You didn't sound this confident upstairs."

"I was giving the official line for the AG's consumption, but whatever it is that sent our guy around the bend, it's not likely to be espionage."

"Senator Young will be happy to hear that."

Maybe it was my tone, or something in my eyes. She frowned and said, "May I be blunt?"

"Please."

"I'm the new girl on the block, okay? I haven't been in Washington four months and I get an assignment like this. They bypass some fair-haired boys and grizzled vets to get to me, so I'm wondering: am I on the fast track, or is there some kind of catch? The assistant director sits me down and explains the stakes for Senator Young, although they're pretty obvious. He says the odds of a bad outcome are low, but if it goes wrong there's no telling what will happen or who'll get blamed. He lays it all out for me—some risk, potentially high reward—and am I game?" She looked at me as if I might have the answer.

"Go on," I said.

She paused a moment, considering her next words. "Look, let me get straight to the point. I don't mean any disrespect, but I don't want to get sucked into anything, okay? All I want is to do it right and let the chips fall where they may. We're not out to kiss anyone's ass but we're supposed to be—what?—*politically astute,* I think that's how he put it. And that's another area where you're supposed to add value. So, how about it?"

"Doing it right is fine with me," I said.

She studied me a moment then nodded. "Okay. By the book, one step at a time."

"Do you think the investigation will take long?"

"I'm not sure. I'm hoping for a telephone call that says he's showed up at home or the office. If we have to find him it could take time." She stood up. "Come over to the Bureau tomorrow morning. I'll have the files there and I'll fill you in on the latest investigative reports. Then we'll go see the senator."

"Fine." I started to get up.

"Stay there," she said. "It's easier if only one of us does this." She stepped behind the chair, opened the door as far as it would go, and squeezed through. Her fingers curled into a wave and she was gone.

Evans rang five minutes later. "Has she left?" he asked.

"She just squeezed through the door."

He lowered his voice; his door to his secretary must have been open. "Well?"

"Well, what?"

"Who does she remind you of?"

"I'm not sure. She's taller than Hoover."

"That actress!" he said. "The one who was in that movie with that Spanish guy . . . what's his name?"

"How much did you tell her about me, Alan?"

The conversation skipped a beat. "About you? You mean, beyond your qualifications?"

"I'll let you know when we learn something."

"You know who I mean. Fernando or Antonio somebody."

"Portland, Alan, as soon as this is over."

2

SO, I AWOKE THE NEXT morning with something to do: find Martin Green, deduce whether national security had been compromised, and determine the outcome of the next presidential election. A full plate. You'd think it would pop me out of bed but the familiar weight of lethargic indifference pressed me to the mattress. The doctors tag-teamed me with assurances that it was to be expected, and they were prepared to write yet one more prescription or tweak the dosages. In truth, I'd grown very weary of medicine and doctors and hospitals, of unfathomable replies to unanswerable questions, of clinging to an outcropping of hope while dangling over the abyss.

I struggled to vertical, showered, shaved, and dressed, then downed a nutritious breakfast of pills and instant coffee. Twenty minutes later I was on the bus, daydreaming about bucolic Oregon hamlets while we crawled along the concrete ribbon toward downtown. Maybe a week or two, Evans had said.

The FBI is ostensibly a branch of the Justice Department but my identification wallet cut no ice at the Bureau. I waited on a plastic chair and watched the world go by while the receptionist tried to locate my new colleague. But for the tight security the lobby could have been any office building in the city. The new breed of FBI agent didn't resemble the square-jawed, white-shirted, Stetson-crowned prototypes of the Hoover era. None that I knew resembled Blair Turner, either.

They finally bestowed a visitor tag on me. I clipped it to my lapel and was remanded to the custody of a close-cropped agent who looked all of seventeen. He took me to a third-floor office about three times the size of mine and left me in front of a desk with a silver nameplate that said SA BLAIR TURNER. The standard Bureau décor was augmented with personal touches: an oriental rug, African violets on the sill, and a large ficus tree in one corner. Some plaques and a diploma from the University of Michigan surrounded a reproduction of Manet's *Railway*. I went around the desk to get a close look at two photographs on her credenza. One was of Blair receiving an award from the director; the other was of a man in army uniform with colonel's eagles on the epaulets. He was staring into the camera with that tight-lipped hint of a smile that was standard for an officer's pose.

"My father." SA Turner was standing in the doorway wearing a navy blue suit with a gold pin on the lapel, looking no more like an FBI agent than my young escort. "He commands the military police at Fort Benning."

"I'll bet it's an interesting job," I said, returning to my chair as she went around her desk.

"I guess so. Don't believe all that crap you see in the recruiting ads. It's still a man's world." She sat down and began to rifle through a pile of messages while I tried to imagine life on an army base for a woman who looked like Blair Turner. Maybe if your father was the head cop it was okay.

"I suppose the FBI is a lot more advanced," I said, smiling. She looked up at me. "I mean, if you persevere and know the right people."

"Maybe not," she replied tersely.

"Why?"

"I take it you saw the *Post* this morning."

As Evans predicted, Green's disappearance was front-page news. The story reported that the FBI had joined with local police in the search for an "important senior staff member" of the Senate Select Committee on Intelligence, who was described by colleagues as "brilliant" and "extremely conscientious." Law-enforcement officials declined to speculate about the reason for the disappearance but noted that there were no signs of foul play. One unidentified source stated that the staffer had seemed "particularly stressed" in the last few weeks, a characterization that contrasted markedly with the photograph of a smiling young man. Senator Warren Young was described as "concerned."

"Now I know what Green looks like," I said.

"So does an agent named Summerfield. And he realized that he had seen him before."

"Where?"

"In the outdoor café at the National Portrait Gallery."

"Doing what?"

"Two weeks ago one of our agents was doing a routine surveillance of an employee of the Hungarian embassy named Magda Takács."

"A spy?"

"Not as far as we were concerned. Just a low-level employee without diplomatic cover. Our resources aren't unlimited, okay? We devote them where the potential payoff is biggest, so we'll only look at people like Takács on occasion and at random. This day she takes the Metro from the Van Ness stop to the Portrait Gallery. She spends a half-hour looking at paintings and heads for the cafeteria. So, Summerfield gets in line behind her with a couple of people in between. She goes from the cash register to the outdoor café. He goes outside two minutes later and she's already at a table with a man."

"Green."

"We didn't know who he was then. All the tables had at least one person at them, so they could have been sharing that one, or maybe they were friends—there was no way to know. The two of them were just talking and eating. It didn't look like a big deal, but Summerfield snapped a couple of pictures, just in case."

"Did anything pass between them?"

"There were some papers on the table in front of Green. They could have been put there by either one of them. I suppose Summerfield would have been more concerned if Takács picked them up, but Green put them in his briefcase when they parted."

"He didn't follow Green?"

"No, there was no reason to. We had his photograph so we figured to identify him later. The photographs were still in the to-do pile this morning. Needless to say, Summerfield is having a bad day. He'll almost certainly take a reprimand for letting her out of his sight, but anyone else would have done the same."

"The whole thing could be totally innocent," I said.

"Maybe, but they both traveled pretty far for lunch, even if it was on the Metro. The museum is over four miles from the Hungarian embassy and a good mile from the Capitol, hardly in the radius of Hill lunch spots. We'll find out if Green was in the habit of going there."

I pondered the implications. Senator Young was about to receive some very bad news, and Blair and I would be the messengers. "Want some coffee?" she asked.

"Please."

I followed her down to a little kitchenette. The coffeepot was empty. "These guys think that only the secretaries should make coffee," she said, annoyed. "They'll walk in and leave, then come back every five minutes until there's a fresh pot." She tore open a bag of grounds as I made myself useful filling the brewer with water.

"Will you question Takács?" I asked.

"It's too early to tip our hand. We haven't got enough for an arrest, and if she's involved in espionage she'd be back in Budapest within twenty-four hours. The best thing to do is to keep her under surveillance and hope they make contact again. And keep searching for Green."

"Any news on his whereabouts?"

"We know a little more about where he's not."

"Evans thinks we could wrap this up in as little as a week."

She frowned. "Don't count on it. It depends on when he makes a mistake, *if* he makes a mistake. Have you ever been involved with a fugitive hunt before?"

"No."

"There are a few basic ways to catch them. Your best

chance is they screw up and get arrested on some other charge. That's not going to happen here. Sometimes they get spotted by a citizen or an alert cop, but you have to put their pictures on television, which we're not about to do."

"But you've got a big dragnet out there. You said you've notified the police in half the country."

"Police and sheriff's departments don't pay much attention to those bulletins unless they're looking for a cop-killer. Ours says that he's a missing person. If Green is arrested by local law enforcement it will be for going through a red light."

The coffee was done; she took the pot and poured two cups. "What do you like in yours?" she asked, bending over to peer into a small refrigerator under the counter. She had that lean, athletic figure that made you want to diet.

"Cream. Milk would be fine."

She poured a little half-and-half into my cup as another agent entered the kitchenette, greeted her, and headed for the pot. He was tall, broad-shouldered, and about her age. He stole a few glances at Blair while he took his time. In his place I'd have been doing the same, wondering about my chances, figuring my best approach. Suddenly, I felt very old.

We walked back to her office. "So, what's our strategy?" I asked.

"He's got to make a mistake. Maybe he'll contact friends or relatives. If he does, we'll be waiting. Or maybe he'll stick to his old habits. We can get him that way, too."

"How do we know his habits?"

"Check registers, credit card statements, interviews

with people who know him. We have a group of agents on it right now."

"So, you figure out where he's likely to go and what he's likely to do, and you try to anticipate him."

"That's it. We're doing the interviews now. I'm going to do some myself."

"I'd like to sit in."

"If I were you I'd start distancing myself from this thing."

"What about you?"

"I don't have any options."

I didn't say anything. I wanted to assure her that if she just did her job and did it right, no one would hold a grudge, but I was the poster boy for a very different reality.

"You want to hear something funny?" she asked.

"There's something funny in this?"

"Did you ever hear of the 'Red Diaper Theory'?"

"No."

"It had currency in the Bureau in the sixties and seventies: 'Old Lefties give birth to New Lefties.' It's either an oddity or a cultural phenomenon—that's the debate—but it turns out that a lot of the leaders of the New Left movement that swept college campuses in the sixties had parents who were Leftists in the forties and fifties, some of them were even Communist Party members. The theory is that these radicals of the fifties inculcated their beliefs into their kids, who sort of picked up the torch and started setting fire to all those ROTC buildings."

"That's interesting, but what does it have to do with this case?"

"Our boy Marty was thoroughly vetted before he got

his security clearance, which required that he list the extended family. It turns out, Grandma and Grandpa attended a few of the wrong meetings in some Bronx basements in the early fifties, and managed to get themselves on the Bureau's list of known Communist Party sympathizers. Like I said, it was only a glitch, but it got Marty a little more scrutiny as a result."

"Which, I take it, he passed."

"Yes, but you know . . ." She shrugged.

"What?"

"We're not infallible." She looked at her watch. "Okay, time to deliver the bad news."

Like most citizens, Blair had never set foot in the chambers of a United States senator before. She tried not to be obvious but as we waited on the leather couch beneath a painting of James Madison, she was taking it all in. However daunting our task might have seemed in her office thirty minutes before, it was surely magnified by our surroundings.

And every stick of period furniture, every painting, photograph, plaque, and memento harmonized to inform that we were in a place where power resides. The first time I entered a senator's inner sanctum it seemed that the air itself was somehow different, and soon I knew it to be true, for inhaling it over time altered biorhythms, stimulated hormones, and according to a body of informed opinion, could produce outright disorientation.

A senator's entrance for a meeting is usually preceded by a staffer or two whose function it is to size up the room, tell you what the boss wants to hear or say, and make sure you don't overstay your welcome. Warren

Young's entrance was preceded by his legislative director, Terry Grantham, a veteran whom I knew from my days with the Appropriations Committee.

"Philip!" he cried, seizing me in a combination handshake and elbow clamp, the preferred fund-raising grip and a hold from which there is no escape. Terry had changed considerably in the years since I'd left, but only rigid discipline could withstand the ravages of life on the Hill: too little sleep and exercise; too much stress, drink and hors d'oeuvres. The lines in his face and the burgeoning waistline and jowls were the badge of congressional tenure.

"I saw Elliott in the cafeteria," he gushed, "and we were saying that we could use a few more Philip Barkleys up here these days." He was already looking over my shoulder with the same stupid grin that Evans wore the day before. His grip on my elbow involuntarily tightened.

"This is Special Agent Blair Turner of the FBI," I said.

"The senator is *really* looking forward to meeting you," said Terry.

"Likewise," said Blair.

They bantered for a few moments while I tried to free my elbow. Finally, he asked, "Philip, do you know Jarrett Sanders?"

"Only by reputation." Sanders was one of the new breed of hired guns who managed political campaigns here and abroad. He first gained notice by engineering an upset victory for an Oklahoma Senate seat by a candidate whose credentials were described, in a classic piece of *New York Times* understatement, as "dubious." He cemented his reputation with the elections of a mayoral hopeful under indictment for securities fraud and an incumbent governor who'd barely survived first-term impeachment. Whenever asked if a candidate's choice of campaign manager had become more important than his credentials or positions, Sanders would deny it, but only mildly, and he always smiled.

"He'd like to meet you," said Terry. He saw my expression change and quickly added, "Just for a few moments before Warren arrives." He excused us to Blair, then used my elbow as a rudder to guide me back through the anteroom and into a small office where Sanders was waiting in a wing chair. "Philip Barkley, Jarrett Sanders," said Terry. An awkward silence ensued until he patted me on the shoulder and said, "I'll just leave the two of you alone. The meeting with the senator will start in five minutes."

The door closed behind me. Sanders remained seated and didn't invite me to take the chair opposite. "Philip Barkley," he began, nodding as if the sight of me confirmed his suspicions. "I remember you." It came out as "Ah remembuh yew," a Georgia drawl, exaggerated as Southerners do when being charming or threatening to Yankees.

"I'm sorry, I can't say the same."

"Well, we've *nevuh* actually met. I thought it was *impawtant* that we do before *yaw'll* meet the senator. I want to be *shawh* that there's no misunderstandin'."

"Misunderstanding about what?"

"Your job."

"That's been explained to me."

"I know, but I thought you should get it from the horse's mouth, so to speak." He slouched in his chair and crossed his ankles, totally at ease. "This spy business is just a pile of *manoowah,* which your investigation is goin' to confirm, I'm sure. That's good news for the good guys and bad news for the other guys. Everything should be just peaches and cream if you don't get any more funny ideas."

"More?"

He sneered at me and steepled his hands under his chin. No jowls there. Like Cassius, he had that lean and hungry look: shaven head, prominent cheekbones, large, sunken eyes, a broad nose. A crocodile on two legs.

"Ever been involved in a presidential campaign, Philip Barkley? I know you've seen 'em, but you ever been in one?"

"No."

"It's a bandwagon, just like the cliché. It starts out slow-like, with a few key people on board, then it gets bigger and bigger as it rolls *awllllllll* around the country, bigger and heavier, gathering that ol' *mooowmentum*. And when it comes your way, you got two choices. You can get on board. Or you can get run *ovah*."

"I see."

"I'm wonderin' if you do. Maybe you didn't learn a lesson last time. Or maybe you got one of them masochist streaks or somethin'. So, I'll make it plain, just like down home. You try to even some score here and you're goin' to get *slapped*"—he smacked the arm of the chair—"like a tick." He paused to let the warning sink in, then smiled. "So you just do your job, Philip Barkley, do your job. Miss FBI out there is going to find out that there's been no spyin' in the senator's commit-tee, and you're goin' to shout 'Amen!' Shout it like a Holy Roller preacher at a revival meetin'. 'Amen!' shouts Philip Barkley. 'Amen!' shouts the attorney gen-eral. 'Amen!' shout the newspaper and TV folks. And when the shoutin's over, when the choir has packed its gowns and the tent is all folded up, you get to climb on the bus and ride into the sunset, all the way to Oregon."

News of my deal with Evans had traveled fast. "I have to get back for the meeting," I said.

Sanders gave me a crocodile smile and made a walking gesture with his fingers along the arm of his chair. "Run along, Philip Barkley. There's work to be done."

I'd known Warren Young. I'd known him for years, before he was a senator. He was just a junior congressman when I left the White House to become minority counsel to the Appropriations Committee. To most citizens Young had the more important job, but within the Beltway there was no comparison. There were four hundred thirty-five congressmen. To be significant required seniority and key assignments. On the Capitol totem pole a junior member of the House was more important than an agency bureaucrat but not up there with, say, the maître d' of a hot restaurant. The Senate Appropriations Committee, however, was a powerful institution and its minority counsel was a player. Lobbyists, journalists, and favor-seekers would trample a junior congressman to corner me at a cocktail party.

But Warren Young wasn't destined to be a junior congressman for very long. He had intelligence, good looks, savvy, and lots of charm. Most important, he had Edward Young for a father, and Edward Young had a blueprint. He didn't create the blueprint, he just borrowed it from Joe Kennedy: a plan to take his son from congressman to senator to president in the wink of a political eye.

Nine years later, Edward's plan was coming to fruition. Warren was a second-term senator with a key chairmanship that he'd exploited to achieve national prominence. Even nature had cooperated as his handsome visage matured into Hollywood's idea of a president. The camera loved him and whatever came through on screen was magnified in person.

We all stood as he strode into the room and went directly to Blair. Like the savvy campaigner he was, Young had the ability to make whomever he was talking to feel like the most important person the senator had ever met. He held on to her hand as he confided how pleased he was that she would be the FBI agent on the case. To her credit, Blair was polite but distant, which only encouraged him to press on. It was only when he had her smiling and nodding that he took notice of me.

"Philip!" He stepped forward and clasped my hand. "It's been a long time!"

"Yes, it has. How are you, Senator?"

He turned somber on cue. "Well, up to a few days ago I would have said 'great.' I don't have to tell you how troubling this matter is about Martin. Of course it doesn't make any sense. The idea that he's a foreign agent is preposterous." He stared at me until I involuntarily nodded my agreement. Out of the corner of my eye I could see Blair watching. Young took a step closer and put a hand on my shoulder. "Philip, however silly the notion is, as the chairman of the Intelligence Committee I am determined to have a thorough investigation. I talked to the president and the AG about this and they both agree that given the political realities, we had to do something to ensure that the public has confidence in the Justice Department's inquiry. When it was suggested that you head the investigation I agreed without reservation. I know you'll be fair and that's all I ask. Put these allegations to rest as soon as possible."   .

I caught myself before I nodded again. "We're going to be thorough," I said.

"Good," he replied, patting my shoulder, then motioned me back to the couch as he settled into a red leather chair that seemed higher than the others. "Why don't you brief us on what the Bureau has turned up?" he asked Blair.

"We're still in the early stages," she began, "but we've developed some significant information. You already know that Mr. Green hasn't been seen since he left the committee office on August 30. Other members of the committee staff say that he was acting strangely for three weeks before he disappeared. He was—"

"What do you mean, 'strangely'?" interrupted Young.

"They said he seemed nervous and quite distracted. He was also—"

Young smiled at his aide. "Half the people around here are nervous or distracted half the time, aren't they, Terry?" Not a good sign: we were thirty seconds into the briefing and he'd already interrupted her twice.

"There's more," Blair said, then stopped and waited. She had to be nervous as hell but was determined not to let it show.

"Go on, please," said the senator, gesturing toward her notebook. The smile on his face was tight. Beside him, Terry's nervousness was plain.

"Mr. Green was observed on two occasions making telephone calls at a public phone at Union Station. By itself, this may or may not be significant but has to be viewed in context." Young shrugged to indicate that he

wasn't impressed. A sense of dread came over me as Blair
continued. "As you may know, Senator, Mr. Green was
on leave during the week of August 6. He said that he
was going to attend to family matters in New Jersey. Our
investigation has revealed that he didn't go home. We—"

"What *did* he do?"

"—don't know yet what he did but we believe he was
in the New York area and we're checking known friends
and associates there. So far we've found no one who was
in contact with him during that week."

The corners of Young's mouth turned upward but his
gaze remained fixed on Blair as he spoke to his aide.
"We probably should find out which female staffer was
on vacation that week, right, Terry?" He was asking for
it. His aide was staring at me now, silently pleading for
intervention.

The door opened. All heads turned as Mrs. Warren
Young swept into the room with a pulse of energy and a
swirl of color. "Good morning, everyone!" she cried. "I
hope I didn't miss anything."

Young sprung from his chair. "Darling! You're just in
time!" I stood as Mrs. Young kissed her husband deco-
rously on the cheek and came around the chair toward
me with her hands extended.

"Philip!" she cried, taking both my hands in hers.
"You're looking well! I'm so glad." At twenty-five Constance Young had been the most pursued woman on
Capitol Hill; at thirty-five, she was better. Her features
were under orders to stand firm against time, although
she permitted some tiny lines around the eyes to add interest and the assurance of experience that supporters
prized. Once she was the cheerleader you coveted in college, now she was right off the cover of *Town and Coun-*

try: prosperous, sophisticated, sensual; a woman at her zenith.

"Thank you, Constance." I gestured toward Blair, who was now standing beside me. "This is Special Agent Blair Turner of the FBI. She's in charge of the case."

"Wonderful!" said Mrs. Young as she and Blair shook hands. "It's good to see that the Bureau is giving women some real opportunities. I fought some of those battles when I was over at Judiciary, and I want to tell you, Blair—may I call you Blair?—there was still a lot of Hoover in that building long after he was gone."

Whether intended or not, the suggestion that Agent Turner owed her career to affirmative action was ill-timed. "The Bureau has been very fair to me," she replied neutrally. Terry surrendered his chair and took one behind the power couple. His forehead was glistening; the arrival of Constance had raised the room temperature and magnified his discomfort.

But my most immediate concern was Blair. Technically speaking, the senator's wife was no longer on the payroll. Her full-time job was manager of her husband's career, the de facto director of the campaign, which, as a practical matter, also placed her in charge of his office. But she was not a government employee and had no security clearance, and if Agent Turner wanted to stand on ceremony, Constance Young had no right to sit in on a briefing that touched upon national security matters.

I caught Blair's attention as Young brought his wife up to speed, and with head and eye movements conveyed a silent plea of my own to go along. The last thing we needed was a showdown. Blair didn't acknowledge the message; she just stared coolly at me then turned back to the senator with her chin raised slightly in anticipation of the next exchange. Finally, Young said, "Go ahead, Agent Turner, you were telling us about Martin's missing week in New York."

"His actions indicate that he was not there for the usual reasons," Blair said. "He took pains not to leave a trail. He left no phone numbers with the office and he didn't use his credit cards, which was his custom when traveling. He apparently used cash because he withdrew twelve hundred dollars from ATM machines here in the days before he left."

"How did you find out that he went to New York?" asked Constance.

"We were lucky. He took the shuttle from National to LaGuardia and ran into an acquaintance on the plane."

"They're still trying to find out what he did up there," the senator told his wife. "I suggested that he might have been meeting a woman, a secret rendezvous."

Constance smiled and said, "Probably. Martin is a good-looking man. The girls in this office certainly seem to be aware of him whenever he's around." The senator nodded at his wife's perceptiveness. He was far more confident with her in the room.

"We're investigating all the possibilities," said Blair. "But this morning we received information that has heightened our concern."

Husband and wife replied as one: "What is it?"

"Fifteen days ago Green and a female employee of the Hungarian embassy shared a table in the courtyard of the National Portrait Gallery. They arrived separately and parted afterward, but spent about thirty minutes together talking while they ate lunch. There were some papers on the table but we don't know who brought them. Green put them in his briefcase when they parted."

"Let me see if I understand this," said Constance with a forced deliberation that signaled danger. "A staff member of the Intelligence Committee was under surveillance and no one told the chairman?" Mrs. Young had taken charge, speaking as if the chairman wasn't even in the room. In fact, the Hungarian story seemed to have put him in a coma.

"No," said Blair. "The embassy employee was the one under surveillance. We hadn't even identified the man as Green until his picture appeared in the newspaper this morning."

"Now I *am* lost," said Constance. "You did an extensive background check on him so that he could work for this committee. You've got a file with his damn picture in it at the Hoover building!" She was getting up a full head of steam and Terry had turned ashen. He knew the senator would take his cue from his wife. If she was irate, he'd be, too, only more so. Warren Young was not a man naturally inclined to anger. Left to his own devices he defaulted to the nice-guy persona that was comfortable but ill-suited to the necessities of political life, and like many of his ilk, he'd been content to let his wife wield the hatchet. In the rarefied atmosphere of national politics that was a risk. The spouse-as-full-partner model played well in some precincts but not in those where voters expected their leaders to wear the pants. The candidate had to be seen as tough without coming off as a hothead who should never have his finger on the button. Sanders's forte was walking that tightrope, and Warren's campaign was planting stories portraying the senator as a down-to-earth guy who knew how to kick a little ass when required.

Warren definitely wanted to kick ass. What happened

next depended on Blair. An abject apology and plea for forgiveness might avoid a major scene, but one glance at that regal profile and I knew the point was moot. There she was, facing one of the most powerful couples in the country, probably the next president and first lady, and there was no outward sign of retreat. Forget knowing the right people; this was all about perseverance. An army officer's daughter, indeed.

"We've done security checks on tens of thousands of people," Blair said evenly. "We have tens of thousands of photographs. Green's face may be familiar to the people who work up here but not to the people at the Bureau. The pictures of him and the Hungarian were slated for review. Eventually he would have been identified."

"*Eventually,*" repeated Constance.

"And what do you make of those pictures, Agent Turner?" asked Young. It was a reasonable question; only the tone portended trouble.

If Blair had more Hill experience she would have known that while brevity is the soul of wit, it could be politically disastrous. "A breach of national security certainly seems more likely," she replied. Terry looked as if he'd been shot. People like Warren and Constance Young perceived every event or utterance as a potential story to be leaked, suppressed, denied, or spun. Blair's succinct response sounded very much like a headline: *Sources Say National Security Breach Likely.* Alarms were going off, survival mechanisms were being activated.

"I don't understand this," muttered the senator. "I don't understand this at all." Blair held her tongue as Young's face contorted with the struggle for self-control.

Constance pounced. "How do you know that Martin and this Hungarian person weren't just friends, or even lovers?" she challenged. "How do you know that it wasn't the other way around—she was providing material to him that was useful to the Intelligence Committee?"

"No one is aware of anything like that," replied Blair. Terry was rubbing his forehead vigorously with the palm of his hand.

"Do your superiors share this view?" Constance asked.

"I haven't discussed this with my superiors. We just—"

"This is *your* conclusion?" Constance cried, rolling her eyes.

"It's not *anyone's* conclusion," replied Blair forcefully. Agent Turner had had enough and was fighting back.

Young had found his voice. "Let's get this over with," he said testily. "Do you have any more information to report?"

"Not at the moment," replied Blair, "but I'd like to ask you a question."

"What is it?"

"According to phone records, on the night before Green disappeared two calls were placed from his office phone to your home. Do you remember them?"

"I don't remember any calls from him," replied Young.

"Are you sure? The calls were late, after ten. One was two minutes, the other almost eight."

Young leaned forward in his chair and fixed Blair with a stare. "I said I don't remember. Perhaps someone else called me using his telephone. I get calls from staff at all hours. We have emergencies, Agent Turner, matters of national security. Do you understand?"

"Yes, I do. We checked with other people in the office. No one recalls telephoning you that night, or even using that phone."

If the proverbial pin had dropped it would have sounded like a crowbar.

"Tell me," said Constance, "did you inform your supervisor that you intended to cross-examine Senator Young today?"

"I don't mean any disrespect, Mrs. Young," said Blair. "I'm just asking questions."

"Now you're patronizing us," said Constance. "Do you have permission to do this or not?"

I recognized the look in Blair's eyes. *The hell with it.* "This is an investigation," she shot back. "I'm supposed to ask questions. I don't need permission."

At that instant an old brainteaser ran through my mind. *A train leaves Chicago going sixty miles per hour. Another train leaves New York going ninety miles per hour.*

"Who do you think you are?" demanded Young. "Where do you come off talking to my wife like that?" The door to the anteroom opened a few inches, then shut immediately.

Terry had managed to stand up and was bent over with his hand on Young's sleeve. "Senator," he began, "I think—"

"*Never mind!*" the senator snarled as he turned on his aide. "Barkley is *your* friend! *You* can escort him— both of them—out of my office!" Then he turned and cast a baleful eye on me. "If you think I'm going to sit by while you ruin everything I've worked for, you need a lot more treatment!"

Blair broke in. "Senator, he's not—"

But Young was already stalking out of the room. Constance stood up and eyed Blair coldly. "I'm going to call the attorney general. I want both of you replaced." She looked down at me and added, "You disappoint me, Philip. I told Warren you were bigger than this." She marched out with Terry in her wake.

Ten minutes later Blair and I were on our way back to the Metro station. She was too angry to speak and I was saving my breath to keep up with her stride. The silence continued until we reached the platform, where she was staring intently into the tunnel, daring the train to be late. "What now?" I asked, speaking to her back. She didn't reply. "I think we should return to Justice. It would be better if Evans heard it from us."

The lights started blinking to indicate the train's approach. She looked at me over her shoulder and said, "I was just thinking about Evans. I was trying to remember how he put it yesterday. I think it was something like, 'Philip has been around. He knows the Hill. His experience will prove useful.'" She turned back to peer into the tunnel again. "Useful," she repeated to herself.

"There wasn't anything I could do," I said.

"It would have been nice to know that going in."

"I'm sorry, Blair."

"I could've handled him if she hadn't set him off, you know? I could always handle guys like him. It was *her* I needed help with." She mimicked Constance's voice: "You disappoint me, Philip," she said, then added, "Join the club, lady."

A steady wind preceded the arrival of the train and

then it glided in on the power of its big electric motors. A two-tone bell signaled the opening of the doors and Blair stepped back to avoid the rush.

"We were married," I said.

She waited until the last passenger departed, then slowly turned around. "*Who* was married?"

"Constance and I. Let's get on."

She blinked. "You . . . and Constance Young."

"Yes."

"Married."

"That's right." The two-tone bell sounded again. "Let's go," I said.

She pushed by me and strode directly to a stone bench. I followed her over, started to sit, then thought better of it. The train glided away and we were alone on the platform.

"Well," she said finally, "at least I don't have to wonder anymore about why the new girl got this assignment. Maybe Constance was right. Maybe there is still a lot of Hoover in that building." She fiddled with the clasp of her bag muttering, "Fast track, my ass," then took out a package of gum. "I quit smoking. I thought it would be better for my career." She looked up and smiled. "Hey! Now I can go back! And I thought I was having a bad day!"

"I thought Evans had told you."

She made a face as if concentrating. "Hmmm. Let me think. Did he mention that you'd been married to Constance Young?" She closed her eyes for a moment then shook her head. "No . . . no, I think I'd remember that one, I really do. But just to be sure how badly I'm screwed, did you and the former Mrs. Barkley have what they call an 'amiable parting,' or did one of you dump the other?" She smiled sweetly and added, "I know that's a very personal question, but at this moment I really don't give a shit about your privacy."

"Constance divorced me and married Warren."

She nodded. "That's perfect. Yet *another* reason to ruin the senator's career. No wonder he went ballistic."

"My bias was supposed to be a cover."

"Evans told me that part," she said. "Mr. Integrity from the opposing party. I could see where people would buy it."

"They'd buy it in the hinterlands, but in this city, politics is a contact sport. They needed cover against the professionals, the rival campaigns, and the media, and as far as those people are concerned, I'm not a player anymore, I've shed my political skin. My value here was as the guy who got the short side of a love triangle. No one would believe I'd go in the tank to help Warren Young, not even in Washington."

Blair looked at me with something like pity in her eyes. I didn't resent it; I *was* pitiful. Mister Integrity. Traded his pride for a ticket to Oregon.

The blinking lights signaled the arrival of another train and Blair stood up. "Well," she said, "it looks like Martin Green put one over on us all." She held out her hand. "Good-bye, Philip," she said. "I'll see you around."

"Are you quitting the case?" I asked.

"No. To *quit* the case you have to be *on* the case. We're being replaced, remember?"

"They won't replace us."

"They won't?"

"Removing us would create a media free-for-all at the worst possible time."

"Our names haven't been announced yet. The media won't know we've been removed."

"They'd know if it leaked."

"I wouldn't do that," she said. "I don't play that way."

"I know."

She stared at me, wide-eyed. "*You'd* leak it?"

"It's not what I'd do that matters."

"I don't understand."

"What matters is that *they can't be sure* what I'd do. I have no career to protect and that makes me unpredictable, and they think I'm unstable, too. Evans told you I was hospitalized?"

To her credit she didn't blink. "Yes, he did."

"Well, put it all together and I'm a risk they can't afford to take."

She looked at me appraisingly. "Evans was right. You *have* been around."

"Right now, espionage is a viable theory. They need to keep the press at bay and hope things aren't what they seem."

"Do you think things *aren't* what they seem?" she asked.

"I don't know. We'll have to ask Martin Green."

There were three pink message slips on my desk, all from Evans, lined up chronologically and in ascending order of urgency. The last said, "Waiting for you." I went upstairs and found him in his chair, practicing his relaxation technique.

"I suppose I should ask for your side," he said wearily.

"It didn't go well."

"I gathered that. The first call came from the deputy—actually, the first *two* calls. Then the AG called."

"We tried, Alan."

"And I just heard from Chip Thurston."

"I don't know who he is."

"He's in Tony Guttierez's shop."

"I don't know him, either."

"Don't know—how long *were* you away?"

"Six months."

He looked surprised. "Six? It didn't seem that long."

"One hundred seventy-eight days."

He snorted. "But who's counting, right?"

"Right." Actually, I hadn't begun counting until I was well past day one hundred and sufficiently aware of my situation to care.

"Guttierez is the president's man on the Hill, the chief liaison, and he's heard a lot about *you,* all in the last hour. Apparently, Constance went through his office like Sherman through Atlanta. Thurston sounded like he just wet himself."

"She was pretty angry when we left."

"Mrs. Senator is a . . . uh, a *determined* lady."

"Mrs. Senator has had some hard knocks."

He nodded vigorously. "Of course she has, of course. I meant nothing by that, Philip. I just meant that Constance is running a very tight ship, that's all. She's been through a lot—you've *both* been through a lot."

"What did the AG have to say?"

"The bottom line is that you and Blair aren't being replaced, but Young is afraid that if there is anything negative to report you're going to make it worse than it is."

"It's a bit late to start worrying about my bias."

"I know, it doesn't make sense but he's not rational about it. He was all for the strategy when he was sure the Green thing was crap, but this Hungarian stuff has got him all shook up."

"Where do we come out?"

"We need to keep you away from the action."

"Oregon is about three thousand miles away."

He shook his head. "You're staying on board in case there's some innocent explanation for this new development. Then it doesn't look like we took a dive."

"That's the plan. All we need now is the innocent explanation."

"Plan or no plan, we'd get killed if we replaced anyone on the first day. You know how those things get around." He looked at me pointedly.

"So, I'm not in Oregon. How far away am I?"

"Leave the actual investigation to the Bureau. If something gets screwed up, a document gets lost or some witness claims his words were twisted, you can't be blamed. Your job is oversight, just as I said. Meet with the agents, get updated, and write nice, neutral reports addressed to me. I know you used to run investigations, so if you've got a suggestion for Blair, fine. Whisper it in her ear or write it in disappearing ink. Just don't do anything that looks like you're putting the screws to Young."

"She may need some help on the Hill."

"So it would seem. You can hold her hand if she has to go up there but stay in the background. It's her show."

"All right," I said, getting out of my chair, "it's her show."

"Philip."

"What?"

He lowered his voice. "What do you think? What does your gut tell you about Green?"

If I was going to keep my distance, that was as good a time as any to start. "My gut doesn't talk to me anymore," I told him.

"*Nothing at all?*"

"It's the medication."

There was another message on my desk when I got back to my office. It said, "Agent Turner" and gave a cell phone number. I reached her in her car.

"Where are you going?" I asked.

"Swimming."

"Is that a euphemism?"

"No, an exercise. Very good for relieving stress. I'm going to break the world record for a thousand meters today."

"I guess you've heard," I said.

"That we're still stuck to tar baby? You were right, I'm impressed."

"There's been an adjustment, though."

"Right, Plan B, under which you can't be blamed. Who does *that* leave?"

"You'll do an investigation that can't be second-guessed and I'll write a neutral, fact-bound report. Whatever happens, we'll all get out of this okay. What's on for tomorrow?"

"I'm taking another agent along to question some of Green's friends in-depth. Maybe they can tell us more about his behavior or where he might have gone. Who knows? One of them might be in contact with him."

"Good luck."

"I want to ask you something."

"Go ahead."

"Are there any more surprises in store, or do I know what I need to about you?"

"I'm an open book," I said.

3

I DON'T LIKE TO STAY on the bench by my daughter's grave. It's too far from her headstone, an impersonal distance. You can't carry on a conversation.

I usually start out there, especially if the ground is cold or wet. But we get to talking and I always move closer when it gets serious. I tell her how I miss her so much it makes me cry at really inconvenient times, and I tell her that someday we'll all be together again. I always end up on the ground. I take out her doll to show her that I have it. Constance wanted me to put it in the casket, and when she found it in the house that was the end of us. Not that it wasn't going to happen anyway, but that was pretty much the end.

I told my daughter about my new assignment. I told her that her mother was still very beautiful. I didn't mention what happened in the meeting. I never talk about the bad stuff, how everything went wrong when she died.

The day after the meeting I showed up for work on time, although I had been effectively benched while the investigation went forward. A manila envelope from Blair was already on my desk. It was Green's file, all the rudimentary details gathered when the government vetted him for access to the nation's secrets, supplemented by the FBI's "first pass" interviews of his friends and acquaintances, a try for a quick solution. The second, more thorough inquiry was now under way and a copy of the witness list was in the envelope. Blair was on one of the two-agent teams at work that very morning, beginning at the outer circle of the bull's-eye and working their way toward the center—those that knew him best—digging more deeply into their subject and pooling information as they progressed.

I spent the morning reading and rereading, drawing on my own intuition to supplement what was known about the alleged spy. It wasn't hard. I knew Martin Green growing up, many people did. He was born in Brooklyn, New York, and raised in a New Jersey suburb. His father was an actuary for a Newark insurance company and his mother a secretary for the local synagogue. The emphasis in the family home was on education. Martin was one of those academic overachievers who spend their high school years avoiding the jocks and toughs as they make their way from band rehearsal to meetings of the Latin Club.

Princeton was more or less an extension of high school. Green joined the Hillel Society for Jewish students and the German Club, but largely abstained from the collegiate experience, spending four years cloistered in his dormitory room, eating cafeteria meals and going home most weekends. I searched for clues, indications of the traumatic moment or watershed event that might have led him to treason. What was it? An influential professor? A summer abroad? Rejection by some gentile goddess or student society? This wasn't the Princeton of *The Sun Also Rises*. If Green was isolated it was likely that his Jewish heritage was less a factor than his own inclination.

But whatever misery and injustice might have befallen him as an adolescent and young adult—all the unattended proms and big games, the unattainable coeds, the invitations to the eating clubs that never came—the serious-minded young man from New Jersey eventually learned, as do we all, that each of us reaches a peak, and later is better and more enduring. The apex of the arc of his life span awaited him in Washington, a Mecca for self-starters imbued with intelligence, energy, and a commitment to making a difference. He began as a staffer for the House International Relations Committee and soon his acumen and industry propelled him upward and opened doors to ever-widening social opportunities. Away from work he joined a thriving synagogue that offered not only spiritual nourishment but, owing to its locale, occasions to debate philosophy, politics, and social responsibility with some of the very people whose views helped frame public discourse. After ten years in Washington, Martin Green's life seemed to be fully realized: a stimulating environment, a satisfying, well-paying job, a circle of accomplished friends, and a live-in relationship with one Diana Morris.

Green's energy was boundless. It seemed there wasn't a worthy cause that was denied his help, and there were plenty. The nation's capital has all the problems of any major city, more than many, and he didn't have to stray far in his Capitol Hill neighborhood to see them up close. Did something cause him to betray the country that nurtured and employed him? Teddy Roosevelt wrote that the "dreadful misery" of a great city could excite the sympathies of a generous young man and turn him to socialism or advocacy of wild schemes. But it was a long leap from advocacy to action, and given all the positives of Martin Green's Washington life, it would have taken an extraordinary experience to transform him into a traitor.

But something had caused him to run. I wanted to be with Blair to hear firsthand from the people who knew him best. I got the secondhand version when she called around noon. "We've done two interviews," she told me. "Both are friends outside of work. One he met as a volunteer at the Holocaust Museum. The other is the chairman of the Neighborhood Advisory Commission. They both think he's a candidate for sainthood, or whatever it is they do for Jews. Neither has any idea why he'd disappear. We had to tiptoe around the spy stuff but it wouldn't have yielded anything."

"Neither one noticed any strange behavior?"

"No. What did you think of the file?"

"I didn't see anything remarkable, certainly nothing to suggest a motive for treason. It looks like these are the best days of his life, or were."

"I know. I'd like to snatch Miss Takács off the street and question her for a few hours."

"Is she under surveillance?"

"Every minute. Nothing. No trips to the Portrait Gallery, no suspicious behavior, no change in routine. If she's missing her Marty, she doesn't act like it."

"Do you think there might have been something between them?"

"I doubt it. They never touched one another. No hand-holding, no peck on the cheek. If there was something between them it was business, but right now it's one big question mark."

"You have to wonder what business they could have had that wasn't espionage. Maybe our mysterious Hungarian was the one providing information, just as Constance suggested."

"Was she suggesting? I thought she was in accusation mode. Anyway, there's nothing to support that theory, and it would have been far removed from what he was working on."

"What was that?"

"He was more involved in process than anything else. How the various agencies effectively coordinate their efforts, the proper balance of human resources and gee-whiz technology, stuff like that."

"What's your agenda for the rest of the day?"

"More interviews. Probably more testimonials to Saint Martin."

"I'd love to go along."

"Sorry, you're grounded, remember? But tomorrow you can write your first report. Got to go. Bye."

I went out to lunch and ate a sandwich in the department courtyard. It was already past two and I had the place to myself. I sat against the fountain, contemplating my options for the afternoon. There was nothing more to be done with the Green file and the thought of returning to my office to write a brief was depressing. The only productive thing to do that I could think of was to follow my doctor's orders to get some exercise. I went out to Constitution Avenue and turned east toward the

Capitol. By the time I reached the National Gallery of Art I had a plan.

According to the *Post*, the Senate Select Committee on Intelligence was holding a public hearing that afternoon. The director of the CIA was going to be testifying about some debacle in an unpronounceable region of Central Asia. Because Chairman Young did not want to make hay at the expense of the White House, it was the CIA's sad lot to be the whipping boy whenever the president's national security adviser gave the boss bum advice. The show would attract the staff's attention, so their offices in the Hart Senate Office Building would be fairly quiet.

A call from the security desk to the staff director got me inside and a few minutes later I was sitting at Green's desk, hoping for an epiphany. Blair's troops had already taken his desk diary, computer, and files, but I had this idea that the surroundings might give me a better sense of our quarry. His office was a corner cubicle separated from the rest of the space by a five-foot-high steel-and-frosted-glass partition on two sides. The wall behind was covered with awards, certificates, and letters signifying his commitment to his country, community, and faith. Among them was an achievement award from the Intelligence Committee, and citations from a homeless shelter, a food bank, and an AIDS clinic.

There was a photograph on the windowsill of an attractive woman whom I assumed to be Diana Morris. There was also a single photograph on the desk, Green with Senator and Mrs. Young. It was taken at a lawn party at Edward Young's vast residence, the most photographed in the Washington area. The senator and

Green were smiling at Constance, who was gesturing happily toward the camera. She was between the two men, the center of attention, the center of the frame. It was, more than anything, a photograph of her.

"Can I help you?" The voice startled me. Standing in the entrance to the cubicle was a young woman with glasses perched on her forehead and an identification card on a chain around her neck.

I took out my own identification and held it toward her. "Philip Barkley. I'm with the Justice Department."

She stared at the identification for a moment with a grim expression. I didn't realize she was struggling for control until she spoke. "Do you think Martin's all right?" she asked, her voice trembling.

"We're trying our best to find out. Do you work for the committee?"

"Uh-huh. I've only been over here six months but I was with the Banking Committee for almost seven years."

"And do you like it here?"

"It's much better. I didn't get along with this one guy at Banking who was hitting on me all the time, so I asked Senator Young's administrative aide if he could help me move."

"I see."

"Senator Young was on Banking until he became chairman over here."

"Uh-huh. Do you know Martin very well?"

"Sure, we were both at Banking, although I was there first. Martin joined us when we held the hearings on the Swiss banks and the Holocaust. That was five, six years ago."

"I remember. That was very interesting."

"Martin's Jewish."

"I see. And you're Jenny Castellano?"

"How did you know?"

"It's on your ID card there."

"Oh." She looked down at the card.

"Jenny, have you been interviewed by the FBI yet?"

"I was off when the FBI was here," she replied, still looking at the card. "One of them called me at home and wanted to know if I had any idea where Martin was. I told him no. He asked me to call him if I discovered anything unusual or missing when I got back to the office. I asked if something had been stolen and he said that they were just trying to get a complete picture of what might have happened." When she looked up there were tears in her eyes. "Maybe they think there was a break-in and something happened to Martin."

"We have to look at every possibility," I said, "but I don't think so. It could just be that something is bothering him and he had to be by himself." She began to look more distressed as she fingered her identification card and looked around the cubicle. "Do you think something was bothering him, Jenny?"

Her eyes went to the photograph on the windowsill. "I'd ask *her*."

"Is that Diana Morris?"

"Uh-huh."

"Does she know?"

"Maybe."

"Why do you think so?"

"Part something I heard and part intuition. I have good intuition."

"Well, I'm interested in both parts. Would you care to sit down?"

She looked around nervously before she sat, keeping one eye on the doorway as she spoke. "The night before Martin disappeared he was here at his desk till late."

"Was that unusual?"

She smiled. "We call him 'the Energizer Bunny.' Sometimes I think working with him is going to give me carpal tunnel. And that's not all he does, either."

"I understand he's very active in the community."

"Sure, and he's going for his master's degree at Georgetown at night."

"A master's? That's a lot of work."

"He's writing a thesis on how different countries dealt with the Holocaust. I helped him get materials from Banking."

"I'll bet he was very grateful."

"Martin is very smart. He's got a photographic memory, a real one."

"That's very rare."

She nodded her agreement. "And he's very nice, too."

"You were telling me about the night before he disappeared."

She took another glance toward the door and lowered her voice. "I was walking down the hall to a little refrigerator we have and I saw his lamp on, so I came in to ask him if he wanted anything. He was facing the windowsill, kind of bent over the desk and holding his head. He was talking on the telephone, real low."

"Did he see you?"

"No, and I didn't realize he was on the phone until I looked in."

"Okay. And he was talking to Diana?"

"That's my guess."

"Why?"

"The way he was talking real low, you know, the way a guy does when he's talking to a girl. It's a different way of talking, different from a business conversation or when he's talking to another guy. It's like the way you talk to your wife, you know?"

"What did he say?"

"I really couldn't hear much, just a word or two, but I'm pretty sure he was upset. It was more the *way* that he was talking, okay? The way he was talking, the way he was sitting, and the look on his face."

"What kind of look?"

"I knocked on the glass and I surprised him because he turned around real fast. He looked real upset. He asked me what I wanted and his voice was kind of mad and kind of . . . upset. I told him I'd catch him later and left."

"And you don't recall any words?"

She gazed at the floor a moment before replying. "I guess it was just the way he was talking and the way he looked." She wiped at her eyes and I handed her a tissue from a box on the desk.

"All right, Jenny, so what does your intuition tell you?"

"I think she was putting the screws to him or something like that," she replied, dabbing at her eyes.

"Did Martin fight with Diana much?"

"I don't know. I only saw her a couple of times when they met outside the building."

"Jenny, do you think Martin has another girlfriend or something? You know, another girl that she found out about?"

"A lot of girls think he's *so* good-looking but I don't think he was dating anyone." She smiled and added,

"The only woman he really paid attention to around here was Mrs. Young."

"Because she was the boss's wife," I suggested.

She shook her head. "No, it wasn't that. I think he really admired her. And she thought he was real smart, too—you could tell. They were always talking about something or other when she was in the office." She pointed to the picture on the desk. "She gave him that."

"It's a nice picture," I said. "What about men friends? Who would you say is Martin's closest friend around here?"

She thought for a moment. "Maybe Mitchell Glass."

"Does he work for the committee, too?"

"He used to. He reviewed budgets and crunched all kinds of numbers. But he moved over to work for the campaign just after I got here."

She agreed to call me if she thought of anything else, then left me alone in the cubicle. I made some notes and took one last look at the photograph on the desk. I couldn't remember the last time I'd seen Constance that happy.

I was deep in thought when I stepped on the elevator and didn't realize who was behind me until a voice said, "You *do* have a masochistic streak, don't you?" The Southern accent was less in evidence. The elevator stopped again and I moved to allow a flood of passengers to fill the gap between us, although I could feel Sanders's eyes on me as we rode down. I thought I was going to have to explain my presence but he just shouldered past the others and stalked off. A woman muttered "asshole" under her breath but he was already well down the corridor, probably heading for a telephone.

It was past five o'clock. I was carried along by a tide

of government servants flowing off the Hill toward homes, bars, restaurants, and gyms. I wasn't expected anywhere by anyone so I strolled back down Constitution Avenue toward Justice, passing a row of newspaper vending machines. The *Washington Times* headline was "Justice Probes Hill Veteran Disappearance." I got the details at my bus stop on Tenth Street, reading over the shoulder of another commuter. There was a quote from Senator Young stating his determination to get the facts. I was described as "a key witness in a probe of campaign finance abuses four years ago." There was more to the story and I was waiting for my fellow traveler to turn the page when a black sedan pulled to the curb with a screech of brakes. Blair was behind the wheel. "Get in," she said.

The commuter looked at Blair, then over his shoulder at me. I stepped around him and got in the car. As I closed the door he grinned and said, "That never happens to me." Blair stomped on the gas pedal and we were off.

"Are you taking me home?" I asked. "I live in Virginia."

She ignored me but turned south at the next corner, heading for the Fourteenth Street Bridge. The car in front of us started to slow for a yellow light. Blair swerved around it and sped through the intersection as the signal went red; I grabbed the handle above the door and held on. A moment later we were on the bridge.

"Do you remember Plan B?" she asked. "Where you leave the investigation to us? I know it's been a whole day since we discussed it."

"Did Sanders call the AG?"

She looked at me sharply. "Sanders?"

"I ran into him. He wasn't happy to see me."

"Jesus Christ, Philip, it just keeps getting worse."

"He didn't call?"

"I don't know what he did. We called the Intelligence Committee to arrange follow-up interviews and the staff director said you were in Green's office right then."

"I wanted to have a look at his surroundings for my report."

We were on the bridge when her cell phone began to ring. She picked it up and snapped, "Turner." She listened a moment and said, "I've got him. I'm taking him home." After another moment she said, "I know," then hung up.

She stewed for a few moments while we sped along. It wasn't until we were stopped in traffic that she said, "I don't want to be relieved of duty on this case. I'm not planning to go off to a new career someplace else. This is it for me, understand?"

"Sure."

"Then stick with the damn program."

"My involvement is supposed to give people confidence in the report. That's not going to happen if all I do is choose the typeface and the margins."

"And you think going to Green's office is going to help?"

"I wanted to get a feel for the guy, that's all."

"And do you have a feel for him?"

"I don't know. So far, I don't see the motive for treason."

She tapped the shoulder bag on the seat. "There's some gum in there. Whenever I'm around you I get the urge for a cigarette." I fished out the gum, took off the paper, and handed her a foil-wrapped piece.

"I live in Springfield," I said.

"Right."

"Did you learn anything today?"

"Saint Martin may have had relationship problems."

"Diana Morris?"

She nodded. "His significant other. A friend of theirs saw them at an engagement party less than two weeks before. Green left. She says that they were barely talking and both looked miserable. Diana alluded to some kind of strife but didn't want to discuss what was wrong."

"Well, you said that he might have had a fight with his girlfriend and jumped ship. Maybe you're right."

"That was before we learned about his Hungarian interlude, and this guy is proving just too hard to find."

"It still could be about a personal relationship gone wrong."

She shook her head. "I've been in a couple of those. I didn't jump in my car and disappear without a trace and neither did the guys, though one of them joined the navy. If Marty and Diana had their problems then all it probably means is that he's a spy with domestic trouble. Do you read Deighton and Le Carré? *All* spies have domestic trouble. It goes with the territory."

We rode along for a few minutes in silence while I thought about the picture of Green that was forming in my mind. "Were you popular in college?" I asked.

She glanced over. "What do you mean, 'popular'?"

"Did you participate in school activities?"

"Swim team, a sorority, and now that you ask, MUSKET."

"What's that?"

"A theater group. Musicals."

"So you had a good social life?"

"Nobody wrote my name in the john but I had a few dates. Where's this going?"

"If Diana's really important to him or he didn't have much experience with relationships, it might have hit him harder than you'd expect. It's something to consider."

"I'll consider it," she replied vaguely. "So, where do you live?"

"That's my building over there." The Commodore was distinguishable at some distance. In a misguided attempt to imbue his creation with "personality," some demented architect specified brick with a yellowish hue and industrial green vinyl panels arrayed in a pattern between floors. It looked like someone had vomited on a checkerboard. Blair turned off the interstate and a few moments later we pulled up in front of the lobby.

"When are you going to interview Diana?" I asked.

"In a few more days. You don't have any plans to go over there, do you?"

"No. I was just curious."

"I meant what I said, Philip. Don't get us fired."

I went to bed that night thinking about Green. I dreamt that I was at a party and Constance, Warren, and I were all standing together. She was smiling and laughing at everything he said. I just stared and wondered why she didn't look that way with me.

4

I SPENT THE NEXT THREE days writing the definitive brief on the Border Patrol's authority to stop and search vehicles riding "suspiciously low." I was keeping busy and staying clear of Blair's investigation. When I finished I looked around for more to do and discovered that Evans had reassigned the rest of my workload. He wanted me focused on writing the progress reports. There was no telling what might make it into circulation.

The sudden vacuum demanded to be filled and, as if on cue, the first FBI "302s"—reports of interview—arrived on my desk. Blair and her teams had interviewed most of Green's friends and associates. Everyone had been cooperative; as far as they were concerned this was a missing persons case, albeit an important person who happened to be very missing.

No one had had contact with Martin, nor a clue where he could be. No one knew why he left. There was, however, some corroboration for the "troubled relationship" theory. One couple reported a last-minute cancellation of a recent dinner date; Diana's explanation was vague. Other friends said that she and Martin seemed less cheerful in the weeks before his disappearance. One longtime colleague reported that his first reaction to the news about Martin was, "They split up."

As Blair predicted, there was no news from the police. The burden was on the FBI and the fault line of responsibility ran right through the desk of the case agent, the field leader of all the investigators hunting for Martin. It was an impressive operation. For starters, Diana's and Green's family members were under surveillance twenty-four hours a day, a massive use of manpower but nothing compared to that required to search for a man who could be anywhere.

Not that the Bureau's hunt wasn't focused. An analysis of Green's spending history, supplemented by the information garnered in interviews, had produced a profile of the man—habits, preferences, and tastes—that enabled the FBI to shrink the prime hunting ground. The missing man was a creature of the city and the densely populated suburb. He'd never lived in the country, gone to summer camp in the mountains, or done a stint in the army. Nor had he formed any attachments to the quaint villages on Martha's Vineyard or the Outer Banks. He was a fish out of water in rural America, and following the laws of probability, the FBI was devoting minimal coverage to the vast web of farms, villages, and small towns that connect metropolitan areas from coast-to-coast, concentrating instead on the terrain that was its quarry's natural habitat.

And not all metropolitan areas received equal attention. Green was born, raised, educated, and employed on the East Coast, so the Atlantic seaboard was the first choice, from Washington north to Boston and south to

Charlotte, Atlanta, and Florida's major population centers. The secondary area of concentration was comprised of Pacific coast cities that were familiar but appealingly distant for a fugitive from the East: Seattle, Portland, San Francisco, Los Angeles, and San Diego. The third was an assortment of cities that were likely to register in his consciousness: Pittsburgh, Cleveland, Chicago, St. Louis, and Dallas.

It is axiomatic that inexperienced fugitives gravitate to comfortable surroundings and activities. No surprise: the FBI had concluded that Martin's faith was a cornerstone of his life, and with the resources that only the Bureau could muster, a plan had been formed to contact every synagogue in the country. Those in the target cities were actually being visited; the rest received a fax bulletin and a photograph. Thanks to the miracle of technology, if Green showed up anywhere seeking spiritual sustenance there was a good chance the FBI would hear about it.

The religion angle was the most obvious, but only one of several. The subject loved Greek food, symphonies, and minor league baseball; every Greek restaurant, symphony box office and ball park had his picture. He jogged for exercise, preferring a particular model of shoe left behind in his closet. All the stores in target cities that carried it had his picture and his size: ten-and-a-half narrow.

It took a couple of hours to work through the material and outline my first report. Writing it was another story. I stared at the computer screen for some time without getting beyond "To" and "From." I didn't want to write; I wanted to act. Actually, what I wanted to do was talk to someone who really knew Martin Green.

The problem was that I was under orders to stay clear of witnesses. Opportunity knocked when I perused the Bureau's interview list and realized that it had omitted a potentially rich source of information. So, I rationalized it: if a man wasn't on the witness list he wasn't a witness, right? And thus the orders didn't apply. Sparing no time for second thoughts, I immediately called Martin's synagogue, explained who I was, and asked to speak to the rabbi. A woman was in the middle of informing me that he was unavailable when she was interrupted by a man's voice shouting "Who is it?" I could hear footsteps, then her voice some distance from the phone, repeating what I'd told her. The man was on immediately.

"This is Rabbi Adler. Is this about Martin?"

"Yes, Rabbi, it is. I—"

"Is he all right?"

"We haven't located him yet. I was hoping you could help us do that."

"Anything! What can I do?"

"I'd like to talk to you to get some more background on Martin. You never know what could be helpful."

"Yes, of course. Are you coming now? Should I come there?"

"I'll come to you," I told him. "I'll be there in twenty minutes." I locked up my documents and took a taxi ride uptown, pleased to be out of the office and doing something to advance the investigation. If I learned anything useful I'd probably have to share it with Blair, who wouldn't be impressed by my technical defense to violating her hands-off decree. I decided to worry about that if and when it happened.

When we pulled up in front of the synagogue a husky middle-aged man wearing a white short-sleeved shirt and black pants hurried down to the curb. He reached through the window as I was paying the driver. "Sam Adler," he said, engulfing my hand in his.

"Philip Barkley, Rabbi. Thanks for meeting me on such short notice."

"For Martin, anything," he replied, opening the door. "Come." He turned on his heel and bounded up the steps toward the entrance. Rabbi Adler had the forearms and wrists of a bricklayer but moved as if he were all coiled springs inside. When we entered the lobby he stooped to pick up a card that had fallen from the bulletin board, then surveyed the assorted notices of seminars, trips, lectures, and workshops for an open space.

"It looks like there's plenty going on," I said.

"We have a very active congregation," he replied, jackhammering tacks with his thumb. He stepped back to survey his handiwork then beckoned me to follow again. A few left and right turns and we were in his office behind the sanctuary. "We have tea," he said, setting a chair for me in front of his desk. "Juice, seltzer water, no coffee."

"No, thanks, I'm fine."

"What do you want to know about Martin?"

"Whatever you can tell me. I'm just trying to get a better feel for him and maybe some idea of why he would just pick up and go."

Rabbi Adler looked surprised. "Do you think that's what happened? That Martin just went away?"

"That's a real possibility. How long have you known him?"

"Since he joined the congregation. I think he came in my second year, so that's—what?—nine years ago? Ten?" He shrugged. "Who remembers?"

"Is he an active member?"

"*Active?*" he cried, rolling his eyes. "He's every-where! In everything! A *mensch*!"

"I've heard that."

"And smart! He speaks Hebrew and other languages. French, I think. And German. Very smart. He knows his Torah, too. That's the Hebrew Bible, some of the Bible. What you call 'The Old Testament.' "

"Yes."

"And he was getting a master's degree in public policy at Georgetown, did you know that?"

"That's what I was told."

"He's taking a course about values, ethics, and public policy."

"That sounds very interesting."

He nodded enthusiastically and kept nodding while he tried to think of more wonderful things to tell me about his congregant. "His mother worked in a syna-gogue in New Jersey," he added.

"I was wondering if you noticed any change in his behavior lately. Did he seem anxious or upset about anything?"

"No, but I haven't seen him much in the last month. He must have been traveling. He has a very important job, a lot of responsibility."

"So you haven't observed any changes in him at all?"

The rabbi leaned back in his chair. "Changes," he said to himself, rubbing his cheek. A moment passed. "Life is about change," he said finally. "There are bless-ings and we are thankful. There are disappointments and we cling to our faith and do what we can. God works His will and we rejoice or we persevere."

"Did Martin persevere?"

The rabbi bit his lip, then tilted his head slowly from side to side like a pendulum while he considered the question. "Martin is like a lot of young people, very idealistic, so he sees things in terms of black and white." He wagged a finger at me. "That's not so bad. The Bible teaches, 'Thou hast commanded us to keep Thy precepts diligently.' That's in the New Testament, too. 'We can be sure that we know God only by keeping His commandments.'"

"The First Letter of John."

"Ah! You know your Bible! What church do you belong to?"

"Methodist. My father was a minister."

"Wonderful! Where?"

"A small town in Ohio, not far from Dayton."

He nodded, satisfied. "So, you understand. Can I tell you a story about Martin? It will illustrate my point."

"Please."

"When he was at Princeton there was a tragedy. A young man killed himself." He threw up his hands. "Jumped off a roof!"

"That's terrible."

"Terrible," he agreed. "He was a senior, a wonderful future. Everybody was very upset, as you can imagine." The rabbi leaned forward, clasping his hands in front of him. "Martin . . . well, he saw things a little differently. He wrote a letter to the school newspaper saying that it was tragic but what the young man did was a sin against God's law." He leaned back again, waiting for my reaction.

"I'm sure that antagonized a lot of people."

"Of course, but that was Martin, you see? Black and white, right and wrong. How can a man like that work up there?"

"By 'up there' you mean Congress."

"For Martin, there were a lot of disappointments. He had preconceived notions when he came to Washington, who doesn't?"

"What were his about?"

"Social responsibility, the ability of government to do good, what motivates public servants." The rabbi sighed. "Young people like Martin think they understand the real world but they don't understand the real world. I think he became very disillusioned with the lawmakers."

"Disillusioned enough to leave?"

"Leave Washington?"

"Or the country. Maybe he found someplace less disappointing."

"Where?"

"I don't know. What about Israel?"

The rabbi's mobile face crinkled into a "no" response. "He was interested in visiting Israel but it was the normal curiosity that most Jews have, that's all."

"What about an ancestral home?"

"He never talked about that."

"Some people at work thought that he was interested in central Europe: Germany, Austria, Poland, Hungary."

"Europe? Well, as I said, he spoke French and German, but he never talked about those places with me." He pondered the notion a moment longer, then said, "Leaving doesn't make sense. What of his family? And there's a girl here in Washington."

"Have you met her?"

"No, he never brought her here. I don't think she's Jewish."

"Did Martin ever speak about her?"

"Just a little. Her name is Diana, I know that much. He would say that they were going here or there or doing this and that, that's all. I'm not being much help, am I?"

"Everything helps. Let me ask you, Rabbi, where would *you* look for Martin?"

The question surprised him. "Where would I . . . ?" He shrugged. "Well, he's from New Jersey so I'd talk with his family there, but I assume you've already done that."

"We have. Any other suggestions?"

He frowned. "I have to tell you, the idea of Martin just picking up and leaving without so much as a good-bye is hard for me to accept. Family, friends, community, they're all very important to him. He treasured his relationships more than position, more than material things. He's not like most people in political life."

"Can you tell me the last time you saw him?"

The rabbi frowned in concentration. "The last time . . . I guess when he returned some books. Martin is an ardent student of the Bible. He picks portions with themes that he's considering and he'll study and reflect. So, he borrowed some works of The Later Prophets and returned them on . . . what day of the week did he disappear?"

"Friday."

"Okay. Tuesday or Wednesday, I'm sure of it." He held up a finger. "Ah! Maybe he *knew* he was leaving. *That's* why he returned the books then instead of waiting till Friday or Saturday."

"Entirely possible."

He shook his head. "So, what else can I tell you?"

"Nothing right now, but if I think of something can I call you?"

"Of course, you can reach me here or at home." He scribbled his telephone numbers on a sheet of paper.

"Thank you, Rabbi, I appreciate your time."

He walked me back to the entrance and we shook hands at the top of the steps. "Can I call you a taxi?" he asked.

"No, I need some exercise, doctor's orders. I'll walk a bit and get one later."

"*Zay gezunt,*" he said.

"Good-bye, Rabbi, and thanks." I started down the steps and realized that I had one more question.

"Rabbi."

He turned around. "Yes?"

"The last books Martin borrowed, The Later Prophets. What was the theme?"

The rabbi smiled. "One of the most interesting," he replied.

"And that is?"

"Betrayal."

—————————

From my bedroom in Ohio I could see a long way. Our clapboard house was on a hill adjacent to a farm, and the vista stretched over miles and miles of pasture. I could lie on my bed and see a silo on the horizon, imagining it to be different things at different stages of my youth: a giant in a faraway land, a spaceship, a lighthouse. I liked that it was always there, spanning seasons and years, a distant beacon that signaled everything was in its place.

Sitting at my apartment window hours after leaving Green's synagogue, I found myself wondering whether that silo was still there. It didn't seem likely; nothing was in its place anymore. Some things should never change, I told myself. Some things should endure. Love. Children. Values, too. Like a distant silo to orient by as you make your way. Perhaps that was what happened to poor Martin. They kept moving the silo. And after years of moving silos, nothing or no one could be relied upon to be steadfast, not even him. That was the nature of betrayal.

The doorbell rang. It never did before, not in the two years I'd been in the apartment. I stared down my short hallway and it rang again, followed immediately by an impatient knock. I hurried to the door and found myself face-to-face with Constance. She was casually dressed, her hair pulled back in a ponytail, revealing diamond stud earrings of serious dimension. "Are you going to invite me in?" she asked.

"Yes, you just surprised me, that's all."

I stepped back and she strode past to the living room, talking as she went. "I'm sorry to barge in like this but I was driving home and decided that I needed to talk to you. It was a spur-of-the-moment thing." She turned and smiled. "I guess I haven't changed much, have I?"

"I guess not," I said.

"I would have called but my cell phone is dead. Warren says that I either have to talk less or carry a spare battery." She inspected the couch before settling on it.

"Can I get you anything?"

"No, don't bother," she replied, scanning the bare walls. "I'll be out of your hair in a few moments. You know, you should have taken some of our paintings. They're all in storage if you're interested." Her gaze returned to me. "Please sit down, Philip."

I sat. "What did you want to talk to me about?"

"I want this kept between us. I want you to promise."

"I'm working on a case, Constance."

She folded her arms and said, "If you don't promise then there's nothing to talk about." A few more seconds passed. "Come on, Philip, you'll never learn what I'm going to tell you if you don't hear it from me."

"All right."

She inhaled and said, "The telephone calls that FBI person asked about were to me."

"Martin called *you* from his office?"

"Yes."

"Why?"

"A few days before, I was at a reception at the Phillips Gallery. On the way home I stopped by Warren's office to pick up some papers I needed for an organizing trip." She shook her head with disgust. "Am I *supposed* to be the one organizing at state level? No. But we've got some dead wood and you know how *that* is. Every donor's got a kid who wants to party through the campaign, then get an office in the West Wing to tell the president how to fix the country. And there isn't one in the bunch who can balance a checkbook."

"So, you went to the office."

"I was also going to pick up a briefing book that Warren needed for a hearing the next day. It was supposed to be on his desk but wasn't, so I went over to the staff offices to see if someone could help me. The only one working late was Martin. He was at the copier, copying away, and he didn't notice me until I was right at his elbow. He nearly jumped out of his skin. On second thought, can I have some water, please?"

"Sure."

"You don't have any bottled water, do you?"

"No, just tap water."

"Do you have anything else to drink?"

"I have some diet cola and some juice, I think."

"Diet cola would be grand."

She followed me to the kitchen and watched as I filled a glass with ice. The tab broke off the first can and I silently cursed it and grabbed another. I could feel her eyes on me the whole time. "I was thinking about some more landscaping for the plot," she said. "I'd like to put in some annuals so there would be color most of the year."

"That would be nice," I said.

"Do you have any suggestions?"

"The annuals sound like a good idea."

"I'm open to whatever you want to do."

"I wish the bench was closer."

"We've already talked about that. It's as close as they can put it and still do maintenance."

"Okay."

"If there was a way to have the bench closer I'd tell them to move it."

"It's okay." I handed her the cola and we went back to the living room. "You said Martin was startled," I prompted.

"More than startled, my dear. He turned pale. Before I could say anything he began stammering about working late to get ready for the hearings and how he could have used some help that night. And as he's talking, he's gathering up all the papers into a stack."

"What did you make of it?"

"I didn't know what to make of it. I thought he might have been doing his résumé or some copying for a friend. You know how the staff abuses the government facilities. It used to be just the copiers and telephones. Now they spend half their time trading stocks on the Internet, for God's sake."

"What happened then?"

"Nothing. He found the briefing book for me and I left."

"Then he called you on August 30, the night before he disappeared."

"That's right. He was upset. I think he was crying. He said that he was sorry. I asked, sorry about what? He said that he'd made a terrible mistake. Those were his words: 'terrible mistake.' "

"What did he do?"

"He wouldn't say. He kept repeating it, though, and then he said something like 'I didn't realize,' but didn't finish the sentence. I think someone must have come into the room or walked by because he hung up."

"But he called again."

"Less than ten minutes later. He told me that he was sorry. I thought he meant he was sorry for hanging up but that wasn't it. He was apologizing for something that he'd done."

"And he never said what that was?"

"No." She sighed. "It's all so sad, really. He's a wonderful man, very diligent, very public-spirited. And he's one of the smartest people I've met up there."

"Do you have any idea why he called you?"

She looked surprised, as if it were obvious. "I suppose

because I caught him at the copying machine that night."

"But if you didn't know what he was copying, why call you to apologize?"

"Maybe he thought I suspected him, who knows?" She began tapping on the nails of one hand with those of the other. I recognized the sign that she was growing irritated.

"All right, so what do you *think* he was copying?"

She grimaced and said, "I think he was copying classified documents."

"That would indicate a breach of national security, Constance." She nodded but didn't reply. "When the FBI agent suggested espionage you rejected it. In fact, you tore into her pretty good."

"That was then, this is now," she said testily. "What did you expect me to do, Philip, agree with her? Warren is resisting that possibility, you saw that. He sees it as the end of his campaign."

"He might be right. Why are you telling me this?"

"Because the truth is going to come out sooner or later, and his candidacy might survive 'sooner.' There's still almost five months to the first primary, enough time for damage control. But if your report doesn't get released until the end of the year, we've got no chance."

"Same question: why are you telling me this?"

"Don't be obtuse, darling, it's not becoming. The FBI woman already believes Martin was spying and I just gave you corroboration."

"That I'm not permitted to repeat."

She shook her head, clearly exasperated. "What I'm

trying to tell you is that you don't have to drag this out to the bitter end. Martin is obviously running and doesn't want to be found. Put that together with what we already know and you don't need what I've told you to reach the obvious conclusion. So, write your report. Say that the investigation is continuing but the signs point to espionage. The only criticism you'd ever face for jumping the gun is from us and we're not going to complain. Do you understand? We're not going to challenge you on this. We're going to agree, by our silence, at least, that the logic is there. Regrets are going to be expressed, new preventive measures will be put in place, and then we'll all move on."

She looked away and sipped her cola, waiting for my reply. When we first met as negotiators over Senate bills she was a skilled player who could keep her agenda well-hidden when necessary. Later, during our courtship and first years of marriage, it seemed relatively easy to read her mind and make her happy. In our final year she became an impenetrable fortress whose thoughts and feelings were as mysterious as her movements.

"There are other parties in interest, Constance. Martin's friends and family, not to mention Martin himself."

"What does that mean? You're *not* going to write your report?"

"I have an obligation to be thorough."

She slammed her glass down and stood up. "You *are* a bastard, Philip! This isn't about being thorough. This is you having your little revenge."

"That's not true."

"The hell it isn't." She picked up her bag, turned to go, then turned back again. "You know what your problem is, Philip? You're weak. You've *always* been weak. When the scandal broke everyone else saw it for the bullshit that it was. They weren't going to surrender everything they'd worked for, everything their families *sacrificed* for, over some tempest in a teapot about fund-raising! Oh, but not you. Philip Barkley, the Boy Scout. Poof!—end of career. Did it feel good, dear? Did you feel morally superior after the dust cleared and everyone else moved on? Or did you feel like a fool?"

"I'm going to see this through."

She stared at me a moment, deciding whether to use a sharper knife. Then she did. "It was the same thing with Bebe."

"Stop now, Constance."

But there was no stopping her. Her eyes were bright with angry tears. "Philip the Boy Scout!" She gave a mock salute. "You played by their rules—right to the end. *Right to the fucking end!*" she cried. "Those fucking doctors did their part, the nurses did their part, and you did *your* part, too! Why didn't you help me fight them? *Why didn't you make them do more?*"

"They did everything possible, Constance. *We* did everything possible. Your confronting them all the time wasn't accomplishing anything. It was just making it harder on all of us."

"You didn't fight them."

"You should go, Constance."

"You didn't fight until she was gone, when it was too late."

"Get out."

"You're through ruining my life!" she shouted. "And I won't let you ruin Warren's!"

She slammed the door when she left. I took her glass to the kitchen, washed it, then rinsed my face in the sink. The nausea hit me first, followed by the dizziness; the usual one-two. I leaned against the window frame and looked out toward the horizon to steady myself. On the street below I saw her speeding away in her convertible, talking on her cell phone.

5

IT WAS THE SAME DREAM; it never varied. I was shuffling down a dark hallway with rooms on both sides. There were people in the rooms lying in beds, and when I passed a doorway the occupant would look at me, then look away. Somewhere, a voice was coming from one of the rooms, and although I couldn't understand the words, somehow I knew it was a message for me. Whichever direction I went, I couldn't get closer to the voice. Then I heard a telephone ringing, which was odd because I'd never heard one in the dream before. And it got louder and louder.

The telephone was still ringing when I opened my eyes. I reached for it but knocked it off the cradle. Then I heard someone calling my name, and in my stupor I thought I'd found the voice.

"Philip?"

"Yes."

"Philip? You sound far away."

With great effort I reached the phone and rested it against my ear. "Yes," I said again, or think I said, because it didn't sound like "yes."

"It's John Hurley at the *Washington Post*."

"John?"

"Right. We haven't spoken since you were at Appropriations. How are you?"

"Fine."

"I'll come right to the point. We're running a story this week about the Green investigation. We're going to say that he's been passing secrets and it's a national security matter. The government regards him as a fugitive and the Bureau is searching every nook and cranny between here and Anchorage. The punch line is that the Young campaign is holding its breath and waiting for the other shoe to drop."

There were a lot of possible implications of a *Post* story right then. More than I could fathom in my current condition.

"Are you still there?"

"Where did you get a story like that?"

He laughed. "Come on, pal, do you have a response or not?"

"You know I can't comment on an active case, John."

"Look, old sport, I know you play by the rules so I'm not expecting any revelations here. I'm calling because we don't want to damage anyone unnecessarily and we don't want to end up with egg on our face. Just tell me if I've got it wrong and I'll believe you. You know I don't make that offer to everyone."

"I wouldn't jump to conclusions."

"You mean it's *not* a national security case?"

"I mean I wouldn't jump to conclusions."

"Okay. What I'm hearing is that the jury's still out on whether Green's a spy. So, let's say that the current betting is that way."

"I couldn't comment on that one way or another."

"And if I say that a breach of national security is a real possibility, I won't have to give back my Pulitzer?"

"Again, I couldn't comment on that one way or another."

"Fair enough. Look, I appreciate it. I want to get it right."

"You're going with this story this week?"

"Yup. You may want to stay clear of Senator and Mrs. Young."

He hung up. I tried to reason my way through all the permutations of what might transpire in the next few days but didn't get very far before I was stumbling down that hallway again.

The next time I woke, it was to a pounding sound. The daylight seeping around the blinds indicated that some time had passed since my conversation with Hurley, of which I was reminded by the phone still resting against my face. I staggered to the door and saw Special Agent Turner through the peephole, looking very unhappy. I opened up while she was in midpound. She eyed me and said, "You're not dead." She seemed disappointed.

"What time is it?" I croaked.

"What *time* is it?" she repeated, brushing past me. "No, let's start with something more basic. How about, what *day* is it?"

"Wednesday," I replied, trying to sound confident.

"Wednesday," she echoed, looking around the room. She picked up a vial and read the label. "How many of these did you take?" she demanded.

"I don't think my medication is FBI business."

She grunted and crossed her arms. "Okay, let's stick to

business. Did you . . . What happened to your pants?"

"What?"

"You've got mud and grass on your pants."

"Why are you here, Blair?"

"Because of *this*." She proffered a copy of the *Post*.

I unfolded the paper; the date said Friday. More than forty-eight hours had passed since Constance drove away, and aside from Hurley's call, I couldn't remember anything that had happened since. A sour taste welled up in the back of my throat. The headline said, "Fugitive Hunt for Hill Aide." According to "knowledgeable sources close to the investigation," Intelligence Committee senior staffer Martin Green was the subject of a massive manhunt in a case involving a "potentially serious breach of national security." The impact on the candidacy of front-runner Warren Young was speculated upon by an array of luminaries across the political spectrum.

"I've got another bulletin for you," Blair said. "Philip Barkley has been the subject of a search, too. He's wanted at the Justice Department ASAP. Is there anything I should know before he gets there?"

"Like what?"

She grimaced. "I'm not the enemy, Philip. We're working together, remember? A national security case? Evans thinks you've only been out of touch since last night but I went to your office this morning and from what I saw you haven't been there since *Tuesday*. That leaves two days unaccounted for and apparently *you* can't fill in the blanks. Now throw in an empty vial of pills, dirt and grass on your pants, a phone that's off the hook, and, last but not least, a *Post* story leaked by someone with an ax to grind. So, I'll ask again. Is there anything I should know before we get to Justice?"

"No."

She stared at me; I stared back. "Screw it," she muttered and headed for the door. "I'll be out front," she said. "I'd shave if I were you—and change your pants."

We never made it to Evans's office. Blair had called ahead and he intercepted us in the hallway. "The AG wants to see *all* of us," he said wearily. We rode up to the fifth floor in silence and walked through the executive corridor toward the office of Owen Hewlett, the attorney general of the United States.

There are a few distinct paths to becoming the nation's chief lawyer. One is public service, usually meaning prosecutor, judge, or legislator. Another is a distinguished record in academia, necessarily coupled with the political acuity to take centrist positions and pick the right horse. The third is private practice in a firm with the right clientele and a history of financial support for the victorious party. That was Owen Hewlett's route. He came to Washington from Wall Street, and with his manicure, ample stomach, and double-breasted suits, he was a caricature of the wealthy capitalist.

At fifty-six, Hewlett had had a long and prosperous career at Chatham & Ball before becoming AG. In reality, though, he hadn't practiced law, in the sense that phrase is commonly understood, in more than twenty-five years. No courtroom appearances, no depositions, no legal opinions or drafting agreements. No counseling or devising strategies, either. And the last time he'd been in a law library, there were no computers. In megafirms, lawyers with brains, ass-power, and common sense were easy to come by. Hewlett was that most valued commodity, a rainmaker. As a still-young associate he sprinted past the competition when he walked down the aisle with the heiress to the nation's twenty-fourth largest industrial concern. That was six million dollars per year in billings. Thereafter, moving in the right circles generated still more business, and his job description evolved to giving good meeting and telephone, and knowing the right restaurants.

Wealth and access to wealth attract politicians, and Hewlett eventually became a player. The job was essentially the same: know enough to have the right people at your elbow and keep your wallet handy. Over time and through his instigation, Chatham & Ball raised its political profile by becoming a home for former officeholders with good Rolodexes. One of them was an ex-senator from Florida who used the firm as a staging area for a run at the presidency. Chatham & Ball—and Hewlett—caught the brass ring.

If the new attorney general had an overarching philosophy about the role of law in modern society, or a grand vision of the Justice Department's mission, it wasn't discernible to his subordinates. To the consternation of many, including his own lawyers, the positions staked out by Hewlett's department showed greater fealty to the party platform and electoral politics than the Constitution and federal law. It seemed that a month didn't go by when some former Justice official wasn't decrying the "politicization" of the department. When it came to tolerance of press leaks, however, his approach was very consistent: it depended on whether they helped or hurt. Evans knew this, and as he marched along the corridor he looked like a man about to have a tooth pulled.

Blair was just angry; she hadn't said anything since she left my apartment and it had been an uncomfortable ride into the city. Protesting my innocence would have required an explanation of my conversation with Hurley, which would only have made things worse. He'd used an old tactic on me and in my stupor I fell for it. If you care enough you want to set the record straight, and I wasn't ready to write off Martin Green.

One of the secretaries led us to the AG's private office. Hewlett was at the head of a small conference table. At his right hand was the deputy attorney general, David Parks, the former managing partner at C&B brought in to oversee the day-to-day administration of the department. As far as Parks was concerned, the job was essentially the same, and although government bureaucracy wasn't nearly Darwinian enough for his tastes, he was remarkably adept at finding ways to make subordinates eat shit. Within the building he was known unaffectionately as "The Blade."

Parks was speaking in low tones and punctuating his words with emphatic gestures that yielded nods from Hewlett. The three of us stood by, ignored, until the AG finally motioned us to sit. Parks stopped talking abruptly and leaned back to glare at us.

"I take it you have all seen the newspaper this morning," Hewlett began.

"We have, General," replied Evans.

"Mr. Parks and I just spent the morning with Edward Young. It wasn't pleasant. He's holding this department responsible for sabotaging his son's campaign. That's what he called it—sabotage."

"He's holding *us* responsible?" asked Evans.

Parks was on him at once. "The story cites sources

close to the investigation. That means inside this department or the FBI." His eyes flicked from Evans to Blair, then back to Evans. That he never looked at me confirmed my position as prime suspect. That was the way things were done in Washington. Dead people could linger for weeks and months before they read their obituaries.

"But we've done dozens of interviews," said Evans. "If he talked to enough witnesses he could have pieced the story together."

"He could figure out there's a manhunt going on," said Parks, "but where would he get the piece about passing secrets?"

"We've asked witnesses about missing documents," said Evans. "It's not much of a stretch to get to passing secrets."

"On the contrary, it's a hell of a stretch."

Evans was venturing into dangerous territory. Fresh from having his own ass chewed, The Blade wanted a piece of ours, and it was about to get ugly when the impatient Hewlett waded in. "What's our timetable here?" the AG asked no one in particular.

"We should have our current list of interviews done in two weeks," Blair replied.

"Good. I take it that the evidence hasn't changed."

"Green had access to sensitive documents, General," said Evans, "but nothing is missing. There's no direct proof that any secrets were compromised. What we've got is a circumstantial case."

The AG nodded, satisfied. "How soon can we have the report ending this thing?" he asked.

Evans's eyebrows arched in surprise. "Ending?"

"We're not going to allow this story to drip-drip-drip

out over the course of the campaign. We have to move ahead."

"We're not done with the investigation," said Evans.

"She just said that the interviews will be done in a couple of weeks," reminded The Blade.

"The interviews, yes, sir. But we may not know for certain what happened until we find Green and—"

Parks interrupted. "And even *then* you won't know. The man's not going to confess, he's going to get a lawyer and protest his innocence." He looked at the AG and added, "This thing could drag on for months. We need a report *now,* and there is no evidence of espionage."

Evans addressed his rebuttal to the AG. "That's not completely true, General. The evidence is circumstantial but you've got a key staffer and a foreign agent in a meeting—"

WHAM. The sound of Parks's hand slapping the table gave everyone a start. "Just . . . hold . . . on . . . mister," he snarled. Evans's face reddened. Assistant attorney generals weren't senators or cabinet officials, but they were too high up the ladder to be addressed like that, especially in front of subordinates. The tinge in Blair's cheeks indicated that she was embarrassed for him, too. The reaction I found most interesting was my own, which was none at all. The miracle of modern medicine: Philip Barkley, unplugged.

"Who the hell said that was a meeting?" said Parks menacingly. "Just two people sharing a table in a crowded public place, that's all."

Evans spoke quietly, trying to reason with him. "They both journeyed a long way to get there, and there's no indication that they did so before or since."

"So, what does *that* prove? There's more than one

museum I never visited a second time. And if they weren't strangers, maybe he was . . . maybe they were lovers or something."

"But they never touched one another," Evans replied.

"How do *you* know?" Parks retorted. "Hell, as far as our great FBI agent knows, she could have been reaching under the table and giving him a goddamn hand job!"

Evans glanced uneasily toward Blair, and the AG laid a hand on Parks's arm. I might have told them that their parochial concerns about mixed company were misplaced but as I said, I was disengaged.

Evans was one of a relatively rare breed: an assistant attorney general who came up through the ranks. He'd spent his adult life in an institution whose values were literally carved in stone. He dug in. "Nevertheless," he argued, "issuing a report at this stage isn't the kind of thing *we* do." The emphasis on "we" was not tactful; the schism between the AG and his careerists was a raw wound at Justice.

The Blade's gaze was locked on the bridge of Evans's nose like a Doberman contemplating a piece of steak while Hewlett drummed his manicured fingers on the table and considered how to deal with this mutiny of sorts. I'd witnessed this scene dozens of times in the White House and the Senate: newly appointed or elected officials being deviled by bureaucrats who didn't seem to grasp political reality.

"All right, then," said the AG soothingly. "From where I sit we've got to balance several interests: the integrity of our department, the public interest in a thorough investigation, and the vital interests of a respected citizen." He leaned forward and folded his hands on the table, prepared to issue his ruling. "Presently we have some circumstantial evidence: some odd behavior, an invented excuse to get off work, a man and woman lunching at a table, and some calls from telephone booths. That doesn't make Mr. Green a spy. It *may* make him a philanderer of sorts, although I understand his domestic situation is one of those modern arrangements. At any rate, there is certainly no justification to destroy Warren Young's chance to be president." He looked from face to face to detect any disagreement; getting none, he continued. "We do have to respect the fact that espionage is a most serious crime, and that it could be years before we are able to know what happened with any degree of certainty."

"Absolutely correct," volunteered The Blade as his gaze swept the room to quash any dissent.

"The investigation will continue until the assistant attorney general determines otherwise, but it appears to *me*"—he looked directly at Evans—"that there's been an improper leak that has created a public . . . uh . . . *misperception,* and we've got to clean up our mess by telling the truth that we currently know, which is that there is no proof of leaks at the Intelligence Committee." For the first time he looked directly at me and said, "The question for the moment is whether Mr. Barkley is prepared to write and sign such a report."

I could feel Blair and Evans looking at me when I replied, "Yes, sir."

"Good," said the AG. "Call it an interim report if you like but I want it issued within two weeks."

The meeting ended. Evans headed back to his office and Blair followed me to mine. She shut the door and leaned against it with her arms crossed. The oversized raindrops drumming on the windowpanes sounded very loud in my cramped little space. I sat down at my desk, now littered with the detritus of three days' bureaucracy: pink messages, green computer paper, blue memos about fire alarm testing and health insurance. Black clouds had rolled in to choke off the daylight.

"We need to talk," she said. The gloom complemented her somber tone.

"What about?"

"I need to know: did you speak to the *Post*?"

"Yes."

She stared at the floor, slowly shaking her head. I could barely hear her over the rain when she said, "I knew it was you. I just didn't want to believe it."

"They already had the story when he called me."

"No, he *told* you they had the story. He was testing you, trying out a rumor, and you fell for it."

"You've got it wrong."

"Really? When did he call?"

"When?"

"Yes, when? Tuesday? Wednesday? Thursday?"

"What's the difference?"

"Christ, Philip, forget *what* was said, you can't even remember *when*!" She grabbed the doorknob and snapped, "I would really love to continue this conversation but I've got a lot of work to do before your report." She turned to go.

"When are you going to interview Diana Morris?" I asked.

She was already out the door but stuck her head back in and glared at me. "Why?"

"I want to be there."

"Thanks, but I'll handle it."

"Fine. You ask all the questions. I just want to hear the answers." Her expression said she was about to argue. "Listen, *I'm* overseeing the investigation and *I'm* the one who has to sign the report. I'm not asking, Blair. I want to be at that interview."

She stepped back into the room and we stared at each other. "Tomorrow at ten, her apartment," she said finally, then left.

6

"*DIANA, WHERE DO YOU THINK HE'S GONE?*"

The question hung there in the small space between them on the couch. I was in an overstuffed chair opposite, a spectator to the skill of Agent Turner. She had wanted to get as close as possible to the person who knew Martin best, and within twenty minutes of introductions had transformed the formality of an interrogation to the intimacy of a condolence call. Blair the good friend, come to hear Diana's story of love and loss.

With the possible exception of her left ankle, our witness was more or less what I'd expected. The report said that she was from a farming family in Nebraska, that she had a degree in communications from the state university, and that she'd wanted more opportunity than could be found in Lincoln. After interning in her congressman's office in Omaha she decided to come to Washington, joining the migratory pattern that maintains the machinery of government. She was attractive: a Rubenesque figure under conservatively cut clothing, fair skin, bright blue eyes, highlighted dark-blond hair, and a predisposition to smile. No discernible makeup and no jewelry except a silver ring on her middle finger. Her friends described her as "a good person" and "caring," and I could see it: looks, clothes, demeanor, they all said Midwest, unpretentious and decent. Sharing a couch with Blair Turner, who was anything but Midwest, Diana was the kindergarten teacher fielding questions from a concerned parent. Is Martin doing well? Is he keeping up in class? Does he obey the rules?

The only incongruity was the tattoo above her ankle, a symbol. Of what? Perhaps something distinctly un-Nebraskan, whatever it was that impelled her to seek adventure in a faraway city. Something that Martin saw, too, I'd bet. I couldn't put my finger on it, and I was wondering if Blair was picking it up as she studied our witness, who was considering the question of Martin's whereabouts as if it hadn't been uppermost in her mind for the past two weeks. Diana sighed and shook her head. "I have no idea," she replied. "I'm sorry. I gave someone a list of everyone that we know, and everyone he knows that I'm aware of."

"We're checking on them, Diana," Blair said. "What about places? Is there someplace that he was interested in, or talked about, or was just curious about?"

"He talked about going to Israel some day."

"That's helpful," said Blair.

"We once planned a vacation to Arizona but Martin couldn't get away."

"When was that?"

"Last spring. We were going to Tucson, Sedona, and the Grand Canyon. Neither one of us has ever been to the Southwest."

"I lived there during junior high school," said Blair. "My father was stationed at Fort Huachuca. We used to take rides into the desert and go whitewater rafting on the Colorado."

"I'd love to do that," said Diana, nodding. "Martin doesn't care for the water. I don't think he's much of a swimmer." Seaside locales just moved down the search list.

"I'd like to ask you something rather personal," said Blair. Diana clasped her hands in her lap and nodded her permission. "Was everything okay between you and Martin—before he left, I mean?"

"I think so."

"You've lived together for two years," Blair observed.

"Almost three."

"Almost three. I lived with a guy for over a year. Things go up and down."

"I guess."

"I have to ask so please don't be angry. Do you think there could have been another woman?"

"No," Diana replied firmly, shaking her head. "We're in love."

"Then nothing has happened to cause concern? No unexplained absences, no funny phone calls or anything?"

Pay dirt. The look on her face indicated that Blair had struck a nerve. "Is there something, Diana?" she asked.

"I heard him on the telephone—one time."

"Talking to a woman?"

Diana nodded. "I heard a name."

"What name?" Blair asked. I waited for Diana's lips to form the shape that would expel the sound that would complete the circle. My hands tightened on the arms of the chair.

"Naomi."

"Naomi?"

"I think it was 'Naomi.' "

"Who's Naomi?" asked Blair. Diana shook her head in reply. "You must have *some* idea."

Martin's significant other glanced at me for the first time. Her eyes were shining; I tried to look sympathetic. "I don't know," she said, her voice shaking. "I really don't."

"If there were some problems, that's not anyone's fault," Blair assured her. "Things happen, that's all."

"But people should talk things out," said Diana plaintively. "If one person does something to make the other angry, they should talk it out."

"You're right," said Blair soothingly, "talking it out is the best thing." She glanced at her outline, then said, "Let's talk about something else. Six weeks ago, Martin wasn't at work for several days. I think he went somewhere . . ."

"New York," said Diana woodenly. She began to twist the silver ring around her finger.

"New York," Blair repeated, looking at her notes and nodding. That Martin had lied about his destination was not public knowledge. "Yeah, I think you're right. For some reason I was thinking New Jersey."

"That's what he said," Diana replied, still twisting the ring. "He said he had some family business there."

"But you know he went to New York?"

"Yes," she said softly, looking more miserable by the moment.

I realized I was leaning forward in my chair. Blair, however, showed no reaction. "How?" she asked.

"He called every day while he was away—my cell phone. The Caller ID showed the number he was calling from. They were New York numbers. I wrote them down."

"Why?"

"I . . . I'm not sure."

"Were you worried about something?"

"He was acting funny before he left and I just decided to write them down."

"Did you check on the numbers?" asked Blair. "To see where he was calling from?"

"No."

"I see."

My heart was pounding in my chest. *Ask her*, I pleaded silently while Blair jotted her notes.

"I have another question," Blair said, still low-key, unhurried, "and I'm sorry to pry, but if Martin said he had family business in New Jersey, wouldn't he be concerned that you'd discover the truth if you called his parents' home?"

Diana's gaze didn't shift from the floor when she replied. "I don't call up there."

Blair nodded sympathetically. "What do you think he was doing in New York?" she asked.

"I don't know," Diana said quietly. "He didn't tell me and I didn't ask."

She was in denial. Why does a man lie about a business trip? *Ask her*, I silently urged.

Blair put her hand reassuringly on Diana's arm and she finally looked up. "Last question and we'll be gone," she said with an encouraging smile. "Do you still have those phone numbers? I'd like to copy them down."

Blair never looked at me while Diana was gone. My stock with her started low and went through the floor with the *Post* story. I didn't care much at first but that was starting to change. In a moment Diana returned with a sheet of paper, perhaps our first real lead.

A short while later we were on the street with me following as Blair marched toward her car. "Can I speak to you a minute?" I asked.

"I've got to get back to work," she said. "Talk while we're walking."

I quickened my pace to move alongside. "What do you think about Diana?" I asked.

"I think their friends were right," Blair said. "The bloom was off the rose."

"Who lost interest, him or her?"

"It sounds like he did, but then again, she might have been two-timing him with the guy in the next office. There's more to Miss Nebraska than meets the eye."

"She's got a tattoo," I said.

"Christ, Philip, *I've* got a tattoo."

"Where?"

She looked at me sharply. "You don't get out much, do you?"

"I'm sorry, that just popped out."

"I don't think it matters one way or another," she said.

"You're right. Lots of women have tattoos."

She shook her head, exasperated. "What I meant is that it doesn't matter who lost interest. This isn't about unrequited love or triangles."

"What about Naomi?"

"My guess is that 'Naomi' is a code name for Magda

Takács. If it's not then Martin may have had something going on the side. But unless she's got a big boyfriend, that doesn't explain his disappearance and it sure doesn't explain the Portrait Gallery. The evidence points to espionage."

"You sound pretty confident."

"I was confident before this morning. This"—she patted the folio containing her notes—"makes me more confident."

"Why?"

"Martin's New York calls were all from phone booths. You can tell by the numbers. Mr. Green was being very secretive, and he wasn't going to those lengths to fool Diana Morris."

"What happens now?"

"We'll locate the booths and have a look around. Maybe it'll tell us something, but probably not."

"Probably not," I agreed.

"Anyway, we're working from inference, right? It's one more fact to suggest that Green was selling out his country."

"I'm writing a report denying that," I reminded her.

"Yes, I heard you yesterday."

"Do you think I should have turned the AG down?"

"You do what you have to do," she replied, looking straight ahead.

"This case was supposed to help your career," I said. "What if it takes down Warren Young?"

"Screw Warren Young."

She was still smarting over the encounter in the senator's office. Apparently, some things were more important than her advertised ambition. I was at once glad for her and sorry because the ability to swallow a little pride was essential for ladder-climbing in the capital. I could have explained this but she wasn't in the mood for career counseling from me.

We reached a corner and she turned right. "My car is this way," she said. "I'd give you a ride but I'm not going directly downtown."

"That's okay."

"I didn't say anything about your telephone conversation with the *Post*."

"Thanks."

"But if there's another leak, I'll nail you. I just wanted you to know." She turned and headed for her car.

Armed with the phone booth locations and, through Diana's cell phone records, the time of each call, Blair's team went to work in New York. Within twenty-four hours they had scrutinized all the sites. On Monday night and three consecutive nights thereafter, Martin called from the same booth, located on Ninth Avenue and Twenty-eighth Street. Between Tuesday morning and Thursday afternoon he used three booths downtown within a radius of several blocks, and two in midtown. One of those was within the New York Public Library, the only inside booth.

The information was at once intriguing and maddening. Was there a pattern? If so, what did it mean? Martin's New York interlude must have had something to do with the case; so, too, his use of phone booths. But what? When I reached Blair for a progress check on Monday she was in New York, she was tired, and she wasn't happy. "There are *only* thousands of stores, offices, and apartments within a couple of blocks of each booth," she complained. "Maybe we'll hand out flyers. Have you seen this man? Did he offer to sell you any secrets?"

"Any progress at all?" I asked.

"We found his hotel, a few blocks from the Ninth Avenue booth. It's a dump called The Lancaster."

"I still don't get the predominance of outdoor booths. Most of the buildings in Manhattan have their own phones inside."

"If they wanted to be sure Martin wasn't being followed it's the logical thing to do. The downtown locations were near squares where surveillance, say, from a high window, would be easy. They could direct him to a phone booth, check for a tail, then direct him on to a meeting site. The library has several entrances so it could serve a similar purpose."

"It makes sense that whoever was involved in this would take precautions," I agreed, "but taking a week off from work and lying about where and why seems pretty risky."

"That part of it was Martin's," she replied. "They probably told him to make up something convincing and he did the best he could."

"You'd think a smart guy like him would be more creative."

"I've got news for you, Philip," she said irritably. "Real-life spies aren't as clever as they are in the movies, and sometimes they're damn obvious. Remember Aldrich Ames? A mole inside the CIA and he spends his payoff money living the high life. Bought a big house, for God's sake. And *he* got away with it for years. Martin's choice of alibi is small potatoes. And let's not forget: he fooled everyone."

"That's true," I conceded. "What do you make of all the calls to Diana? Doesn't sound like they were on the rocks."

"I make nothing of it because, as I told you, I don't believe their relationship, whatever its condition, has anything to do with this case. But since you raise it, maybe he calls her so she doesn't try to call him. That would make sense. Maybe he's keeping her happy while he's planning his exit. Or maybe his conscience is bothering him—who knows?" There was a pause and I could hear her giving instructions to one of her agents. She sounded confident, in charge, and the responses I could hear were tinged with respect. No, the notion of Blair Turner as director wasn't far-fetched at all.

She was back in a moment. "How is your report coming along?"

"I'll make the deadline."

"How are you going to play the phone booth thing? It's going to make your conclusions a bit more vulnerable, wouldn't you say?"

"It could. Then again, it shows that he had a habit of using public phones, and those calls we were able to trace were to his girlfriend."

"That's pretty good. You'll be in Portland before you know it."

"I've already fallen on my sword, Blair. It isn't fun."

"Don't bullshit me, Philip. You're rooting for Green."

"What does that mean?"

"You identify with him."

"No, I don't," I said defensively.

"Martin Green, oasis of virtue in the moral desert of Capitol Hill. Despite any evidence to the contrary you're resisting the idea that he's sold us out. And you're not doing it for the Portland deal, and you're sure as hell not doing it for Warren Young. What's your fantasy? That Martin's got the *real* goods on Warren, something more damaging than espionage? Perhaps another campaign finance scandal! Do you think he was shadowing Warren's campaign in New York?"

"Warren was in New York that week?"

"Fund-raising. First Mrs. Warren, then the two of them. Hey! Maybe Martin's writing some kind of an exposé! Wouldn't you just love it?"

"Maybe you should spend less time analyzing me and more on figuring what this case is all about."

"No, Philip, I *already know* what this case is about. I know because we're out here gathering facts and examining them *objectively*."

"Look, why don't we have a different conversation than usual?"

"How so?"

"This time, *I'll* end it."

And I did. I hung up. Arguing with Blair would have been uncomfortable even if her analysis of my psyche didn't cut so close to the bone. The fact was that once upon a time I took a very proper, very public stand and got my ass handed to me by an entire city. Even those who praised the message were privately wary of the messenger. In the aftermath, estranged from my colleagues and, increasingly, my own wife, it seemed that there was only one person in the whole world who thought I was still the same wonderful guy. When she died, Humpty Dumpty fell off the wall, and all the king's doctors couldn't put him together again. And every day Humpty rides the bus to purgatory and dreams of deliverance. Then along comes an interesting case. Martin Green, industrious, virtuous Martin Green, is making everyone very nervous, and can I help? If it gets me out of purgatory, sure.

But that doesn't mean I can't have a rooting interest in the outcome.

7

"*Good afternoon. Young for President.*"

"Good afternoon. Mitchell Glass, please." The conclusions of Blair's investigation being foregone, I no longer had any qualms about pursuing my own inquiry.

"Mitchell Glass."

"Mitchell, this is Philip Barkley. I'm—"

"Is there news about Martin?"

"No, I'm afraid not. We're still investigating."

"Oh . . . Why are you calling me?"

"I understand that you and he are friends. You worked together at the Intelligence Committee."

"I told that to the FBI. I don't have any idea where he's gone." I could hear someone nearby saying his name, trying to get his attention. "Hold on a minute, will you?" he said and put me on hold before I could reply. It was a full five minutes before he came back on, and he wasn't apologetic. "Is there anything else?" he asked impatiently.

"Only the grand jury."

"The grand jury?"

"I have some questions for you and I'm on a tight timetable. If you're too busy to speak to me now then you'll have to come to the grand jury."

"Oh . . . Can I transfer this call to another phone?"

"Go ahead."

A series of clicks and he was back on a moment later. "I'm sorry, Mr. Barkley, I didn't mean to be rude but I'm under tremendous pressure here. I do the campaign finance reporting and it's fourteen-hour days, seven days a week. I go into the bathroom here and they're talking to me while I'm in the damn stall."

"It sounds like life is tougher than it was at the committee."

"It is, but here at least there's a chance for a reward. I tried to tell that to Martin, you know? That he should come over here, too. If you've got a chance to work for the guy who's probably going to be the next president of the United States, you should maximize the opportunity."

"Maximize?"

"What's he going to do for the Intelligence Committee staff if he's elected except show up at the farewell party? But if you work on the campaign, well . . . it's the spoils system, right?"

"Right. Martin wasn't interested?"

"Nah, he marched to his own drummer."

"Mitchell, you and Martin are friends. Did you notice anything peculiar about his behavior before he disappeared?"

"He wasn't himself. There were definitely things on his mind. He was preoccupied or worried about something but I don't know what."

"Do you think it could have had anything to do with his girlfriend?"

"Diana? I don't know. At one point they were thinking about getting married but I don't know what happened with that. Martin never talked about it and it wasn't the kind of thing you ask about. One day it was a subject, the next day it wasn't."

"Was there someone else?"

"I don't know. He's a good-looking guy with plenty of opportunities, but if he was taking advantage of them he never said anything to me. Then again, he's a very private guy. He could have been having liaisons every night and you'd never know about it."

"I guess that would make him unique around here," I said.

"Can I ask you something?"

"What?"

"Is the stuff in the paper true?"

"I don't know. What do you think?"

There was a long pause while he considered his answer. "Ever since I read the story I've been going back over things, you know? Martin Green, a spy? Like I said, he's a very private guy so maybe it fits, but it still sounds crazy to me. He seemed to genuinely care about things, not just the work, but about people. How does a guy volunteer for everything that helps his neighbors, then screw all of us at once?"

"Well, it makes a great cover, doesn't it?"

"I guess. Maybe it's all some grand scheme to put the screws to the candidate. That's crazy, too, but it makes more sense than spying."

"Put the screws to Young?"

"Yeah, it's bullshit, I know. We're breathing each

other's exhaust around here, and the level of paranoia, mine included, is through the roof. I've taken to reviewing everything Martin ever said or did, looking for the hidden meaning."

"That's what you do in situations like this."

"Sure."

"So . . . did you come up with anything?"

He laughed quietly. "I don't know what it means but we had a funny conversation about a week before he disappeared. I didn't tell this to the FBI. I wasn't holding back, I just didn't think of it."

"Fine."

"Actually . . . I did think of it but it didn't seem relevant to the questions they were asking, okay?"

"Okay. Go ahead."

"I went back up to the Hill to attend this big party for Erskine's retirement. That's the guy from Oklahoma. Martin and I were standing in a corner, kind of taking it all in, and in walk Senator and Mrs. Young and I . . . uh . . . well, you know her."

"We've been divorced for years. Go ahead."

"All right, well, they walk in and it's like the golden couple have arrived, the football hero and his cheerleader girlfriend. Warren is tan, manicured, with a perfect haircut. He's rich, a senator, probably the next president, and if all that's not enough, on his arm is this . . . goddess."

"I get the picture."

"Hey, I know we've got to take responsibility for our own lives, but—*damn!*—this guy won the big sperm lottery, didn't he?"

"Right."

"So, we're taking it all in and I'm kind of kidding

around, saying that there's no justice. One guy has all the luck."

"And what did Martin say?"

"He said, 'Things aren't always what they seem.'"

"What did he mean?"

"I've got no clue. The subject was closed, and with Martin, closed is *closed*. Listen, they're piling up outside to see me. Is there anything else?"

"One thing. You keep track of all campaign expenses?"

"I sure as hell hope so. If not, we're going to have a big problem with the Federal Election Commission."

"I take it that Martin didn't do any campaign work."

His voice went up an octave. "Whoa! *No one* crosses that line. If anyone on the public payroll is spending time on campaign activities, that is *totally* without my knowledge!" There was a moment's pause while he decompressed, and when he spoke again the concern was obvious. "Did someone say that happened?"

"Relax. I just have to double-check everything for a report I'm writing. Do you have the expenses for August yet?"

"I've got a computer run of all but the last week."

"Why don't you fax it to me in case I have to substantiate the point that Martin's work for the senator didn't extend to campaign activities. It probably goes without saying, but just in case . . ."

"Sure, you'll have it in ten minutes. And please let me know if something develops."

"I will. I may be calling more of Martin's friends."

"Sure."

"I'll probably start with Naomi."

"Who's she?"

"I'm sorry, it's not 'Naomi,' I can't read my own writing. Anyway, I'll let you know if there's some big development."

When I was a prosecutor I would get these hunches that were almost always right. After a while I learned to trust my instincts, even if the proposition seemed like a long shot, and I actually developed a reputation of sorts. The thing is, you can lose your career, your family, your prestige, even your confidence, but the instincts remain.

———————————

"Town Limo. Your service is our pleasure." The voice was tinged with that unique mix of haste and world-weariness common to New York commercial-speak.

"Good morning, my name is Philip Barkley. I'm calling in connection with the Young for President campaign."

"Yes, sir. Do you need to schedule a car?"

"No, not today. Whom am I speaking to?"

"Mike."

"Mike, I'm actually handling a campaign finance matter. I have an invoice here for a car and driver furnished to Constance Young for August 8 through August 10."

"Okay. Something wrong with the invoice?"

"No, not at all. It's just that we're required to distinguish campaign use from any personal use for accounting purposes. I was wondering if you have a log or something showing times and destinations that I can use to document any necessary splits. We have to be very careful."

"Hang on," he told me, and then his voice was replaced by Sinatra's singing "The Lady Is a Tramp."

I supplemented the list of expenses I received from

Mitchell Glass with some on-line research. The week
Martin was in New York, Constance was staying at the
Plaza Hotel. She was the main attraction at a fund-raiser
in Armonk on Wednesday evening, then had meetings
with the New York State campaign organization and
various important personages on Thursday and Friday
morning. Warren flew up Friday afternoon to join her at
the site of Saturday's fete, the estate of one of the twelve
thousand investment bankers leaving their marks on the
topography of Eastern Long Island.

Two people in a city of eight million.

Mike was back. "All right, I've got them here . . .
Logs for Wednesday, Thursday, Friday, and . . . okay, it
looks like we went till Friday night. Took her to an address in Southampton and that was it. You want
copies?"

"Can you fax them?"

"Your service is our pleasure," he repeated. "Ten
minutes."

I'd just begun perusing the logs when I was interrupted by a call from Evans. "I need you to do something," he said. "I'm afraid 'no' isn't an option."

"What is it?"

"You have to update Edward Young on the investigation."

"No."

"He's expecting you tomorrow morning."

"I'm working on a classified report about a case,
Alan. We're the Justice Department and he's a private
citizen, not a king."

No response, but I could hear him doing his breathing
exercise. "Okay," he said finally.

"Okay?"

"So, do I just tell The Blade to go to hell, or should I say that you turned me down? Same result, but with the first option I go out with a little more dignity, don't you think?"

"That's a great management technique, Alan, taking yourself hostage."

"Crude but effective. What do you hear from Wonder Woman?"

"Wonder Woman?"

"I'm still trying to figure out who she looks like."

"She's in New York. They've visited the phone booths Green called from but there's not much to go on from there. Something about Manhattan being a big place."

"We're still going to meet the deadline, right?"

"I'm doing my part, and I think she's firmly in control of her end."

"I'll bet. Do you know Dean Lustigard over at the Bureau?"

"No."

"Well, he told me a little story about our Agent Turner."

"No locker room stuff, Alan."

"No, no, this isn't what you think. She was in her second or third year, right? And she goes with another agent, a guy named Broderick, to interview the ex-girlfriend of a fugitive named Thatcher who murdered a guard during a bank robbery. They're questioning the girlfriend and this Thatcher guy comes out of the next room and starts blasting away. Broderick hits the floor but Turner pulls her gun and fires twice. Lustigard says there were two holes in the guy's chest that you could have covered with a quarter!"

"That's very impressive."

"I didn't notice when she was here, but where do women agents carry their guns?"

"I think she keeps hers in a garter belt."

There was a moment's pause while he conjured up the image. "Turns out she's an army brat," he said. "Learned to shoot from the national pistol champion or somebody like that. Dean says they gave her a medal and she was on her way. What do you think of *that*?"

"I think I wouldn't let her hear that Wonder Woman stuff."

Evans laughed. "Yeah, she's definitely not a woman you'd want to piss off."

"Alan, the Portland ticket, it's in your drawer, right?"

"Tomorrow, ten o'clock. At the palace."

Edouard Lejeune, an Alsatian by birth, emerged from World War Two homeless and destitute. According to his authorized biography, by 1950 he had amassed a small fortune by "moving goods and materials from where they were needed to where they were *more* needed." He emigrated to the United States, anglicized his name, and began to apply the lessons learned in the European black market to the burgeoning American economy. Young was a student of leverage—the concept of applying resources, capital and information to maximum effect. When he invested in an enterprise it was before the initial public offering. When he acquired real estate it was the key parcel needed for some future assembly. And when it was useful to know something he knew it first. By 1965 he was one of the richest men in the country.

Early on he recognized the difference between wealth and power, which was wealth multiplied by influence.

Power could facilitate the accumulation of even more wealth. Moreover, wealth without power wasn't fulfilling, and certainly wasn't exciting. Young set out to amass influence. Applying the principles of leverage to influence is the essence of politics, so he began to assist candidates for city and state offices but soon realized that participation on a national scale was required. He moved from New York to McLean, Virginia, where he built a replica of an Alsatian chateau on twelve acres encircled by an eight-foot iron fence. It became known in Washington circles as "The Palace," a prominent terrain feature on the political landscape. And from its windows one could almost see the highest leverage point in American politics, 1600 Pennsylvania Avenue.

The sentry at the main gate scrutinized my Justice Department identification and after confirming my name on a printed schedule, cleared me to proceed up a long cobblestone driveway to a courtyard where two manservants beckoned at the porte cochere. One took my keys and the other led me inside to an anteroom. At five minutes before ten I was escorted to Young's office. It was oval, bigger than the White House version, and with a better view: a panorama of the Potomac and the city to the south.

The room was empty so I took advantage of the opportunity to browse part of what was reputedly one of the world's finest collections of eighteenth-century American art. The paintings adorned all the wall space with the exception of the area behind the desk, which was devoted to photographs of the patriarch with assorted dignitaries. I moved along the rows, a who's who of American politics in the last fifty years, beginning with Vice President Nixon.

At precisely ten o'clock another door opened noiselessly; it was set into the wall and almost invisible. I didn't notice it until I glanced away from a painting and saw an elderly man standing in the doorway, scrutinizing me with a dour expression. "I was just looking at your collection," I said. He didn't reply but turned to shut the door, which he did slowly and with some effort, then shuffled toward his chair. I moved away from the paintings to a spot before his desk. "I'm Philip Barkley," I told him, "from the Justice Department."

"Philip Barkley," he said in a creaky voice, motioning me to sit. His gaze shifted to a water glass on a silver tray by his right hand. He held it with both hands as he drank, then replaced it carefully on the tray. He was in his eighties and looked all of it. He was thin, with parchment-like skin that showed veins and liver spots, and there were deep vertical lines etched around his mouth that accented the virtual absence of lips. With wisps of gray-white hair on the sides of his head and moist eyes enlarged by the thickness of his black horn-rimmed glasses, he gave the appearance of an aged owl.

It became apparent that he was waiting for me to speak. "I've been asked by the attorney general to meet with you."

"Hewlett," he said.

"That's right."

"You're here to tell me about the investigation," he informed me.

"Yes," I replied. He motioned impatiently for me to begin. "We haven't found Martin Green," I said.

The sudden strength of his voice surprised me. "I know *that*," he said testily. "If you'd found him I would have read it in the newspapers."

"There have been other developments."

He waved a hand dismissively and reached for the water glass again. I waited while he drank. "Get on with it," he commanded as he set the glass down.

I told him about the interview with Diana Morris, including the troubled relationship with Green and the overheard mention of "Naomi." I described the clandestine trip to New York and use of phone booths. Young vacillated between annoyed and disgusted as he sat there, occasionally sipping water and muttering to himself.

"Is that it?" he asked when I paused.

"There's one more thing. Green shared a table with a Hungarian embassy—"

"I know all about that," he interrupted, then spat, "more nonsense." He ran his fingers along the polished surface. His flesh was so thin I thought it would tear. "You're going to write a report," he said.

"That's right."

"And you'll say that these espionage stories aren't true."

I felt myself flush. Why was I there to tell him what he already knew? "It's an interim report," I said. "It is hard to say what the final conclusions will be."

"Do *you* believe this man is a spy?" he asked.

"I just analyze the facts. At the present time the evidence is very circumstantial and there's no proof that secrets have been compromised."

He nodded. "I see . . ." Another moment passed while he raised the water glass again to drink. In his shriveled condition he required frequent watering.

"That's all I have to report," I said. By then I was wondering why I'd been summoned. To the extent he cared, he could have learned everything I'd told him in a telephone call to the attorney general, if he hadn't already.

He set the glass down again and stared at me, making up his mind. "You were married to Constance," he said finally. "That's the reason you were chosen for the assignment."

"I know that," I said, wondering how much input the man in front of me had in the decision. For all I knew it could have been entirely his idea. I might be a marionette, dangling at the end of strings worked by those veined, spotted hands.

Young's gaze went to the view of the city down river. "Constance is a great help to Warren."

"She's very talented," I replied, reaching for my briefcase.

He frowned and said, "She's a woman with"—his head swiveled around as he searched for the word—"appetites." His eyes locked on mine, probing.

I hoisted my briefcase into my lap. "If there isn't anything else you want to know about the investigation, I need to get back to the office."

He wanted to question me about his daughter-in-law; I could see it in his face. "Good-bye, Mr. Barkley," he said finally. "I'll look forward to your report."

8

FRIDAY MORNING I WAS BUSY at my desk, gilding the lily. A ten- or twenty-page fact-laden discourse might have persuaded anyone with the time and inclination to actually read it, but this was Washington, and so my report had to be of sufficient size to carry the day when merely dropped on a desk, hefted in a briefcase, or waved in front of a television camera. I supplemented the wheat with the chaff of biography, background, and explanatory material about everything from the protocol of manhunts to the intelligence-gathering methods and capabilities of former Eastern Bloc nations operating with diminished resources and realigned priorities. I even threw in some impressive charts portraying the manpower and costs associated with the investigation. The report was taking shape, a web of circumstance and inference ultimately resting on a simple premise: if you were not inclined to believe Green was a spy then there was nothing in the report to change your mind. Of course, if you were a real cautious type when it came to national security there was nothing to give you much comfort, either. My account wasn't going to settle the issue but it would accomplish its purpose: keep Warren Young afloat through the primaries. Once he secured the nomination he could deal with the espionage question from more of a distance, and from a position of strength.

Blair called midmorning to tell me that they were working on a possible Green sighting in Miami that had promise. I told her that I was making good progress on the report but would be sure to hold the presses if there was a break in the story. I mentioned that I was going to be out in the afternoon and she was instantly wary.

"Tell me this isn't more investigation," she said.

"I'm taking some personal time," I replied, which was literally true, and before she could follow up I added, "I've got to get going. Leave me a message here or at home as soon as there's news."

It was just past noon when I left my office and caught a taxi for National Airport. The morning had been devoted to government service and team play; now I was on my own. I took the one o'clock shuttle to New York and another taxi to midtown Manhattan. It was a hot day for September. The streets were full of businessmen with unbuttoned collars and women in sleeveless dresses with their hair pinned up off their shoulders. Everyone looked happy. It was still summer and—thank God—Friday.

I arrived at Seventy-fifth and Lexington thirty minutes early. I killed a little time window shopping, ate a late lunch under an umbrella at a hot dog stand, and was back at the corner when a Lincoln limousine rolled up at three-fifteen. The passenger window glided downward and I peered into the dark interior. "You Barkley?" said a gruff voice.

"That's me. Mr. Murphy?" I shaded my eyes to make out the driver, a dark-suited guy in his early fifties, with thinning white hair, a thick neck, and a cleft chin.

"You got identification?"

"Sure." I proffered my ID through the window and he took it.

His eyes went to the photo and back to my face. "You got older," he said.

"It's the sun," I replied. He flicked the switch on the electronic door lock and I got in. The window glided upward and the heat and noise receded, masked by dark glass, air-conditioning, and background jazz from the stereo. The car idled while Murphy studied the credentials for another moment.

"Thanks for meeting me," I said.

"No problem," he replied, handing me back the ID, "it's on my way. I've got one of my regulars downtown at four-thirty. Every Friday it's the place in the Hamptons." He checked the sideview mirror then pulled the car into southbound traffic. With both of his hands on the wheel, I could see a gold ID bracelet with an engraved "Michael" on his right wrist and a Rolex on his left. The condition of his nose and the fingers on his right hand suggested that he enjoyed a cocktail and a nonfiltered cigarette when he wasn't driving, but except for a slight paunch he looked pretty solid, and tough. "You got mutual funds?" he asked.

"A little bit."

"This guy manages one of those funds—Benchmark, Benchley, Bench-something."

"A place in the Hamptons, he must do real well."

He smiled as he glanced in the rearview mirror. "These days, they *all* got places in the Hamptons, my friend, and I can pick better stocks throwing darts at a board. The guys who manage my pension fund ought to be indicted for stupidity." We stopped at a red light and he looked over at me. "So, this is an investigation?"

"Yup. With an election next year we're looking hard at any potential violations of campaign finance laws. There's some allegations that the Chinese have been putting money into everybody's campaign again. We've got to check it out."

"So you want to know if the senator's lady got her manicured fingers in the cookie jar?"

"That's it."

He laughed and said, "I'll tell you something but you can't quote me." He looked over for assurance.

"Go ahead, strictly between us."

"I wouldn't trust that bitch as far as I could throw her. She ain't seen the line yet she wouldn't cross."

"The logs say that you drove her around for three days. I guess it wasn't fun."

"I picked her up at LaGuardia on a Wednesday and took her to some chi-chi beauty salon on the East Side, then on to the Plaza. Later we went up to Armonk, one of those parties where you part with ten thousand bucks for a meal you eat standing up. I took her to another one of those in the Hamptons on Friday. Maybe she met some of your Chinese friends there, but I don't know."

"I doubt it, there were reporters all over both events. Do you know if she met any people at the hotel?"

"I was in the lobby a couple of times and I don't recall seeing any Chinese guys walking around, but I wasn't looking real hard."

"Sure. The log says you drove her to another address in Manhattan on Thursday."

He nodded. "To Bliss."

"Is that a restaurant?"

"A spa. Down in SoHo. It's where the rich ladies go to get nails and new skin." He shook his head and snickered. "I'll tell you something, though. I've dropped a few there and they look a lot better comin' out than goin' in, so there must be something to it."

"I suppose so."

He glanced at me and said, "You look a little disappointed."

"Do I?" I was about to deny it but he put a hand on my arm.

"Hold on, I'm not done. This may not be the Chinese thing but it could make your trip."

"What is it?"

"We made a stop on the way to the spa—not even on the way. We made a U-turn and went across town."

"Where to?"

"The Waldorf-Astoria, a little farther down Lex from here. She was in there for about an hour. I don't know who she met."

"Did you know she was going there when you picked her up?"

He shook his head. "Nope, and neither did she."

"How do you know?"

"She missed her appointment at the spa. She got another one, though. After she got back in the car she called and told 'em she'd been delayed and needed to move her appointment back an hour. I guess she didn't like the answer because she got pissed off and told 'em to put the manager on the phone." He shook his head. "I'll tell you something, I feel sorry for Senator Young. If he gets one-tenth the shit she gave that manager—"

"How did the Waldorf thing come up? Did she just change her mind?"

"No, it wasn't like that. She was talking to somebody on the phone and I heard her say 'Waldorf-Astoria.' Then she asks me how long it will take to get there. I tell her that we got to turn around and go crosstown. With traffic, it could take thirty, thirty-five minutes. She didn't like hearing that, either. What the hell am I supposed to do, right? This is Manhattan."

"Did she get that call or did she make it?"

"I think she got it."

I thought about trying to get a look at registration records but that was a big undertaking and there was no time for it right then. "I'd like to stop at the Waldorf," I told him. "I want to make a phone call of my own."

"Use my phone, no charge."

"It's long distance and I have a charge card," I told him. "Besides, I'd like to take a peek inside. It will only take a minute." We entered the Waldorf's block and he pulled to the curb just south of the Lexington Avenue entrance. I went inside, through the lobby, and out the Forty-ninth Street entrance to a phone booth off the corner, a steel and Plexiglas totem pole. I confirmed that it was one that Green had used, then went back into the hotel and out the front entrance to the waiting limo.

"Thanks," I told Murphy, who was looking in the sideview mirror.

He nodded but his eyes remained on the mirror. "Something must be going down," he said.

"What do you mean?"

"See the black Ford back there, behind the UPS truck?" The truck was parked on the other side of the avenue, in the middle of the block. Behind it, two men were sitting in a sedan staring straight ahead.

"What about it?" I asked.

"It's a stakeout," he said. "Trust me, I know."

"You were a cop?"

"For twenty-eight years, most of 'em in this borough. Two guys sittin' in a sedan, trying to look inconspicuous. One of them got out of the car and walked down to the corner to look down the street."

Which could have meant he saw me at the phone booth. "Are they NYPD?" I asked.

He shook his head. "Probably federal, maybe FBI or DEA. I guess they're waiting for someone." The light at the corner turned green and he pulled into traffic again. The black car remained parked.

"So, what else do you want to know?" Murphy asked.

"What time was Mrs. Young's spa appointment?"

"Eleven o'clock. She got a new one for twelve-thirty. I remember because there was a big argument over it being lunch hour and a tough time to slot her in."

The phone near the Waldorf was used at ten-forty. Green had to have called Diana while he was waiting for Constance. "Listen, I appreciate the information," I told him. "If you should think of anything else about the Waldorf stop, will you let me know?"

"No problem," he replied, smiling. "The war on crime is a never-ending battle."

———————————

Saturday I went to the cemetery. Constance had been busy. The grave was adorned with flowers and the patchy grass had been replaced with sod. My former wife was never one to dawdle between decision and action, or to embrace half-measures. I puttered around the new plantings, smoothing and shaping in places that didn't need it while I told my daughter a story I'd read about the sea lions at the National Zoo. We always had to visit the sea lions. Eventually I got around to Oregon. I said that we could still talk all the time and I'd come back every year on her birthday. Then I ended the conversation with my usual promise that, someday, we'd all be together again.

My work done, I lay on the bench and closed my eyes, listening to the droning of insects and airplanes. I was aware of the cool stone on my back and warmth of the sun on my face when it peeked around the swaying leaves. Then the surroundings slowly dissolved into the sound of my own breathing and the aroma of flowers.

Sometime later I was jarred awake by the slamming of car doors close by. I lifted my head to see pall bearers carrying a mahogany-colored casket toward a mound of earth fifty yards away. Then more slamming doors, portending a black tide of mourners. I lay back and closed my eyes once more, and soon the hum of prayer blended with the ambient sound. I heard, ". . . your servant, Robert . . ."

Rest in peace, Robert. *Requiescat in pacem.*

I dozed again until I was stirred by the crunch of shovels biting into the mound of earth. Family and friends had departed, committing Robert to the care of strangers who were talking animatedly while they covered him. After several minutes the work stopped and cigarettes were lit. One of the men went to a sack and brought out a small cooler. The others gathered around and crouched, checking in all directions before passing around the cans. They drank and smoked and talked, then finally drained the cans, tossed their cigarette butts on poor Robert, and began work anew. I got up and began walking purposefully in the opposite direction, onto a road that wound through the cemetery. I trudged around, noticing the dates on each headstone I passed and automatically calculating the life spans.

I forced my thoughts back to the case. With the notable exception of the Portrait Gallery interlude, all of Green's words and deeds seemed to point to an affair with the chairman's wife. My trip to New York had more or less confirmed it. Logically, an affair didn't prove Green *wasn't* a spy, but the odds that one man was simultaneously harboring two devastating secrets seemed less than remote. If Martin was successfully engaged in espionage, why risk a most dangerous liaison?

No, I decided, it was an affair, and a mismatch to boot. Poor, righteous Martin, moping around New York, awaiting his inamorata. An affair with the boss's wife would have been stressful under the best of circumstances, but this boss was a candidate for president, and the lady in question . . . well, how did her father-in-law put it? Constance was a woman with appetites. And in our last year together it became obvious that she was indulging them with someone who turned out to be Warren.

I circled the cemetery and made my way back to my bench. I explained to my daughter that if I did my job, if I followed through, it could make things very hard for all of us. I told her that Mommy had changed, that she had had a very bad time when her little girl went to heaven, and that sometimes people break, just like toys. Then I made up my mind. I was supposed to write a report saying that there was no evidence of compromised secrets at the Intelligence Committee, and there was no proof that Martin Green was a spy. It wasn't the whole truth, but it was nothing but the truth, and what difference did it make? I'd finish the damn thing, tie up loose ends, and be gone within a month. Senator and Mrs. Young could have America; I only wanted a piece of Oregon. And if Martin Green finally showed up at Constance's door howling like some Ivy League Stanley Kowalski, well, that would be someone else's problem.

I walked down the path to the road where the hearse had parked. Off to my right there was a woman in a wheelchair stopped at the curb, stymied by the six-inch drop. She didn't notice my approach. "Can I help?" I asked.

She smiled. "I was going to do an Evel Knievel off the curb, but as long as you're here . . ."

I lowered her to the road. "Not a very accessible place," I said.

"The worst," she replied. "I'm going to open a cemetery for the handicapped."

"You'll have no competition."

"People will be dying to get in."

"Ouch."

"Sorry, couldn't help it," she said, laughing. "Can I impose a little more? I'm going down to the administration building to make a call. The same guy that forgot the curb cut was supposed to build a ramp over there."

"My pleasure." I stepped behind the chair and began pushing her down the road. She looked at me over her shoulder and extended her hand upward.

"Susan Edwards," she said. She had an interesting face: a quick smile that contrasted markedly with the hardness in her eyes. A survivor.

I took her hand. "Philip Barkley. Nice to meet you."

"Who were you visiting?"

"My daughter."

"Oh. How long ago did she pass away?"

"Just over three years ago. Who were you visiting?"

"My husband. We were in a car accident on the Beltway seven years ago. That's how I got my ride." She patted the arms of the chair.

I appreciated her matter-of-fact tone, and that the mention of my daughter didn't prompt the usual spasm of sympathy and cross-examination. How old was she? Oh, my God. What was it? Oh, how awful. How long did she have it? Who was your doctor? What kind of treatments? On and on, followed by the inevitable segue: I have a friend whose nephew . . . I hated it. I hated it when my daughter was in the hospital, too. Ignoring the phone. Avoiding my friends. Fleeing all those concerned expressions in a futile effort to submerge myself in work for just a day, or an hour. Sorry, can't stop now, I'm late. Yeah, well, we're taking it a day at a time. Yeah, that's all you can do. Sure, I'll do that, and thanks.

"Are you a lawyer?" she asked.

"Does it show?"

"Everyone around Washington is a lawyer, at least every guy with a tie. What kind of lawyer are you?"

"A government lawyer. The Justice Department."

"That's an important job."

"Not as important as a lot of other things."

"Are you a crime-fighter or something?"

"No, I just write briefs."

"My husband was an antitrust lawyer. Do you do any antitrust?"

"No, that was always too complicated for me."

"Me, too. I didn't understand much of it. I got the price-fixing stuff but that's as far as it went." We were approaching the administration building. "I lied to you," she said.

"Lied?"

"Yup. I need still *another* favor. There's a pay phone inside those doors. Believe it or not, it was installed by the same guy who forgot the curb cuts and the ramp. If you'll dial the cab company for me, I promise not to make you pay for the call."

"I can do better than that. Where are you going?"

"Thanks, but I've imposed enough."

"I'm in no hurry," I said. "I'll be glad to drop you."

She laughed again. "A cabdriver actually did drop me once. The poor guy was more frightened than I was."

"I'll be careful."

"I'm not going directly home. I'm going to McDonald's to get a hamburger with large fries and a strawberry shake. I go there every time I leave the cemetery and I get the same meal. I have absolutely no idea why." She turned around. "Do you have any idea why?"

"Because they're wheelchair-accessible?"

She grinned. "That's good! Are you sure you're a lawyer?"

We went to my car, where she showed me how to help her into the passenger's seat and fold her chair. Ten minutes later we were at the drive-thru window ordering lunch. "Where do you want to eat this?" I asked.

"How about right here in the parking lot? We can turn on the radio and have a little music with our food."

I pulled into a spot facing the highway. "I've told you what I do," I said. "What about you?"

She was squeezing several foils of ketchup on her French fries. "Why don't they make a box that stands up?" She asked. I thought she was ignoring my question but then she bit into a French fry and said, "Research."

"What kind of research?"

"Government programs, agency regulations, reports, statistics, stuff like that. I work for a little company that does research for clients interested in what the government is up to. I basically divide my time between the Library of Congress and working at home using the Internet. I read a lot of regulations and stuff put out by the Government Printing Office. It's very exciting, perfect for insomnia, but the Internet is interesting. It's absolutely amazing what you can get off the Web these days."

"That's what everybody says."

"You're not much of an Internet guy, are you?"

"No."

A conversation stopper. We ate in silence until she said, "Well, have you written any good briefs lately?" We both laughed. "I'm reaching!" she admitted.

"That *is* reaching," I said.

"Okay, forget briefs. Can I ask you a personal question?"

"What?"

"What happened to your wife?"

"We're divorced. Why do you ask?"

"Just curious. I'm pretty direct, aren't I?"

"It's okay."

She bit into her hamburger, chewed a moment, then

said, "I used to be coy but . . . you get past certain things, you know?"

"I know."

"They don't seem to matter anymore."

"You learn what's important."

She nodded, then held up a French fry. "Like hamburgers and fries!" she said.

"And strawberry shakes," I added.

I drove her home, a nice five-story condominium outside Alexandria. I held her chair while she slid into it, and pushed her up to the entrance. "Let's exchange business cards," she suggested. "Maybe we'll do another power lunch sometime."

"I don't have a card with me but give me yours."

"It's all there," she said, handing me one from her wallet. "Phone, fax, and e-mail. I'm very reachable."

I nodded but said nothing. Owing to three stays in the hospital and all the medication, I hadn't been on a date since my divorce, and now wasn't the time to start a relationship in Washington. Nevertheless, I still fretted that she'd misunderstand my reticence. There probably weren't a lot of dating opportunities for her, even if she was direct.

"Well, good-bye, Philip," she said suddenly, pushing off, "and thanks for everything."

"Susan."

She stopped and turned her chair around. "Yes?"

"I don't see anyone," I said. "I mean, I don't go out."

"That's okay," she replied, "but if you should change your mind I'm a good listener. And if I have to, I can do the talking *and* the listening."

When I got back to the apartment there was a message on my answering machine from Blair: "*I don't know where you are, but I hope you get this message in time. You've got a meeting with the AG tomorrow morning at nine o'clock. You'll get the news then, but if you're still working on your report, you can stop right now."*

9

I CONSIDERED THE SITUATION FOR the final time on the bus. The first possibility was that the case was finished, but if they'd found Green she would have said so. The second possibility was that *I* was finished. Did they know that I'd been moonlighting? I couldn't conjure up a third, but I comforted myself with the knowledge that one way or another, my days in Washington were coming to an end.

I walked into the small conference room ten minutes early and was the last to arrive. The room was quiet, save for the voice of the AG, instructing a secretary who was hunched over his shoulder and nodding in sync with his speech. I took the chair next to Blair, who was making notes in the margin of a report. She looked up to regard me neutrally before returning to her task. To my left, with bold ties and identical haircuts, sat two earnest-looking assistants to the AG, probably former associates at Chatham & Ball. They were watching the boss but peeking at Agent Turner whenever it was safe.

On the AG's right flank sat The Blade, whose head was cocked at an odd angle as he listened intently to his master's voice. On the left, providing a kind of sociopathic symmetry, was Jarrett Sanders, doubtless there to remind anyone who needed it that the case had its political aspects. His presence was confirmation that something disagreeable was about to happen.

Between Sanders and Blair sat poor Evans, fidgeting with his fountain pen and avoiding eye contact with The Blade. Blessed only with intelligence, integrity, and the capacity for hard work, he had gone as far as he could in a political hierarchy. He may have understood the game at the upper levels but was ill-equipped to play. The irony was that I used to thrive in that game. After several years on the periphery, I came to a truce of sorts with the realpolitik when I decided that the true system of checks and balances was not among the branches of government, but between its servants wedded to self-interest and those to principle. The system required both, and I came to see myself as a sort of balancing pole, one of those that kept the high-wire act of government aloft as it inched along from Congress to Congress and Administration to Administration. But it's a dynamic environment, and I eventually inched myself in deep enough to know where those proverbial bodies were buried, but not so deep that I'd lie about it. In the capital, that's no-man's-land.

"We're all here," the AG announced, "so let's get started. I'm sorry to bring you in on a Sunday but there's been a development in the case and Agent Turner will fill everyone in." Blair passed packets of documents around the table. The AG, Sanders, and The Blade let theirs lay untouched, indicating that a more exclusive briefing had already occurred. The documents were bank statements from a small savings and loan in New Jersey. The account was in the name of Martin Green; the address was his parents' house. The statements went back three years and began with a balance of just over two hundred dollars. Other than a few dollars of interest each quarter, there were no changes until the last statement, which showed a deposit of fifty thousand dollars four days after Green disappeared.

"Green had this account since high school," explained Blair. "It doesn't show up in any credit report or loan application because it only had a small balance and he never used it. That last deposit was wired from a bank in Liechtenstein. We're trying to trace it but we're not optimistic."

"It's a payoff," pronounced the AG.

"That's our theory," agreed Blair.

"Betrayed for filthy lucre," drawled Sanders.

"Is the money still there?" asked The Blade.

"Yes, every dollar."

"Why, do you suppose?" asked one of the haircuts. "He cleaned out his Washington account."

Everyone stared at the impertinent assistant until Blair directed a reply toward the head of the table. "Fifty thousand dollars is a lot of cash, General. If he withdraws it he attracts attention, and it's a lot to carry around. If he hides it someplace he's got to go back for it, not a smart move for a fugitive. And if he just transfers it to a new bank he's got to open an account and risk drawing attention again. He's better off just letting it lie and hoping we'd never find it."

"How did you find it?" asked the AG.

"The local field office got a telephone call on Saturday from a woman who wouldn't give her name, almost certainly a bank employee. She'd seen the newspaper stories and wanted to come forward."

"Have we made any progress on what he gave them for the money?"

"Green had access to lots of material that would interest the Hungarians. Certain intelligence estimates were found misfiled. There's only supposed to be one secretary handling them, and she's certain she wouldn't have made such an error. They have Green's fingerprints on them."

"Sounds damn compelling to me," said The Blade.

"Absolutely," agreed the AG. "There's our case."

"Looks like a duck, quacks like a duck," added Sanders. The haircuts bobbed in agreement.

Evans cleared his throat. His pained expression indicated dissent. "What is it?" demanded the AG.

"General, if they're documents that Green would have used his fingerprints won't prove anything. It comes down to a filing error and . . . well, that's not a very compelling case." He was right, of course, but his timing was all wrong. When the politicos went into heat it was best to allow a cool-down period before burdening them with reality.

The first reaction was a thrust from The Blade. "We're dealing with a spy, not an idiot," he said menacingly, clearly implying who was who. "He's not going to steal sensitive documents. He's going to copy them when no one's around. What kind of evidence do you expect?"

"I understand that," replied Evans defensively. "I'm just pointing out that it won't be very compelling to a jury and—"

"That's for another time," interrupted the AG. "We've got more immediate concerns than what a jury might do." He paused as if he was considering the matter anew, then said, "This bank account development changes things entirely. We now have proof that secrets were compromised and I'd say our planned interim report is no longer an option. Does anyone disagree?" No one did. "Well," he continued, "that means we're going to have to change the report and lay out the complete story as soon as possible."

There was a moment of silence as the AG's gaze swept the table; Sanders's eyes remained on me. The brain trust, no doubt with Warren's input, had finally landed on the solution Constance had staked out in my apartment.

"General," Evans said quietly, "if we apprehend this man it could lead to a trial for espionage."

"Of course," replied the AG. "What's your point?"

The assistant attorney general blinked at the prospect of explaining the basics of criminal law and the Constitution to the nation's chief law enforcement officer, in front of a room full of witnesses to boot. "The Justice . . . *we* don't report the evidence against a defendant before we prosecute. It would raise due-process concerns, the right to a fair trial. The first thing his lawyers would do is to move to dismiss the case on constitutional grounds."

"Defense lawyers are always filing motions like that," snapped The Blade. "They rarely succeed."

Evans was committed now. There was a principle involved and he was genetically incapable of backing down. No, definitely not the skill set for higher office. "Defense lawyers don't usually have a case like we'd be handing them if we condemned Green before he was even tried," he said. He looked at the AG and added, "This would be a lynching before trial. Our motives would be questioned."

Perhaps unwittingly, he'd played the right card. The AG may not have understood the Constitution but he grasped the implications at once. An unprecedented step would be seen for the blatantly political ploy that it was, and opponents would have a field day. The AG was boxed in and clearly unhappy. He looked around the table for rescue and it came from an unlikely source.

"General, can I make a suggestion?" asked the other haircut. "Why don't we indict him now? An indictment is public unless it's sealed from view and there are no barriers to reciting as much or as little evidence as we want. We could lay out the entire case and leave nothing for the press to root around for."

The AG pursed his lips, considering the point, then looked at Evans. "What about it?" he asked.

"Well," Evans replied, frowning, "that's true as far as it goes . . ."

"So, what's the problem?" demanded The Blade.

"There's more work to be done," explained Evans, "and there could be coconspirators that still might be caught. In this type of situation we seal the indictment to avoid compromising the investigation. We don't unseal it until we've arrested the people involved and are about to charge them in court. We haven't even arrested Green and can't say when—or if—we will. It's just too early to reveal what we know."

Sanders took his cue. "*Ah* don't know nothin' about this sealin' and unsealin' business," he said. "What ah know is that if this thing isn't nipped in the bud, one of

them minority members is gonna call for an investigation by a select committee, and they're gonna keep this
on the front page for *months*."

The AG didn't have to be hit over the head. "We'll
continue with the investigation," he declared. "We'll
commit all the resources of this department and the Bureau to apprehending any coconspirators. However,
there's public interest in this case and even though it's
not good news for Senator Young, I think we have a
duty to act." He looked around and asked, "Does anyone disagree?"

A few feet away, Evans was biting his lip. Gratuitous
remarks about public interest and duty notwithstanding,
the paramount interests were clearly those of Senator
Young and his party. The integrity of the department
was up for auction and the AG was about to bring down
the gavel when I made my decision.

"I disagree," I said. Every head swiveled toward me
but no one said anything for a long moment.

"You disagree?" asked the AG finally.

"That's right, General."

"You believe the indictment should be sealed?"

"I believe there should be no indictment at this time,
sealed or not. Treason is the most serious crime in the
federal code. If the case against Green were prosecuted
on the current evidence it would be dismissed out of
hand and this department would look foolish."

"That's bull—that's ridiculous!" cried The Blade.
"We've got pictures of this man in a meeting with an
agent of a foreign government!"

"It was only the other day," I reminded him, "that
you argued there was no meeting at all."

The Blade's eyes narrowed. He didn't appreciate being trapped by his own words, uttered in what he regarded as the distant past. "We didn't know then about the payoff," he said. "That changes everything."

"The money indicates that *something* was going on but we don't know what. You can't convict a man of espionage if you're not prepared to prove that any secrets were compromised."

"What about conspiracy?" asked the other assistant. "We don't have to prove an actual transfer."

It was an amateur's question and I treated it dismissively. "You still have to prove that treason was the purpose," I said. "How are you going to do that based on sharing a table at lunch? You can't prove that the Portrait Gallery incident was about espionage, and you certainly can't connect it to the money. It's a good theory, maybe even a strong one, but it's still a long way from proof beyond a reasonable doubt, and this department has rules about bringing cases that lack sufficient evidence to convict."

The AG blinked at the directness of my message; The Blade grunted in disgust. Sanders was staring at me as he pantomimed slapping ticks on the arm of his chair. I avoided Blair's eyes although I could feel them. "I'd like to confer with the deputy and Mr. Sanders in my office," said the AG finally. "We'll be back shortly."

Five minutes after they were gone the AG's door opened again and Blair was summoned by his secretary. That left Evans and me with the two assistants, who were whispering excitedly over the prospect of an actual lynching. Evans motioned me to a corner. "You used to be more tactful," he said. "The AG is in there breaking up the furniture."

"When they come out, Alan, whatever happens, stay out of it." He looked at me, wide-eyed. "I'm telling you as a friend. You serve at the president's pleasure. Don't chuck your career over this because there's no need."

He looked dubious. "Why not?"

"Trust me."

The AG's group returned twenty minutes later. Blair's face was impassive but the others looked very unhappy. "We've considered the situation and I've decided that we won't seek an indictment right now," announced the AG. "Agent Turner advises me that there's a good chance the evidence against Green will soon improve, and so, for the sound reasons stated by the assistant attorney general, I've decided to await developments. Are there any questions?" He looked around the table, bypassing me.

Back in my office I made a copy of my draft report and put the disk in my shirt pocket. Then I opened a new memo on my computer screen, typed "Notice of Resignation" on the subject line, and stared at the blinking cursor. The sensation was not unlike drowning: my whole life was passing in front of me as I sat with fingers poised on the keyboard.

"Seems like a good idea," said the voice behind me.

Blair was sitting on the corner of my desk, looking over my shoulder. "Short and sweet," she suggested. "No whining."

"No whining," I repeated.

"Right. What will you do now? I don't think your transfer to Portland is coming through any time soon."

"I'll find something out there myself," I said.

"They'll have a clear field to indict Marty when you're gone."

"No, they won't. My resignation is like pouring gasoline on the case. I can throw a match from anywhere and they know it."

She frowned. "Well, since I'm close enough to get burned, maybe this would be a good time for you to stop holding out on me."

"Holding out?"

"Look, either you know something about this case that I don't or . . ." She paused, considering her next words.

"Or I've got real problems?"

"Don't try to turn the tables on me, Philip, I've been thinking it over. How would you know something about this case that I don't?" She reached over and pressed a key. A series of question marks appeared on the screen. "What sources do you have?" She pressed again; more question marks. "I keep coming back to the same answer." She typed slowly with one finger: C-O-N-S-T-A-N-C-E. "I'm right," she said. "I can see it in your eyes." She put her hand on my chest and tilted me backward, then bent over so her lips were right by my ear. "Did she tell you Green was innocent?" she asked softly. "She was using you, Philip. She was lying to protect Warren. Tell me what she said."

I didn't have the energy to lie or stonewall. "She swore me to secrecy."

"Of course she did. She was making sure you couldn't check out her story." Blair swiveled me around so we were almost nose to nose. "Well, that was then, this is now. Constance and the senator have had a change of heart. They've just made that very clear. They want to get the truth out quickly, so whatever bullshit story she fed you was just that—bullshit. So, tell me: what was it?"

"She caught Green copying documents. Later, he called her and essentially confessed. Those were the calls you asked Warren about."

Blair straightened up slowly. "Son of a bitch," she muttered, "you *knew* he was guilty. You had the evidence all along." She grimaced and reached for her pocketbook. "There's one thing I don't understand," she said angrily. "Why tell *you*? Even if she knew you'd keep your promise, why reveal something like that?"

"She said that the truth would come out eventually, and the sooner it happened, the better their chances to repair the damage before the primaries. It's the same point the AG and Sanders were making today."

"If she wanted the truth to get out, why not come forward? Why swear you to secrecy?"

"She said Warren and Sanders weren't seeing things the same way, not then. They wanted to circle up the wagons and dig in. She was ahead of them, she was always smarter than the men she worked for. By letting me know Green was guilty she was hoping to accelerate our timetable. She assured me that she'd bring them around by the time I issued the report. Warren and his people would accept the findings and concentrate on damage control. No one was going to throw rocks at the messengers."

"Well, they're all brought around now, and thirty minutes ago everyone was ready to go forward except you, the one person at the table who had the missing piece of the puzzle, the one the rest of us had to take on faith. You single-handedly brought the case to a grinding halt so you could drag it out as long as possible."

"That's not true."

"Sure it is. You're determined to destroy Young's

chances. That's why you went along with the interim report. Were you counting on us to break the case in time to hurt him bad? Or were you going to use Constance's admission against them later, when it would do the most damage?"

"I wasn't going to use it at all."

"And why is that?"

"Because she lied."

Blair blinked. "What?"

"We were married. I know."

She unshouldered her pocketbook and sat down on my desk again. "I really want a cigarette," she said. "Have you got one?"

"No, but I can get you some gum or something."

She didn't hear me; she was talking to herself. "Well, *of course* Constance was lying. I mean, why should anything in this case make sense? Mrs. Young wants to be first lady so bad she'll crush anyone who gets in her way, so she tells her ex-husband a lie that can wreck the campaign. And, naturally, the ex-husband, who's got every reason to nail the *current* husband, agrees to keep it a secret." She closed her eyes and began to run her fingers through her hair, long strokes from front to back. "So, why did she lie?"

"There can only be one answer."

"Go ahead."

"The truth is worse."

She stared at me, waiting for more. "I'm listening," she said.

"That's it." I wasn't ready to share my theory about Constance and Martin.

"Not espionage, huh? What other explanation can there be for the fifty thousand dollars?"

"I'm working on that, but the timing of its discovery is interesting, isn't it?"

"What are you saying?"

"What I said a moment ago: they wanted to accelerate our timetable."

"So they arrange an anonymous tip?"

"And she leaked the national security angle to the *Post*."

Blair went to the window and leaned against the frame with her arms folded, staring at the traffic below while I watched the play of light and shadow on her profile. Finally, she said, "I suppose if I interview Constance she'll deny everything. She couldn't explain why she didn't tell her story about Martin when he first disappeared."

"That's probably true."

"So, let me see. We can't indict Green with the evidence we've got because they're afraid you're going to blow the whistle. I can't judge for myself whether Constance has what we need because she won't talk. And although you think evidence is being planted to steer us away from the truth, you can't—or won't—tell me what that truth might be. Does that sum it up?"

"I guess so, for now."

She came back to the desk and picked up her purse. "Good-bye, Philip Barkley," she said. "You're an interesting man. I wish I'd known you back when."

"Likewise."

She nodded toward my computer screen. "Make it straightforward. It will be the only thing in this case that is."

———————

"May I speak to Mrs. Young, please? It's Philip Barkley."

A moment later she was on. "Philip?"

"We need to talk, Constance."

"I don't think so. Warren is very angry. *I'm* very angry."

"Imagine how angry you'd be if the truth came out."

"What does *that* mean?"

"The spot at Roosevelt Island," I told her. "Four o'clock."

"I'm not sure I can get away."

"Try very hard."

She showed up thirty minutes late to demonstrate that she wasn't worried. She sauntered in wearing resort casual: beige linen slacks, white silk top, sandals, and a wide-brimmed straw hat. Her sunglasses were tinted a frosty blue. "Sorry, I'm late," she said nonchalantly. "I couldn't find my cloak and dagger."

"I wouldn't joke about espionage, Constance. It's the most serious of crimes. Life imprisonment, no parole. To even be accused would be ruinous."

She removed a bottle of mineral water from her bag. "Your point being?"

"They want to indict him, but you already know that."

"I do try to keep up with things. What does indicting poor Martin have to do with me?" She took a sip of water.

"That's a good question. I think I have the answer but maybe you'd like to help."

She laughed. "Stop being so dramatic, Philip. I have no idea what you're talking about, I assure you."

"Been to the Waldorf-Astoria lately?" I asked.

"I prefer the Plaza," she replied coolly. "Is this the spot where we used to picnic? Or was it on the other side of those trees?"

"Remember when I was a prosecutor? I was very good at it."

"I don't remember what you were very good at, Philip."

"You know what I learned? When you've got the right answer, *all* the pieces fit, not just some. And the pieces I understand have nothing to do with espionage but everything to do with Martin and you. What happened? Did he take it all too seriously? My guess is things spun out of control. You couldn't know he'd run off and create a manhunt, but now he's out there somewhere licking his wounds. A bit overdramatic, but then he's a very serious young man, some might say a little rigid."

"Philip, dear, you really need to adjust your medication. Do you truly believe I'd frame a man for espionage to cover up an affair?"

"You're right, it's all out of proportion, totally crazy—unless the presidency's at stake. So, let's put the question this way: would you sacrifice Green to save your marriage and Warren's chance to be president? Well, as they say, to ask the question is to answer it."

"I've heard enough," she said. "You left the hospital too soon, dear. You need help."

"Listen to what I'm saying. I'm not going to permit this man to be destroyed, no matter how much circumstantial evidence you create. I'm going to keep at it until I can prove what really happened, so if I were you,

I'd figure out a way to free Green from this web you've woven."

"How graphic," she replied, looking at her watch. "Well, I really must be going. I've got another appointment at five." She looked me up and down and said, "You're thin. You must take better care of yourself, Philip. You were always too focused on work."

A rough measure of what you've accumulated is the ease with which you pick up stakes. After fifteen years in Washington, almost forty on this earth, I had a job, an apartment, and a doctor. A visit to pick up copies of my medical records took a morning. The apartment market was good so the landlord was pleased to cancel my lease, as was the company from which I'd rented the furniture. That left the job.

I told Evans I didn't want a send-off. No announcement, no party, no cake. He came down to my office carrying my identification wallet, which he placed in the cardboard box on my desk. "Take it," he said. "Officially, you lost it, so it couldn't be turned in."

"Thanks," I replied. He stared into the box, looking miserable. "What is it?"

"They're bypassing me," he said. "They're pressing Turner for proof that Green gave the crown jewels to the Hungarians."

"They'll never find it," I told him.

He summoned a wan smile. "I heard one of the AGs assistants tried to muscle her. He won't do it again."

"He's lucky she didn't hurt him."

"Yeah, she'd do it, no question."

He walked me to the elevator and punched the

button. "It shouldn't end this way," he said.

"It's going to be fine. It turns out I can withdraw some retirement money if I pay a small penalty. I'll get settled in, take the bar, and open a little office. I'll do a few wills and some contracts, maybe an occasional divorce and DUI. When things are slow, I'll go fly-fishing."

"Sounds good. Maybe we'll make it a partnership."

The elevator door opened, we shook hands, and I was on my own. All in all, it took less than forty-eight hours to sever my ties. Family, career, relationships, attachments, possessions, memories: they all fit neatly into the trunk of my car. I planned to leave early the next morning to beat the rush-hour traffic, so I filled the tank and drove to a seafood restaurant for the dinner buffet, my last supper in the capital. I was in bed by ten with my clothes and my shaving kit on the chair beside me. At two A.M. I was still listening to tractor-trailers on the interstate and hoping for sleep. I felt as if I could float.

The telephone rang at seven. I bolted upright, arms flailing, heart pumping, and grabbed the receiver. "Yes," I slurred.

"Philip?"

"Who . . . ?"

"Blair. They found him."

It didn't register.

"Are you there?" she asked.

"Green?"

"Yes."

"Where?"

"The Alta Vista motel in Reading, Pennsylvania, less than an hour ago."

"Are they questioning him?"

"No."

"Why not?"

"He's dead. He killed himself."

10

TIMING IS EVERYTHING. THAT'S WHAT was going through my mind as I sat in the visitor's lobby in the Hoover Building waiting for Blair to return. As a former public servant formerly investigating the disappearance of the formerly alive Martin Green, I was not invited to the meeting then in progress in the AG's conference room. I wasn't even supposed to be in the visitor's lobby. They let me wait because I had a Justice ID. But for Evans's gift I'd have been on line with the tourists being marshaled around in groups, a peripatetic parade of complicated sneakers, hats, and T-shirts espousing a fair cross-section of the American experience: Yankees, Packers, VFW lodges, Nike Swooshes, Caterpillar tractors, auto parts dealers, feed stores and granaries, big cities, exclusive islands, rock tours, political slogans, rhetorical questions, conventions, beers, motorcycles, sex acts, and messages I wasn't hip enough or something enough to decipher.

And I wondered how I'd fare in that place outside the Beltway. Washington and government service were the only world I'd known since adulthood. Now my only link to that world was the identification in my breast pocket, a ceremonial passport bestowed as a souvenir. Timing was indeed everything.

Blair entered the lobby just before noon, striding toward the employees' entrance. I stood up and she saw me. "Are you here for the tour?" she asked. "Be sure to see the fingerprint exhibit. It's a humdinger."

"I was hoping we could talk."

"You're not on the case anymore."

"Please."

She looked around the lobby, then at her watch. "I'll be down in fifteen minutes. We'll go to lunch. You're buying."

We walked over to a tapas restaurant on Seventh Street with me once again pushing to keep pace. The sidewalks were thick with tourists and government workers, and it seemed as if everyone—men and women—stared or at least glanced at Blair as we passed. It was, I decided, a combination of looks and attitude. If I manufactured sunglasses I'd hire Blair Turner to wear them and just walk around. There was a knot of construction workers on Eighth Street. They were poking each other as we approached and she veered toward them. Here we go, I said to myself. I figured she'd shoot one and just slap the others around. We passed within three feet but before the first crack was uttered she turned her head and said, "Good afternoon, guys." The leers vanished; a few mumbled "good afternoon" and the rest kept their mouths shut. Over my shoulder I saw them staring in her wake.

"Is that how you usually handle it?" I asked.

"Handle what?"

We got a table in a back corner. Our waiter struggled mightily trying to explain the specials until Blair said something in Spanish and he lit up, relieved. The rest of the process went smoothly with her serving as interpreter, then they bantered for a few moments before he walked away laughing. When I looked up she was smiling. "What?" I asked.

"He wanted to know if you'd eaten tapas before."

"What did you tell him?"

"That you don't get out much. Are you all packed?"

"I turned in my apartment key this morning. Everything I own is in the trunk of my car."

I wanted her to look disappointed but she just laughed. "Very collegiate. When do you head for Portland?"

"I was going to leave this morning but after your call . . ." I shrugged. "It's hard to just drop something like this."

"I guess so."

"How did he die?"

"It was relatively painless. He swallowed a handful of pills, climbed into a warm bath, and slit his wrists with a razor blade. Then he just lay there and watched his life run out. The coroner says—are you okay?"

No. Definitely not okay. I was swallowing hard, trying to force down a sob that was lodged around my Adam's apple. She politely busied herself with a bottle of mineral water while I struggled for control. Until a few days before, I thought I would save him. I'd save a decent man who deserved it, then ride off into the sunset.

"Drink this," she instructed, handing me a glass.

"Are you sure it was suicide?"

"He left a note, Philip. It requires a little interpretation but it's all there."

"Go ahead."

"Basically, he was a very disillusioned man. He despised politics and its compromises. He felt we were unethical, not only in the way we governed ourselves but in the way we treated other peoples. He felt powerless to change things and thought he was acting on principle by taking matters in his own hands. Apparently, he realized we were on to him and went off to figure out what to do. He was terrified by the prospect of arrest and punishment, so he found a way out."

"Is that everything?"

"He condemned politicians for being greedy and forsaking the cause of the downtrodden. So what's new?"

The food arrived. I pushed it around the plate while I thought about what I'd heard. Did I believe it? Only if I believed he was a traitor, which I'd already rejected. But now there was a confession. "Are you sure the letter is genuine?"

"It's time to get back to reality, Philip."

"I'm just asking."

She put down her fork. "Do you really believe he could have been murdered? Why? Did Diana drug him and slit his wrists for dumping her?" She leaned forward and lowered her voice. "The letter was at the lab by eight this morning. It's written in his handwriting and has his fingerprints on it, no one else's. The pen used to write the letter was on the desk in his room."

"And the paper?"

"Motel stationery."

"What sedative did he take?"

"Rohypnol, very powerful stuff."

"Was it prescribed for him?"

"No."

"So how did he get it?"

"It was in an ordinary vial with no label. He could have stolen it or bought it on the street."

"Bought it on the street?"

"Yeah, it's the so-called date-rape drug." She held up her hand before I could say anything. "The only fingerprints on the vial are his, and before you ask, Diana doesn't have a prescription for it, either."

"She's been notified?"

"This morning, right after his family. They want to bury him the day after tomorrow and the AG wants us to accommodate them. The autopsy began"—she looked at her watch—"three hours ago. It should be over and his body already on its way to the funeral home in New Jersey."

She finished her lunch while I digested the facts. A few minutes later we were walking back toward the Hoover Building. When we reached the entrance she turned and offered her hand. "I guess this is good-bye," she said.

"Can I call you?"

"I'm seeing someone."

"I mean, about the case, the autopsy and whatever."

She shook her head. "God, you're easy. Yes, you can call me. I'll tell you what I can. You know the way to Portland? I won't have to look for you, too, will I?"

"North to Pennsylvania, west till I hit the ocean."

"Sounds right. Well, good-bye again, and good luck. I really mean it."

"Good luck to you, too. I think Evans was right. You're a shoo-in for director." She turned to go. "Blair?"

"What?"

"Green was opposed to suicide. It's forbidden by his religion."

She sighed, then said, "Everyone is opposed to suicide, Philip—right up to the decision to kill themselves."

By evening I'd reached the outskirts of Columbus, Ohio. It wasn't the most direct route to Oregon but I planned a detour from Dayton to visit my first home on the way to my next one. I ate dinner in a truck stop and spent a fitful night at a motor court as images of bucolic hamlets clashed with all the autopsy photos I had ever seen. By sunrise I was stopped at a light just north of the entrance to the interstate. The options were painted on the green sign directly in front of me. Right and west to the future, a new day with fresh possibilities. Left and east to failure and pain and loss. And a troubling case about the death of a man I'd never met.

West, I commanded, but the damn car had a mind of its own. East, it said. Time to pay our respects.

———————————

I reached northern New Jersey by dinnertime. I called the synagogues in Green's hometown until I found the right one. I arrived early the next morning and took a seat in the last pew. A few elderly men were already seated. Their lips moved and bodies rocked as they chanted in occasionally audible voices. People began to arrive in clusters. Middle-aged aunts and uncles, adolescent cousins, and contemporaries from Washington and

Princeton. Jenny Castellano arrived with a group from
the Intelligence Committee. Diana Morris entered alone
and sat with her head bowed in a corner in the back row.
The pews filled, then people began to line the walls. Warren and Constance were escorted in by someone who
seemed to know what he was doing, and sat in the second row, behind immediate family. Warren looked
somber but not grief-stricken, a sort of middle ground
that was probably carved out by his advisers as appropriate for the funeral of a colleague who had been pub-
licly linked to a serious offense. The decision to show up
at all must have been a tough one, but given short notice,
a trip out of the country wasn't feasible. No doubt an
appropriately balanced statement would be put out by
his office.

People were whispering, hugging; some were crying. A
door opened and the casket was rolled in. The crying and
murmurs grew more audible. A woman began to wail and
was comforted by the people around her. An elderly rabbi
entered, followed by the immediate family, all wearing
black ribbons pinned on their clothes. Two young men
were supporting Martin's mother and his father shuffled
behind. Rabbi Adler followed the procession and took a
seat on the platform, facing the congregation. He saw me
but didn't react.

It wasn't a long service. The elderly rabbi said that
Martin was a righteous young man trying to make his
way in a world that seemed to grow ever more confus-
ing. He recited a biblical verse about man's lifetime being three score and ten years, four score if he were
strong. He said that some men are not granted the full
span of days, and that every life should be measured in
terms of the love given and received, and by good

works. By that measure, he assured us, Martin had lived a full and rewarding life. Martin's brother and a cousin followed and talked about episodes in his life, prompting murmurs of agreement, a little laughter, and more tears. Rabbi Adler was the last speaker. He said that Martin was an active member of his Washington congregation, a pillar of his community, and a student of the Torah until his untimely death. The service closed with more prayers and the usual announcements.

I watched from inside as Senator and Mrs. Young expressed their condolences to Green's family before leaving for the airport. The candidate looked genuinely heartbroken as he hugged Martin's mother while the cameras flashed. Constance said something to Martin's father and kissed his mother's cheek. Then they were gone. The funeral procession began to form up in the parking lot. I went to my car, planning to head for the interstate as soon as the others had left. The hearse began to roll slowly forward, followed by a limousine bearing the family, then a line of private cars. I saw Diana Morris go by, still alone. The S-curve of the procession brought the hearse directly into her line of sight and I saw her chin sink to her chest and her shoulders begin to shake. I got out of my car and walked up to her window.

"Remember me?" I asked. "Philip Barkley from the Justice Department. I came to your apartment with the FBI agent." She stared at me through her dark glasses, then nodded. "Do you want me to go with you? I'll drive, then you can drop me back here afterward."

"That would be very kind," she said, her voice breaking.

We were at the rear of the procession. I concentrated on keeping up with the cars in front, not an easy matter as we rolled through stop signs, red lights, and around drivers who didn't seem to know or care that they were in our way. Diana stared out the passenger window saying nothing until we passed a row of newspaper vending machines in front of a coffee shop. "There's a story in the *New York Times* this morning," she said softly. "It says Martin was spying and he killed himself because he couldn't live with what he'd done. It says he left a letter."

"Who said that?" I asked. "Is it a press release?"

She shook her head. "It wasn't official. It said, 'sources close to the investigation.'" She turned and looked at me. "Was it you?"

"No, it wasn't."

"It's going to be official soon. They've made up their minds about Martin but it isn't true, Mr. Barkley. The letter can't be real."

Up ahead the hearse moved to the center of a four-lane street and signaled a left turn. The tall iron fence indicated that we'd arrived. The procession turned into the cemetery and then stopped to wait while some last-minute processing took place. Ten minutes later we rolled through the cemetery grounds, turning left and right until we stopped near a newer, more open area. I got out of the car and stood by the door, thinking about my last visit to a cemetery as I watched them carry the casket out of sight. Five minutes passed. It was totally still except for Diana's muted crying. Then the funeral director signaled and car doors opened and we all walked toward the grave.

We were in the outer ring of mourners. The rabbi

prayed and led the gathering in a prayer in Hebrew. Then I heard the sound of a shovel biting into the earth. I wanted to leave, to run, but Diana was holding on to my arm and we were actually moving *toward* the sound, and then I could see what was happening: men and women were taking turns, each throwing a shovelful of dirt onto Martin's casket, and then a man was looking at me, proffering the shovel, and Diana let go of my arm. I stepped to the edge of the grave. A small part of casket was still visible. Martin's father was holding on to his wife, staring at me, silently pleading with me to bury his son, to end it. It doesn't end, I wanted to say. It never ends. I drove the shovel into a mound of dark earth and threw some on that last visible spot.

At the cemetery gate most of the cars followed the limousine to the family's house to begin the ritual sharing of memories and prayer and food. Diana and I went the other way, back toward the funeral home. "Are you going to his house?" I asked.

She shook her head. "I don't think they want me there. I wouldn't be comfortable."

"Was it the religious differences?" She nodded. "I'd like to ask you something. When I was at your apartment I saw a book on your shelf about conversion. Were you planning to convert to Judaism?"

"I thought about it," she said, "but the more I thought, the more stressful it became. I'm a Lutheran, Mr. Barkley. I've attended church all my life. My father's first cousin is our pastor. My conversion would've been very hard on my family, and I think it would have been hard on me, too. So I didn't."

"How did Martin feel about it?"

"He never pushed it. He never even mentioned it. It was my idea and when I told him that I'd consider converting he handled it so perfectly. He said that my relationship with God was my own and I should keep that uppermost in my mind. Either way, he'd love me just the same. That pretty much made up my mind."

"I assume it was marriage that made you consider it."

"With both of us coming from religious families we knew marrying was going to be very stressful. We were still wrestling with what to do when I found out that I couldn't have children. That was a very tough time for us but I guess every cloud has a silver lining, right? We were very happy with our lives together. We decided that if we weren't going to have children we'd continue as we were until one of us wasn't satisfied anymore. Then we'd make a decision."

"I guess that makes sense."

"Do you believe Martin was a spy?"

She caught me off-guard; the "no" was out of my mouth before I even considered something more prudent.

"Well, they have to listen to you, don't they? Maybe you'll convince them that they're wrong."

"That might be very hard to do, Diana. I have another question. It's a difficult one to ask."

"Go ahead. If it could help, ask me anything."

"When you were interviewed by Agent Turner you were very certain that Martin couldn't have been seeing another woman. I was wondering if you still feel that way."

"Martin wouldn't have done that, Mr. Barkley."

"Well, I understand why you say that, him being the

kind of man he was, but things can happen that we don't expect and—"

She reached into her bag and took out a rolled-up document tied with a ribbon. "I was thinking about putting this in the casket but I decided he'd want me to keep it."

"What is it?"

"A *ketubah*. A traditional Jewish marriage contract. It's a promise between a husband and wife to love and care for each other with forgiveness, compassion, and integrity. It's a Jewish tradition. It's signed before the wedding."

"Whose is it?"

"Ours. This contract is written for an interfaith marriage. We had our own ceremony in a private spot at Dumbarton Oaks. We signed this contract and then we read vows that we wrote to each other, and passages from the Old and New Testaments. We regarded ourselves as married, Mr. Barkley, although we never told anyone. So, do I believe Martin Green would break his vows and our contract? From what you know of him, what do you think?"

We said good-bye back at the parking lot. She thanked me profusely for driving her to the cemetery, and for anything I might do to prove the stories about her Martin weren't true. Then she was gone. I set out for the highway that led to the interstate that led to Oregon. I filled up at one of those combination gas stations and convenience stores. I bought stale coffee that I drank while sitting on my fender, then went to a phone and dialed Agent Turner's pager. She called back a moment later.

"How was the funeral?" she asked.

"You had someone there?"

"The investigation isn't over, Philip. It takes at least two to spy: one agent and one controller. We photographed everyone. You know, I love this digital stuff. Your picture came up on my computer screen twenty minutes ago."

"Were you surprised?"

"Not really. How's Diana doing?"

"She says that Martin couldn't have been having an affair."

"That wasn't my theory, it was yours."

"What if we're both wrong?"

"You must have missed the news: it was espionage. We got it straight from the horse's mouth."

"What about Magda Takács? Are you going to interview her now?"

"Gone. Left the country last night."

"Dammit!"

"Nothing we could do, but it's one more indication that the encounter at the Portrait Gallery wasn't innocent . . . Are you still there?"

"I'm here."

"Well, making his funeral was a nice gesture. Now you can move on."

"Right."

That was greeted by silence. Then: "You're not going to Oregon, are you?"

"I have to make a stop first."

"You're not on the case anymore. You don't even work for the government anymore."

"That's true."

"I'm going to have to report this, Philip. The AG will

cough up blood, and that's less than Warren Young will do."

"Well, like you said, I don't work for the government anymore. I've got to go."

"Philip."

"What?"

"If we're both wrong, it could be dangerous."

11

THE LANCASTER HOTEL WAS IN an area between
Tenth and Eleventh Avenues that was largely the domain
of trucking companies and remnants of light industry in
Manhattan. It catered to travelers who didn't know any
better, tourists from places where sixty-five dollars
meant a color TV, a pool, and a breakfast buffet. The
clerk remembered Martin Green; he'd already told that
to the FBI. Stayed four nights and paid cash. Went out
each day and never asked directions. No visitors, no
messages, no mail or packages. The FBI copied the registration cards and searched the room, too.

Green's former room was a set out of film noir: a sagging bed, a chest and lamp, a torn shade. The only thing
missing was the blinking HOTEL sign that threw shadows
on the wall while you dragged on a Lucky and wondered
how it had come to this. I opened a window opaque with
grime and stood where he had stood, surveying the same
dreary scene. Why are you here? I wondered. Why are
you here? he replied.

I emptied my suitcase into the drawers and spread a

map of the city on the bed. I circled the locations of the phone booths and wrote down the dates of the calls. I'd visit each one the next day, a quick tour to see if something jumped out at me. Then I'd go back and start digging. With the rudiments of a plan, I showered and went to bed. Sleep didn't come. Another side effect. Sleep could be a problem, the doctor said. And anxiety. And you may feel a little flat as we even out the highs and lows. And your libido, well . . .

Headlights traveled across the ceiling. The symphony of city noise dissolved into footsteps and television and conversation seeping through the walls. The rhythmic clank of cars rolling over steel plates marked the passage of time. Somewhere, someone shouted, "Shut up."

I watched. And listened.

And wondered how it had come to this.

The next morning I took the subway downtown to the first phone booth, used by Green at midmorning, Tuesday, of his New York trip. It was on Broadway, directly opposite the park that fronted City Hall. There were plenty of stores and office buildings in the vicinity and I immediately sympathized with the magnitude of the task facing Blair and her team. If Green had business there it could have been in any one of thousands of places.

The second booth was only seven blocks north of the first, near the intersection of Lafayette and Worth Streets, near Foley Square. Green was there near noon on Wednesday. It was familiar territory to tens of thousands of lawyers because the east side of the square was dominated by the state and federal courthouses. Once again, there were plenty of stores and offices, including

the New York Department of Health, but the most intriguing possibility lay less than a football field to the
south, a building I'd visited many times in my days as a
prosecutor: 26 Federal Plaza, the New York offices of
the FBI. Since this was supposed to be a quick tour to get
an overall picture, I wasn't going to dwell on the implications of that.

The third telephone Green used was the one in the
New York Public Library, but the fourth was only a few
blocks southeast from where I was standing. I crossed
Foley Square and circled around to the rear of New York
Police headquarters to the site at the corner of Pearl and
Madison Streets. To the south was a high school and a
building belonging to the telephone company. I stood
around for a while watching cops and students come
and go, then headed for the subway and a ride uptown.

It was at the New York Public Library that the first
possibility of a lead materialized. The booth Green used
was in a row of them near the Forty-second Street entrance. I walked down a short hallway and spotted a
sign over the entrance to a reading room: DOROT JEWISH
DIVISION. The two librarians advised that they had one
of the world's largest collections of commentary on all
aspects of Jewish life, as well as Hebrew- and Yiddish-
language texts on general subjects. I showed them my ID
and a picture of Green; neither recognized him, although
they were both on duty the day he was in the building.
We spent an hour rooting through a chronological collection of registration cards and call slips, but no luck.

I'd already visited the booth by the Waldorf-Astoria,
so I decided to walk back to the Lancaster for exercise
and a chance to think things over. No booth or combination of booths indicated what Green was up to in New

York. As Blair had said, the downtown sites were adjacent to open areas that would make surveillance easier. They were also near major institutions, City Hall, the FBI, the courts, and the police—among thousands of other possibilities. The library could have been a destination or a checkpoint. That my tour had yielded no insights wasn't surprising, yet I couldn't help but feel disappointed and a bit overwhelmed.

So, day one was a zero. I stood in the shower with the spray pounding my neck and thought about day two. I needed a hypothesis, a theory to work against, so I had a conversation with myself. Why does Martin go to New York? Broadly, to get information or to give it. "Give" was the espionage scenario, but Martin wasn't a spy any more than he was Constance's paramour. That left "get." He was investigating, but what? Motive is revealed by action. What he did before the trip was unknown, but afterward he called Constance, who lied about why.

An investigation involving Constance, or Warren, or both. Not Constance, Martin worked for Warren. So did she, in a manner of speaking. It was about Warren, the man who has everything, including money. What was it that Martin told Mitchell Glass? Things aren't what they seem. So, he goes to New York to prove the truth, or to get the truth. From people? Institutions? He went to different places because of what or who was there. Different people with the truth, scattered around New York? No, not people, *places*. Information that you can gather. Public institutions? Public records? The library would fit. There were public records available near all of the locations.

I'd go to all the agencies around the sites, any place

with records. I'd show his picture to the clerks. If there were sign-in sheets, I'd examine them. I'd ask about security cameras and tapes. Something might come up. Private companies would be the last resort.

Revived, I went looking for food and found a pizza parlor with posters of Greece and a fan that blew the bug strips around like streamers. I was the only customer. The proprietor heated two slices and returned to his *Daily News*. In no hurry to return to the hotel, I took a seat near the fan and ate slowly, considering my nascent plan. What if nothing turned up at the agencies? I envisioned myself going floor-to-floor in every office building, knocking on hundreds, thousands of doors. And then what? Maybe passing out leaflets, as Blair had joked. My confidence began to ebb. A clock between the Parthenon and the Aegean Sea said that I could be sleeping a hundred miles away by midnight. A hundred miles closer to Oregon. And no one could fault me. Not Blair, not Diana, not even Martin.

My feet hurt. I untied my shoelaces and noticed the dried earth in the welts. Martin was passing his second night in New Jersey. No headstone yet, just a darker patch on the ground. I'd have to drive right past him. I'd stare straight ahead all the way to Pennsylvania.

I heard myself grunt. When I looked up the proprietor was staring at me. "Yes?" I asked.

"What?" he replied.

"What?"

"Another slice?"

"No, I'm full. It was good." I tied my shoes and stood up. "It was good," I repeated. I walked back to the hotel and tried not to think about the odds. Something would happen, I told myself. It was just a matter of time.

I climbed the two flights to my floor. A fat, unshaven man in a T-shirt was standing in the open doorway of the room opposite mine, glaring past me down the hallway. "This f-in place is too much," he grumbled as I reached the door. "This is gonna be the second night with no TV."

"It sure isn't the Waldorf," I agreed.

"You got pull here," the man said. "Can you get the f-in maintenance guy to show up?"

"I don't have any pull," I said.

"How'd you get him to come to your room?"

"My room?"

"Some Puerto Rican was in your room this afternoon with his toolkit. I asked him to take a look at the TV and he gives me that f-in 'I don't speak English' smile and walks off. Did he fix your TV?"

"I'm not sure," I said.

"They're gonna hear about this bullshit," he said bitterly. "Wait till they hand me the bill. Then maybe I won't speak English, either."

I searched the room thoroughly. Nothing seemed out of place; no additions, no subtractions. I took the phone apart: normal. Everything seemed as it was. The lamp that worked still worked; the one that didn't, still didn't. The shower still dripped. The television with the rabbit-ears antenna worked—sort of. I called the front desk and asked if the maintenance man had been in my room. The clerk said he didn't know and asked if anything was missing. Nothing, I told him. Then he asked if something was broken and I said no. The silence on the other end of the phone was a question: so, what's the problem?

Maybe nothing. Maybe everything.

The next morning I went to breakfast at a diner near the hotel. There was a line of empty taxis out front and I figured that cabdrivers, like truck drivers, probably knew the good places to eat. I showed Green's photograph to the owner and he brought over the cashier, who'd been interviewed by the FBI. He told me what he told them: the guy had been in a few times for breakfast several weeks before, maybe once for dinner. He ate his food and didn't bother anyone. He was always alone.

I ate breakfast at the counter. Several cabdrivers came and went; all seemed part of a group at one table speaking Arabic. The short-order cook nodded toward the assemblage and said, "Welcome to the Gaza Strip."

"Regulars?" I asked.

"I don't know how we got so lucky. They nurse their coffee and take up a table during prime time. Some of 'em will sit there until they get a fare."

"They get fares here?"

"Sure, some of 'em."

The chatter stopped when I approached the table. One driver, a husky man in his forties with a moustache and a few days of beard, seemed to be presiding. "Yes, mister, you want a cab? Where are you going?"

"No, I don't need a cab right now. I was wondering whether any of you could help me."

The leader frowned. "We don't want to buy anything, mister, we're cabdrivers."

I took out Green's picture and held it out for all to see. "I'm looking for this man."

"You are a policeman, mister?"

"No, I'm helping his wife. He's been missing for a few weeks and she's very upset." The leader said something in Arabic to the group and took the photograph. There was more discussion as it passed from hand to hand until a younger man in a New York Mets T-shirt called out and poked the photograph excitedly. That set off an animated conversation between him and the leader, who finally asked, "This is a Jewish man? An Israeli?"

"No, not an Israeli, but a Jewish man, yes."

More animated discussion. Then the man in the Mets shirt looked at me and said, "I take him."

"You remember him?"

The man nodded. "We talk about Arafat. It was on the radio. We had a . . . a . . ." He said something in Arabic to the leader.

"This is Gamal," said the leader. "All the time he talks about the Palestinians. A lot of Jewish people in New York. He fights with them about the Palestinians and makes everyone mad. They had an argument about Arafat."

I asked Gamal, "Do you remember where you took him?"

"Downtown," he replied, then said something to the leader that included the word "Broadway."

"He doesn't remember the number but he can take you," said the leader. "You should pay him something extra, okay?"

"Okay," I said. Gamal got up and motioned me to follow him out of the diner and into his cab. We drove down Ninth Avenue and then east to Broadway. He drove fast with one hand on the wheel and the other keying his CB handset as he engaged in shouted conversation with other Arabs that could have been about traffic. We went south on Broadway, down to the vicinity of City Hall, when he pulled to the curb and announced, "This place!" The good news was that we were a stone's throw from the first phone booth, which was a form of corroboration. The bad news was that we were in front of the Woolworth Building. I tipped him ten dollars for the service and Gamal roared off, shouting into his handset.

In college I'd toyed with becoming an architect. My introductory course included a lecture on the evolution of the skyscraper. I remembered that the Woolworth Building was the tallest in the world until the Chrysler Building came along, that its architecture was something called Neo-Gothic, and that President Wilson pressed a button in Washington that turned on its lights. There were all kinds of famous firsts associated with the design that I couldn't recall, including something about its power plant, but as I was standing in front of the entrance, looking straight up, the only thing running through my mind was "needle in a haystack."

The so-called Cathedral of Commerce was undergoing a sorely needed renovation but its lobby was still ornate: wide marble staircases, lacelike wrought-iron cornices covered in gold leaf, Tiffany glass, and huge frescoes. In the midst of all the opulence and exquisite detail was one incongruous feature: a cheesy directory with about fifty tenants' names in raised white type floating on a sea of black vacancy. The surprisingly small number was heartening, although I had absolutely no idea of what I was looking for. I scanned the list and when I reached the Js I found something called "Jewish International Labor Guild." Figuring it was as good a place to start as any, I rode the elevator to the twenty-fourth floor. The wooden door to the guild's office was locked but light showed underneath. I pushed a button: nothing. I waited a moment to be sure, then knocked.

"Who is it?" asked a woman's voice.

"My name is Philip Barkley," I said.

"What do you want?"

"I'm from the Justice Department. I'm conducting an investigation."

The door opened a couple of inches and an elderly woman peered at me through the crack. I held out my identification and she opened it all the way. "Come in," she said, stepping back to admit me. I barely cleared the threshold before she closed the door and turned the handle to test the lock. "You have to be careful," she advised. The receptionist had to be near eighty, bent by age to something less than five feet tall, with red-orange lipstick and a matching wig that seemed in danger of shifting as she shuffled ahead of me to her desk. The reception area wasn't in its prime, either: faded beige walls, spotted brown carpet, and two yellow vinyl chairs flanking a "wood-grained" Formica table. The only decoration was a poster of an Israeli flag with the legend "1948–1998."

She reached her chair and lowered herself slowly. "We're closing early today, in just a few minutes."

I took out Green's photograph and placed it next to an ashtray filled with red-orange cigarette butts. "I was wondering if you've seen this man," I said.

She studied it and asked, "Is he the one?"

"The one?"

"The one they're looking for," she said.

Before I could reply another elderly woman entered from the hall behind the receptionist. She was wearing a black coat and carrying two bulging shopping bags. "I'm going, Terry," she said, then noticed me.

"He's from the police, Helen," said Terry.

"The Justice Department," I corrected.

Helen nodded vacantly. "He's got a picture of someone," said Terry.

I showed the photograph to Helen. "I was wondering if anyone has seen this man before. His name is Martin Green."

She shook her head. "I thought it would be the Spanish," she said, "or the Blacks. There's always trouble with them."

"Mrs. Singer was nice to them," said Terry. "She treated everyone nice."

"She was a good person," agreed Helen. "She shouldn't have died like that."

"In her own apartment," added Terry.

"When did this happen?" I asked.

They looked at me quizzically. "The night before last," said Helen. "They broke into her apartment."

"I thought that's why you're here," said Terry.

"I'm sorry, I didn't know." I put the picture away. "This man had nothing to do with it," I said.

"I told you," Helen said to Terry. "It was the Spanish or the Blacks. There's always trouble there."

"I'm very sorry," I said. "Is there anyone else here I can show this picture to?"

"We're the only ones," said Terry. "We're closing up for the funeral."

"I've got to get something from the bakery," Helen told her. "I'll see you by the subway."

Helen and I waited together for the elevator. She stared forlornly at the tiled floor, sagging under the weight of her shopping bags and her grief. "Can I help you?" I asked. She looked up at me, glassy-eyed. "With the bags," I added, but she shook her head. The elevator finally arrived. We got in and began the long descent. The only sound was Helen's labored breathing. It must be frightening, I thought, to be old and defenseless in a threatening place, scurrying past alleys and doorways to the sanctuary of a few rooms in a brick warehouse full of people like yourself. And then to die there, huddled in a corner in your final moments as you listened to the splintering of your own door.

"Did you know Naomi?"

I turned around. "I'm sorry?"

Helen looked at me. "Mrs. Singer—did you know her?"

"No. No, I didn't . . . Her name was Naomi?"

"Naomi," she confirmed, nodding. "She was nice to everybody."

"And she died the night before last?"

"It was the Spanish," she said. "Or the Blacks."

Naomi Singer had a niece who lived in a six-story apartment building in the Flushing area of Queens. According to Helen, that was where the family was sitting *shivah,* the observation of a period of mourning. The door to the apartment was open and the chatter and aromas drifted down the hallway. People were standing shoulder-to-shoulder, balancing plates and glasses while they commiserated. Two aluminum folding tables covered with platters and cake boxes were set up in the dining area. Helen was at one of them, cutting the string on a white bakery box. I noticed Terry's wig over the shoulder of a man in one corner. In the center of the room a woman in her forties was seated on a cardboard box, kneading a tissue. There was a black ribbon pinned to her dress. Helen saw me and beckoned me to the table.

"You got here," she said.

"Yes. I just wanted to pay my respects."

"You should eat something. I'll make you a sandwich."

"Thank you, maybe in a little while. Is that woman Naomi's niece?"

"Frieda," Helen said. "I can introduce you." She took me by the sleeve and led me over. "Frieda, this young man wanted to say hello." Frieda stared at me, trying to place the face.

"Philip Barkley, Frieda," I said.

"Oh, of course. Please sit down." She motioned toward an ottoman.

"Let me know if you want anything," said Helen.

"I was very sorry to hear about your aunt," I told Frieda.

"She spent her whole life helping people."

"She was a good person," I agreed.

Frieda sighed. "Her whole life. She came to America during the Depression with nothing but she worked hard. And look what happens."

"Where did she come from?"

"Hungary. She had nothing!"

"Did she work for the guild a long time?"

For a moment I didn't think she heard me. She took another tissue from a box on the floor and blew her nose. Finally, she said, "Only a few years. She just worked a little bit. She wasn't happy being retired, so she went back." She looked at me and shrugged. "She went back to what she knew, helping people. She wasn't what she used to be. I had to take care of things, her checkbook, her bills, but she still wanted to do good."

"What did she do before she retired?"

"The Hebrew Immigrant Aid Society. Over thirty years!"

"That's wonderful."

"You should have seen the party they gave her. Max Ornstein gave her a plaque and a beautiful watch. It's inscribed."

"She must have been very proud."

"They didn't get it," she said angrily.

"They . . . ?"

"Those drug bastards. I've got the watch. She gave all her jewelry to Nancy and me years ago. Those drug bastards didn't get anything to buy their poison."

"Do they know who did it?"

She shook her head. "They'll never catch them, those drug bastards." She wiped her eyes and looked at me. "They come into your home to steal, and if you can't give them what they want"—she began to weep—"they hit you with a bat."

Another woman hurried over and knelt beside Frieda. "Darling, come lie down," she said.

"That's a good idea," I said.

"Eat something," said Frieda as she was led away.

Helen came back with a pastry on a paper plate. "Have some Danish," she said.

"I've got to go, Helen, but thank you."

"Everyone says it was drug addicts," she said. "That picture you had didn't look like one of them."

"No, he wasn't one of them," I agreed.

"Turner."

"It's Philip."

"Tell me you're in Oregon."

"New York. In a phone booth."

"Uh-huh."

"I think I've found Naomi."

Silence.

"That's the name—"

"I know what it is."

She listened without comment while I made my report. There was more silence when I finished. "Do you have any questions?" I asked.

"Why are you telling me this?"

"Why?"

"What do you expect me to do?"

"I thought you'd want to follow up."

"Oh. Okay, but I'll have to report this to the AG first, so let's hear how it sounds. 'General, I need more resources for the Green case. It seems that his former girlfriend thought she overheard him say 'Naomi' in a telephone conversation. Actually, she's not sure, but it *sounded* like 'Naomi.' And Philip Barkley—you remember him, General—well, it seems that he's still on the case, even though he quit, basically doing his own thing. Anyway, Barkley showed Green's picture to a bunch of cabdrivers who eat *in the very same diner* that Green ate at, and—surprise!—one of them volunteered, for a fee, to show him where he supposedly took Green. So, this cabdriver drops Barkley in front of a Manhattan office building and it turns out that one of the *thousands* of people who work in that building was *also* named Naomi, and she was killed during a break-in at her apartment in Brooklyn. Are you still with me, General? So, all things considered, it looks like we'd better forget Green's confession and the fact that we've gone public with a solution to the case, and get right on this amazing development.' How'd I do?"

"It's more than the name. She worked for a Jewish organization."

"How odd! And in New York!"

"You can drop the sarcasm."

"Fine. Did anyone in Naomi's office recognize Green's picture?"

"No."

"And even if someone did, what would *that* mean? There was a connection based on religious affiliation, so what?"

"Martin and Naomi died within two days of each other."

"You know what your problem is, Philip? You've become one of those conspiracy buffs, like the guys chasing around the Kennedy and King assassinations. You don't like the official conclusion that makes eminent sense, and so you chase around and around until you find an interesting fact or a coincidence and then you shout 'Aha!' The government doesn't work that way, Philip. We can't run around shouting 'Aha!' every time we find a coincidence, because there are *always* coincidences. We can't be stirring people up and making the whole country nuts because a woman who may or may not have known Green happens to get killed in a high-crime neighborhood."

"Who said anything about a high-crime neighborhood?"

More silence. Then: "Don't get paranoid on me, okay? You said she was killed by someone who broke into her apartment in Brooklyn. I assumed it was a high-crime area. Are you saying it's not?"

"No."

"You see? I drew an inference. That's what we do,

Philip. We draw inferences based on logic and experience and we don't ignore the obvious. So let's put a few pieces together and draw an inference. A man with access to top-secret information, unusual behavior, a meeting at the Portrait Gallery, fifty thousand—"

"You can stop now, Blair. You've made your point."

"Go to Oregon, Philip. Get on with your life."

12

"BRENNAN AND O'CONNELL."

"Frank O'Connell, please."

"And who shall I say is calling?"

"Philip Barkley. Please tell Mr. O'Connell that Mr. Brennan introduced us when I worked in the White House."

"Of course. One moment, please."

"Philip?"

"Hello, Frank. I'm not sure if you remember me."

"Sure I do. You were in the counsel's office with Jeff Brandt."

"Right. That was a long time ago. There's been a lot of water under the bridge since then."

"For both of us."

"Yes, and belated congratulations. On everything."

"Thanks. My wife and I are trying to figure out whether we're about to have our third anniversary or our sixth. Do you start over or total them?"

"I think the answer to that one is on a mountaintop in Tibet."

"You're probably right. By the way, I read about that Green case. Must have been an interesting assignment."

"That's why I'm calling, Frank. I need a favor, and before I go any further, there's something you should know. I've left Justice but I'm still working on the case, doing some investigating on my own in New York."

"From the papers, I thought it was essentially over."

"Well, officially, that's true, but I think Justice has got it wrong."

"I've had some experience with that. What do you need?"

"Some information from the New York Police Department on a pending murder case. I read that you used to be an assistant DA up here and I was wondering if you could put me in contact with someone who could help."

"Sounds like the Green case is just getting interesting."

"If I'm right, 'interesting' isn't the half of it."

"Well, my chief investigator is a certified NYPD legend. If he can't get you inside, it can't be done."

"Seven-Oh squad. Detective Morrow speaking."

"Detective Morrow, my name is Philip Barkley."

"Oh, yeah, the guy from Washington."

"Yes, but I'm up in New York at the moment."

"You want to know about Singer, right?"

"That's right. I could be in Brooklyn in an hour. Can I buy you a cup of coffee?"

"Make it three hours and you can buy me a Guinness. There's a place on Third Avenue called Judge 'n Jury."

At six o'clock Detective Paul Morrow and I were seated at a table in an Irish pub in Bay Ridge. He was taking his first sip of a Guinness while a waitress named Erin stood by with her arms folded and an expectant look on her Irish face. "Bubbles," said Morrow. "There's some carbonation in there."

Erin shook her head. "The carbonation is in *there*," she declared, tapping his crown. She pointed at his mug and said, "Smooth as a baby's arse," then threw a towel over her shoulder and marched off.

"I love to get under her skin," he said, chuckling. "It's easy to do." He took another, longer drink, and nodded approvingly. "Smooth as a baby's arse," he mimicked, then wiped his mouth with a napkin. "So, what can I tell you about poor Mrs. Singer?"

"What do you think happened there?"

"I think a couple of the indigenous gangbangers broke into her apartment to steal anything that wasn't nailed down. And I think Mrs. Singer was in the wrong place at the wrong time."

"How did they get in?"

"The tried-and-true. Down the fire escape and through the window. Broke a pane of glass near the lock and they were in."

"Why her apartment?"

"You mean, as opposed to any other apartment in the building or on the block? That's a good question. There could be a million answers. Maybe they heard that she had money or jewelry or a nice TV. Maybe they thought she dissed one of them when she was walking home from the supermarket. Maybe she was the only one with the light off. Maybe they can't count floors and thought it was somebody else's apartment. Who knows? Around here, violence is totally unpredictable. You're walking down the street or riding the subway and you make eye contact with the wrong guy. Next thing you know you've got a knife in your gut. Crazy shit."

"You think it was more than one person?"

"Probably. They gave the apartment a thorough going-over. That's a lot of work for one guy. Usually, if one of these hopheads kills the occupant he panics and won't spend much time there. He'll yank off a wedding ring and go through a few drawers. This place was turned upside down *after* they killed her. That's unusual."

"Maybe they weren't drug addicts."

"Maybe, but that's usually what you get around there, gangbangers and hopheads. Professionals aren't going to waste time in a neighborhood like that. Anyway, we're pretty sure they were hopped up."

"Why?"

"They gave her a dozen whacks with a baseball bat and one would have done the trick. Way more than necessary. These guys were hopped up. They did her, then took the place apart."

"What did they get?"

He shook his head with disgust. "A goddamn box of books. That's worth it, right?"

"What kind of books?"

He snorted. "Fuckin' hopheads. This is somethin' only they could do. The old lady had diaries, not the 'Dear Diary' kind, but the kind that you use for work."

"You mean, appointment books?"

"Yeah, but the hardbound kind, with the gilt edges, the kind you buy in a fancy stationery store, or American Express gives you if you're a big customer. She had a whole collection of them from her years at work. Her organization used to give them to big donors as thank-yous. The assholes probably saw the gilt edges and thought they were valuable."

"How many did they take?"

"We figure around thirty. She worked for that Hebrew Immigrant place from 1949 to '81, but they stopped giving the books away around '79. The people she worked with said she used her books to jot memos and phone numbers, keep her to-do lists, that kind of stuff. This was a meticulous person. You could tell by her apartment, what was left of it." He took a deep breath and shook his head. Just telling the story was getting him worked up. "So, anyway, we're asking every pawn shop in the borough to be on the lookout for the books. We'll probably find them in a trash can someplace when these guys come down off of whatever they were on and realize they killed someone for nothin'— not that they'd give a shit."

"Did they take anything else?"

"She didn't have anything else to take. She gave away all her jewelry and I don't think it was an estate-planning deal, either. She probably figured that in her neighborhood it was only a question of time before they got her." He grimaced and rapped the empty Guinness mug on the table. At the bar, Erin looked annoyed. "Fuckin' gangbangers and hopheads," he muttered. "People get old around here and it's like the lambs and the wolves."

"Do you have any suspects?"

"Like they say, my friend, anybody and everybody." He waved his empty mug at Erin. "Anybody and everybody," he repeated.

The next morning I was back at the Woolworth Building. Terry opened the door, this time wearing a blond, curly wig. "It's you," she said. "I didn't think we'd be seeing you anymore." She opened the door to admit me and locked it again. "Helen won't be in for another hour."

"That's okay, you can help me. I was wondering if I could see your telephone bill for last month."

She made a face. "The telephone bill? Why?"

"There may be some information there that can help the investigation."

"But we don't know the man in the photograph."

"I think Naomi knew him. I'd like to check the phone bill to see if she called him."

"I thought you said that he didn't do it."

"He didn't. It's hard to explain, but if they knew each other it may help me and the police." Terry's hand went reflexively to a pack of Chesterfields. She looked unconvinced. "I just want to look at a couple of dates," I said soothingly. "It'll only take a minute."

"Helen isn't here," she repeated.

"I'm sure she wouldn't mind."

Terry lit a Chesterfield and took what seemed to be a remarkably deep drag for such a small person. It seemed to fortify her. "Okay," she said finally. She got up and shuffled through a door, leaving her cigarette burning in the ashtray. In my heart I knew that Naomi Singer was the one; I had no doubt of it. But the possibility loomed that Green had initiated all their contacts and there was no proof to be had.

She returned with the bill a few minutes later and I had my first break: a call to Green's home number; the timing was right, too. "Do you have a copier, Terry?"

"Inside," she said. "Is there something there?"

"It looks like Mrs. Singer spoke to the young man in the picture. He may even have visited her here."

"He could have, for all I know," she replied. "I've been in and out since March, and when I'm not here there's no receptionist." She leaned forward as if there were other ears in the office. "We don't get many visitors here," she confided. "Most days I just sit here and lick envelopes."

"Terry, I was wondering if I could see Mrs. Singer's office."

She reached for her cigarette. "Her office? Like a police search?"

"I'm not with the police. I showed you my identification, remember? Have the police been here to search Mrs. Singer's office?"

"No. No one took anything from there. It's just the way it was."

"Good. I won't take anything, either. I just want to see it."

"Maybe we should wait for Helen."

"Terry, this may be very important. You're helping the investigation and time is always critical to solving a case. Why don't we look together? You can make sure everything remains as it was."

Naomi's little office had no window. There was a desk, a chair, and a two-shelf bookcase with a few spiral binders and knickknacks. The desk was bare except for a telephone and a small pile of manila folders. There was a telephone book in one drawer and the others were empty. "Terry, did Naomi keep an appointment book?"

She nodded. "It's in Helen's office. We looked inside, just for curiosity."

"Of course. Please let me see it."

"There's nothing in there. Naomi didn't have appointments or conferences. She just put mail in envelopes."

"Then could I see it?"

I waited again until she returned with Naomi's appointment book, another hardbound type but without the gilt edging. I turned to August and began flipping the pages. There was an entry on August second, two lines surrounded by a penciled border. The first was "Martin Green" and had the Washington telephone number. The second said, "Sonia Denes."

Terry was looking over my shoulder. "Do you know Sonia Denes?" I asked her.

She shook her head. "I can check our mailing list."

There was no one named Denes on the list. Terry made me a copy of the phone bill and promised to ask Helen about Sonia. Before I left I got the address of the Hebrew Immigrant Aid Society.

Sonia Denes. I was on autopilot as I wandered up and down Broadway trying to hail a cab. Two more events to add to the chronology. Martin and Naomi discuss Sonia Denes. Four days later he takes a trip to New York to conduct an investigation. He goes several places and he visits Naomi. Seven weeks later they're both dead.

The Hebrew Immigrant Aid Society had a case-file index card with the name Sonia Denes. I was given a file number and referred to the YIVO Institute for Jewish Research on Sixteenth Street, which was the repository of HIAS files. My Justice ID eventually got me to an archivist, who was waiting for me when I stepped off the elevator at the tenth floor. He was a tall man dressed in a plaid shirt, corduroy pants, and what people called "sensible" shoes. A YIVO identification card and a pair of reading glasses hung around his neck.

"Samuel Berman," he said, extending his hand. "You're the man from Washington."

"Philip Barkley. Yes, I'm with the Justice Department. I was referred to you by Adam Rifkind over at HIAS. I have a case-file number of an immigrant that we are interested in."

Berman beckoned me to follow him into the stacks where steel shelves were filled with documents stored in acid-free folders and gray boxes. He looked at the number that I showed him. "And what is the name of this immigrant?" he asked.

"Sonia Denes," I said. "I believe she came here from Hungary."

Berman stared at me. "Sonia Denes? Again, Sonia Denes?"

"Someone else inquired?"

"A young man; several weeks ago. The one in the newspaper."

I took out Green's picture. "This young man?"

He glanced at the photograph and nodded. "What a pity. We talked about Washington and politics. Very nice, very knowledgeable. The newspaper said he committed suicide and there was something about spying."

"Yes, that's correct."

"Does it have something to do with Sonia Denes?"

"Indirectly. It's a matter of utmost urgency that I see the Sonia Denes file."

He ran his finger along the shelves until he located a dusty manila folder with black marker numbers that matched. "Sonia Denes," he said. He began leafing through the contents. "She was born in Budapest on January 3, 1928. According to the record of contacts with her there by HIAS, she was considered to be religiously observant, of good moral character, and enthusiastic about emigrating to the United States. There appears to be no other family."

"She was alone?"

"Not unusual," said Berman. "Okay, there are the usual guarantees of housing, and of employment with . . . let's see . . . the Paramount Hat Company here in Manhattan. There's a certification that she will not be replacing a U.S. worker. I've got a petition for issuance of an immigrant visa here that was obviously granted . . . She emigrated from Genoa and arrived in the United States on August 31, 1950. Her ship was met by Naomi Singer of the HIAS Port Reception department, and Sonia was taken into the temporary care of the United Service for New Americans."

"Who petitioned for the visa?"

"Her immigration was sponsored by a synagogue. That's not unusual."

"Is that everything?" I asked.

"Everything," he said. He studied me. "You're disappointed."

"Well . . ."

He held up a hand. "I understand. That young man was disappointed, too."

As I rode the subway uptown my mind was focused on the riddle of Sonia Denes, but something else was pressing on my consciousness. Not at the outer perimeter; that was the onset of fear. Something much closer. I pushed the riddle aside to make room for other concerns that were stacking up and circling like planes over an airport. A video of the walk from YIVO to the subway was running inside my head. There was a car parked just down from the building entrance. As I walked by, the passenger looked away toward the driver, but I had this sense of déjà vu. It came to me as I climbed the steps to the street. My last trip to New York: the car parked across the avenue from the Waldorf. Two men in a car, a clean-shaven passenger with a short haircut, wearing a white shirt and tie. I reached the corner and looked back toward the subway entrance, then up and down the avenue. I didn't see the car but there could have been other cars, other men.

I decided that I wouldn't be going out that night. I stopped in a grocery store and bought a sandwich for dinner. Back in my room, I locked the door and considered my next move. A call to Evans would inevitably lead to Blair Turner, and at that moment I wasn't sure whether she was part of the solution or the problem. There was something there, out on the perimeter with the fear, the blurry image of some truth that could have been a mirage. Viewed up close, the laws of probability said nothing was awry. But every now and then you have to step back and look at the big picture. I was embarked on a journey to find the truth and I'd just discovered a shadow. It would have been troubling under any circumstances, but the road kept running into funerals.

I spent the evening sitting at the window with the lights off, watching doorways and parked cars. The temperature hadn't dropped with nightfall. Rivulets of sweat migrated down my chest and pooled at my waist. The hours passed; the clank of the metal plate on the avenue signaled a decline in traffic. Nothing on the street.

No moving shadows or glowing cigarette butts. I tried to convince myself that if someone really wanted me dead, I'd already be dead. I could be imagining danger; I could be imagining the whole thing. What if Green really did kill himself? What if Naomi really was the victim of some dope-fiend burglar?

No. They were out there, circling, and I was too stupid to see—not stupid, too something, too . . . suppressed. I considered the options, then picked up the phone and dialed a number I knew by heart. The return call came in minutes.

"Philip?"

"Doctor Blake?"

"Are you all right? My service didn't say what it was about."

"I just wanted to check with you about something."

"I'm glad you called. I was told that you picked up your files. I was very concerned."

"I'm moving to Oregon."

"Oh. Do you have a doctor out there?"

"No. I don't know anybody in Oregon."

"You'll need to get someone, Philip. Your condition needs to be followed. I can recommend someone after I do some checking."

"Okay."

"You left a New York number. What are you doing there?"

"I'm working on a case."

"Working? Your office said that you've left the Justice Department."

"I still have this case."

"Oh." There was a pause while he considered whether

to believe me. "What did you want to check with me about?"

"I want to go off my medication."

"Why?"

"I need to feel more like myself."

"Well, we put you on the medication so you wouldn't feel that way."

"I need to be more alert. And I need to sleep. I can't sleep."

"That's not unusual with the medication, Philip. We talked about that. It's a matter of getting the antidepressant and the tranquilizers in the right balance. Why don't you come see me and we can discuss other—"

"I can't come right now. I really need to get off the medication, Doctor Blake."

"That could be dangerous. You've had several hospitalizations."

"I know that . . ."

"You've been making progress. Why go off the medication now?"

"It's hard to explain."

"I have an idea. Why don't you see a doctor in New York? I'll arrange an appointment for tomorrow."

"Maybe. Let me think about it."

"Philip, don't go off your medication, okay?"

"Okay, I understand. Thanks."

"Take care of yourself."

"All right. Good-bye, Doctor Blake."

I went back to staring out the window. More time passed. I'd essentially been adrift for years, but I'd never felt farther from shore than in those hours of watching. The telephone became a lifeline.

"Hello?"

"Susan?"

"Yes?"

"It's Philip."

"Philip! It's so wonderful to hear from you!"

"Is it too late?"

"No, no, I'm a night owl."

"I kept your card."

"I'm glad."

Suddenly, I couldn't think of anything to say. "I'm in New York, in a hotel."

"Oh. What are you doing there?"

"Working. How are you?"

"I'm fine. Nothing new, really. I was at the cemetery on Sunday and I visited your daughter. I hope you don't mind, I just wanted to see her resting place . . . Philip?"

"Okay."

"Are you all right?"

"Thank you."

"It's beautifully done, with a bench and a tree, very peaceful. I said a prayer for her."

"Me, too. I say prayers for her . . . I just wanted to say hello."

"Fine. You can call me whenever you want."

"Thanks . . . Good-bye, Susan."

"Call me. Good night."

I crawled into bed thinking about Susan. I imagined myself paralyzed, maneuvering from a bed to a wheelchair and from a wheelchair to a car seat. I lifted my head with great effort and looked at my feet, then wiggled my toes. I fell asleep and dreamt I was at the cemetery. Susan was sitting on the bench under the shade tree with her head bowed. As I approached I could see she had a book in her lap. She was reading to my daughter and they were both smiling. Susan found her, I thought to myself. She found her and she's alive. My daughter's lips were moving and I realized that if I got close enough I could actually hear her voice again, but somehow I knew that if I got too close she would disappear. So I watched from a distance and it was all so sad.

13

IT WAS A KNOCK THAT woke me but I didn't know it at first. A bright sun and the metallic clank from the avenue indicated that I'd slept longer than intended. The knock again. I called out and a muffled voice replied from the hall. I opened the door a crack; a Hispanic woman was pushing a cleaning cart. "I come back," she said over her shoulder.

I wobbled into the bathroom and rinsed my face, then stared at the vials on the sink. *Recovery requires a period of adjustment, Philip. The best medicine is to become reengaged. Without engagement we dwell on the past.* Well, they're still out there, and now I'm fully engaged. What was the saying? Nothing so concentrates the mind as the prospect of being hanged in the morning. But I needed my senses fully deployed, my instinct for self-preservation on high-gain. I opened the vials, poured the pills into the toilet, and flushed. They swirled around, then left me on my own.

I showered and dressed, then went down to the desk. The clerk was dealing with an unhappy man in a Miami

Dolphins jersey, explaining hotel telephone charges in the automated cadence of a flight attendant demonstrating seat belts. Each protest was adroitly deflected until the disgruntled guest scribbled on the MasterCard chit, hoisted his Samsonite, and marched out muttering under his breath. The clerk turned to me, ready for the next problem. "What time do you start cleaning the rooms?" I asked.

"Six-thirty, seven," he replied. "Do you need something? I can have 'em do yours now."

"No, it's okay. Do they start knocking on doors that early?"

He shook his head. "They're supposed to do the check-outs first, the ones we know are empty. I keep tellin' 'em, no knocking until eight, but some of 'em don't understand the King's English."

"Is that kind of standard—no knocking till eight?"

"Eight, eight-thirty, at least in the places I've worked at. Earlier than that, guests are still sleeping or getting dressed. What time did they get you?"

"They didn't. I was just curious."

He frowned. "I got a note here that you called about maintenance."

"It's okay."

He showed me the note with my room number. "Maybe it's a mistake," he said, as if a cop interrogating a recidivist.

"No, it was me," I admitted.

"What's the problem?"

"There's no problem. Is the maintenance man Hispanic?"

"This is New York. You sure there's no problem?"

"There's no problem," I repeated.

He nodded but his face said it all: another asshole. He returned to his newspaper and I went off to the diner for breakfast. The Arabic cabdriver clique was at its usual table, presided over by the same leader. I ordered breakfast and thought about Sonia Denes. It was clear I needed help. I took my coffee over to a phone by the rest rooms and called Susan.

"Susan? It's Philip Barkley again."

"Philip!" A hell of a benchmark at life's midpoint: the only one who's happy to hear from you is someone you barely know.

"I'm sorry about last night."

"Don't be ridiculous. Call me whenever you feel like it."

"Thank you. That's wonderful to hear."

"I hope you didn't call to apologize."

"Well, that and something else. I *am* working up here. I'm actually doing some investigation and I was wondering if you were interested in helping."

"Really? I'd love to! It would be such a welcome change of pace."

"It would involve some Internet sleuthing and maybe some work in the Library of Congress when you're there."

"I've got goose bumps already!" We both laughed.

"Great. I was afraid that I'd be imposing. Let me just say this because it's a little awkward: I'd want to reimburse you for any expenses, okay?"

"Okay, but I doubt there'll be any. My company gives me unlimited long distance and access to the Internet and all kinds of databases. And I'll do the library stuff while I'm there on other things."

"That will be a big help, especially the telephone."

"So, I'm on the case! What's my first assignment?"

"We're looking for someone. A woman named Sonia Denes."

"What do we know about her?"

"Not much, I'm afraid. She was born in Budapest on January 3, 1928, and came here in 1950. She was met on arrival by a woman named Naomi Singer who worked for the Hebrew Immigrant Aid Society back then, and, more recently, for the Jewish International Labor Guild."

"Does Sonia live in New York?"

"There's a decent chance of that. I've got a Manhattan phone directory in front of me and there are several Deneses in it, though no Sonia. There are probably a bunch more in the New York area."

"Should I try to find Naomi Singer, too?"

"Well, this is the thing: she's dead."

"Dead?"

"She was murdered a few days ago by someone who broke into her apartment."

"Philip, are you in any sort of danger?"

"No, not at all. It was a burglary. She was in the wrong place at the wrong time."

"Does this have something to do with your case in the newspapers?"

"The Green case, yes."

"I read that he confessed to being a spy. Are you looking for accomplices?"

"Well, I'm trying to tie up some loose ends."

"Okay, I'll concentrate on New York first. What do I do if I find Sonia Denes? She might answer my telephone call."

What to do, indeed. "Tell her that you're calling on behalf of the Hebrew Immigrant Aid Society. Say that Naomi Singer has died and the organization is contacting people she worked with in case they wanted or needed to know. Maybe you can expand on that, solicit a donation or something. I'll leave that to you."

"All right. How do I reach you?"

"I'm out and about all the time. Let me call you, okay?"

"You're sure there's no danger?"

"No, there isn't." My tone was firm, intending to be reassuring, but she didn't hear it that way.

"Okay," she said quietly. "I'm just concerned about you, that's all." It had been a long time since anyone worried about me for free.

"I'm sorry, Susan, I didn't mean it that way. Listen, just to be on the safe side, don't leave your real name or telephone number with anyone, okay? I'll feel better if you don't."

"Don't worry. My nom de guerre is . . . Barbara Cohen!"

"Barbara Cohen?"

"I just made it up."

"All right, Barbara, good hunting."

"If she's alive, I'll find her."

I hung up, started to go back to the counter, and it hit me.

If she's alive, I'll find her.

That's the first question, isn't it? And if Green wasn't sure, he'd start with death certificates. The phone book listed the Bureau of Vital Records at 125 Worth Street, the Department of Health building adjacent to the second phone booth. I went out and approached the table of cabdrivers. They were listening intently as the leader was speaking in low tones and writing on a piece of paper. He stopped and turned the paper over when he noticed me. "Hello, mister," he said. "You want a cab today? You want Gamal?"

"I'd like two cabs today," I said.

"Two cabs," he repeated. "One now, one later."

"No, two cabs now. One cab to take me and one cab to follow."

"Why, mister?"

"I want to know if anyone is following me."

The leader looked around the table, silently polling the group, then asked, "You are in trouble, mister? The police maybe?"

"Not the police but it could be some trouble. I'm willing to pay for help."

"Is it Israelis?"

"No, like I told you, the man was not an Israeli. There are no Israelis involved. It's a long story but his wife is very worried."

A middle-aged man in a short-sleeved white shirt said something in Arabic and everyone began talking at once. The leader's eyes flicked from speaker to speaker as the conversation grew more animated. The first speaker began talking more loudly than the rest and, one by one, they fell silent. When he finished everyone looked at the leader expectantly. "Gamal will take you," he declared. "You are his customer. Two cabs will follow."

"Two?"

"It is too hard with one. Nabil and I will go," he said, pointing toward the man who had done the loud talking. The other men nodded in agreement; the matter was not to be debated.

"How much?" I asked.

"One hour. Fifty dollars for each cab." He produced a cell phone from his shirt pocket and dialed a number. There was a brief conversation in Arabic and then he asked, "Where do you want to go?"

"Downtown. Worth Street."

He said something into the phone and put it back in his pocket. "Ten minutes."

I went back to my breakfast, peering out the windows as I ate. Nothing suspicious: no men in cars, no one reading a newspaper or lounging in a doorway. I began to feel foolish about wasting my money. The leader and Nabil walked past. Nabil was fiddling with a small camera with a zoom lens. "Maybe we get pictures," said the leader. He stuck out his hand and said, "I am Sayed."

Nabil held up the camera and smiled. "A photographer person," he said, pointing at himself.

They went out to their cabs and drove away. A moment later Gamal pulled to the curb and I went outside. "Taxi, mister?" he asked with a broad smile. I got in and we were off in a cloud of dust, west toward Tenth Avenue, then north, then back east toward Ninth. We actually slowed as we approached the avenue, missing a green light to allow a truck to back into a loading platform. This was virtually unheard of in the annals of New York livery and apparently a tactical ploy to allow our entourage time to get into position. Sure enough, a few minutes later we proceeded down Ninth and passed Sayed and Nabil five blocks beyond the diner. Gamal spoke into his CB and got an immediate reply from both.

We proceeded downtown in heavy traffic with occasional snippets of conversation in Arabic and English. We turned west, then south, then west again. Gamal was following a snaking route downtown, not unusual for a taxi trying to get somewhere in Manhattan in good time, and perfect for detecting a tail. Near Canal Street there was a long burst of Arabic from Nabil. Gamal responded and glanced repeatedly into the rear- and side-view mirrors. "There is a car following, sir," said Gamal. Then a single word came over the speaker: "Ford." Gamal repeated, "A Ford." Up ahead, the light turned red.

Gamal kept his gaze on the sideview mirror while we waited. I avoided the urge to turn around. The light changed and we were off again. Then another burst of Arabic, this time from Sayed. "There is a second car," said Gamal.

"We're being followed by two cars?" I asked.

Gamal spoke into his handset and got an immediate reply. "Yes," he said. "A taxi. A Chevy taxi. It is behind Nabil."

Two cars. It made sense. They'd change off to avoid detection. "Don't go to Worth Street," I told him. "Turn into the first street you can."

Gamal relayed his intention and did as instructed. As we approached the far end of the block the light changed and we stopped. Nabil and Sayed confirmed that all the cars were in the block. The Ford was two cars behind us. Nabil was behind it. Two cars farther back was the Chevy. Somewhere behind it was Sayed.

Sayed spoke again and a longer conversation ensued among all three men, punctuated by an "okay" from Gamal. "Would you like to lose them?" asked Gamal.

"Yes, if you can do it without acting like we know we're being followed."

More discussion. The light finally changed and cars

started to move. Gamal shut off the engine, jumped out of the car, and raised the hood. Parked cars on both sides made us impossible to pass. Horns began sounding immediately, a chain reaction that spread quickly backward, toward the last intersection. Gamal was fiddling under the hood. All of a sudden, Sayed came running up, screaming in Arabic. Gamal stepped around and met him on the driver's side. The two men began arguing, pointing at the car. Sayed put his hands on the car, indicating that they should push it out of the way. Gamal pulled Sayed's hands off the car and shoved him. The two men began shoving and shouting. Passersby stopped to watch. Horns blared. The driver immediately behind us stepped out for a better look. Then I saw Nabil coming up the sidewalk on the passenger side. He stopped at a spot two cars back and pretended to watch the confrontation while stealing glances at the Ford. The camera came up to his waist and then dropped. Then again and again before he walked back to his cab.

"Enough!" I said to Gamal. The two men separated and Sayed walked back to his cab, continuing to shout at Gamal. I got out of the cab and told him to meet me at the diner with the pictures at four o'clock. I walked around the corner, went down into the subway, then across to another entrance and up again, emerging on the other side of the avenue. I waited in the stairs until a crowd of teenagers came up, and walked east using them as a screen.

Thirty minutes later I entered the Office of Vital Records at the City of New York Department of Health. I filled out an "Application to Consult Indexes," paid fifteen dollars, and was given a pass to the Special Handling Search Unit. There on the shelves were books entitled "Deaths and Still Births," one for each year, beginning in 1949. I started in 1950. The entries were in alphabetical order: name, medical examiner case number, age, date of death, borough, and death certificate number. There were three sets of columns on each page and it didn't take long. Soon I opened the book for 1955. I reached the "D" entries and ran my finger downward: to "De," then to "Den," then to "Dene."

A Sonia Denes died in the Bronx on April 17, 1955. Unlike in the vast majority of records, there was an entry in the box reserved for the medical examiner's certification, meaning that her death was "unnatural," just like Martin's. Objectively, it could have been a coincidence but I knew it wasn't. This was Martin's Sonia. That was the clincher. It all made sense but when the pieces fall in place and experience bends to logic, it's still the most extraordinary feeling. My hand was trembling as I copied down the information.

If Martin wanted information that only Sonia Denes could provide then he'd hit a wall, but if he was seeking information *about* Sonia Denes, then he'd try to find people who knew her. She came to America with no immediate family, but that didn't preclude the possibility of relatives. There may have been some here when she arrived, or they could have emigrated after she did, people who survived her, who may have been mentioned in a death notice. Now it was clear why Green had gone to the New York Public Library right from Vital Records. I called Susan again.

"Barbara Cohen," she answered.

"Either you knew it was me or you're carrying this sleuthing thing too far."

"It's Caller ID," she replied, laughing. "New York

number, same exchange. And so far, Barbara has struck out. I haven't found a Sonia Denes in New York but I'm going to branch out."

"Wow. You're fast."

"Barbara doesn't fool around—at work, anyway."

"Susan, I think I found her. She died in 1955."

"Oh, no. What does that mean for your investigation?"

"I'm not sure yet. I've got to figure that out."

"I was just getting into character."

"It's possible that I'm wrong, so you should go ahead and track down the others. If we haven't got the right one yet, then we'll have to start calling all the Deneses."

"Barbara Cohen, at your service."

"I really appreciate this."

"When you get a chance, can you tell me what this is about?"

"Yes, as soon as I can."

The rows of steel drawers in the Microform Reading Room at the New York Public Library were labeled by newspaper and year. I picked a film of the *Daily News* that covered April and May 1955 and loaded it onto a reel for viewing. I skipped to the notices the day after Sonia's death but there was nothing. Nor was there anything in the notices for the next ten days, so I went back to the beginning and started on the front page.

The article was on page three. The headline read, "Bronx Woman Killed in Rooftop Plunge." The story kept to the essentials. Sonia Denes, age twenty-seven, was killed in the early morning hours when she fell from the rooftop of her six-story apartment house on Morris Avenue in the Bronx. Her body was found in a courtyard and there appeared to be no eyewitnesses. Neighbors said that Miss Denes, a Hungarian immigrant who lived alone and worked for a Manhattan millinery company, had appeared despondent in recent weeks. The detective in charge of the case, Joseph F. X. McSorley, declined to say whether foul play was suspected.

I began reading the papers for the following days. There was nothing for weeks, then, finally, a short piece forty-two days after the first. The lead said it all: "Bronx Plunge Called Suicide."

I left the library and began walking down Fifth Avenue. I turned west and headed across town, periodically window-shopping to check behind me. I reached Sixth Avenue and entered a hotel that turned out to have real phone booths, with seats and privacy. I called Frank O'Connell. His secretary said he was on the phone but would call me back in twenty minutes.

Time to kill. I thought again of calling Blair. With this new evidence she'd have to concede that the Green case needed a new perspective. I dialed her cell phone, had second thoughts, and hung up before it rang. A lot had happened, but nothing to ease my concerns about Agent Turner. There was time, however, to possibly make some headway on that front. I called information and got the telephone number for the Alta Vista motel in Reading, Pennsylvania. First things first, I told myself.

"Alta Vista."

"May I speak to the manager, please?"

"Speaking. Can I help you?"

"My name is Philip Barkley. I'm calling in relation to the Martin Green incident that—"

"You want to speak to one of the owners. Hold on, please."

A moment later: "This is Harold. Can I help you?"

"Harold, this is Philip Barkley, calling from Washington on the Martin Green matter. The FBI agents who were there were working under my supervision."

"Okay."

"I've gone over reports and I want to make sure that I understood one part. What time was Mr. Green's body discovered?"

"I'm the one who found him."

"Right. I knew that."

"Just what I told the agents—six-fifteen."

"Then the report is correct. I need to be clear on what prompted you to go to his room at that hour. It's too early to be entering rooms unless you thought the guest had already checked out."

"Well . . . my statement said that a light was on and, uh, you know . . . on all night . . . and . . ."

My statement said. Interview enough witnesses and you learn to spot the red flags. I changed my tone when I cut him off. "Should I *rely* on this statement, Harold? I'm asking because if I put this statement in evidence before the grand jury and there's a problem with it, then bad things happen."

"Well . . . wait a minute . . ."

"Maybe it would be better if we brought you to the grand jury and—"

"Wait a minute . . ."

"Do you have a calendar available? I'd like to schedule you for next week."

"Whoa. I was told there wasn't going to be any trouble over this."

"There doesn't have to be."

"I did the right thing. A little delay, is all."

"I haven't got a lot of time."

"This is what happened. A guest checked in around twelve-thirty and I give him a room. He calls me twenty, thirty minutes later and says he saw some guys sitting in a car in our parking lot when he pulled in, and just wanted us to know. So, I'm thinkin', thanks a lot for waiting thirty minutes. Do you understand what's been going on around here?"

"No, tell me."

"We got problems with break-ins—not just us, all over the area, all the way up to Scranton. These guys pick somebody with a nice car and knock on his door. They tie him up, steal everything he's got, and leave him with a privacy tag on the doorknob. By the time we find him they've used up the credit cards and the car is somewhere in a million pieces."

"How long has this been going on?"

"Nine goddamn months, pardon my French. And if you don't mind my saying so, the FBI hasn't been a big help."

"So, the caller said that there were these men in a car."

"Right. So, like I said, I'm thinkin', thanks a lot. I go out and take a look and everything's quiet. You can't tell much, you know? But there's nobody in the parking lot and everything seems okay. A few lights are on in the rooms, but it's only around one, and people are still up. I go out at three and only a couple of lights are on. At four, this one light is still on and I'm startin' to wonder a little, but lights go on, lights go off."

"Sure."

"Come six o'clock, this light is still on. It's been on all night. A single guy, Michael Davis—that's the name he used. They always break in on singles. It's probably nothing, fell asleep with the light on or something, but since it's on, I'll jingle. Hold on a minute. I've got to do this."

He put me on hold. Two minutes seemed like two hours.

"Hey, I'm back."

"You decided to jingle."

"Right. No answer. But he could be on the shitter, pardon my French. I give it five minutes and call again. No answer. Now I'm a little nervous. I go over and knock on the door, then I knock louder, then I'm pounding. That's it, I'm using my key. I go in and the bedroom looks okay but the bathroom door is closed. I knock, call his name, and knock again. Then I gotta open the door."

"And you found him."

"Jesus Christ," he muttered. "Jesus Christ."

"Right." Neither one of us could say anything for a moment.

"I never saw anything like that. We had a few people pass while they were here, a couple of heart attacks, a guy choked on a pizza. But nothing ever like that. Anyways, you understand why I didn't say anything about the guys in the car? It wasn't important to what happened. People read stuff like that and all they're going to remember is break-ins at the Alta Vista. And we got a lot of regulars who live in the area—you know what I'm talking about."

"Go on."

"So, I just said that I saw a light on all night and decided to check it out."

"And later you decided to do the right thing."

"Well . . . you know . . . that agent comes a couple of days later and the two of us go into my office and I tell the story. I get a funny look, then comes the threats."

"Threats?"

"First of all, an FBI agent shouldn't go around threatening citizens, right?"

"That's right."

"And a woman shouldn't talk that way to a man. 'Squeeze my balls till my eyes pop.' What the hell is that shit?—pardon my French."

"Not appropriate."

"Not appropriate. So, I tell her the whole thing and I explain why I left out part the first time, just like I explained it to you."

"And what did the agent say?"

"Well, I asked if I was in any trouble and she said that we could keep this to ourselves, but if she did me a favor I'd better not make her look bad by shooting my mouth off. I told her—hey!—my lips are sealed. I thought she was a lady of her word because I signed the statement they prepared for me and there was nothing about the guys in the car."

"Okay."

"You know, I feel bad about that poor guy, even if he was a spy. Dying like that. I wouldn't wish that on anybody."

"Thank you, Harold."

"One more thing. I don't remember her name but if you know the agent I mean, do you have to mention this conversation?"

"I know who you mean. Like she said, we'll keep this to ourselves. Good-bye, Harold."

I felt claustrophobic. I opened the door to the booth

and began to take deep breaths. The phone rang a few minutes later. "Frank?"

"Hi, Philip. Sorry to make you wait but I was on a conference call."

"That's all right. I hope I'm not making a pest of myself. I really appreciate your investigator setting me up with Morrow."

"No problem. He loves an excuse to call on his pals up there and they love to do him favors."

"I need another one."

"Shoot."

"I need to get access to a police file on a woman who died, a suicide."

"This case is getting more interesting all the time. When?"

"April 17, 1955."

"*Nineteen-fifty-five?*"

"I know."

"Philip, I can tell you based on my own experience that the NYPD wouldn't retain a file that old unless it was an unsolved murder case. It would have been destroyed years ago."

"I see."

"Is there any other way to get at the information? My investigator can be very creative."

"What would you say the odds are that the investigating detective is still alive?"

"Not great, but easy to check if you have the name."

"Joseph F. X. McSorley."

"An Irishman. Your odds just got better. If he's alive he's probably drawing a pension somewhere. Call me at six o'clock."

I went into the hotel coffee shop and ordered a hamburger. I had fifty minutes till my appointment with my taxi armada at the diner. I picked up a *New York Post* and began turning the pages as I ate. Palestinians. The Euro. Lotteries. Tiger Woods. I imagined how the stories might look in fifty years. I was too tired to begin sorting things out but unless McSorley was around, I was done in New York. I'd already had a good hunch about the last place Green had gone: One Police Plaza near Foley Square, in search of the Denes file that had been destroyed years before.

Suicide. They got it wrong, and when I awoke that morning there was still a chance I had it wrong, too. But one car pursuit, one death record, and one lying motel operator later, Portland was no longer an option. I sat back and looked around. People eating and talking, a few were reading; all going on with their lives. I left the coffee shop and started walking west again. There were two cops sitting in a patrol car parked on Seventh Avenue. *Excuse me, officer, I'd like to report a homicide. Right. The Bronx, Morris Avenue. Fifty years ago. Yeah, they got it wrong.*

When I arrived at the diner, Sayed, Nabil, and Gamal were at a table by themselves. "You are okay?" Sayed asked as I sat down. He looked genuinely concerned.

"I'm fine. Did you get the pictures?"

Sayed replied, "Nabil got the pictures of the men in the Ford—two men." He put a heavy hand on my shoulder and looked at me gravely. "You should leave New York, my friend. Okay? It's no good with these people following."

"You're right," I said. "What do I owe you for today?"

"One hundred and fifty dollars." He removed a thick

envelope from his shirt pocket. "And seven dollars for the pictures."

I counted out the money and took the envelope. "I'm not going back to the hotel," I told them. "I'm leaving New York today. I need you to get my car from a garage and bring it here."

"Gamal and Nabil will go," said Sayed. "And they will follow you to the tunnel to make sure you are alone."

"Thank you. Thanks to all of you." I opened the envelope and began flipping through the pictures. The passenger in the Ford was the same one I'd seen near the archives and in the car across from the Waldorf. Same man, different cars.

"You are in trouble, yes?" asked Nabil. "Like you said before."

"Yes," I replied. "I'm in trouble."

14

AT SIX O'CLOCK I WAS in a telephone booth in Jersey City, hoping I wouldn't have to return to New York. I wasn't sure what I'd do if McSorley was dead, maybe call Evans and get myself in the Witness Protection Program. I didn't know whether to laugh or cry. Slowly, but ever so surely, I'd managed to maneuver myself into a very bad place. There was no going back, and maybe no going forward, either. Running around in circles until some very bad people put me out of my misery. There was a tremor in my fingers when I dialed the phone, a palpable reminder that I'd picked a hell of a time to go off medication.

Frank O'Connell's voice was a beacon in a storm. "I've got good news," he said. "Joseph F. X. McSorley, age seventy-six, is alive and well and living in Mesa, Arizona."

"Thank God."

The relief in my voice startled him. "Philip, is there anything else I can do? Just name it."

"No, nothing. You've done plenty, Frank. You've been a tremendous help."

"Well, you've got my number and don't hesitate to use it. It's not an imposition."

No, not an imposition. That wouldn't be the word for involving him in something that could get him killed. I thanked him once more and resolved not to call on him again.

Arizona. I could phone or I could just go. The thought of a cold call to stimulate a fifty-year-old memory wasn't the ideal way to tug on my only lifeline. Then again, it was a long trip to come up empty. I opened up another roll of quarters and dialed McSorley's number.

"Hello?"

"Hello, my name is Philip Barkley. I'm calling for Joseph McSorley."

"Are you selling something?"

"No, sir, I'm from the Department of Justice."

"If this is about the Social Security check, it still hasn't been replaced." The voice was strong and the speech crisp. Please be McSorley, I prayed.

"No, sir, it's not about that. I'm calling because a matter has come up related to one of Detective McSorley's old cases."

"Which case?"

"Is this Mr. McSorley?"

"Maybe, tell me again who you are."

"Mr. McSorley, my name is Philip Barkley and I'm a lawyer with the Justice Department in Washington, D.C."

"Washington, D.C. . . . and you're calling on one of *my* old cases?"

"That's right."

"How old?"

"Nineteen-fifty-five."

"*Nineteen what? Fifty-five?*"

"Yes, sir."

He snorted. "I'll be a monkey's uncle. Which case?"

"A woman named Sonia Denes. She fell from a rooftop."

Silence. Ten seconds. Fifteen seconds.

"Mr. McSorley?"

"How do I know you're who you say you are?"

"I'd come out there with identification if you remember anything about the case."

"When?"

"Probably the day after tomorrow. Do you remember anything about the case?"

"First the proof, then we'll talk."

No credit cards. That's what I'd decided. I might've already caused the death of Naomi Singer; I didn't want McSorley on my conscience, too. Credit cards left a computer trail. So did airline travel, although that would have to be finessed. I checked into a motel near Newark Airport, opened the Yellow Pages, and plotted my departure. Then I called Susan.

"It's Philip."

"I was getting worried."

"Everything's fine. How'd you make out?"

"I reached two of the three Sonias. I don't think either one is her. One is a twenty-six-year-old teacher in Brockton, Massachusetts. The other is a mother of three in Winnetka, Illinois. Neither ever heard of Naomi Singer or the Hebrew Immigrant Aid Society. Should I start calling all the Deneses?"

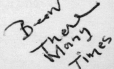

Been
There
Many
Times

"Not yet. I'm a little more certain I've found the right one. And I've made an appointment with someone who might be able to confirm it."

"Who?"

"A retired New York cop named Joseph McSorley who lives in Mesa, Arizona. He actually investigated Sonia's death."

"My God. Sonia Denes was murdered, too?"

"Supposedly, it was a suicide."

"What do these deaths have to do with Martin Green?"

"I don't know. I'm trying to find the connection between them, and McSorley may have some answers."

"You read things and see things on television but somehow this is much more real, a little scary but in a way, exciting."

"Scary but exciting. That's a good way to put it."

"What do I do now?"

"Right now, just sit tight."

"That I can do," she replied, laughing.

"I'm sorry, Susan, that was stupid."

"Don't be sorry. I lost the use of my legs, not my sense of humor."

"Right . . . Well, I'm going to fly to Arizona the day after tomorrow. After I meet McSorley, I'll call."

"Please do. I'll be waiting to hear from you."

"Okay . . ." I wanted to say something more but I got tongue-tied.

"Philip . . ."

"What?"

"Be careful, okay?"

"Careful is my middle name."

I spent the next day running errands in the New Jersey suburbs. I bought a small suitcase to replace the one I'd left at the Lancaster, stuffed it with enough clothing to keep me going for a week, and put the rest of my belongings in storage. Then I went to a travel agency and bought a one-way ticket to Phoenix because I didn't know where I'd be going next. Finally, I took care of my cash shortage by selling my car. Ninety-five hundred dollars, less than I'd hoped but enough to fund my investigation. I put a thousand in a new money belt and converted the rest to traveler's checks. By evening I was back at the motel and studying my chronology yet one more time.

Susan had asked the obvious question. Three people die over a span of fifty years: one murder and two suicides that were almost certainly two murders and one suicide, and probably three murders. What was the connection? To my chronology I added the men in the car at the Alta Vista and Blair's agreement with Harold to keep it a secret. And then there was the surveillance of me in New York.

Green had it right: things weren't what they seemed.

The next morning I produced my driver's license to the gate agent for my Phoenix flight. My ticket said I was "P. William Barker." "Philip W." or "P. William" was a distinction without a difference to the airlines. "Barker" versus "Barkley" was a distinction masked with a well-placed index finger. I spent the flight conjuring up scenarios for my meeting with McSorley. In my fantasy he had the key that unlocked the door. In my more realistic moments I pictured him giving me a big shrug.

The Valley of the Sun was a mecca for retirees of all

stripes. The wealthy settled in Scottsdale and the mountain golfing communities to the north. The middle class was spread among communities like Mesa. McSorley's neighborhood consisted of modest houses on postage-stamp lawns uncluttered by bikes and kiddy pools. It was life on fixed income, life after downsizing, and a testimonial to the miracle of compounding: small sums at low interest rates over a lifetime of hard work. The notable exceptions were in the carports, the big sedans of a generation weaned on the Harley Earl designs of Detroit in the fifties.

There was no sign of life at the house. The blinds were closed and it was quiet. I knocked on the screen door and silently prayed while the seconds passed. Behind me, I could hear my taxi driver talking into his cell phone. I knocked again. "Please don't be dead," I prayed. The driver took the phone from his ear and turned his hand palm-up. "Another minute," I called.

When I turned back the door was open. A tall man with a ruddy complexion and a full head of hair was standing on the other side of the screen. "Mr. McSorley?" I asked.

"Did you bring that identification?"

"Yes, sir." I took out my ID wallet and held it up to the screen. "Philip Barkley, from Justice."

"Well, send your cab away and come on in."

The door opened into a living room that was more appropriate to New York than the Sunbelt. A Queen Anne sofa with a rose-colored satin print, wing chairs, and a mahogany tea table. Over the sofa were two photographs: a woman and a man who had to be McSorley's father, both in the dress of the twenties. On another wall was a framed wedding photograph of McSorley and his bride. He was wearing an army uniform with corporal's stripes and three rows of ribbons. His bride was a pleasant-looking woman with dark curls and a benevolent smile.

"Come on back here," he said, "and I'll get us something cold." I followed him down a hall to the back of the house, where the second bedroom had been furnished as a den. He pointed me to a loveseat and left. The walls were covered with the usual array of family photographs and a lot of professional ones of suited men sitting under lodge banners. There was a portrait photo of McSorley in a police uniform, and another of him receiving an award from Mayor Wagner. And there was a framed newspaper photograph of him in a trench coat and fedora, with a grip on the elbow of a man in handcuffs.

McSorley entered carrying two glasses. "It's just iced tea, if that's okay, and I've got artificial sweetener if you want it."

"That's okay. And thank you for seeing me."

He handed me a glass and sat down at a kneehole desk that looked like another family heirloom. His clothes complemented the décor, a combination of Sunbelt and New York: tan golf shirt over brown dress trousers, and ancient wingtips that had probably been resoled countless times. "So . . ." he began, wiping his mouth with a handkerchief, "Sonia Denes."

"I saw the newspaper articles. That's how I got your name."

"Why the interest?"

"I was looking into the disappearance of a man named Martin Green. He was on the staff of the Senate Intelligence Committee and it was considered a national security matter."

"Was?"

"He's dead. He was found in a motel bathtub with his wrists slit." I paused for a reaction, then remembered he'd seen a lot worse. "It's been ruled a suicide," I added.

He picked up on my tone. "And you don't believe it."

"No, I think his death had to do with Sonia Denes."

His eyebrows arched in surprise. "What's the connection?"

"Green took a week off work, supposedly to tend to family business in New Jersey, but he actually spent the time in New York. He registered in a flophouse under a false name and tried to leave no record of where he went and what he did. The government thinks the reason was espionage. I think he was conducting an investigation that had to do with Sonia. I saw the notes of a woman he met with in New York and Sonia's name is written next to his."

"What woman?"

"Her name was Naomi Singer. That doesn't mean anything to you, does it?"

He thought a moment. "No."

"She used to work for an organization called the Hebrew Immigrant Aid Society, and she's the one who met Sonia's ship when she immigrated to New York in 1950."

"I don't think I ever heard of her but that was five years before Sonia died."

"I guess the circumstances of her immigration didn't come up in your case."

He shook his head. "No. Why would this Green fella be interested in her?"

"I have no idea. That's why I'm here."

"So, you think he was murdered and it had something to do with Sonia?"

"It's all circumstantial but that's what my gut says."

He nodded appreciatively. "Well, the gut is important."

"Was Sonia Denes a suicide?"

He didn't answer. He opened one of the desk drawers and took out a shoebox with "1954–1955" written on its side in black crayon. "I kept my notebooks," he explained. He removed one marked with an index card and began to thumb through the pages. "I thought I remembered the case until I looked at these notes. I guess it's just been too many years." He found the page he was looking for and read to himself. "This wasn't long after I'd gotten my gold shield and I was working nights. It says here that the call came at six-thirty in the morning. The super found her. She landed in an enclosed courtyard at the rear of the building, took some clotheslines with her, too." He looked up and added, "That's how we knew she went from the roof."

"Nobody heard anything? No screams or . . . her hitting the pavement?"

"Well, it can still be pretty chilly in New York in April, especially at night. Windows were probably closed."

"That makes sense. Did she live alone?"

"Yeah, she didn't have any family. We talked to the neighbors and the people at work. She made hats for"— he turned some pages—"the Paramount Hat Company on West Thirty-eighth Street. Her coworkers said Sonia pretty much kept to herself. Did her work and went home. No boyfriend, no social life. Same thing from the neighbors: went to work and came home, no real friends. Paid her rent on time and didn't make any noise."

"Any financial problems?"

"Wait a second." He turned some more pages and said, "A savings account with fourteen hundred and twelve dollars, pretty good for those days. And it says she didn't owe any money. We checked that angle pretty closely. You know, people didn't borrow like they do today and there were no credit cards."

"Did you get any more from the neighbors or coworkers?"

"The neighbors said she'd been looking distressed, though nobody could say why. Like I said, she wasn't the talkative kind."

"I take it there was no note or anything."

"No, nothing like that." He tapped one page with his finger. "Here we go. There was this one girl who lived in the neighborhood, Esther Müller. Her I remember. She was another Hungarian, and she and Sonia were around the same age and chummy, or as close to chummy as Sonia ever got. I was pretty sure Esther knew something but she stonewalled me. I tried to twist her arm a little but nothing doing. Maybe if I'd had a little more experience I might've handled her, but when you're starting out you don't realize how much you don't know. But I thought she knew something, all right."

"You sound like you had some doubts about suicide."

He put the notebook down and tugged at the creases in his pants. "This is where it gets interesting," he said. "The spot she went over, the wall was almost as tall as she was. Five feet high. She was five-five." He shook his head. "I remembered that without looking at the notes.

It's funny how some things stick, right?" He held up his hand. "Here's another thing: there was nothing to help her get over the wall. No step, no crate. She had to shinny up on top, then go."

"That's possible."

"It is, but she was wearing her robe and nightgown, and she had on these shoes, leather, no heel—'flats' they called them."

"I know what you mean."

"Well, they had polish on 'em, see? The liquid kind that you put on with an applicator brush. We found the bottle in her bathroom. And when she fell she landed on her back. Crushed the back of her head and broke everything. But the toes of the shoes weren't even scuffed."

"Couldn't she get over the wall without scuffing them?"

"I had several women try it. Men, too. Average-strength and strong types. There's no way to do it without the toes scraping the wall. She could've been an Olympic gymnast and she would've scraped her toes shinnying over a brick wall her own height."

"So she was thrown over."

"That's the way it looked."

"When we spoke on the phone it sounded like you remembered the case. Is that why?"

He sighed and said, "I'll tell you what I remember. That case about cost me my gold shield. Less than six months after I made detective, I nearly lost my shield over that case."

"Why?"

"In a police department a lot of things get said without getting said. Do you understand what I'm talking about?"

"I'm not sure."

"It came from the top down but I was too new to read the signs. I was just a dog with a bone. You know what that's like? There are other cases to be solved but most of the time it's obvious. The husband did it, the wife did it, the best friend did it. He grabbed a hammer, she grabbed a knife. He killed her in the bedroom, she killed him in the kitchen. But *this* one, this one's a real mystery. Why her, a young girl who kept to herself and never hurt anybody? It wasn't a burglary because she had nothing to steal, and it wasn't a sex thing. So, why? A real mystery, and it's *my* case."

"I understand."

"The law of gravity," he muttered.

"What's that?"

He looked over. "Just a saying we had."

"Meaning?"

"The guy who did it has to fall."

"Right."

"All I had to go on is the shoes and my gut. I'm figuring there's something about Sonia that I don't know and I'm pressing everyone I can, the coworkers, the neighbors, everyone. I'm bugging the senior detectives, too. What am I missing? Every chance I get, I'm back on Morris Avenue or at the hat place. Then it starts."

"Then what starts?"

"It was low-key at first. There's other cases, so move on. But the shoes, I say. Then I start getting a little heat. Move on, let it go. No problem, I say. I'll do the other stuff and work the Denes thing on my own time. Then one day I'm over at the DA's office on another case and I wind up in a room upstairs. The guy in charge is one of the principal assistants, a real political guy. What's going

on with Denes? he asks. So I tell him: nothing yet but I'm working it. End of conversation. No encouragement, just some stuff about how there's lots of crime and you can't solve 'em all."

"That's all he said?"

"You see, I'm too new to read the signs. I didn't understand."

"Did you ever figure it out?"

"I think so, but it'll be hard for a guy your age to understand. You didn't live in those times."

"Go ahead."

"The next day I get called into the lieutenant's office and get told point-blank that it's time to wind it up. I'm so stupid that I say I'll stop working it but keep it open, just in case we get a break."

He stopped to drink some of his tea, then noticed my glass. "Want some more?"

"No, thanks. So, you're going to keep it open . . ."

"Right. We don't close murder cases, that's procedure. Well, the lieutenant comes right out of his chair and hollers he's not going to have an unsolved on the books just because some Commie broad does a header on Morris Avenue. Those were his words. He says—this is almost a quote—'Them Hungarians are always offing themselves, so fuck the shoes and close the damn case. It's one less Red.' "

"I don't understand. He called her a Communist because she was Hungarian?"

He shook his head. "No, no. That was the thing, see? It didn't turn up in my talks with the neighbors and coworkers, but Sonia belonged to the Socialist Workers Party. There were plenty like her in the garment industry in those days. Today, that might not sound like much, but in 1955, that was a big deal. Communists were like the Japanese and the Nazis. People were worried about the 'Red Menace.' And this lieutenant, he's a Korean War veteran, see? You can imagine how *he* felt. He said that if it was murder, then the Party probably tossed her because she was behind on her dues."

"So, they wanted the case closed because she was a Communist?"

"If there was another reason for the pressure, I never found it."

"You say you didn't get it from the friends and coworkers. How did you find out about her Party membership?"

"I got it from the lieutenant, just the way I told you."

"Where did he get it from?"

"Who knows? Maybe from our own intelligence division, maybe from the FBI. I'll tell you, though, there wasn't a lot of sympathy for Communists and Socialists in those days."

"So, what happened?"

"Case closed—suicide." He drained the rest of his iced tea and set down the glass. "I had a lot of bad nights after that."

"Nothing else was ever learned?"

He shook his head. "That's the whole story. The next time I heard the name Sonia Denes was when you called two days ago."

"Did you investigate Esther Müller?"

"Sure. I was looking for something to open her up. Zero."

I couldn't think of another question. I threw out my catchall, one last, desperate stab. "Mr. McSorley, is there anything you thought I was going to ask that I haven't?"

He shook his head. "No, nothing."

"Is there anything else in your notebook that might help me? Anything we haven't talked about?"

The old detective began going through his notes again, slowly, meticulously. The silence of the house contrasted with the Lancaster and the ferment of New York. Down the hall, the refrigerator began to hum. I couldn't watch; I stared at the floor, listening to the whisper of turning pages. This is how it ends, I thought. Just like it began. The same man turning the same pages of the same notebook, maybe even wearing the same shoes. It was like this years before I was born, when he stood in a courtyard over poor, broken Sonia, the girl who never hurt anybody.

Finally, he closed the notebook. "Nothing," he said. "I'm sorry."

I was empty but I forced out the obligatory words. "I appreciate your seeing me, Mr. McSorley. I . . . well, I really appreciate it. Could I use your phone to call a cab?"

"I'll do better than that, I'll drive you." He waved off my protest. "You came a long way, it's the least I can do. And it'll give me a chance to show you my pride and joy."

"I'd like to go to a motel. Something near the airport."

"You might still catch a plane today."

"No, that's okay. I'm going to stay over and do some stuff."

We drove back in his pride and joy, a 1958 black-and-white DeSoto. I stared forlornly out the window as we passed bungalows, convenience stores, strip malls, and billboards for HMOs. He sensed my disappointment. "I'm going to think about the case some more," he assured me. "If I come up with something I'll call you."

"I'll be staying under the name Barker." He looked at me questioningly. "It's hard to explain," I said lamely.

"Are you really from the Justice Department?"

"Yes . . . and no. I left the department a few days ago."

"Then why are you here?"

"It's like you said: a dog with a bone." I waited a moment, expecting more questions, but he seemed satisfied. "There's a reason I'm not using my real name," I confessed.

"I figured that."

"I was followed in New York."

"By who?"

"That's even harder to explain. I'm not sure I understand what's going on or who I can trust, but there's something else: Naomi Singer was *definitely* murdered, a few days after Green. She was beaten to death in her apartment and the police think it was a burglary gone wrong."

"My God," he muttered, "no wonder . . ."

"Yeah. Well, anyway, I took precautions coming here. There's no reason to believe there's any danger but I thought I ought to tell you." My words of assurance were tinged with guilt. Whatever I thought about the risk I never gave him a choice about taking it.

He read my mind and waved it off. "Don't worry about it. At my age a little danger is good for the circulation."

We turned into a motel with a sign that said VACANCY over CABLE AND POOL. He pulled up to the office and winked at me when we shook hands. "Good luck, Barkley—or Barker," he said. I pulled my bag out of the backseat and then he was gone.

I got a room near the pool, which turned out to be closed for maintenance. I stretched out on the bed and thought about what to do.

You might still catch a plane today. I might, if I had a place to go. There were people out there looking for me and they knew how to look. They had my background, my habits, and my preferences. If I left that motel room, the chances of getting caught grew with distance and time.

Maybe I'd put an ad in the newspaper. *I quit, you win. I couldn't figure it out. No need to crush my head or slit my wrists or throw me off a roof. All I want is safe passage to Oregon.* Or I could stay right there, curled up in the fetal position inside my cinder-block fort. I'd claim motel sanctuary in the name of P. William Barker and exchange traveler's checks for pizza and whatever else they deliver.

It was dark when I was awakened by the crunch of tires on gravel. The slamming of a car door was followed by footsteps on the walkway. Pass by, I prayed. Please.

A knock on the door. Thoughts of the Alta Vista were fresh in my mind. I got up silently and placed a chair against the door so it was just below the knob. Another knock. I opened the door and peered through the crack at the silhouette of a man wearing a hat. His words sounded like some bizarre code.

"Esther Müller lives in Florida."

I removed the chair and opened the door. McSorley stepped into the room wearing a suit and a narrow-striped tie. "It's a long shot," he explained, "but she's the only lead."

"Esther Müller," I repeated.

"Right. It's funny, isn't it? Fifty years go by and it's still down to Esther."

"How did you find her?"

"I had her Social Security number in my notes. With a computer and the right contacts, it only takes a few minutes."

"You have a computer, Mr. McSorley?"

"Sure, I even get e-mail. Listen, my name is Joe. What do people call you? Phil? Philip?"

"Philip."

He nodded. "Okay, Philip, why don't you throw your bag in my trunk and we'll get started."

"Your trunk?"

"I don't like to fly. We'll be in Miami in two days if we take turns at the wheel."

"Miami . . . You and I . . . Tonight."

He smiled. "Philip, I've got news for you."

"What?"

"Our case isn't getting any younger."

15

WITHIN AN HOUR WE WERE on the interstate heading east, with McSorley behind the wheel, still wearing his fedora. I'd placed a quick call to Susan to say I was heading to Miami to see a lady named Esther Müller. When I mentioned that my transportation was a 1958 DeSoto driven by a seventy-six-year-old detective, she was understandably curious. I promised to fill her in when we got there.

"So," he said, "it's your turn."

"It's a long story."

"We've got lots of time. I want to hear the whole thing."

I told him all of it, glad for an audience. I related Martin's background, his mood change, his cryptic comments, and his odyssey in New York. I told him about the Hungarian embassy connection, the late-night calls to Constance, the fugitive hunt, and the events at the Alta Vista motel. Then I reprised an odyssey of my own: my Washington inquiries, the encounters with Constance and Edward Young, Martin's funeral, and being under surveillance while I retraced his steps. Finally, I told him about Blair: her investigation, her intuition about Naomi Singer's neighborhood, and her pact with Harold.

It took almost two hours and he never said a word or took his eyes off the road. It was nerve-racking. I craved a grunt, a nod, some positive sign that portended progress. In my heart of hearts I wanted him to tell me that he'd figured it out: it was Constance, or Blair, or Warren and Edward, or the entire Hungarian government. He could have told me that the butler did it and I might have cried with relief. Not a word.

"That's a heckuva story," he muttered, then fell silent again. Fifteen minutes passed as I sank deeper into despair. "So, how did you get into this thing in the first place?" he asked.

I took a deep breath and launched into the rise and fall of Philip Barkley. To his credit, he kept the DeSoto on the road when I mentioned my marriage to Constance. "Washington is a heckuva place" was all he said, then looked over at me and smiled. We both laughed. For a moment it felt as if we were partners, two detectives working a case, and it lifted my spirits. "So," he continued, "you're on the outs and they pull you back in for this case?"

"When Green disappeared a national security breach was a real possibility and a threat to Warren's candidacy. But espionage can be very hard to prove. They needed a credible report that said just that—no proof. If I wrote it there was a good chance it would stand up, at least through primary season. So, they offered me a deal."

"What kind of a deal?"

"The report in exchange for a fresh start in Oregon. I

was lined up with a job in the U.S. Attorney's Office. But after that picture of Martin at the Portrait Gallery and the fifty-thousand-dollar transfer, my report wasn't going to fly. If the administration couldn't get a favorable report, it needed a quick one. I wasn't ready to brand Martin a traitor, so I quit."

"You started your own investigation and now you're here."

"And now I'm here."

"A heckuva story," he repeated, shaking his head. "So, your first idea was that he had something going on with the senator's wife."

"That's right."

"It seems reasonable."

"Her father-in-law thought so, too. And if their affair became public it would have been the end of Warren's candidacy. That theory provided plenty of motive for murder but it didn't explain all the other things."

"That's true," he agreed, "*if* it's all one story, but maybe it's *two* stories. A young, handsome guy and the boss's wife—that's an old one. Do you think she's the type to fool around?"

"She's the type."

"Okay. Say they're playing footsie—"

"What?"

"Footsie. It's an expression."

"Okay."

"And the father-in-law finds out. Big trouble. They meet in a hotel in New York. 'What are we going to do, la de dah.' He decides to take it on the lam and—you're smiling."

"It's nothing, the expressions you use, that's all. Go ahead."

"He decides he's got to go and he calls her. Good-bye, sweetheart. But the father-in-law has a lot of money and he puts it to work. Eventually, they find him at the Alta Vista."

"So, it's about an affair, and all the other stuff is . . . ?"

"Other stuff."

"A long shot," I said. "Considering Green's background and his unofficial marriage to Diana, I'd say there wasn't an affair."

"Okay, you're satisfied, maybe *I'm* satisfied, but what if the father-in-law wasn't? He could've made a mistake."

"That would explain Green's death but it wouldn't explain Naomi's."

He held up a finger. "Unless the cops are right about Naomi, in which case what happened to her has nothing to do with anything."

I looked at him. "Do you believe that?"

"Probably not. I just wanted to talk it through before we moved on. I'm the slow and steady type, I guess." The speedometer corroborated him. It appeared that making Florida in two days was another one of those long shots. "If we drop the love affair theory," he continued, "then we need one that fits all the facts. That's a heckuva theory."

"I haven't come up with it yet."

He turned on the radio. I fully expected the Tommy Dorsey Orchestra or the Andrews Sisters, but it was Willy Nelson. Traffic sailed by as we puttered along in the right lane to "Funny How Time Slips Away."

"Every mystery has a beginning," he said, then fell silent.

"Okay," I prompted.

"What I mean is that the world is going along and then something changes. What's Martin's world?"

"His job, his relationship with Diana, and his faith and charitable work."

"First you thought the part with Diana had changed. They were on the rocks and he had an affair."

"But I was wrong. And I haven't come across anything relating to his faith or his community work, so it comes back to the Intelligence Committee. That's where the change took place, and that's where the pieces have to fit."

"Right," he said. "So, we're back to espionage and we need one theory, and with Green as a good guy. Okay?"

"I'm with you," I said, glad for a fresh perspective.

"Life is going along and one day he gets some new information, new input. His mood changes. The theme that's on his mind is betrayal. He decides to conduct an investigation, which is what you figured. The search takes him back to the early fifties, to a Hungarian immigrant with funny politics. He finds stuff out. He looks at Warren and says that things aren't what they seem."

"It's possible," I agreed. "Go on."

"That means Green wasn't giving Takács information at the gallery, he was getting it, which makes sense. The FBI agent saw him putting a piece of paper in his pocket." My respect for him was growing by the minute. He listened to two hours of detail and got it all. "Do you think the Hungarians could've been helping him?"

"Anything's possible, I suppose. The world has changed since the breakup of the Soviet Union."

McSorley held up two fingers. "That leaves a couple

of pieces that have to fit. You're the expert on Constance. What about her?"

What about her, indeed. "I'll tell you something a senator said about her before we were married. This guy was one of the most notorious womanizers on the Hill—anything in a skirt—and we were standing in a corridor when Constance walked by. He elbowed me and said, 'If she worked for me I'd keep her on the payroll even if I couldn't screw her. It'd be hell on earth, but it'd be worth it.' "

"So, she's smart."

"Very."

"What else?"

"You can take this with a grain of salt if you want, but she's ruthless."

His eyebrows arched at that one. "I'd have to explain," I said. "Things happened to us and she changed."

"I don't want to pry," he said. "Let's leave it at that: she's smart and ruthless."

"And ambitious," I added. "I think that if she gets to the White House she's going to even a lot of scores, and that's what motivates her these days."

"So, she'd protect her husband."

"I think so. If she was aware of the threat posed by Green's investigation she'd take action."

"How would she be aware of it?"

"She might've heard it from Martin himself." I told him about their relationship and the picture on Martin's desk.

"All right. We've got a theory on Constance. Maybe she just tried to talk him out of it in New York, or maybe she took it a step further. That remains to be seen. It might be a tough fit but no tougher than your FBI agent."

"No."

"You have any background there?"

"She's the daughter of a career army officer. She's ambitious and she's gotten a lot of recognition in the Bureau. She's tough, too. Supposedly, she killed a fugitive in a gunfight."

"Anything else?"

"Let's say you'd notice her in a crowd."

He smiled. "I guess she's the wild card in this thing."

"That much is clear."

"Well, if there's something going on that reaches up to a senator who may be the next president, then there's no telling how wide it is, or how deep."

A Cadillac pulled alongside and kept pace to allow its driver to admire the DeSoto before roaring off. It was followed by a blur of cars and pickup trucks and tractor-trailers. The DeSoto rocked back and forth in the jet stream. The speedometer indicator looked like a painted line pointing at fifty-five. Fifty-five miles per hour. Nineteen-fifty-five. The gauge was a calendar and we were frozen in time. I leaned back and closed my eyes. "So, what do you think?" I asked.

He exhaled and said, "You can see the outline of a story there, vague, but still an outline. A spy ring that goes back a long way, one with some real interesting new members. That gets you to betrayal, things not being what they seem, and a motive for murder. If I could have the answer to just one question, it would be the one I asked before: What got Green interested in Sonia? If we knew that we'd be a long way down the road."

"And you think we might get the answer from Esther Müller."

"Well, one step at a time," he said.

"Right. Slow and steady."

Nighttime in the desert and I'm riding with a ghost. He had to be a ghost because he couldn't be real. Everyone else was dead. Sonia was dead. The super who found her was dead. The neighbors were dead. The Paramount Hat Company was dead, too. Everyone, even Naomi. And Martin. So, how could he be real? A ghost carrying me across generations, back to the beginning, before there was a Philip, a Constance, a Blair, or a Martin, back to the time of Sonia and Naomi, and Esther Müller.

It was a dream. And like all the really bad dreams, it was black all around, everywhere but the next hundred feet of highway, and beyond that, somewhere in the on-rushing dark, monsters. I stared out my window at his reflection, lit by the dashboard glow. McSorley. A name in a newspaper so old it wasn't even a newspaper, just a picture of a newspaper, a strip of film on a shelf in the basement of a library. This is as it should be, I decided. This is how it would get done. Going back in a time machine, piloted by a ghost.

"I joined the force after the war."

I shifted in my seat to face him. His gaze remained fixed on the road.

"Nineteen-forty-six. I was twenty-one years old."

"You were a corporal. I saw your picture."

"Company B, the 116th Regiment, 29th Division. We were assigned to the First Division on D-Day."

"The D-Day invasion?"

"Omaha Beach. You read about it. Everyone has read about it."

"Sure. It was . . . I was going to say 'terrible' but that sounds . . ."

"Terrible is a good word . . . It's a good word. I got home, though, and I got married to a girl named Eileen."

"I saw the wedding picture. She looks very kind . . . very gracious."

"Yes, she was. She passed two years ago. We were together almost every day we were married. A few times she visited relatives when I couldn't go, but that's all . . . She used to write me letters."

"When she was away, that's nice."

"Not only when she was away. Sometimes I'd come home and there'd be a letter on my dresser."

"That's wonderful."

He was lost in thought. "You were telling me about joining the force," I said.

"Right. I didn't plan on being a cop when I finished high school. I was going to be an electrician. But when I got home from the war I didn't want that anymore. I didn't know what I wanted, to be honest."

"It must have been hard getting readjusted."

"You know how I felt? Clean."

"Clean?"

"Like I'd been scrubbed clean on that beach and I didn't want to get dirty again. It's hard to explain but when you're growing up you get into all kinds of things, some of them pretty stupid. Maybe you don't respect the things you should. You think the world started when you were born and you don't owe anybody anything. But when I came home I felt like I was some kind of knight, home from the Crusades."

"Well, in a way, you were."

"In a way. And the thing of it was, I had to choose, see? I could continue to be a knight, or go back to what I was before. Does that make any sense?"

"Sure. So, you decided to become a police officer."

"Not only to be a police officer, but to do it right."

"Like a knight on a quest."

"That's it. A knight on a quest. So, you do the job a certain way. You look like you're supposed to look, do what you're supposed to do. And when you see what some other cops might be doing, you make different choices."

"It isn't easy."

"That's right. Cops didn't make much money in those days but there was side money if you wanted it. The local businesses would contribute, although a lot of them weren't happy about it. And then you had the gamblers and the pimps, and, later, the drug dealers. There were lots of opportunities to improve your standard of living. Some cops bought houses on Long Island, or boats, or sent their kids to private schools and went on big vacations. These were real differences from how a cop could live on just his salary."

"And they rationalized it."

"All the time. 'We don't get paid what we're worth.' 'Nobody gets hurt.' 'Everybody's doing it.' 'I got a family to take care of.' These guys thought they were men of the world, and guys like me, we were choir boys, holier-than-thou jerks."

"But you did it right."

"I had a smaller bedroom but I slept better. You understand?"

"Yes."

"I could always look people in the eye."

"How did Eileen feel about it?"

"She felt like I did, and that's no small thing. I saw some situations that went the other way, too. Some wives put on the pressure. I don't know for certain what would have happened if she had, but thank God, we both felt the same way."

"I'm glad to hear that."

"Later, things hit the fan with the Knapp Commission. You remember that? No, you're too young."

"I read about it. The police corruption investigation. Frank Serpico. They made a movie about it."

"I had twenty-five years in when that happened but I had no worries. You know, most of the smart guys never did get caught. They went all the way through, doing what they did, and they convinced each other that they were pretty slick." For the first time, he took his eyes off the road to look at me. "But here's the payoff," he said.

"Go ahead."

"I've lived long enough to know how it turns out. Understand? Some of those smart guys live right there in Phoenix, in nicer places than I could ever afford, but it took a toll on them. You can see it in their faces: no self-respect. They're rotten inside. Their own kids hate them and they hate themselves." He looked over at me. "What I'm trying to say is that the reward for doing it right may come way down the road, but that's when it counts most."

He fell quiet again. The hum of the tires and the air rushing past the windows had long since diminished into barely audible background noise and we rolled along in relative silence. "Thanks," I said finally.

"I'm the one who should be thanking you."

"Me? Why?"

"You know what I did yesterday?"

"What?"

"I went out and bought the morning paper and stuff for lunch. And later I went out to buy something for dinner. I shop for one meal at a time to have something to do. That's my routine."

"You're still coping with your wife's passing."

"I needed something to get me in gear."

"And now, here we are. A couple of crusaders."

"Here we are," he agreed. "On a quest."

The statistics say that women usually outlive their husbands. The Sunrise Apartments complex appeared to be proof. We were waiting on a second-story breezeway between rows of apartments that faced a central courtyard. With few exceptions, the residents sitting in lawn chairs along both sides, top and bottom, were women. They sat awhile, went inside, then came out and sat some more. They all seemed to be waiting. "Waiting for a visit," observed McSorley.

We were waiting for Esther Müller. With our assurance that we were discreet, her neighbor, Minnie, confided that Esther had a doctor's appointment, then went on to share Esther's entire medical history, right up to her recent bursitis. The transition into a guided tour of her own anatomy was seamless. We heard all about her arthritis, bunions, and cataracts, and were working our way through her colon when, fortuitously, Minnie's son and daughter showed up with the grandchildren. After declining an invitation to a four-thirty dinner out, McSorley and I took up station on the breezeway, hoping that Esther hadn't had any complications.

"This is funny," said McSorley. "I used to wait on Esther to come home from work. For a while I was there three, four times a week, trying to wear her down."

"Let's hope that fifty years did the job."

It was after six when a short, sturdy woman with curly white hair shuffled along the walkway below us and stuck her key in Esther's door. We waited ten minutes then knocked. When she opened the door she was wearing a house dress and carpet slippers. She looked worn out.

"Miss Müller? My name is Philip Barkley. I'm with the Department of Justice in Washington." Her eyes ricocheted between the ID and my face a half-dozen times before she spoke.

"Washington?" she mumbled.

"Yes, ma'am." Her gaze followed the identification into my breast pocket. "This is my partner, Joseph McSorley. We're working on an official matter and would like a few moments of your time."

"I live alone," she said anxiously. "I don't know from Washington."

"It's not about Washington, Miss Müller. It's—"

"Is it about Mrs. Fuentes? I thought they caught that man."

"No, it's not about Mrs. Fuentes, ma'am. It's about another matter and it will only take a few minutes. May we come in? Or we could sit out here and talk if you want." I motioned toward a grouping of lawn chairs.

"I have to make dinner," she said. Her eyes went to McSorley.

He removed his fedora and gave her a practiced, gentle smile. "It would just be a short visit," he assured her.

"We've come a very long way to see you. We haven't had anything to eat or drink since this morning."

"I've got ginger ale," she said. "I could bring it outside."

"I can't have sugar," said McSorley.

She looked at him like he was crazy. "Who uses sugar?" she asked, then closed the door saying, "I'll be right out."

We arranged the lawn chairs so she'd be sitting between us. Esther was out in a moment carrying a tray with two glasses of ginger ale and a plate of cookies. "There's no sugar in the cookies," she told McSorley, passing the tray. She settled into the chair and arranged her house dress. "Just a few minutes," she said, glancing around. She noticed two women watching us from above. "Oh, the two *yentas*," she whined. "By tomorrow everybody will know my business!"

McSorley gave me a knowing look. "Do you think they'll figure out we're from Washington?" he asked quietly.

Esther contemplated this bonus. "Of course!" she complained. "By tomorrow it will be all over the building!"

"How long have you lived here?" I asked.

"Twelve years. I used to have that apartment over there"—she pointed above us—"but the elevator is always broken and who can walk stairs?"

"I have trouble with swelling in my legs," said McSorley. "The doctor gave me a prescription but it doesn't seem to help much."

"And I'll bet it was expensive, too," she replied. "That's the game they play. They give you something expensive. Did you ask for generic?"

"No. Maybe I should."

"Generic," she said firmly. "Don't let them give you the fancy names. And get it at Publix. Do you have Publix?"

"No," he replied, "but I've got a discount place that's good."

"Ohhhh," she said, nodding. "Give me the name before you go." She turned to me and said, "So, what is it?"

"Miss Müller, I believe that years ago you lived in the Bronx, on Eastburn Avenue." I was going to take this in small steps.

Her brow wrinkled. "Eastburn Avenue? . . . That was a long time ago."

"Yes, a long time ago, we know. And you had a friend in the neighborhood named Sonia Denes. Do you remember her?"

Her mouth opened, and shut again. "Why are you asking me about her?" she cried.

"It's hard to explain but her name came up in a case that we're working on and we need to learn more about her."

"The police asked me questions when she died."

"Well, then maybe you won't mind giving us the same information."

"It was so long ago. Who remembers?"

"It's important to try, Esther. May I call you Esther? You and Sonia were friends."

"Not friends, acquaintances," she said firmly.

"Acquaintances, okay. I understand that she worked for a millinery company."

"I don't remember."

"That's fine. What did you do?"

"Me?" She looked uneasy.

"Uh-huh."

"Why?"

I smiled. "I'm just interested, that's all. I get to meet all kinds of interesting people in my job."

"Are you a lawyer?"

"That's right."

"I had a nephew who was a lawyer. He handled car accidents and falls in supermarkets."

"A personal injury lawyer. That's a very interesting job."

"He had a heart attack."

"Oh, I'm sorry to hear that," I said, and waited.

"So, what do you want to know?"

"I was just asking what you did."

She sighed. "I worked in a photography studio."

"In the Bronx?"

"No, Manhattan. I worked for Leonard Montague on Madison Avenue. He was very well known, *very* well known. He took Milton Berle's picture. And Georgie Jessel's."

"That must have been very interesting."

"We did portraits. We did society weddings. And advertising. Models would come in to pose for their portfolios. We had some of the real famous ones. You know who else came in for a picture?"

"Who?"

"George Raft."

"No kidding? What did you do there?"

"I was the office manager. I helped set up, too. Lighting and props."

"It sounds like a great job. Did you ever talk about it with Sonia?"

Her face fell. "I don't know *anything*," she bawled.

I was one misstep away from losing her completely. At that moment a neighbor walked by, slowed for a look, and waved. Torn between her distress and a golden opportunity, Esther called out to her. "These gentlemen have come a long way from Washington, Ida. I can't talk." As Ida scuttled away, Esther muttered, "Another *yenta,*" and turned her attention back to me, the source of her distress.

"I live in a retirement community," said McSorley suddenly. Esther looked at him. "Near Phoenix."

"You sound like you're from New York," she said.

"I am. We moved to the Phoenix area when I retired."

"I thought you said Washington."

"I'm back on special assignment for this case."

"Your wife is in Phoenix?"

"She passed a couple years ago. I'm alone now."

"Ohhh. Do you have any children?" This kind of conversation was more to her liking.

"No, we never had any."

"I was never married," she said.

"The reason we came to see you is about a young man who died. Philip here went to his funeral just about a week ago and met his parents."

"Oh." She looked at me. "A young man?"

"Yes," I said, "the family is sitting *shivah* now."

"Ohhh, how terrible," she said.

"His name was Martin. He was very active in his synagogue."

"Oh, my God," she said softly. "What happened to him?"

"We're not sure, Esther. That's part of what we're trying to find out."

"What does this have to do with Sonia?"

"The young man was looking into Sonia's life. We don't know why, but it might have something to do with how she died."

"She fell from the roof."

"She did. What can you tell us about that?"

"I don't know anything."

"Of course, but if you know something about Sonia, maybe what she was doing before she died, or if she said something to you, that might help."

"I don't know *anything*," she repeated.

Fifty years later and she was still stonewalling. I could feel the frustration welling up inside me but McSorley remained patient. "Martin's parents want to know what happened, Esther," he said softly. "It's very hard, not knowing. Isn't there anything you can tell us about Sonia that could help?" She bit her lip and slowly shook her head.

McSorley looked at me and shrugged, then stood up and said, "Esther, you're tired. You've had a long day. Suppose we come back tomorrow for a visit? We can talk about something else."

Esther looked up. Now she was conflicted. Distressing as it was, another visit from Washington officials—with sufficient lead time to lay the proper groundwork—was a public relations bonanza. "We can talk about something else?" she asked, looking from him to me.

"I think so, Esther," I said. "I'll try to get permission from my boss but he's pretty demanding."

"I have a picture of Sonia," she said suddenly.

"You do?"

"Sometimes I would bring a camera home and make extra money. Mr. Montague didn't mind, if I paid for the film. There was a man who had a pony. I would take pictures of neighbors' children sitting on it and we would split the money."

"How did you get a picture of Sonia?"

"Mister Montague was always looking for interesting faces. He would say that he wanted faces etched by experience. I would take him pictures of people I thought were interesting but he never used them."

"And you took him a picture of Sonia?"

"It was the only one he really liked. He said, *'That's experience!'* But before I could bring her . . ." She started to weep. "I kept it. I couldn't throw it away."

"I'd love to see it," I said.

She pushed herself up and went into her apartment.

"I'm sorry, Philip," said McSorley. "It looks like fifty years hasn't changed her mind. Maybe we'll have better luck tomorrow."

"I hope so. I'd love to know whatever she's been keeping inside all this time. What do you think it could be?"

"I don't know," he said. "We'll have to talk about it later. Here she comes."

Esther handed me the photograph. "Sonia," she said. It was the picture of a grim-faced woman wearing a dark skirt and a white blouse rolled to the elbows. She faced the camera squarely with her arms at her sides, as if for an identification photo or a police lineup. On the back there was a date in pencil: "3/7/55."

"Can we keep this?" I asked. "I'll have a copy made and return the original when we come back."

Esther chewed her lip a moment, then nodded. "Will you be back tomorrow?"

"Probably," I said. "I'm going to check with my boss. Will you think some more about Sonia?"

"I'll try," she promised. We said our good-byes. Mc-

Sorley walked her back to her apartment and I went to the car. I was staring at the picture of Sonia when he got behind the wheel.

"We have to figure out our next move," he said.

"Unless she comes up with something tomorrow, there aren't any left. We're at the end of the line."

He took off his fedora and rubbed his face with his handkerchief. "I guess so," he said softly. We stared through the windshield and separately pondered the meaning of the end of the case. A resident of the Sunrise Apartments using a walker slowly crossed our field of vision. I watched McSorley watching her, probably contemplating the return to his empty house in Arizona, a world without Eileen. Would it be harder now? For a few precious days he was back on the job, working a case, working *the* case.

I held up the picture of Sonia and spoke directly to her. "What's your secret?" I asked. McSorley looked over. "Here," I said, passing the photograph to him. "Have you ever seen a picture of her alive?"

He shook his head. "I saw the autopsy photos and I saw her in the courtyard." He tapped the photograph and grunted.

"What?"

"It's been too many years. I forgot about this."

"Forgot about what?"

He tilted the photograph toward me, pointing to a dark spot on her arm. "The tattoo."

"A tattoo?"

He nodded. "A number, from a concentration camp. Isn't that something? She survives a concentration camp and gets thrown off a roof in the Bronx."

"Jesus Christ."

"I know. It's a heckuva thing."

"Jesus Christ."

"I . . . What's the matter?"

"Your big question about the connection between Martin and Sonia."

"What about it?"

"I think it just got answered."

16

I CALLED SUSAN WHEN WE stopped for gas. "Okay," she said, "I'm on the edge of my seat, kind of."

"I'm in Miami with McSorley. We just left Esther Müller and we're heading back to Washington."

"Does that mean the trail leads back here?"

"I'll fill you in when I see you."

"Will you be back tonight?"

"No, we're driving. We should be there tomorrow night or the following day. It depends on how long we stop."

"Anything I can do in the meantime?"

"Susan . . . it may not be a good idea for you to be involved."

"I thought I was already involved."

"There were people following me in New York. I lost them but they're certainly looking for me, and they're dangerous."

"What does that mean, 'dangerous'?"

"They've probably killed two people."

"Oh . . ."

"I don't know who they are but they've got a long reach. We'll try to avoid attention in Washington but it would be best if we kept you out of it."

"I'm not afraid, Philip."

"I understand that but—"

"It's nice to be excited about something again."

"Well, let me think about it. We'll talk when I get back."

"Okay. Be careful. I keep saying that, don't I? Be careful."

"Keep reminding me."

Twelve hundred miles to Washington. I took the wheel of the DeSoto and McSorley stretched out in the backseat. I was exhausted but more than rest I craved quiet time to consider things anew. Logically, the national security angle was still the best fit, but I was sure that the line from Green to Sonia Denes ran through the Senate Banking Committee and its Swiss banks inquiry. But it was a blurry line.

My adrenaline carried us as far as Jacksonville before McSorley sat up and announced he was hungry. We found a near-empty pancake house near the interstate where a woman doubling as waitress and cashier told us to sit anywhere. I went off to the men's room to wash up and was caught off-guard by the image in the mirror. The fatigue was plain but closer inspection revealed the fear I'd been living with since New York, now amplified by the reality that I was no longer the only one in harm's way. My guilt over McSorley was mitigated by his enthusiasm and experience, but what about Susan? *It's nice to be excited about something again.* I'd recruited her in my hour of need, enticed her with the opportunity for a little sleuthing, and now I was on the verge of cutting her loose. It didn't seem fair, but then again, fair had nothing to do with it. What did? When it came to Susan I wasn't sure. I leaned toward the mirror. The bearing of a crusader was nowhere to be found.

McSorley was in a booth; his fedora hung on the hat rack alongside. Without it he seemed transformed from his detective persona to ordinary senior citizen, another Florida retiree. The fluorescent lights revealed that the trip had taken its toll but he hadn't uttered a word of complaint and never would. The waitress came over with coffee. We ordered a midnight breakfast and he began fiddling, following a routine born of a thousand such places, polishing the silverware with his napkin, getting his coffee just so. I watched him with an odd sense of pride. "Have you got it figured out?" he asked, adding another half-packet of sweetener.

"No, I'm only at the starting point. Warren Young was on the Banking Committee when Green joined to work on the Swiss banks inquiry. Part of Green's job was to research old files."

"I remember there was a Swiss banks thing, but that's all."

"I sat through some of the hearings when I was still at the Senate. When the Nazis came to power a lot of people moved money to Switzerland, including thousands of Jews who were subsequently murdered during the Holocaust. When their heirs tried to recover the deposits after the war the Swiss banks essentially stonewalled them, and they kept stonewalling for fifty years. The hearings produced a lot of embarrassing revelations about that and Switzerland's image took a heavy hit. The result was major concessions by the banks. They agreed to search for dormant accounts, and they put up over a billion dollars to settle a class-action lawsuit by the heirs."

"And you think this somehow connects Green, Warren, and Sonia?"

"Yeah, I do. Sonia was a Holocaust survivor. The hearings were about Holocaust events. And Martin recently went back to look at those files."

"That's worth investigating."

"I like this angle more than espionage but I don't know where we go from here."

He sipped his coffee, thinking it over. The waitress brought his soft-boiled eggs and an omelet for me. "Well," he said finally, "let's come at it another way. There's a hundred crimes and a million ways to commit 'em, but there's only a handful of motives, and the list hasn't changed since the Garden of Eden. Basically, you're looking at money, power, love, and revenge, and you pretty much eliminated love."

"Where do we start?"

"With old number one. Your campaign finance scandal was about money, so was the Knapp Commission thing. So, let's see how money plays in our case."

"Swiss banks have money."

"Lots of it."

"The hearings were about the deposits of Holocaust victims."

"That's two. You also have to ask how the money relates to your primary actors."

"First, there's Green."

He shook his head. "He's not an actor, he's an investigator like us, skip him."

"Well, then there's Warren. Staging for the presidency and running a campaign requires tons of money."

"He's got tons of money, or his old man does, anyway."

"True, but he couldn't use it for a presidential campaign. He had to go outside."

"Why?"

"First, like everyone else, his father is limited by law on what he can contribute directly to his son's campaign. Warren could spend his own money freely but he'd look like some rich guy trying to buy an office. Self-financing has been tried in congressional campaigns, and sometimes it works, but it's always an issue and it costs votes."

McSorley nodded. "That makes sense. He sure wouldn't get my vote. So, where could the Swiss banks fit in?"

"I'll tell you something interesting, Joe. As a presidential hopeful, Warren came out of nowhere to overtake more-established pols, including the vice president himself. He was a fund-raising machine. By the time Forsythe was able to react Warren was earning IOUs from the key party people and the most important organizations."

"How did that happen?"

"Do you know the difference between 'hard money' and 'soft money'?"

He smiled. "Not coins and paper?"

"The terms come from campaign finance law. 'Hard money' is contributed directly to a candidate's campaign for federal office, and there are strict limits on who can give and how much. 'Soft money' is donated to political parties for more general use and there are no limits. The political parties use it very effectively to advocate on certain issues like abortion or health care, which in turn helps or hurts specific candidates. They also use it for get-out-the-vote drives and to help candidates for state office. Today, the major parties raise more soft money than hard, and politicians who can get people to open their checkbooks accumulate IOUs and support."

"And Warren was one of those."

"In the years he was staging for the presidency he went around the country raising an incredible amount of soft money, and there's a long, long line of people who owe him big-time. It's been said that if he got the nomination, he'd win it before the primaries were even on the horizon."

"Where did the money come from?"

"Everywhere and anywhere. Individuals and committees, and fund-raisers that would yield astronomical sums. Everyone thinks it was his father's connections that got him started."

"Maybe a bunch of it was Swiss money funneling in."

"Illegal but certainly possible. Foreign sources can be very hard to sniff out. The question is, why would they help him?"

"What if he had them over a barrel? Maybe there was something the banks didn't want to come out, something embarrassing or a real bombshell."

"And Green found out about it, is that it?"

"Right, but why the delay? You said the hearings ended years ago."

"Supposedly, he went back to the files because he was working on a paper for his master's degree. So, maybe he found something he overlooked the first time."

"Maybe the paper story was just a cover," he said.

"Maybe he discovered something that sent him back to the files."

"Something about Warren?"

"Maybe."

"Getting our hands on those files may not be easy."

McSorley wiped his mouth with a napkin. "Where there's a will there's a way," he declared.

I smiled at another vintage expression. "So, what do you think of our theory?"

"It's not bad. It's still about Warren becoming president and it still explains why Constance is so involved."

"Constance is fixated on Warren becoming president," I agreed.

"Money ties to the presidency," he said. "The presidency ties to power. And if Constance gets to the White House, it ties to revenge, too. Money, power, revenge. That's a lot of motive, Philip."

"Yeah," I agreed, "a lot of motive."

"*Philip!*"

It seemed that I'd just closed my eyes in the backseat when McSorley's voice pierced my consciousness. I sat up, groggy. "What . . . ?"

His attention was divided between the road ahead and the rearview mirror. "We're getting off at the next exit." His tone said it wasn't up for discussion.

"Why?"

"I think we've got a tail." I turned around and saw only blackness. It wasn't until we were on a long straight stretch that the headlights materialized. "There," he said.

"We're not the only car on the interstate, even at this time of night."

"They've been back there a long time," he replied, "keeping their distance—no closer, no farther, even when I change speeds. The other cars have gone past like we're standing still."

That I could believe. "Where are we?"

"Georgia, between Brunswick and Savannah."

We passed a sign saying there was an exit in two miles. "That car can't be following us," I said. "No one knows where we are." He didn't reply. The one-mile sign came and went. "Do you really want to get off here?"

"Better safe than sorry," he said.

The exit came up. He turned off without signaling, down the ramp and around to the intersection with a state road. We stopped and waited: nothing . . . nothing . . . the beam of headlights coming around the curve. McSorley made a quick left turn onto the highway, following a sign for gas and food. "What are we going to do?" I asked.

"We're looking for a place that's still open, maybe a gas station or a bar."

We drove along the dark two-lane road past a few clapboard houses and corrugated-steel buildings. Lights in the distance indicated a town up ahead. I checked behind us. There was nothing visible but the road was curvy. We passed under a streetlight and into darkness again. McSorley turned off the headlights and slowed to a crawl as we approached the next bend in the road. A second later, the headlights materialized. The car passed under the streetlight and now the silhouettes of the two men inside were visible. My hands were sweaty on the upholstery. McSorley accelerated around the bend and turned the lights back on. Soon a brightly lit service station appeared in the distance. "Those places have a back door," he said. "We'll pull in and go inside. I'm going out the back. You stay inside, by the front counter. Start a conversation with the clerk or something, but stay visible from the road."

I leaned forward. "What are you going to do?" I asked. As I spoke I saw the glint of metal on the seat. A gun. He picked it up and put it in his jacket pocket. "Why don't we keep going until we find the police?"

"Then what?" he asked, still watching the mirror. "They'll just deny following us and there's nothing the police can do."

"If they've got guns they'll have to explain them."

"This is rural Georgia. Lots of people have guns. And even if they have trouble with the police, they or whoever they're working for will just come after us later, and next time we won't see them coming." He looked at me. "Listen, we're in this thing together. If you want to take the chance, then okay, we'll go to the police, but I think this is as close as we'll get to having the advantage."

I stared back at him. A seventy-six-year-old man with a gun in his pocket. A bad dream. "Okay," I heard myself say, "I go in and stay visible. Then what?"

"Just wait. If something goes wrong you'll know it, and then you go right out the back and run. Get yourself to a police station and call anyone in Washington you can count on. Here we go."

It was a combination gas station and convenience store. He parked close to the entrance and we hurried inside. There was only a clerk, a man in his early twenties with a wispy moustache. "Bathroom this way?" asked McSorley, pointing. He didn't wait for an answer. I heard the back door open and shut.

"Wrong door, Dad," said the clerk, shaking his head and laughing.

The car that followed us drove slowly past the station and out of sight.

"He'll come around," I said. "Listen, how long to the South Carolina border?"

"About an hour and a half, give or take."

The glint of headlights through the bushes bordering the parking lot showed that they were turning around; the road in front of the station was briefly illuminated before it went dark. The car remained out of sight.

"Are there any restaurants in the area?"

"There's nothing right around here open this late," the clerk said. "There's a Hardee's about eight miles down the road that might still be open."

"That would take us farther from the interstate," I said, watching the area near the bushes.

"Well, we got chili dogs and nachos, if you like that stuff. The chili dogs are pretty good." No one was approaching the station.

"How long have those dogs been turning on the grill there?"

"Since about four," he said. "They're done, don't worry about that." I watched the area around the bushes: nothing. They were going to wait us out. The thought of McSorley dealing with the two men by himself became unbearable. "Had much trouble around here?" I asked.

"Trouble?"

"With robberies. I used to work in one of these places. I got robbed twice and they wound up giving me a gun."

The clerk snorted. "Shit, mister, I been robbed *four* times—twice by the same guy! I told 'em, 'Let me bring my gun and there won't be no next time, no how,' but the owner's scared I'm gonna pop some kid grabbing a candy bar or somethin'." He held up a baseball bat with the top quarter sawed off. "*This* is what they gave me. Can you believe that shit? Some motherfucker walks in here with a Magnum and I'm supposed to pop 'em with *this*?"

"Let me see that," I said, taking it out of his hand. "I'll bring it right back." I walked directly out the door and headed left toward the line of bushes, then moved in a crouch toward the street with the bat cocked. I should have been scared out of my mind, taking a baseball bat to a gunfight, but I'd been afraid for so long that the idea of fighting back brought a rush of adrenaline. The bat felt like a feather in my hand. I wanted to fight them, to make them pay for what they'd done.

I reached the end of the bushes and peeked around. The dome light in the car suddenly went on—I'd been seen! I couldn't contain the surge inside me. I jumped up and ran around the bushes, bat raised high—and stopped short. The two men were still inside the car but they had their hands on the dashboard. McSorley was at the back passenger door, pointing his gun with a two-hand grip. Without looking at me he said, "You're just in time."

He moved closer to the passenger. "What're you carrying?" he asked quietly. There was no reply. The gun swung against the side of the man's head; the passenger grunted and blood spurted from the gash.

"A Glock in the shoulder holster," said the man. The calm voice acknowledged no pain or fear.

"My friend here is going to reach across and take it. If your hands move, I'll kill you. Do you understand?"

"Yes," he replied.

"The same goes for you, driver, understand?"

"Yeah," said the driver.

"When you get out of the car we're going to search you real thorough. If I find a second gun I'm going to shoot you through the kneecap. I won't say anything, I'll just shoot. You understand?"

As calm as the passenger was, the remarkable voice was McSorley's. It wasn't the voice I'd been hearing for days. It was a younger, authoritative voice, perhaps the same one that criminals heard fifty years ago, and it left no doubt about the speaker's intent. At that moment I had absolutely no doubt that McSorley would kill them without hesitation, and neither did they.

"There's a thirty-two in an ankle holster," said the passenger, again, without emotion. McSorley nodded to me and I opened the door and retrieved both guns. He took the Glock from me, flicked off the safety without taking his eyes off the two men, and handed it to me. Then he told the passenger to get out, drop to his knees, and lie flat on the ground. Then he told me to kneel on his back and press the gun into the base of his skull. The driver was told to slide over to the passenger's side. McSorley retrieved a gun from a shoulder holster and a second one from the small of the driver's back. Then he made him lie next to the passenger. A pickup truck came down the street; he closed the door to shut off the dome light. The two men on the ground were hidden from the road by their car, and the truck went by without stopping.

I got up and peeked around the bushes at the convenience store. The clerk was still behind the counter, watching the street, no doubt trying to figure out what had happened. I went back and searched both men from their necks to their ankles, following McSorley's instructions. The passenger had a cell phone, which McSorley told me to keep, and there were credit cards and drivers' licenses identifying them as being from Minnesota. I found a knife in a scabbard strapped to the driver's calf. When I showed it to McSorley, he kicked the man hard in the groin. The driver groaned, then vomited.

On McSorley's instructions I opened the trunk and found two overnight bags with clothes, a wooden box filled with steel chain, and another bag with two rolls of duct tape and two pairs of work gloves. He glanced at the stuff and said, "The chain and the tape were probably for us." I shuddered, the gun practically vibrating in my hand. He told me to use the duct tape to gag and bind the two men. Then we put both of them in the trunk after moving everything else to the backseat.

"I'll drive this car," said McSorley. "You drive the DeSoto. Go back toward the interstate and turn off at a road that looks like it leads someplace private. I want to go deep into the woods."

"What are we going to do?" I asked.

"Try to find out who they work for."

We drove back toward the interstate, passed underneath it, then went about another mile until I saw a dirt lane. I killed the headlights and turned in, continuing under the illumination of a three-quarter moon. I made another turn down a firebreak and drove far into the woods before I stopped. McSorley pulled up and immediately opened the trunk and pulled our passengers into a sitting position with their legs dangling over the rear bumper. Then he took the baseball bat.

"How did Naomi Singer die?" he asked, hefting the bat. "Remind me."

I swallowed. "She was beaten to death with a bat."

He nodded. "It's a lousy way to go. We once found this guy under the Grand Concourse. He'd been worked over with a Louisville Slugger so bad you could have poured him into a hatbox." With that he suddenly swung the bat and cracked the driver just below his left knee. The man's body levitated with pain and the back of his head struck the inside of the trunk with force. Even with the duct tape across his mouth, the scream was quite audible.

The passenger didn't react. He sat there, stock-still. His eyes showed no fear whatsoever. There was no question that we were dealing with professionals who could kill an old woman without hesitation. I thought about Naomi and I stopped shaking. I wanted McSorley to hit the passenger. He did, in the same place, with the same result. Then he hit the driver again, this time on the right shin, and then the passenger, on the right shin. The rear of the car bounced up and down with their writhing.

"That was by way of introduction," he said, his tone matter-of-fact. "My name is Joseph F. X. McSorley, and I like baseball. Do you fellas like baseball? You look like a couple of baseball fans to me. When I was young we played a lot of baseball with fellas like you, and I liked it a lot. What we're going to do right here, right now, is have an Old Timer's Game. And since I'm the only Old Timer, I get to pitch *and* hit. I pitch questions, see? And when I don't like the answers, I hit." He ran his hand slowly up and down the bat and his voice turned ominous. "And I'm going to keep hitting until I know everything I want to know, starting with your mothers' maiden names—their *real* maiden names. If what I hear doesn't sound like a real maiden name, I hit." He looked at the driver. "It's the first inning, fella. When my friend here takes the tape off your mouth, I want to hear it: first, middle, last. If I don't like the answer, it's a hit. If I like the answer, then I'll throw another pitch. If you hesitate, that means you're stupid or you're going to lie. That's the two kinds of people I hate most—stupid people and liars. Either way, I hit. Now, nod if you understand the rules."

The driver nodded. McSorley gestured to me to remove the tape.

"Alice Marie Higgins," said the man.

McSorley swung the bat. *Crack!* The man screamed and the car bounced. "That's an Irish name," said McSorley. "What's her real name?"

"Alice Marie Higgins!" screamed the driver.

"You're Irish?" said McSorley. "Now that makes me *real* mad." He swung the bat. *Crack!* The man screamed again. Tears flowed down his face. He was lying down in the trunk now, his legs still over the lip. "Sit him up!" ordered McSorley. I pulled him into the sitting position. "Here we go. You hesitate, you get hit. Got it?" The driver nodded vigorously. "What's your Social Security number?"

"Seven-one-three-four-two-eight-nine-three-two."

"Faster! Place of birth?"

"Milwaukee."

"*Faster!* Date of birth?"

"January 3, 1964."

"Real name."

Hesitation. McSorley swung the bat. More screams. "Pull him up again." I pulled him up.

"Michael Alan Shea! Michael Alan Shea!"

"Did you kill Naomi Singer?"

Hesitation. McSorley raised the bat. "Yes!"

McSorley hit him. A long wail came out of the man's mouth. "That's for hesitating," said McSorley. "Did you kill Martin Green?"

"No," said the man, gasping for air. "Just Singer."

"Who killed him?"

"I don't know," the man said, sobbing. "There are others we don't know." McSorley raised the bat. "*I swear!*" he bawled. "We were told to do her and get any records in the place, anything with writing on it. That's what we did."

"What did you do with the stuff you took?"

"We burned it. That's what we were told . . . *Ohhh, fuck!* It . . . hurts . . . Jesus!"

Another swing of the bat. It didn't produce the same sound as before, more squish than clunk, and the man fainted. "Don't take the Lord's name in vain," said McSorley. "Put the tape back on his mouth."

I did as ordered and he moved to the passenger. "How do you want to do it?" he asked. "The hard way?" The man shook his head. "You sure?" The man nodded. "Same rules," said McSorley. "Only this time, I don't hit singles, I go for the fences, understand?" More nods. "Take off the tape," he told me. I pulled it off; the passenger took a deep breath.

"Name?"

"Hector Espinosa."

"Social Security number?"

The man responded instantly.

"Did you kill Naomi Singer?"

"Yes."

"Did you kill Martin Green?"

"No. Like he said, just Singer."

"How did you follow us?"

"A transmitter under your bumper. The receiver's under our seat."

"How'd it get there?"

"We put it on down in Miami."

"How did you know we'd be in Miami?"

"We got a call. We got told to go and wait. We waited two days, then we got another call. We got an address and what your car looked like. We were there when you got there."

"Who called you?"

"I don't know." McSorley swung the bat. The man screamed and fell backward; his head hit the trunk.

"Sit him up!" I pulled the man forward. He'd bitten his tongue; blood flowed from his mouth and down his chin. He spit more blood onto his pants. "*I don't know!*" the man cried. "We got hired by phone. We got told what to do by phone. We never had anybody to call. There was only a voice on the phone talking through one of them voice-disguisers that makes it sound like it's coming from a tunnel or something."

"Give me a name of someone else involved in this."

An agonized Espinosa looked at him. He was close to fainting himself and could barely speak for all the blood. "You can beat me till I'm dead," he blubbered, "but you're gonna get the same answer. I got hired by phone. I went to a place and picked up cash and I met Shea. We didn't even know each other. He got hired like me. We got sent to Brooklyn for the Singer thing. And we got sent to Miami to wait, then follow you. That's the whole story."

"Were you going to kill us?" I asked.

Espinosa shook his head. "We were supposed to follow you and wait for new orders."

"Lay back," said McSorley. Espinosa did as ordered. "Wake the other one," he told me. I shook Shea repeatedly for several minutes until he opened his eyes, then sat him up. "Can you hear me?" McSorley asked. Shea nodded dully, his eyes clouded by the pain. "Your pal Espinosa talked while you were off in dreamland. Now I know who you're working for. I'm going to give you one chance to give me the same answer. If I get a different answer I'm going to start working on your elbows, understand?" Shea's eyes opened wide. The look on his face was pure terror. "Take off the tape," McSorley told me.

As soon as the tape was off, he was talking. "I don't know!" he whimpered. "I got a call. He said he got a call. We never called anybody. It was just a crazy voice on the phone . . . *Dammit!* There's no name! I don't care what he said! *There's no name!*"

"Sit the other one up," McSorley ordered. It seemed likely that he was going to kill both men. At that moment I don't think I would have tried to stop him. "Give me those drivers' licenses," he said to me. I gave him the Minnesota licenses bearing phony names but real photos of Shea and Espinosa. He wiped them clean with a handkerchief, then turned Shea sideways and pressed his thumb against the plastic-covered license, expertly getting a print. He did the same with Espinosa, then rolled the licenses carefully into his handkerchief.

"What now?" I asked.

"Give me that phone you took from them," he said.

I retrieved it from the DeSoto. "What are you going to do?"

"Tape a confession," he said, turning to the men. "I'm going to ask you some questions about the Singer thing," he told them, "one at a time. You're going to answer real quick just like before, or we play some more baseball, understand?" The killers nodded vigorously. "You know how to use that thing?" he asked me.

"Yes," I said. He told me a phone number that I recognized as his own in Arizona. I dialed and listened. An answering machine came on: *This is Joseph F. X. McSorley. Please leave a message.* I heard the beep and handed him the phone.

"This is Joseph F. X. McSorley," he said. "I'm a former detective with the New York Police Department and I'm interviewing two men about the murder of Miss Naomi Singer of Brooklyn, New York." He placed the phone next to Shea's mouth. "What's your name?" he asked.

"Michael Alan Shea," came the instant reply.

"Did you kill Naomi Singer in Brooklyn?"

"Yes."

"Who was with you?"

"Hector Espinosa."

McSorley fired more questions: how they were hired, paid, and traveled to Brooklyn. He elicited details of the murder that only the killers—and police—would know,

including a description of the apartment, Singer's clothing, the approximate number of times she was struck
about the head and body. Question, answer; question,
answer. It took about three minutes. Then he did the
same thing with Espinosa, getting more details, including a description of the gilt-edged diaries that they took
and burned. When it was finished McSorley spoke into
the phone again: "That concludes this interview," he
said, and handed me back the phone.

"I got your names," he told them. "I got your pictures, your fingerprints, and your taped confessions. I'm
giving all this stuff to a lawyer. If I die, the lawyer gives it
to the police. If my friend dies, the lawyer gives it to the
police. Understand?"

"Yeah," said Espinosa.

"Okay," said Shea.

"You keep your mouths shut and disappear, you're
only going to have to deal with your maker when your
time comes, got it?"

Both men stared at him in surprise. "You gonna let us
go?" asked Espinosa.

"It's your lucky day," replied McSorley. "I'm seventy-
six. What you've got to hope for is that I live to be a
hundred."

I crawled under the DeSoto and found the transmitter. McSorley threw it into the woods when we drove
off. "Are we really going to let them go?" I asked.

He shook his head. "We'll deal with them later."

By the time we returned to the interstate the adrenaline rush was over and the unreality of the last hour began to sink in. I looked down and realized my hands
were trembling. Had he noticed? He was sitting for-

ward, peering through the windshield with his hands in the prescribed ten-and-two position on the wheel. He seemed calm.

"That was a good idea, using your answering machine," I said.

"I saw that on a TV show. I hope that gadget got it all."

"I'm sure it did."

He looked over. "Philip . . ."

"Uh-huh?"

"Just to be safe, better write their names down. My memory isn't what it used to be."

17

I WAS FLOATING IN THAT haze marking the boundary of consciousness, watching a video projected by my own anxiety. When the image of Shea appeared to the sound-track of wood on bone, the spasm jarred me awake. The DeSoto was parked and I was alone. I could see the branches of an oak tree hung with Spanish moss, and smell saltwater tinged with something sweet. Soon, my breathing began to slow. The time machine was safe, impervious to monsters, and I was so tired.

There was the sound of footsteps and then McSorley's face was in the window. "You're up," he said. A second face appeared over his shoulder, another senior citizen, deeply tanned and wearing a baseball cap that said SEA PINES. "This is Lou Brickman," said McSorley.

"Welcome to Hilton Head," said Lou, extending a hand through the window. "You look like crap."

"Lou was on the job with me," said McSorley, as if to validate Lou's judgment.

"Philip Barkley," I croaked, shaking Lou's hand. I looked questioningly at McSorley.

"We need to change cars," he explained. "Lou is giving us his. The DeSoto is staying here."

Lou opened the door and I struggled to a standing position. We were parked in a driveway in front of a two-story, wood-framed house. There were similar houses on both sides and across the tree-shaded street. Lou led the way inside to a living room that was empty save for two canvas beach chairs. "We just closed two weeks ago," he explained. "Sold our place in Florida. I'm up here dealing with painters and a carpet guy."

"It's a nice house," I said.

"Fabulous golf," said Lou. "You guys can relax while I go out and get some food. We've got a couple of inflatable mattresses set up in the bedrooms, too. There's some juice in the refrigerator and glasses in the cabinet."

Lou left us in the kitchen. McSorley poured two glasses of orange juice and handed me one. "How are you doing?" he asked.

"Fine. Are we okay here? Whoever hired our baseball friends is probably looking for us."

"They don't know we're here," he replied. He drank his juice and set his glass on the counter. "But they knew we were going to Miami." He looked at me questioningly.

"I told Susan, that's all."

"Who's Susan?"

"She's a friend in Washington. That's the call I made when we left Esther's."

"Did she know that we were going to see Esther?"

"Yeah, I called her when we were leaving Phoenix."

"Do you think she told anyone?"

"No . . . I don't know."

He frowned. "How good a friend is she, Philip?"

"I trust her."

"What does Susan do?"

"She's a researcher for a marketing company, mostly out of her home. She's got a computer and access to all kinds of databases. I asked her to help me find Sonia."

"How long have you known her?"

"A couple of hours," I replied. He blinked in surprise. I described the meeting at the cemetery and our impromptu lunch date.

McSorley walked to the window and peered out at the backyard. "Was this after you got involved in this case?" he asked.

"Yes."

"Maybe the meeting at the cemetery was a setup."

"No, I approached her." I was feeling defensive; my response was automatic. *Did* I approach her? Or did she position herself in my path? I tried to reconstruct the scene in my mind.

"Philip, she's the only one who knew about Esther, unless she told someone else. Either way . . ."

"Maybe we were followed from Arizona."

"It doesn't figure, but who knew you were coming to see me?"

"Susan."

"Who else?"

"Just her," I admitted.

"Whose phone did you use when you told her?"

"I was in a phone booth." The logic closed in, pressing on my chest. Susan was one of the few good things going on in my life, maybe the only one. "What if her line was tapped?" I said. "Someone could've been listening."

"Why would her line be tapped?"

"I was in my hotel room when I first called her from

New York. Whoever was following me could have gotten the phone records."

"It's possible . . ."

"But?"

"But we're not going to bet our lives on it, right?"

My heart sank. "No . . . no, we're not."

"Good. What else did you tell her?"

"That we were coming back to Washington."

He grimaced. "This is going to make it a lot harder."

"Maybe now's the time to go to Justice. We've got a story to tell."

He pushed his empty glass slowly along the counter with his finger. "We'd have to tell the *whole* story. That would be the end of our investigation."

"No question about it."

"What do you think would happen then?" he asked.

"I don't know. The last thing they'd want is to reopen the Green case, but if they had to, they'd opt for the most expedient solution possible."

"And the FBI is going to handle it. That means your FBI lady, and we don't know where she stands in this thing."

"We don't know where *anybody* stands."

"Look," he said, "I think we're the best chance for catching some murderers. What do you think?"

"We're the best chance," I admitted.

"And it's *our* case. I've been living with it since 1955. That gives me seniority and now you're my partner. So, let's get some sleep and leave tonight. When the sun comes up tomorrow we'll be in Washington. What do you say?"

A bad dream, I said to myself, a bad dream. But what I said to him was, "Okay."

"Good. I'm going to get some sleep." He started toward the bedrooms, then turned. "One more thing," he said.

"What?"

"We're going to stay away from Susan, right?"

"Yeah, we're staying away from Susan."

"Okay. You should get some sleep, too."

"I want to make a phone call when the government offices open."

"Who to?"

"Someone who can get us access to those Banking Committee files that Green wanted."

"This is someone you can trust?"

"Right."

"Uh-huh. How long have you known this one?"

"About twenty minutes."

McSorley looked at the floor and sighed. "Washington is a heckuva place," he said softly, then left.

I called the main number for the Intelligence Committee promptly at nine. It was Jenny Castellano who answered the phone.

"Jenny, I don't know if you remember me. This is Philip Barkley. We talked—"

"I remember."

"Can you talk now? Is there anyone around?"

"I'm the first one in."

"Do you remember telling me that you helped Martin get materials for the paper he was writing?"

"Uh-huh, the files at the National Archives. He wanted to see them again."

"Could I see a copy of what you gave him?"

"The newspaper said you weren't working on the investigation anymore. It said you left the Justice Department."

"That's true, Jenny, but I'm still investigating."

"Mr. Barkley, do you believe what they're saying about Martin?"

"No, that's why I'm calling you for help."

"I don't believe he killed himself."

"Why do you say that, Jenny?"

"There's just no way," she replied.

No way. She knew Martin and that was enough, end of story. It was sweet and innocent, and after all my running around, if we had to go to court right then, I couldn't do any better. Ladies and gentlemen of the jury: no way; there's just no way.

"Well, I want to prove what really happened," I told her. "Will you help me?"

There was a moment of silence while she thought about it. "I'd have to go over to Banking and look on the computer, or ask someone else to do it."

"Jenny, this is important: don't ask anyone. If you can't get the list yourself we'll have to think of something else." We arranged that she would try after work and I would call her the next morning from a place with a fax machine.

"Everybody misses Martin so much," she said.

"I'm sure they do."

"Mrs. Young was standing by his desk yesterday, just staring at it. I told her it was terrible."

"What did she say?"

"Nothing. She just nodded, that's all."

We arrived in northern Virginia the next morning in Lou's 1997 Oldsmobile. I phoned Jenny from a twenty-four-hour copying center. She had come through. "The list's not that long," she said.

"It's not?"

"Martin wasn't one of the regular researchers. He helped the senators prepare for hearings and deal with all the interest groups." With the encounter of two nights before still fresh in mind, I made her promise yet one more time to keep our arrangement confidential. The fax machine eked out two double-spaced pages and soon we were on our way, doing forty-five miles an hour on the Beltway, heading for the National Archives in College Park.

As with the FBI, my Justice ID cut no ice at the National Archives. The pleasant woman behind the desk pointed us toward the computer stations along the wall where we were supposed to register electronically. Using a false name wasn't an option; the next step required our drivers' licenses. Biding for time, I made a joke about Big Brother watching over the research. Apparently, similar concerns were routinely expressed by those who rooted around in the government's closet. The woman quickly assured me that other agencies would not have access to my record.

McSorley and I were registered, photographed, and issued "Research Cards" with our pictures imposed on the Preamble to the Constitution. We went upstairs to the Textual Research Room and filled out request forms using the first group of file numbers from Green's list, just making the scheduled ten-thirty "pull time." By eleven-fifteen we were seated at a table with a steel cart loaded with twenty gray boxes of files.

I'd spent time in the archives when I worked at the White House and there was something special, almost magical, about documents that might not have been read or touched for generations: onion skins, carbon copies, and originals impregnated with the inornate Courier font of the manual typewriter. And these were extraordinary documents, the administration of history's greatest upheaval and its aftermath, and notwithstanding the leaden government prose and the urgency of our mission, it was impossible not to become engrossed in their contents.

Some boxes were files of the Foreign Economic Administration pertaining to German and Swiss banking activities during the war. Early on, the role of the Swiss as bankers and money-launderers for the Nazis was understood. They exchanged francs for gold plundered from the central banks of occupied countries, enabling the Nazis to purchase war materials from neutral states. After the war there was an attempted reckoning that required tracing plundered gold and national treasures. But all of this had to occur in the context of rebuilding the war-torn economies of Europe, and these same Swiss banks, their coffers engorged from years of profitable neutrality, had an important role to play. This considerably dampened the Allies' appetite for hard-bargaining with the Swiss, and they settled for the return of a small percentage of the looted gold.

Other boxes contained more pertinent records: the efforts of Jewish organizations and individuals to force the Swiss to account for so-called heirless assets. The Allies were focused on other matters and provided no more than moral support, and so the files documented frustrated attempts to recover bank deposits and insurance policies of relatives who died in concentration camps.

After three hours we were famished. We had to wait for the next delivery of boxes so we decided to stretch our legs and get some lunch. We left the building and drove to a bar with lots of televisions, near the University of Maryland. McSorley brightened with the prospect of a hamburger and a few innings of baseball. The waitress brought us two beers and took our order. "How long till we get a ball game?" he asked.

"Orioles and Yanks tonight," she said. "Mussina's back in town. That SOB broke my heart. *I* could break into the O's rotation this year."

McSorley was sympathetic. "You've got to have pitching," he said. "Any afternoon games on at all?" She promised to check with the bartender.

"That was pretty interesting stuff in those files," he said.

That was my cue to voice the latest doubt rattling around inside my head. "What if Green really was working on a course paper? Maybe the connection to Sonia Denes has nothing to do with those files."

He waved it off. "Nope, you've got it pegged, don't worry. It's just going to take a little time. This is what being a detective is all about: telephone calls, knocking on doors, wading through paper."

I smiled. "And every now and then, a little baseball."

"Every now and then," he agreed.

The food came but I was too preoccupied to really taste it. I told myself that the theory really did make sense, and unless Green managed to get the documents out of the building we were on the verge of finding the key. Lost in thought, I was startled by McSorley's tone when he said, "Get up and walk to the car."

"What?"

"Don't rush, just walk naturally. I'll take care of the bill."

I kept my eyes riveted on him. "What's wrong?"

"Just go. Keep your head turned toward the window and go. Do it now." His gaze was fixed on something over my shoulder. "Jesus," he whispered.

I followed instructions, resisting the urge to look around. I went directly to the Oldsmobile and slouched in the passenger's seat, shielding my face with one hand while I waited. A few minutes later McSorley walked nonchalantly out of the bar, but his eyes darted left and right as he approached and got in the car.

"What the hell is it?"

"Your picture was on television."

"Why?"

"Esther Müller is dead."

"*What? Oh, no!*"

"She was strangled in her apartment."

There was a sudden tingling sensation in my hands and arms, followed by dizziness and palpitations. I couldn't get any air. I tried to take deep breaths but the car was smothering me and I knew that I'd die if I didn't get out. McSorley was already backing up but I fumbled with the door and pushed it open, half-falling into the parking lot. He stopped the car, jumped out, and ran around to my side. "What is it?" he asked nervously. I couldn't answer; I just circled him, sucking air. "Is it your heart?" I shook my head. "Are you on medication?"

"Give me a minute!" I gasped.

"We can't be standing around out here!" he said, his voice low and urgent. He yanked open the rear door and pushed me onto the seat; I curled up and shut my eyes tight. A few seconds later we were moving again. "Philip! Can you hear me? Do you need a doctor?"

"No doctor," I mumbled. I tried to slow my breathing, fighting for control as the car turned and accelerated. Why Esther? Why now? I was so dazed I almost forgot why I fled the bar. I raised my head. "My picture?" I croaked.

McSorley answered without taking his eyes off the road. "Yeah," he said bitterly. "Everybody's looking for us."

I wasn't sure how long we'd been driving when the car left the highway and made a series of turns, then stopped. The attack was subsiding but I was nauseous and soaked with perspiration. "We're at a motel, by the back fence," he said. "I'm going to get us a room. Are you okay?"

"Go ahead," I mumbled.

"You're sure you don't need a doctor?"

"Yes."

As soon as we got in the room McSorley turned on the TV and began flipping through the channels for news. Still nauseous, I went into the bathroom, struggled out of my clothes, and got into the shower. I rested my head against the tile and let the water pelt my neck. Esther Müller was dead. I went to Arizona, a man opened a notebook, and now she was dead. Another funeral. I sank into the tub and lay curled up under the spray until another wave of nausea hit. I leaned out of the tub and vomited into the toilet, retching until I was empty.

McSorley knocked on the door. "Philip, are you okay?"

"I'm okay." I struggled to my feet, finished shower-ing, and went back into the bedroom wrapped in a towel. The television was still on. "Anything?" I asked.

"They've got a picture of you and a lousy drawing of me. I'm an unidentified white male."

"What did they say?"

"We're wanted for questioning and we could be in the Washington area. You know the rest."

I sat on the edge of the bed and rested my head in my hands. "They're going to kill everyone who knows any-thing about this."

"No question."

"Susan could be the next victim."

"Unless she's one of them," he warned.

"I don't think so."

"But you're not sure."

"Right! When will we be sure? When we see her pic-ture on television?"

He held up a hand. "All right, take it easy. Let's try to find out if her line is tapped."

"How?"

"See if someone got your phone records from the ho-tel." He used Espinosa's cell phone to call the Lancaster, claiming to be an FBI supervisor working on the Green matter. The desk clerk gave him the number of the ho-tel's management. It took a little while, but he finally reached a woman who said that a copy of the bill had been sent to Mr. Barkley.

"To me?"

"Your office said you needed it for your expense re-port. She faxed it herself."

"That proves it! They found out about Susan and tapped her phone."

"Maybe," he replied. A methodical approach had served him all his life; he wasn't going to be rushed into anything stupid. I stared anxiously at the television, half-expecting to see Susan's picture at any moment, while he considered the matter further. Finally, he said, "If her phone is tapped, they could be keeping an eye on her, too. They probably are."

"She's under surveillance?"

McSorley nodded. "*If* she's not one of them."

"Then all we've got to do is spot them and we'll know!"

"Without getting ourselves killed."

"And then we can sneak her out of there."

"Without getting ourselves killed," he repeated. "And if we pull *that* off, we have to hope we haven't missed anything or—"

"I know: we'll get ourselves killed."

"I thought this case was hard fifty years ago," he said, shaking his head. "I had no idea . . . You said you were at her place once before. What's the layout?"

"It's an L-shaped building tucked into a kind of natural bowl near Alexandria. There's a parking lot in front and a ridge that runs along one side and around the back. There are trees all around."

"That could work for us. Look, if there's a stakeout I'll spot it, don't worry. And if she's being watched we'll find a way to get her out of there. What you've got to figure out is how to contact her, because we can't call and a letter would be a little slow."

A letter. "Not mail, *e-mail*," I told him. "I have her e-mail address and you've got an e-mail account. We'll send an e-mail telling her to call us on Espinosa's cell phone. No one will know where we are, including her."

"Okay, that works for me, but tell her to call us at nine this evening."

"Why so late?" I asked.

"We want to look for the surveillance before we're expected. Otherwise, it could be *her* friends waiting *for us*."

"Good point."

"And if we're going out you need a disguise."

We drove to a nearby pharmacy where he bought a Washington Redskins hat, sunglasses, and bandages that covered my nose and left cheek from chin to ear. "All a smart stick-up guy ever needed," he told me, and it worked. The next stop was one of those Internet cafés near the university, where we sent an e-mail entitled, "Message from Philip." The first part done, we bought two pair of binoculars at a sporting goods store and returned to the motel to wait.

McSorley placed a chair under the doorknob and closed the blinds. At six o'clock I turned on the television to watch the local news. The lead was a car-bus collision in downtown Washington. Then my picture appeared behind the news anchor. *The search has widened for a former White House and Senate lawyer wanted for questioning in connection with a murder in Miami.*

"I've got you into one hell of a mess," I said to McSorley.

"Yup," he replied absently. He removed two guns from his bag and set them on the night table between us.

"You don't look scared," I said.

"Sure I am."

"No, I don't think so."

"Well, I've got an advantage on you," he said.

"What?"

"I've been to the end of the line. Everything looks different now."

"Joe, just because you're seventy-six doesn't mean—"

"It's got nothing to do with age." He sat down on the bed and began untying his shoes. "You know, a few weeks ago I was in my living room, just standing at the window. It was another one of those sunny days and no one was out there, nothing was moving . . ." His voice trailed off.

"And?"

"And I was daydreaming that the doorbell rang and it was Eisenhower."

"President Eisenhower?"

"General Eisenhower, then. And he looked me up and down and said, 'It's time to go.' "

"Go where?"

"It was D-Day, and I was young again. My legs were strong, my arms were strong, and I was going to get my equipment and join the boys in my platoon. They were waiting for McSorley."

"That's quite a dream."

He stretched out on the bed and spoke to the ceiling. "Even knowing what I know now, I would have gone."

"I understand."

He smiled. "And a few weeks later the bell *does* ring! A young fella on a mission."

"I'm afraid I'm no Eisenhower."

"Well, I'm not the young McSorley, either." We both laughed, then he turned serious. "We'll just have to do the best we can."

I rolled onto my back again and began to think about our plan. It seemed straightforward just two hours before. "Joe?"

"Umm?"

"What happens if there's no one watching her building? Do we get her out or just leave her behind?"

"Let's cross that bridge when we come to it."

"It may come down to a gut thing."

"That's right," he agreed, "a gut thing."

"Okay."

"Philip?"

"What?"

"If the time comes to use those guns, I won't hesitate. You shouldn't either."

"Okay."

Soon, the only sound was his regular breathing. He'd waded ashore almost sixty years before and never really stopped. There were different battles on different terrain against different enemies, not all of them to his front. Corporal Joseph F. X. McSorley had done his bit, that and more. He should have been on a porch somewhere, reading his newspaper or fretting about crabgrass while Eileen pasted pictures of the grandchildren in the family album. But Eileen was gone, and there was no porch and no grandchildren. He was back where he started, an enlisted man. General Barkley and his senior-citizen army of one.

"This is a hell of a situation, isn't it?" I said quietly, more to myself than to him.

He didn't open his eyes when he replied. "No one ever said being a crusader was easy."

———

It was seven-fifteen and still light enough for surveillance when we drove past the driveway leading to Susan's building. "This is the acid test," said McSorley.

On the other side of the wooded ridge bordering the

eastern end of the property was a four-story office building. We parked, entered the woods, and climbed to a
spot just below the top of the ridge and peeked over. We
had a good view of the parking lot below. While McSorley scanned the cars with his binoculars, I took mine and
worked my way around to the back of the building.
There was a loading dock with an overhead door that
was closed, and a ramp leading to a rear entrance to the
lobby. I watched for twenty minutes, then went back to
McSorley. "There's a rear door," I told him, "and everything looks good. We could pick Susan up there when
she comes down the elevator. Have you seen anything?"

"There's no one in the cars," he said, "but look at
that van way back there." I focused my binoculars on a
Chevy van with dark-tinted windows. It was backed into
a spot at the far corner of the lot, abutting the woods
that marked the western boundary of the property.
"There could be a couple of guys in the back watching
the building," he explained. "They could slip out the
back door and into the woods to change teams."

"So, what do we do?"

"We wait until we know whether someone else is
watching or we can't wait anymore. Then it's decision
time."

We spent the next forty-five minutes scanning the
parking lot and checking the van for signs of life. I fretted about Susan the whole time. Then McSorley tapped
me and pointed at the van. I didn't see anything. "Use
your binoculars," he said.

Something had changed. "The window!" I whispered
excitedly. The front passenger window had been closed.
Now, it was open about two inches.

"Yup, it's getting stuffy in there."

"What do we do?"

"We wait an hour and hope she got the e-mail."

It was nine o'clock and quite dark when the phone rang. "Hello?"

"Philip?"

"Yes, it's me, Susan."

"Thank God," she muttered. "They're looking for you . . . Philip?"

"I'm here."

"They're looking for you. That woman in Miami."

"I know."

"I didn't know what to do. I thought about calling the police to tell them you didn't do anything, but I wasn't sure if it was the right thing to do."

"Good. Where are you now?"

"I'm using the public phone in the lobby of my building. Why couldn't I use my own phone?"

"This is hard to explain but I think your telephone is tapped."

"Tapped? . . . Why would *my* telephone be tapped?"

"There were people following me in New York. They got the record of my telephone calls from my hotel. They probably tapped your phone and heard me tell you about Esther Müller."

Her voice became taut. "What are you saying? That woman is dead because of our call?"

"It's my fault. I was careless."

"Oh, God, that poor woman . . ."

"There's something else."

"What?"

"I think there are people watching your building." That was met by silence. "I don't think you're in any

danger but it would probably be better if we took precautions."

"Why would I be in danger? I don't really know anything."

"The people that were following me can't be sure of
that."

"Philip, if you're trying to scare me you're doing a
good job!"

"I'm sorry, Susan. I've made a lot of mistakes."

There was another moment of silence before she gathered herself. "What kind of precautions?"

"How would you feel about leaving your place for a
while?"

"Leaving? When?"

"Uh, right now."

"Now? To go where?"

"I'm not sure but you can't stay there."

"I'm dreaming, right? This is all a dream."

"I'm really sorry, Susan."

"It's not your fault, Philip. I know how terrible you
must feel." The confidence returned to her voice. "Okay,
just let me think . . . I have a key to a weekend place in
Annapolis. It belongs to friends who are away."

"Where are they?"

"In South America, a two-year assignment for the
World Bank. I'm invited to use the place but I don't go
out there very much."

"That would be great. Go upstairs, pack enough
clothes for a week, and I'll call you when we're ready to
pick you up. Can you manage a suitcase?"

"I'll manage."

"What I'm going to do is call your phone number and

hang up after one ring. That's your signal to come down-stairs, okay? Just go right to the back door. I'll be wait-ing there."

"I feel like Mata Hari."

"If something goes wrong I won't call but you'll get an e-mail tomorrow."

McSorley and I slipped out of our own surveillance spot and made our way through the trees back to the car. "You lie in the backseat," he instructed, "and I'll drive in and go behind the building. It'll be one guy in a car. If everything still looks good, you'll call her."

"I'm ready."

He patted my arm and said, "I'm glad it worked out."

"Never a doubt," I said, smiling. "Never a doubt."

18

BY TEN O'CLOCK WE WERE on Route 50 on the way to Annapolis. The look on Susan's face said it all: she was happy to see me, but the circumstances left a lot to be desired. The "weekend house" turned out to be a big contemporary on two acres overlooking Clements Creek, which fed the Severn River on its way to the Chesapeake Bay. It took an hour to get there and I needed every minute to explain what I'd gotten her into. She was understandably shocked by parts of my story and asked a lot of questions, but it wasn't until we were settled in the family room, having coffee, McSorley and I on a couch, Susan in her wheelchair, that she offered an opinion.

"To me, it's like a jigsaw puzzle without a picture. You can't organize the pieces. All you can do is try to fit them together two at a time."

McSorley agreed. "Throw in that we're missing some key pieces and that sums it up."

"We have a loose theory," I told her. "Martin is researching for the Banking Committee's Swiss banks inquiry and comes across something involving a Holocaust survivor named Sonia Denes. Maybe he overlooks it the first time around, or maybe it has been suppressed, but years later something brings him back to those files. Then he begins to investigate."

"Which gets him to Naomi."

"Right."

"And to the meeting with the Hungarian at the Portrait Gallery."

"That, too, although we don't know why. But Martin pieces together a story and, being Martin, is intent on exposing the truth. And that's very embarrassing, or worse, for Senator Young. We're only guessing but we think money's involved."

"I like it," she said. "It explains Warren's motive, and Constance's, too. She's in this thing up to her neck and she tries to throw sand in your eyes with that story about Martin being a spy."

"That's it," said McSorley.

Susan had the scent now and was keen to follow the clues. "All right. So, Martin has to die, and since he's involved Naomi, she has to die, too. And Esther Müller has to die because . . . why? Because you went to see her?"

I wasn't prepared to hear it put so plainly. It was a knife through my heart. "That's why," I mumbled.

"These characters want to kill anybody who knows even a piece of the story," said McSorley.

"They were going to kill you on the highway," said Susan, nodding. Her clinical tone threw me at first, but I reminded myself that she was a survivor, and that underlying toughness would have to steel her against the unavoidable inference that now she was a target, too. "I've got two questions," she said. "First, where does the FBI agent fit in?"

"That's anybody's guess," said McSorley. "She's the biggest question mark of all."

"What's the second question?" I asked.

She grinned. "When do we eat? I'm ravenous."

There weren't many people who'd be thinking about food at a time like that. A survivor, indeed. We wound up with Chinese takeout that we consumed with a bottle of Merlot from the wine cellar. Susan opened a fortune cookie that said, "Tomorrow brings big news."

"That proves it," she declared. "We're going to figure it out."

"Absolutely," I said.

"We're with you," said McSorley.

Now we were all laughing, but I was only laughing on the outside and it must have showed. "Philip, don't worry about me, okay?" she said. "I'm not sorry I got involved. In fact, I'm *glad*."

"That's what I've been telling him, too," said McSorley.

"Well," I said, "if we're going to figure it out then tomorrow's certainly the day. We've got to find a file with Sonia's name on it."

"It's going to happen," said Susan. She looked at me and affected a mock-serious tone. "Susan Edwards *always* gets her man." We all laughed but something in her eyes said she wasn't kidding. Later that night, staring at the ceiling, the usual fears gave way to a replay of that moment. I fell asleep feeling pretty good.

———————————

It happened at ten-twenty in the morning. For the record, it was the fifth box of files. I was scanning a Treasury Department memo when, without a word, McSorley placed a document on the table in front of me. It was a letter from the American embassy in Bern, dated June 23, 1955, two months after Sonia's death.

Miss Sonia Denes
1728 Morris Avenue
Bronx, New York

Dear Miss Denes:

In response to your recent correspondence, I regret to inform you that this office is unable to be of assistance. Please be assured that we are sympathetic with your attempt to locate the account allegedly established by your father with a Zurich bank. However, our diplomatic mission and resources are completely unsuited for the type of investigation necessitated by your request.

That being said, an informal, limited query by the undersigned met with no success. You may wish to review the accuracy of your information, if possible, or to undertake a more conventional inquiry. You may also wish to pursue your claim through the Swiss Compensation Office.

I regret we cannot be of further assistance. Your material is being returned herewith.

Sincerely,

Bruce L. Conway
Second Secretary of Embassy
Economic Section

Enclosure

CC: Miss Naomi Singer
Hebrew Immigrant Aid Society

425 Lafayette Street
New York City, New York

There were two envelopes attached. One had held the letter; it was addressed to Sonia and bore a stamp RETURN TO SENDER with a check in a box that said NO LONGER AT THIS ADDRESS. The other envelope was smaller and had "Enclosure" written on it. It was empty.

"Let's go through the rest of the stuff," said McSorley. We made copies of everything, then examined the remaining boxes. Knowing what we were looking for facilitated the search, but when we finished at midafternoon we'd found nothing more about Sonia's claim.

It was a quiet ride back to Annapolis as we confronted the possibility that we'd reached the end of the line. We split up in the house. Susan went directly to her bedroom. McSorley said he needed a drink and headed for the wet bar. I went out on the back porch to a wonderful view of the creek and the Severn River beyond. A good breeze had set the scenery in motion. The mast of a sailboat was rhythmically swaying side to side, as if a metronome keeping time for the creaking trees and the ripples migrating across the water. It was much like I pictured Oregon. I closed my eyes to empty my mind, succeeding to the point of being surprised by my own tears.

Behind me, the glass door slid open, then closed; McSorley appeared alongside me. "It looks like rain," he said.

"Yeah," I agreed, staring up at the sky while I tried to be inconspicuous about wiping my eyes.

"I love the rain," he said. "I should live in a place like this."

"Why did you go to Arizona?"

"Eileen was real fond of the sunshine. Wanted it every day."

"I like the rain, too. I think Oregon would be like this."

"No desert up there," he said.

"No, no desert."

The door slid open again. Susan backed her chair up to the edge of a six-inch drop to the porch. "Will one of you guys do the honors? I told my friends that if they want me to freeload off them anymore, they're just going to have to build some ramps." I eased the chair downward and pushed her up to the porch rail, which turned out to be at her eye-level. "This is going to have to go, too," she declared. She looked from me to McSorley and her smile faded. "A grim bunch," she said.

We avoided talking about our enterprise. Susan told us that she and her husband had a sloop they'd sailed on the Chesapeake, spending weekends skinny-dipping in private coves and cruising to places like St. Michaels and Oxford. She kept the boat for two years after the accident. Sometimes she'd go to Annapolis to look at it and remember. "It took a long time to sell that boat," she said, "but eventually I had to let go." She wasn't looking at me when she said it.

"Should we get at it?" asked McSorley. "We need to talk about our next move."

"If it's okay with you guys," said Susan, "I'd like to lie down for a little while before we begin. I didn't get a lot of sleep last night. I guess it was the excitement."

"Sure," I said. "I can use a little time myself."

We all retired to our bedrooms. Mine had wicker furniture and wallpaper with a floral motif. I lay on the bed and studied the patterns, a little avoidance behavior, circling but not engaging, yet drawing nearer to reality with each passing moment. From that day a lifetime ago when I'd struck out from Washington to run in circles, it had always been a decaying orbit. Inevitably, the centrifugal force would be overcome by the gravity of the situation. Now, impact was near.

A distant rumble and fading light signaled the approaching storm. Soon the flowers were only visible in lightning flashes and the room was filled with the sound of rain on leaves and water gurgling through the downspout. The darkness, the sound, the comfort of the bed, they all conspired to draw me downward, to compel a surrender to the pull.

The clock said eight-twenty when the knock came. I got up and opened the door to McSorley. "It's time to talk," he said. We went into the living room. Susan was in her chair with a blanket across her lap, wearing a black turtleneck with her hair back in a bun. When she smiled there was no warmth in her eyes. It was plain that she was anticipating surrender and intended to resist.

"Did you get in a nap?" I asked, trying to probe. "It was a good afternoon for one."

"I tried but I couldn't stop thinking about it," she said—"it" being our situation.

"I've been thinking, too," said McSorley.

"Let's focus on what we found," I said, spreading copies of the letter and envelopes on the coffee table. "Sonia believes her father established an account with a Swiss bank. He probably deposited the money when the Nazis came in, or sometime before. We know she went to a concentration camp. The parents probably did, too."

"And died there," added McSorley.

"Right, but she survives and has a claim."

"And she must have had some kind of proof," he said. "But why was her claim different? The letter says that she was asking them to do something unusual and suggested she take a conventional route."

"Maybe it was the nature of her proof," I said.

"I'd sure as heck would love to know what was in that envelope," said McSorley. "Do you think Green found it?"

"He must've. There doesn't seem to be anything in the letter to get him excited."

"If only we had it . . ." mused Susan.

"The guys who killed him could have it now," said McSorley.

"I don't think so," I said. "If they did, Esther Müller would still be alive and we wouldn't be in any danger."

"Why?"

"Because Esther was just a link in the chain that led to whatever was in that envelope. If they already had it there'd be no need to kill her—or us, for that matter— because the trail seems to go nowhere."

"That makes sense," said Susan. "So, where is it?"

"I'm sure Green had it. Who knows what happened to it after that. It's not in his apartment. The FBI turned the place upside down searching for any Intelligence Committee material. A fifty-year-old document would have gotten their attention."

"Well, what do we do next?" asked McSorley.

"We could go through every box at the archives that might have more on Sonia's claim. That would be everything the Committee looked at and maybe more."

"How long would that take?"

"Months, at least. They had a lot of help."

"We don't have time for that," he replied. "If we keep showing up we'll attract attention and eventually get recognized. And sooner or later, someone's going to notice that Susan here is missing, too."

"Maybe we can all put bandages on our faces," she said, smiling.

"We could talk to everyone who worked on the Banking Committee," said McSorley. "Maybe the name Sonia Denes would mean something to someone."

"There's also this Swiss Compensation Office," I said. "If its records are still around, maybe something could be arranged through diplomatic channels." No one said anything for a moment. "No matter which way we go from here," I added, "we're looking at a huge job."

"By 'huge job,'" said Susan, "I take it you mean something beyond the three of us."

"We've gone as far as we can go," I replied. She looked at McSorley for confirmation.

"We're only three people," he agreed.

Susan's face was a mask. "So, Philip, what now?"

"I see three choices. One is to go on with our lives like nothing's happened."

They both smiled. "What's Plan B?" asked McSorley.

"Hide out here in Annapolis forever, eating Chinese food."

"Too much MSG," said Susan. "Go to C."

"We come in from the cold. I suggest that we go to Evans's house in Chevy Chase. We've got a story to tell, and whatever anyone might want to think about Naomi's death, what happened to Esther Müller is proof that there's more to the Green case than currently known.

We'll have to trust that Evans can arrange for our safety and somehow get a real investigation going despite the AG."

"What would you tell him about Turner?" asked McSorley. "I'd feel better if they had her under wraps."

"She covered up what happened at the Alta Vista. She's got a lot to explain." I looked at both of them. "So, do I call Evans?" McSorley shrugged. I reached for the phone.

"Don't," said Susan.

"I know how you feel, Susan, but—"

She stood up from her wheelchair and the blanket fell to the floor.

The gun in her hand had a silencer.

19

IT WAS MCSORLEY WHO SPOKE first. "What the hell . . ." he muttered as he gripped the arms of his chair.

"If you try to get up," said Susan calmly, "I'll shoot you in the face." It was the same tone she used when she offered me an egg roll. That she was standing was surprise enough, but she was nearly six feet tall, and her turtleneck accented shoulders that didn't come from propelling a wheelchair. The gun remained leveled as she reached into her pocketbook for cigarettes and a lighter. She tapped the pack against its barrel, then removed a cigarette with her teeth and lit it.

"What the hell is this all about?" asked McSorley.

She blew a jet of smoke toward the ceiling, then said, "It's about being thorough, Joe. If you're sloppy, if you leave loose ends lying around, they can get picked up— tomorrow, next week, next year, even fifty years later. So, we have to be thorough."

"Those old women were no threat to you," I said.

"Thorough is as thorough does. Don't blame yourself for Naomi, by the way. That was in the works before you went to New York."

"Am I supposed to feel better?"

"No, you're still responsible for Esther"—she waved the silencer toward McSorley—"and now, poor Joe. You've kind of forced our hand on Diana, too."

"She doesn't know anything!" I cried. I started forward in my chair, planting my feet beneath me.

Susan extended her arm and I looked right down the barrel of the gun. "Stay still," she said. "Last warning."

"Why wait till now?" asked McSorley. "Why not in New York or Arizona? Or Miami, when we got there?"

She picked a piece of tobacco off her tongue, examined it, then said, "Philip here has been helping us find loose ends. It seems he's much better at it than he is at women." She looked at me and smiled. "You were thinking about it, weren't you? Getting in the sack with the paraplegic girl? Yeah, I can see it in your face." She shook her head and took another drag on her cigarette. "Anyway, the idea was to follow you to those loose ends until it was time to step in. After you left Esther in Miami the decision was made. We were going to start with you two but it didn't work out."

"So you started with Esther."

"Not ideal, but you know how old ladies like to gab, and we just couldn't let Esther share her adventure with all of Miami. Sure, I knew you'd be suspicious but I figured we'd find you sooner or later. You kind of caught me by surprise last night so it took till this evening to arrange a proper reception. And now it's time to call it a day."

"There's still the enclosure from the letter to Sonia," I said. "That may be the only loose end needed to unravel the whole thing."

"Maybe. It wouldn't be at the archives because Green would never have left it behind. We pressed him pretty hard about what he did with it, and all we got was babbling and scripture." She shook her head. "Take it from me, don't even *bother* drugging one of those devout types."

"So, tell us," I said, "what was in the envelope?"

"That's *the* question, isn't it? Don't ask me. My employer keeps things strictly need-to-know. I don't even know what the hell this whole thing is about." She affected a what-the-heck smile. "But it must be pretty important because it cost a lot of money."

"It cost a lot of *lives*," I replied.

She shrugged. "Whatever."

"Who is your employer?" asked McSorley. "You might as well tell us."

"A fair question," said Susan, tapping the silencer against her cheek. "The problem, I'm afraid, is that I don't know that, either." She looked at me and added, "I really don't. I'm just the general contractor, hired for a job. I got money, a briefing, and instructions, all without meeting anyone. I brought in subcontractors and it went from there. Strictly professional."

McSorley snorted and said, "It always turned my stomach to hear your type call yourselves professionals—'contractor,' 'subcontractor,' like you're real businessmen. You're just low-life scum and cowards, that's all."

Susan pretended to pout. "I respect our senior citizens, Joe, but don't push it, okay? There's lots of ways to die, and all at once is better."

"I've got a question you *can* answer," I said. "How did you find Green?"

"We never lost him. We were supposed to stay close until we got new orders. I guess it made sense, didn't it?

The pressure builds: big manhunt, lots of newspaper stories. Plenty of reasons to kill yourself." She looked out
the window. "It's dark and the neighbors are all settled
in for the evening. Time for a walk. We've got some
friends waiting out there in the woods, that reception I
told you about."

"Where are we going?"

"We're taking a short boat ride to the middle of the
bay." She stepped back and waved the gun toward the
door. "Let's go, fellas. Don't worry about the mess, I'll
clean up later."

We went through the front door and into the dusk.
The trees around the house had been cleared for landscaping; the woods fifty yards away were barely visible
in the gloom. With McSorley on my right and Susan behind us, we began walking across the lawn when a figure
emerged from the woods ahead. Susan ordered us to
stop. "Here comes our escort," she said, pressing the
gun into my back. "If you try to run, Philip, I'll paralyze
you."

"You're going to drown us anyway."

The figure got closer. I recognized the walk before I
could make out any features. My heart sank and I
groaned. "Shut up," ordered Susan. "Don't go out like a
wuss."

She stopped about forty feet away, just close enough
to see her face. Her arms hung loosely at her sides but
her right hand was slightly behind her.

Behind me, Susan muttered "What the hell . . ."

"*FBI, Julia!*" called Blair. "Let your gun fall to the
ground and step away from it."

In one motion, Susan stepped behind me and struck

McSorley behind the ear with the barrel of the silencer. He collapsed into a heap.

Blair didn't move. "There's no way out of here," she said. "The others are already in custody and there are agents on all sides."

Susan's face was right next to mine. Her teeth were bared like a wolf's and the silencer was pressed under my jaw. Out of the corner of my eye I could see a red dot playing across her forehead. "Philip and I have a date!" she spat. "We're running late, so be a good girl and fetch the car, will you?"

Blair shook her head. "There are snipers in the trees. They can kill you right now."

"I've got all the slack out of this trigger!" yelled Susan, loud enough for the snipers to hear. "If I'm shot, Philip is going to blow his top, he really will. So, get the car or I'll kill him now!"

"Go ahead," said Blair. "He's been a pain in the ass anyway."

"Hey, FBI girl, read your manual! I've got a hostage here and I'm going to kill him if I don't get a car!"

Blair shrugged.

Susan whispered in my ear: "You know, I've already been paid. The professional thing is to do you right here."

"I'll see they get a refund. Just tell me who they are."

Susan's eyes were darting left and right. "I already told you," she said, biting off the words, "I don't know."

"Give up, Julia," called Blair. "What's the point of dying here?"

Susan snickered and said, "What do you think, Philip? Can I drop the FBI girl before they drop me?"

"She'll kill you, Susan."

She grunted. "Isn't this *a bitch*? Two women in a gun-fight over a guy who hasn't fucked either one. I guess the only question is whether I waste a bullet on you first."

"One final act of mercy may get you into heaven."

"I'm not going to heaven, Philip." Now there were three red dots clustered on her face. "I'm definitely not going to heaven."

Nothing happened for a few seconds that seemed an eternity. We were frozen in that bizarre tableau, as if someone had hit the Pause button. Then a sudden breeze stirred Blair's hair, a signal that Play had been pushed again. Susan took a deep breath as her grip tightened on my shirt. "What the hell," she muttered, "one act of mercy."

It happened so fast the snipers didn't have a chance to react. Susan yanked me to the left as she crouched and swung her gun toward Blair. As I fell I could see Blair's right arm swing upward. The blast from her gun covered the spit of Susan's silencer. I landed on a stump that knocked the wind out of me and instinctively covered up.

Silence. I raised my head and looked around. Susan was on her back, staring at the sky. There was a dark spot just below her left eye. I rolled onto my knees and struggled for air.

Then Blair was crouching beside me. She was wearing body armor and still holding her gun. "You told her to shoot me!" I gasped.

"Yeah," she replied, frowning. "Women—they *never* listen!"

———————

Agent Turner was on her cell phone. McSorley was getting his head examined. I busied myself being confused.

When she finally came over I shot her a look. She folded her arms and said, "Hey! I'm the one who told you to go to Oregon."

"You used me, and you used that old man in there."

"We were trying to protect you."

"Great job. Tonight was our second brush with death in three days."

"Well, if you hadn't been so damn clever about getting out of New York, Mr. P. W. Barker, we would have followed you . . . What do you mean, *second* brush with death?"

I ignored the question for one of my own. "It was *your* people following me in New York?"

Suddenly she looked uncomfortable. "Not exactly. We were following the people who were following you."

"Oh, now it's all clear."

"Look, as far as the AG and Senator Young were concerned, our investigation was supposed to be in wrap-up mode. We had to stay off their radar screens just to keep it going. Evans said you were good at piecing things together, so it made sense to let you go your own way and keep tabs. We no sooner located you at the Lancaster— predictable, by the way—than we realized you were being watched. Within twenty-four hours we had them identified. Two were professional killers, two others we'd never heard of, which probably meant they were *very* professional killers."

"And I became bait. I thought you wanted me to go to Oregon."

She waved a hand dismissively. "Give me a break, Philip. There was no way you were walking away from this case. You're Dudley Do-Right, for God's sake."

"You knew Green was murdered all along," I said accusingly.

"Let's say that was my feeling. You told me Constance was lying about Green to cover up something worse. Then he turns up in a motel as a suicide but the medical examiner is a bit suspicious about the angle of the cuts on his right wrist, and the motel manager might've seen the murderers."

"Speaking of Harold, he wants you reprimanded for bad language."

Blair smiled. "You got to Harold, did you? Did you threaten him?"

"Not like you did. Why didn't you tell me you suspected murder?"

"Everything we reported was going right to Warren Young. I decided to keep things on a need-to-know basis while we tried to figure it out. You had no need to know, and you weren't exactly impressing me as reliable."

"Thanks. You still might have told me I was bait."

"You would have acted differently and spooked them. Look, it was a golden opportunity to break the case. If we could watch them and intercept their communications we had a chance to figure out why Green was killed and catch them all in one net. But after you slipped out of New York we didn't pick up your trail again until you called Julia from Miami. How did she get involved in this, by the way?"

I told her about our first encounter at the cemetery. "I called Susan—Julia—when we were leaving Arizona, too. I told her where we were going."

Blair frowned. "So *that's* how they got to Müller so fast."

"They were watching her apartment when we arrived. One of their teams followed McSorley and me from Florida to South Carolina."

"How do you know that?"

"That was our *other* brush with death. It was the two guys that killed Naomi Singer."

It was the first time I'd seen Blair Turner at a loss for words. "But where . . . how do you know that?"

"McSorley convinced them to play ball."

She sank into the chair opposite mine. "You're joking, right?"

"No, we've got their names, fingerprints, and a taped confession."

She was staring at me, open-mouthed. "And you let them go?"

"Trust me, they'll be easy to find. You intercepted my call to Julia. How did you come across her?"

She was still stunned. "What? . . . Oh, from your hotel phone records. We made a pretext call, pretended to be your office."

"That was *the FBI*?"

"Sure. You don't think we were going to walk in there and identify ourselves, do you? Your safety depended on us keeping our distance."

"If you were tapping her phone, then why didn't you react to my call from Arizona? If you had gone to Miami, Esther might still be alive!"

She glared at me. "Hey, *Mister Prosecutor,* we need a warrant to tap a phone, remember? This woman was a professional. Her false identification was absolutely flawless—built over *years*. We didn't know Susan Edwards was Julia Masters until we got her fingerprints. My affidavit said that you'd just headed a national security investigation and professional killers had you under surveillance in New York. Then another killer in Virginia was in contact with you using a false identity. It didn't seem like a coincidence. That convinced a judge to give us the warrant, but you must've been well on your way to Florida by then."

"I see . . . I'm sorry. Esther's death is my responsibility, not yours."

"It's not yours, either."

It would take me a long time to accept that. I exhaled heavily. "When were you able to link the guys following me directly to Julia?"

"Not till tonight. We had her home and cell phones tapped but they must've been using another line of communication."

"Probably e-mail," I said. "I'll explain later."

"Anyway, the first call we picked up from you said you were leaving Esther Müller and heading for Washington. Hours later Esther was dead and soon the Miami police had come up with your name."

"I'll bet *that* got some reaction."

"The AG didn't know what we were up to, but he assumed Esther's death had something to do with the case and wanted you found and shot on sight. Actually, that was a break for my team because now we were *supposed* to be looking for you. We planned to intercept you before you made contact with Julia but she got out of her building without being seen."

"That was us again."

Blair shook her head in disbelief. "You know, you make it real hard to keep you alive."

"You're the one who dared her to shoot me!" She wasn't going to dignify that with a reply. She had her eyes closed and was tilting her head side to side to stretch that lovely neck. Soon, my curiosity overcame my indignation. "So, how'd you find us?" I asked.

"We followed Julia's friends from New York. They left for an Annapolis motel late last night. Tonight she finally used her cell phone to give them directions to the house. They were supposed to wait in the woods. We got there first."

"And here we are," I said. "So, can we break the case now?"

Blair frowned. "That's what *I* was going to ask *you*. Whoever's running this thing is very careful. Julia may have been giving instructions but we never learned who she was working for."

"Neither did she."

"She told you that?"

"It was her dying declaration."

The doors to the treatment room swung open and a nurse pushed McSorley into the waiting area. He was in a wheelchair and looking very unhappy. "Will you get a load of this?" he grumbled.

"Hospital regulations," said the nurse. "You ride until you reach the door."

"I told her these things can be dangerous," he said. "She doesn't believe me."

Agent Turner gave us an option. We could promise to stay put in a safe house or she could arrest us for impersonating federal officers in Miami. So, we took a Bureau car to a Victorian house in Takoma Park. I rode up front with an agent named Fuerst, and Blair and McSorley sat in the back. They were very chummy, gabbing about law enforcement and the army, and it was disgustingly obvious that my partner had a weakness for long legs and a quick draw. Just wait, I said to myself, wait till she threatens to squeeze our balls till our eyes pop.

We stopped to pick up a pizza and some beer, courtesy of the FBI, and soon the three of us were in the kitchen of the safe house. I felt better than I had in a long time. It felt good to be alive, and circumstances aside, it felt good to be with Blair. McSorley caught me staring at her when she wasn't looking and got this twinkle in his eye. I decided to get back to business.

"When the AG hears you were in a gunfight with a woman holding me hostage, he'll probably be curious."

"I'd say so," she replied.

"What do you intend to tell him?"

She wiped her mouth with a napkin and said, "What else? The truth."

"The truth," I repeated.

"The whole and nothing but. We've got three murder victims and I just shot the chief suspect. What am I supposed to do—lie?"

"I guess not."

"So, let's hear it. Everything that happened since you left Washington."

I put down my beer. "You remember I told you that I'd found Naomi?"

"Yes."

"She'd been contacted by Green. There was a note of the conversation in her office diary, actually, a name."

"What name?"

"Sonia Denes. She was a Hungarian brought to America after the war with the help of Naomi's employer, the Hebrew Immigrant Aid Society. Naomi met her ship. Sonia lived alone, worked for a millinery company in Manhattan, and fell from a rooftop in the Bronx in 1955. It was ruled a suicide. Joe here was the investigating detective, so I went to Arizona to ask him what he knew about the case. He always suspected it was murder, so we decided to join forces and follow the only lead we had."

"Esther Müller."

"That's right, but Esther stonewalled Joe fifty years ago and the passage of time hadn't changed her mind."

"Did you learn anything at all?"

McSorley remained expressionless when I looked her in the eye and answered, "No."

"Go on," she said.

"There was nothing more to do in Miami. If there was a next step it would be taken in Washington or New York, so I called Susan—Julia—and we headed north. We were in Georgia when Joe realized we were being followed." I told the story of McSorley's bravery while he sat there, quietly drinking his beer. Maybe it wasn't a big deal to him, but it was to me, and I wanted Blair to feel the same way. I suppose it was one measure of how I felt about him.

"Amazing," she muttered when I finished, "but why didn't you contact us? You had proof of the conspiracy behind Green's death."

"But not of why he was killed. We weren't ready to share anything."

Blair nodded appreciatively; we were preaching to the choir. So far, so good, I thought. I was obeying an important principle of deception: lie as close to the truth as possible. But it was about to get harder.

"So you drove on to Washington," she prompted.

"Right. The only one who had known our whereabouts in Florida was Susan." I explained how we decided to avoid her, then changed our minds when Esther was murdered and it seemed Susan might be next. "We contacted her by e-mail and went to stake out her building."

"E-mail," repeated Blair. "You're right, that's probably how she stayed in contact with the others. She probably had a wireless modem, too. They could set up addresses all over the Internet and publish them in the personals of any newspaper."

"We still weren't sure where she stood," I said, "but when we saw your van in front of her building, she passed our test. We took her out the back door. You know the rest."

Blair's gaze went from me to McSorley and back again. "Let me get this straight," she said. "These people murdered Green, they murdered two witnesses, they almost murdered you, and now it looked as if they have your girlfriend—"

"She wasn't my girlfriend. She helped when I was trying to locate Sonia."

"Okay, so now they have your *assistant investigator* in their sights, and you *still* don't call for help?"

"I already told you, we needed time to figure things out."

"You were real determined to keep the AG out of this," she said.

"So were you," I shot back.

She stared at me. "And there's no big clue you haven't told me about?"

Her cell phone rang before I could answer. From her clipped responses, the person on the other end of the line wasn't happy. "What was that about?" I asked, changing the subject.

"Things are getting complicated," she said. "The agent in charge of our Baltimore office wants to know why he wasn't informed about our operation."

"Refer him to the director," I said, but she didn't reply. She seemed to be concentrating on her beer. "The director *does* know, right?"

She frowned and said, "He's been keeping his distance. I tried to brief him but he cut me off. I guess if he actually knew what was going on he'd be required to do something about it. It was his way of giving me the green light."

"Then he doesn't know what happened in New York?"

"No."

I shook my head in disbelief. "And he doesn't know you've been chasing after suspects?"

"No." She was starting to get angry. "Not just him, the assistant director is out of the loop, too. They've left me on my own but that ends tomorrow. I'm to meet with the director in"—she looked at her watch—"six hours. Then I've got a session with the shooting team to review what happened tonight. Sometime after that we'll surely be meeting with the AG. It wouldn't surprise me if he wanted you there, too."

"When you tell the 'whole' truth, does that include Constance coming to me with Green's confession?"

"Why not? If Green was murdered, his suicide note is phony. That means the espionage scenario is in doubt, and so is Constance's story about his confession. I know you made her a promise and I've kept your little secret till now, but she's got some explaining to do."

"You want to solve this case, don't you?" I asked.

"Of course."

"Then I suggest you not start a panic. Keep the case about espionage and don't point a finger at the next first lady just yet. That'll give you more leeway. Once you've got the proof, no one can stop you."

"Is that your advice as an investigator?"

"No, as a politician."

Blair considered a moment. "Okay," she said, "I'll leave Constance out of it—for now."

"Good. What do you think will happen tomorrow?"

"I think it will work out. Sure, we kept things on a need-to-know basis but it was our best shot at a tough case."

"Do you think the director will back you up?"

"Why wouldn't he? He took himself out of the loop so the investigation could go forward, and it paid off. We've made some arrests and we're a lot closer to breaking this case. And don't forget, the director and the AG have a tight relationship. He actually did the AG a favor."

"How?"

"The AG can't be expected to tell the senator what he doesn't know. No one can blame him for holding back."

"Okay," I said. "I was just asking."

Dinner was over. I walked Blair outside to her car. "I'll call you in the morning and let you know what's going on," she said.

I took her arm. "Blair?"

"What?"

"Whatever happens, you're an amazing woman."

The sentiment took her by surprise. She smiled, then said, "You're not going soft on me, are you? A close brush with death can do that."

"That must be it."

She turned and started walking to the car. I headed back to the house. "Philip," she called.

"What?"

"Evans was right about you."

I went back inside and found McSorley still at the table. "You held out on her," he said. His tone didn't indicate how he felt about it.

"That's right."

"A few hours ago we decided to let the government carry the ball. You were just about to call your friend in Chevy Chase. What changed?"

"The whole landscape. Tomorrow, the director is going to serve Agent Turner to the AG on a platter. She's finished."

McSorley's eyes widened in surprise. "Why?"

"Because he's a smooth politician and the AG's reaction is predictable. His first priority is Warren Young's candidacy. That means he's got to keep the Green affair off the front page, but tomorrow he'll be confronted with three murders, a truckload of conspirators, a dead suspect, and FBI agents gone off the reservation."

"Those are the facts."

"The facts don't matter, there's an election at stake. Unless he's compelled by irrefutable proof, the AG is not going to accept a new scenario in which Green is a victim and Warren is an ex-candidate. He may not be able to kill the investigation but the clamps will be on real tight to keep it under control. That means having investigators with the right priorities. Agent Turner no longer qualifies."

"What's going to happen to her?"

"When the sun sets tomorrow, Blair Turner will be an

overly ambitious agent who deceived her superiors and compromised an important espionage case."

"They'll can her."

"No question. Joe, I *had* to hold out on her. With Blair as its advocate, our Banking Committee theory would be dead on arrival. Even Evans couldn't get the investigation expanded to do the things we suggest. All she'd succeed in doing is tipping off our progress. That would make our job a hell of a lot harder and maybe get us killed."

"So, we're on our own again."

"That's right."

"Then that advice to leave out any mention of Constance, that wasn't for her benefit, it was for ours."

"If we're going to continue this investigation I don't want them to see us coming."

McSorley began to peel the label off his beer bottle. "I was just wondering . . ."

"What?"

"What's more important to you, the case or the girl?"

He took me by surprise. "What does *that* mean?"

"You know what's going to happen to her, she doesn't."

"You heard her: her mind is made up! Do you think *anything* I'd say would make a difference?"

"Maybe, maybe not."

"Look, if she played any games with the director tomorrow her team would have to tell the same lies. She'd never expose their careers to that kind of risk. She only agreed to hold back on Constance because she'd kept that to herself."

"You're right about that," he conceded. He rubbed his face. It was the first time I'd seen him close to upset.

His nascent bond with Agent Turner was tugging at him. "Washington is a heckuva place," he muttered.

"You've said that."

A few minutes passed while he peeled the label. Finally, he put a hand on my shoulder. "You're right, Philip, the only thing we can do is solve the case. If we're in the driver's seat, we can save her."

Right. Solve the case.

No problem.

20

AT ONE THE NEXT AFTERNOON I was in an anteroom
waiting for a summons while Blair conferred with the
AG, the director of the FBI, and the usual suspects. The
meeting had been delayed to await the arrival of Jarrett
Sanders, who stopped by to drop off his raincoat and
glare at me before entering the conference room. Thirty
minutes passed, then sixty. I hadn't gotten much sleep in
the safe house and was on the verge of nodding off when
the AG's secretary finally opened the door and announced, "They're ready for you now."

I got up and walked toward the conference room. Its
door suddenly opened and Blair strode out, her jaw
tight. Our eyes met. "I'm suspended," she said, and kept
going before I could reply.

Conversation stopped when I entered. I went around
the table to the far end, which had more or less become
my spot. The director was sitting immediately to the
AG's left, wearing a black double-breasted suit and a
gold tiepin. His hair was smoothed straight back. He'd
started life as a Chicago police officer and made lieu-

tenant by the time he graduated from law school. In private practice he stayed close to local politics and eventually landed a federal judgeship. For most, that's the last stop, but he grew bored on the bench and set his sights on the FBI job when the new administration came to power. The people who backed him had delivered Cook County for the new president, and he got it.

The AG began as my back touched the chair. "Agent Turner has briefed us on this rather remarkable series of events," he rumbled. "It would appear that the Bureau's own procedures were flouted, although I'm sure you don't care about that. So, let's talk about your role in this sad affair. Summing up, you misused classified information to conduct your own unauthorized, unwarranted, and probably unlawful intrusion into an ongoing national security investigation. The result of your bungling is that said investigation has been compromised, an FBI agent's life was put at risk, and two innocent people are dead." The Blade led a murmured amen chorus and heads bobbed or shook with disgust. The lone dissenter was poor Evans, who sat silently by. "Is there anything you'd like to say?"

"If I may, I'd like to note that my investigation led to the discovery of the conspirators."

"Don't break your arm patting yourself on the back!" snapped The Blade. "Your major accomplishment was getting some people killed; people who were key to breaking the case wide open. You tipped off our investigation and these Hungarians rolled up their own network before we could, only they did it *their* way! And if Turner hadn't ignored her own instructions, you'd be just another victim!"

"And what have you got to show for it?" asked the AG. "It appears that this spy ring might go back for decades but we'll never nail them because our only link was severed last night—unless you've got something else to go on?"

Every head turned my way. That was the question I was there to answer. They wanted to know whether there was anything else in store. Would there be more grist for the media mill or was it safe to close the books? Warren Young was probably wearing out the oriental rug in his chambers that very moment, waiting for the word. I paused for dramatic effect before shaking my head. The Blade snorted and Sanders looked especially pleased as he lightly slapped the table. As for the AG, he could barely conceal his relief when he intoned, "Then the FBI will continue the investigation as best it can, although I fear that there's not much more that can be accomplished, given the circumstances. In the meantime, of course, there will be no further public statements other than one regarding the events of last evening." He turned to Evans. "You've prepared something?"

The assistant attorney general nodded. "There was actually an old warrant for Julia Masters in Nevada. She skipped bail on an extortion charge twelve years ago. The story is that we received an anonymous tip on her whereabouts and were trying to arrest her when she elected to shoot it out."

"That'll do," replied the AG. "Mr. Barkley, do you understand that you are *this* close"—he held his thumb and forefinger an inch apart—"to being arrested for interfering with federal law enforcement officers and misusing confidential information?"

"I understand."

"Then I take it that you will cooperate by neither doing nor saying anything to compromise this investigation further?"

"I assure you I won't."

"And that police officer you've involved in this—what's his name? McBride?"

"McSorley."

"I understand he's retired."

"That's right."

"Well, it's time for you to join him. Go to Arizona, or Oregon, or wherever. It would seem that there's nothing here for you anymore."

"Nothing," echoed The Blade. Sanders was smiling behind his hand.

"There's no question about that," I conceded. "I do have one request, though."

The AG frowned. "What is it?"

"That the department issue a press release saying that I'm not a suspect in the Esther Müller slaying. I don't need *that* following me around."

He looked at Evans. "Handle it," he instructed.

"Thank you," I said.

Having demonstrated that he was tough but fair, the AG radiated satisfaction. "Then if there's nothing more, this meeting is over." He smiled at the director and said, "I trust that you'll be able to wind this up without undue delay."

"You can count on it, General," said the director. "I'm sure we're on the right track now."

"Good," he replied, the smile widening. It abruptly disappeared when his gaze shifted to me. "Good-bye, Mr. Barkley. I know this is our last encounter."

The meeting broke up. I went directly to the anteroom to get my raincoat and was heading out when Sanders blocked my path. He let out a low whistle and cackled, "Now, if you ask me, that *theah* was a good, old-fashioned ass-*whuppin'*! I mean, *son,* that old boy handed you your walkin' papers, *knowwhutahmean*?" He began to put on his raincoat, talking softly to himself. "Nothing for you here anymore," he repeated with a chuckle.

For the briefest moment I was torn. I was supposed to slink out of the building and a few weeks before that's probably what I'd have done. He had one arm in his raincoat and the other halfway into the sleeve. I snatched his tie, wrapping it around my hand and yanking upward, drawing him too close to shrug on the raincoat or slip it off. He tried to wriggle free, then drew back his fist to throw a punch. I grabbed him by the balls and squeezed. He went limp and began making gurgling sounds.

"Listen to me, asshole," I hissed through clenched teeth. "Can you hear me?" I squeezed a little harder and he squealed. "Is that a yes?" He gave another, short squeal. "Good. Now, what do you think would happen to the senator's chances if the press found out that he was fucking my wife while we were still married? What would all those good churchgoing voters think about him taking her to his little getaway place on the Eastern Shore?" Sanders's face was contorted in pain. I relaxed my grip just a bit and snarled, "Answer me, you little prick!"

His face was beet-red. "They'd . . . uhhh." He began to sink but I had leverage on him.

"I can't hear you. They'd what?"

"Be mad!" he gasped.

"That's right. And the next time you even look my way I'll call the *New York Times,* got it?"

Tears were streaming down his face. "Y-y-yes!"

"And I'll make damn sure Young knows who's responsible. I'll tell him you baited me into doing it even after I warned you, and as fast as you can snatch a fly with that lizard tongue of yours, you'll be back on the farm with pig shit between your toes. Do we understand each other?" I squeezed his scrotum real hard and his eyes bulged as he began flapping like a fish on a line. When I let go he dropped to his knees, then collapsed onto his side and tucked into a ball. I picked up my raincoat and walked out. One of the AG's secretaries was standing in the hallway with her mouth open. I straightened my tie and said, "We were just talking politics."

We decided to begin the next phase of the investigation with some head-clearing exercise on the towpath beside the C&O canal, once an important commercial thoroughfare and now a tree-shaded boulevard for hikers, joggers, and bicyclists. We strolled along, enjoying the warm breeze off the Potomac and hoping for inspiration. A woman runner appeared in the distance. McSorley watched her until she passed us, moving at a good clip. "They don't bounce like you'd expect," he said.

"It's called a jogging bra," I said.

"Jogging bra," he repeated, smiling. Two more women passed us from behind, then another came toward us. He looked at me with eyebrows raised. "Is it Ladies' Day on this road?"

"There are usually more women than men. They're more disciplined about exercise."

"You know, you guys today have it better than we did."

"How so?"

"The women's lib stuff. I think guys are the big winners. Women used to stay home. If a guy wanted to see a ball game or get some exercise, his wife probably wasn't interested, and the things she liked probably didn't interest him, either. Now women exercise, play sports. These young guys and gals have things they can do together and that's good for a relationship."

"You should write an advice column, Joe."

He chuckled. "Actually, I heard it on television, but I think it's true . . . You know, Eileen loved baseball."

"Baseball? That's great."

"Crazy about it, couldn't get enough of it. We'd go to the doubleheaders at Yankee Stadium on the weekends. She used to read the box scores and knew everything about the team. One time I took her over to the old Grand Concourse Hotel where the Yankees stayed and she met Mickey Mantle, Whitey Ford, and Hank Bauer in the bar. Ford was giving her an autograph and she says, 'They're taking too big a lead on you.' Now everybody's listening. He looks at her and says, 'What are you talking about?' And she says, 'Going from second to third, they're getting too big a lead. You and Rizzuto need to keep 'em honest.' Can you believe it? Everybody was laughing and kidding him. His face was red, let me tell you." He grinned at me and said, "We had a lot of good times talking about the Yankees."

"It sounds like it."

We walked along a little farther and then he said, "In my day there weren't many women cops, either."

I could see where this was going; he was taken with Blair. "You want to talk about her or work on the case?"

"Okay," he said, "we're working on the case."

"We'd need an army of investigators to tackle the National Archives, and official help to get into any Swiss records. As far as something the two of us could do, I'm fresh out of ideas."

"Okay," he said, "then let's review one more time, putting together what we know and what we assume. Sonia's father opens an account with a Swiss bank in Zurich. The family winds up in a concentration camp but Sonia survives, comes to the States, and pursues a claim for the account."

"With some proof that she sends to the U.S. legation in Switzerland," I said.

"Right, and before she gets an answer, she's murdered, and her proof winds up in a government file. Forty years later, the Senate Banking Committee—"

"—with Senator Young as a member—"

"—conducts hearings. Martin Green, a staff guy, finds Sonia's proof. Nothing happens then but a few years later, Green, who now works for the Intelligence Committee—"

"—again, under Senator Young—"

"—retrieves the material and begins to investigate Sonia."

"Which gets him to the Hungarian embassy."

McSorley stopped and looked at me. "That's interesting. Do you think Green went to the Hungarians to ask about Sonia?"

"It makes sense. She was the focus of his investigation up till then."

"Why would they know about Sonia?"

"I have no idea."

"Okay, we'll come back to that." We started walking again and he continued. "The other big piece is Senator and Mrs. Young. Speaking about one or both of them, Green says, 'Things aren't what they seem,' and Mrs. Young takes a definite interest in the investigation. She meets him in New York, and he calls her before he disappears."

I picked up the thread. "Then things are staged to suggest Green was engaged in espionage: the fifty thousand dollars in his savings account, the supposed confession to Constance, and the suicide note."

"And then he's murdered, too," said McSorley.

"A supposed suicide, just like Sonia."

We continued to stroll along in silence while we turned the problem upside-down and sideways. More joggers passed and McSorley seemed to be having a good time. Finally, he said, "It's still all knotted up."

"Right. We don't have the enclosure and we don't know where to look for the next clue."

"There was this guy in my squad who everybody thought was the best detective in the house. When you could get him to talk, people would listen, and I remember this one thing he used to say: 'If you're stuck for an answer, you're not asking the right question.' "

"That makes sense."

"So, here's a new question: What's so special about Sonia's father's account? What's so troubling about it that people have been getting killed for so long?"

"I can't even begin to guess. Were there different kinds of accounts? Different ways to establish them? Did people like Sonia's father make some special kind of arrangement?"

Through the trees we could see two tanned, shirtless fishermen sitting in a boat near the far bank. McSorley watched them and said, "There's nothing like a little local knowledge for fishing."

"Are you making a point?"

"Green knew the terrain better than we do, the background of the case."

"He certainly knew a lot more about the Holocaust. He was a volunteer at the Holocaust Museum."

"And that's a place we haven't visited."

I thought about it. "You know, they probably have a record of Sonia Denes there, too, at least that she was in a concentration camp, maybe something more."

"It's worth checking."

"I have a contact who can get us an appointment with the right people there."

He grinned. "How long have you known *this* one?"

"Since my White House days."

"Good, because if it gets back that we're still on this case, that'll be trouble."

"Okay, we've got something to do. Are you ready to turn back?"

"Hold it, here comes another one." We walked until she ran by. "No jogging bra," he said.

"Right."

He smiled after the bouncing ponytail. "You know, change isn't always for the best."

"Yeah," I said, looking at him, "some things should last forever."

21

THE NEXT MORNING WE WERE in the office of Paul Kopelman, the chief of staff of the United States Holocaust Memorial Museum. Uncertain about the nature of my visit, but well aware of my publicity, Kopelman had prudently decided to include a witness, Aaron Nadler, the director of museum programs.

"I, uh, read the story this morning," said Kopelman, glancing at Nadler.

"So, you know that I'm not a murder suspect."

"I . . . yes, I guess so. I don't know the situation . . . what it's all about."

"Mister McSorley and I saw Esther Müller just before she was killed. We were working on an investigation."

"You were working on Martin's case before you left the Justice Department."

"That's right. That's why we're here."

"But you're not with Justice anymore."

I leaned forward and lowered my voice. "I know you understand how sensitive things are handled. I can tell you that I met with the attorney general and his deputies yesterday, and he gave me certain instructions that I'm not at liberty to discuss at this time."

Kopelman shifted in his chair. "I thought the investigation was over."

"Did you know Martin?"

"Of course, we both did. Martin was a volunteer here for years."

"Do you believe the stories about him?"

"Believe? The stories said that he left a note admitting that he was a spy. So . . . what are you saying?"

"Shut the door," I said. Kopelman's eyebrows arched in surprise. He looked at Nadler, who quickly complied and returned to his chair. Their gazes were riveted on me when I said, "What I'm about to tell you is highly confidential."

"I understand," they said in unison.

"By confidential, I mean that you are about to be entrusted with information that, if revealed, could compromise an effort to redeem Martin's reputation. You can't tell *anyone*." They both nodded solemnly. "Not even your wives," I added.

"*Especially* not my wife," replied Kopelman.

"I'm not married," said Nadler. I looked at him. "But I've got a girlfriend," he added, hopefully.

"For reasons I can't go into at this moment, Martin's knowledge of the Holocaust may have been a factor in what happened." They stared, transfixed. "I want to share something with you, a name. We need to know anything that you can tell us about this person."

"Who?" they asked.

"The name is Sonia Denes. She was a Hungarian who was interned in a concentration camp."

"That would mean Auschwitz," said Kopelman. "When they rounded up the Hungarian Jews, they were taken there."

"Sonia survived and emigrated to the United States in 1950. She died in a supposed accident in 1955."

The word "supposed" had its intended effect. Kopelman looked at Nadler. "Does the name mean anything to you, Aaron?"

Nadler shook his head. "No, but if she was a registered prisoner we should be able to look her up. Beyond that, I don't know what else we could tell you, but there are certainly people here who are experts on the Holocaust in Hungary."

"Was Martin?"

"Martin was knowledgeable about Holocaust matters," said Kopelman, "but I don't think he considered himself an expert on any particular aspect, at least not that one. The Holocaust in Hungary was one of the most terrible chapters of one of the most terrible stories in human history. Do you know much about what happened in Hungary in 1944?"

"The Nazis occupied the country," said McSorley. "It was only a few months before D-Day."

"They crossed the border in mid-March with Adolf Eichmann leading a special commando unit of the Gestapo," Kopelman explained. "The Hungarian Jews were the only ones that had thus far escaped the Final Solution, and with the outcome of the war decided, Eichmann was racing against time. A few days later, working from east to west, they began rounding up all the Jews in the provinces. They shipped them in railroad cars to Auschwitz, where they had prepared a special railway ramp and additional gas chambers and ovens to handle the influx. Even with the extra facilities they couldn't kill them as fast as they were arriving. Eichmann was sending five trains a day. They had to plead with him to slow down to three. By early July the Nazis had shipped four hundred and thirty-seven thousand men, women, and children. Four hundred thousand were murdered immediately upon arrival. The rest were used for slave labor. Churchill said it was probably the greatest and most horrible crime in the history of the world."

"My God," whispered McSorley, "it had to be."

Nadler said, "By July they'd swept the provinces. The last group of Jews left unscathed were about two hundred and fifty thousand in Budapest. Before Eichmann could round them up, the regent, Admiral Horthy, stopped the deportations under international pressure. Thereafter, Budapest Jews were systematically deprived of their property and their freedom, but as bad as things were, they got much worse in October when Horthy was deposed with German assistance and the Arrow Cross Party took over. They were rabid anti-Semites, and Eichmann was back in business. The end of the war was imminent. The Russians were advancing toward Budapest. Jewish males were rounded up to build fortifications east of the city. That left the women and children to be dealt with. Because trucks and trains were needed for movements of troops and material, Eichmann decided to march them the one hundred and twenty miles to Hegyeshalom at the Austrian border, where they were to be loaded on trains for Auschwitz. With no food and no protection from the cold, it was a death march. Bodies littered the road. Most of those that didn't die were gassed at Auschwitz."

Kopelman continued the story. "The street outside is named for Raoul Wallenberg. Do you know who he was?"

"The famous Swedish diplomat who assisted the Jews," I replied.

"Yes," he said. "One of the 'righteous gentiles,' non-Jews who committed heroic deeds to save Jews from destruction. Oscar Schindler was one, too, and there were others. Wallenberg was a hero of the Holocaust in Hungary. It was his rescue of perhaps two thousand of those wretched souls on the road to Hegyeshalom that made him a legend. He drove up and down to intercept the death columns, saving as many as he could with nothing more than bluffs and sheer audacity. He put phony passports in the hands of hundreds of the condemned, then insisted they were under Swedish protection. He pulled it off, plucked them right out of Nazis' hands and delivered them from the jaws of death."

"It's an amazing story," I said.

"Can I ask a question?" said Nadler. "What was the connection between Martin and this Sonia Denes?"

"We're not sure," I replied.

"Well," said Kopelman, "we'll check our records and see what we can find out."

"I have to emphasize again how confidential this is," I told them.

"Don't worry," he replied, "we get these kinds of requests all the time."

"How long do you think it will take?"

"I'll say it's a priority. We might have something for

you by late this afternoon. It just depends on how deep we have to dig."

———————

"We've got time to kill," I told McSorley after the meeting. "It's a beautiful day and we're in Washington. What's your preference?"

"I'd like to visit Arlington National Cemetery."

That's what we did. We took a tour bus to Arlington and visited the Tomb of the Unknown Soldier, President Kennedy's grave, and watched a funeral complete with a twenty-one-gun salute and the playing of "Taps." We walked among rows of mostly white tombstones memorializing mostly curtailed lives, and then up a long flight of steps leading to Arlington House. We sat there with a commanding view of the cemetery and the city across the river: Lincoln's memorial and Jefferson's, the Washington Monument, the red roofs of federal buildings along Constitution Avenue, and finally the Capitol, where this whole odyssey began in a Senate office. Was it only weeks ago, or years?

McSorley was quietly taking it all in. I said, "Can I ask you a question?"

"Sure."

"What goes through your mind when you look at a scene like this?"

He didn't answer right away. He looked down at his lap where his hands were twisting the brim of his hat, then out at the horizon. Finally he said, "It goes pretty fast."

"You mean life?"

He nodded. "It goes pretty fast. It's important to put the setbacks behind and make the most of it."

"Sometimes that's hard to do."

"Sometimes that's hard to do," he agreed, "but you have an obligation to try."

"Why?"

He inhaled deeply, then said, "On Omaha Beach we had to get supplies to the people that needed them. Sometimes a man would get shot while crawling or running with a box of ammunition. Then another man would have to pick it up and run a ways, and maybe he'd get hit. Then another man, and so on and so forth until the job was done. You understand?"

"Sure."

"Life's a little like that. Somebody comes along with something to share with you. And when she can't go on, you've got to carry it with you and share it with someone else, and so on."

"Are you talking about Eileen?"

"We came here once. I think we sat right here, on these steps."

"When?"

"In '51, for a funeral. It was a fella I knew in the service who stayed in and got killed in Korea. They buried him down there somewhere. Afterward, we sat on this hill and talked. I was feeling down. Part of it was the funeral, I guess, but part of it was what was going on in my own life. I was thinking that maybe I should've stayed in the service myself."

"Why?"

"I was a little—what's the word?—*disillusioned,* is that it? Things weren't the way I expected."

" 'Disillusioned' is a good word."

"Well, that's what I was. I was disillusioned about my

job. There were things going on that I didn't like."

"Right, the things you told me about before."

"That and other stuff. The police department wasn't like I expected and I was thinking about throwing in the towel."

"But you didn't."

"Eileen talked me out of it. She said some things that I never forgot."

"What?"

He wiped his forehead with a handkerchief. "She asked me what I'd do if I quit. I said I wasn't sure, maybe become a salesman because it was a people job and you could make good money."

"What did she say?"

"She said if that's what I really wanted to do it was fine with her. She said she was sure I'd make a good salesman just like I'd made a good cop, but there was one thing she wanted me to think about."

"Which was?"

"She waved her arm at all these tombstones and said that these men and women died protecting us, and that if I was a good cop I was honoring them in a way a good salesman could never do." He chuckled to himself. "I told her that she should be the district attorney because she knew how to present her case."

"I guess she did."

"It's a funny world, isn't it?"

"It's a funny world."

"You go along worrying about all kinds of stuff. You dwell on things that have happened. You know life is too short and you do anyway. But a place like this changes your perspective. You're born, you're here a little while, and you're gone. Maybe a lot sooner than you ever thought."

"And while you're here?" I asked.

"You try to do worthwhile things."

"Like Eileen said."

"That's what she shared with me," he replied, looking at me.

Neither one of us spoke for a while. Another funeral must have been going on somewhere because we could hear the rifles firing a salute, then the faint sound of a trumpet. Worthwhile things, I thought to myself.

"What if we never figure out what happened to Martin?" I asked.

He put his fedora on and said, "It's all in the doing. You don't always get there, but you have to keep moving forward, one foot in front of the other."

"And you try to share something along the way."

"You've got it."

We got up and started walking down the hill to the tour bus stop. I was passing tombstones, looking at dates of birth and death, and suddenly remembered that my daughter's birthday was only three days away. Constance and I had an arrangement: she would visit the cemetery in the morning and I'd go in the afternoon. One time, for no good reason, I went early and watched her from a distance as she pulled weeds and fussed with flowers. Then she sat on the bench and cried. I wanted to go to her, to tell her that it wasn't my fault, that she shouldn't hate me anymore. Before she left I saw her put a piece of paper under a rock by the tombstone. It said, "Mommy loves you."

"Philip?"

"What?"

"Now that you've lost your deal, what will you do in Oregon?"

"I'm not really sure."

He winked at me. "Well, I hear there's good money in sales."

―――――――――――

"I think we found her," said Kopelman. "There was a prisoner named Sonia Denes registered at Auschwitz on November 14, 1944."

"That's got to be her," said McSorley.

"What can you tell us?" I asked.

"She was registered, which means that she wasn't selected for the gas chambers when she arrived, but you knew that. She was processed and assigned a prisoner number, which would have been tattooed on her left forearm."

"She did have the tattoo. What else?"

"That's essentially it. We've talked to several of our most knowledgeable people on the Hungarian chapter but no one recognized her name."

"November 14," repeated McSorley. "Sonia could have been one of those marched to the border when Wallenberg was on the scene."

Kopelman nodded. "The timing fits, so it's certainly possible, but I don't know where that gets you."

Then there was silence. I waited for them to say something, a suggestion, an observation, anything to create another lead. The investigation had teetered on the brink so many times . . . I looked at McSorley. His face was a mask of concentration as he wrote deliberately in his little spiral notebook. No dash ahead, no jump to conclusion. That could take you over the edge. A step at a time. That's how he'd gotten off Omaha Beach, that's how he'd lived. When he finished he looked up at Kopelman. "Maybe we can canvass the other people that Martin knew here at the museum. He might have mentioned Sonia to any one of them."

"You're welcome to try but I think if her name were recognizable the people we spoke to would have known it."

"How many people work here?" asked McSorley.

"Over two hundred, not including a few hundred volunteers."

"Well, we may be back," he said. "Thanks for all your help."

————————————————

That evening we had a quiet dinner at a restaurant in Bethesda, a few blocks from our new motel headquarters. "What's on your mind?" McSorley asked as he buttered a roll. "You haven't said ten words since you ordered your food."

"We're dead in the water again."

"We learned something today," he said.

"And tomorrow?"

"We keep moving forward. I'm going back to the museum. There's lots of people there and someone might know something."

"I suppose that's the only thing left for us to do."

"Not us, me. There's a special job for you."

"What's that?"

"Get her back on the case—with us."

"Why don't I just stick this fork in my eye?"

"She's smart and she knows the case."

"I don't know where she is."

"You'll find her."

"Tell me this isn't some cute plan to bring us together."

He grinned. "Strictly business."

22

I ALWAYS ENJOYED WATCHING SOMEONE who could really swim, just knife through the water and do those somersault-style turns and power on. Blair was freestyling, her cobalt-blue suit gleaming in the lights as she clicked off fifty-meter laps without any discernible drop in speed. Power and grace. She'd been at it for twenty minutes since I arrived and hadn't noticed me yet. We were alone. It was ten-thirty and the health club was in between the early birds and the lunch-hour rush. She finally stopped at the far end and hoisted herself out of the water with remarkable ease. I intended to call out but delayed to let her shake out her hair. Then she began toweling off. More delay.

A guy in sweatpants and a club T-shirt entered the pool at the far side and nodded to her. He began picking up towels and noticed me. "Can I help you?" he called. I shook my head and waved him off. He said something inaudible to Blair and she turned. Her gaze followed me as I walked the length of the pool, giving her my most winning smile.

"Hi," I said.

"Why are you here?"

"I figured you didn't carry a gun while you were swimming."

"I don't have a gun, I'm suspended."

"I'm really sorry."

"But not surprised."

"No."

"Then *I'm* surprised. I would have thought you'd try to protect me, or at least warn me. I think I deserved it."

"I'm here to protect you now."

"It's too late."

"No, it's not. If we solve the case we're in control. We'll set everything right."

"Solve the case, is that all?" She tossed the towel over her shoulder and said, "Good-bye, Philip."

She turned to go but I caught her hand. "I held out on you."

"Meaning?"

"We know more than I told you the other night. We can solve the case." I was going out on a limb but I was desperate.

She stepped toward me; we were inches apart. "You lied to me," she said through clenched teeth.

"Yes."

"Why?"

"Because you were going to tell the truth to the director. I was concerned about what would happen."

"Happen to the case, not to me. The case was more important."

"McSorley asked me that—what's more important."

"And what did you tell him?"

"I dodged because I wasn't sure." She stared. I took a deep breath and said, "I'm sure now."

She looked down at my hand, still clasping hers, but she didn't pull away. "What do you want?"

"To buy you another lunch."

"It's too early."

"We'll talk, then eat. I'll explain everything." Now I was very aware of the feel of her hand in mine. My brain registered the sensation and liking it, caused my fingers to close a little tighter. A moment passed. When she looked up the challenge in her eyes had given way to something else.

"Do I get to change or do I go like this?"

"Go like that."

It hit me as she walked to the locker room: her tattoo still wasn't visible.

———————————

McSorley was waiting outside the Holocaust Museum as agreed. He smiled when he saw us approach. "I brought the reinforcements," I said. "She's up to date and ready to go."

"I hope he didn't have to twist your arm," he said to Blair.

"He squeezed my wrist a little but I'm okay."

"Anything?" I asked him.

He shook his head. "No, but that might change. I had a short conversation with a guy who's here as a 'visiting fellow' or something like that. He's supposed to be a big expert on the Holocaust in Hungary, and he said that he talked to Green before he disappeared. I didn't have a chance to follow up because he was about to take some VIPs on a tour, but he's going to meet me in his office in fifteen minutes."

"How many people did you talk to today?" asked Blair.

"Twenty, twenty-five. They all thought Green was a prince of a guy but nobody ever heard of Sonia Denes."

Simon Hirsch looked too young to be an expert on anything, about sixteen, I'd say, but the University of Chicago diploma on the wall was a doctorate. He was lean with black wavy hair and a five o'clock shadow that seemed to complement his dark eyes. He was good-looking and intense, perhaps the Martin Green of the museum staff. McSorley introduced us as being from Justice and the FBI. I showed my ID as corroboration; Blair only had to smile.

"You're still investigating what happened to Martin?" Hirsch asked.

"That's right," said McSorley. "We met with Paul Kopelman and Aaron Nadler yesterday, and we're interviewing the other people who knew him."

"Well, I'll tell you what I can."

"We understand you spoke to him shortly before he disappeared."

"Right, he was writing a paper for his course work at Georgetown and was interested in the Hungarian chapter of the Holocaust."

"Did the name Sonia Denes come up?"

Hirsch considered a moment. "No, I don't think so."

"Have you ever heard that name before?"

He frowned. "Sonia . . . Denes . . . No, who was she?"

"She was a prisoner at Auschwitz."

"Is there anything special about her that I should know?"

"Well, we're not sure, but you feel certain Martin didn't mention her?"

"I'm fairly sure because I pretty much recall the conversation. We talked about Eva's Diary."

"What's that?"

"An important artifact that surfaced about thirty years ago, a first-person account of the events in Budapest from March to November 1944. It was written by a young woman, probably a teenager, identified only as 'Eva.' As you can imagine, it's a tragic story."

McSorley looked at Blair and me, then said, "We'd like to hear it."

"Well, do you know anything about what happened?"

"Aaron and Paul gave us an overview yesterday. It was horrible."

"There was widespread fear among the Hungarian Jews, who had hoped they might survive the war in relative safety. The day after the Nazis crossed the border and before the round-up began, Eva's family was visited by a representative of a Swiss bank. He predicted—correctly—that the Nazis were going to confiscate Jewish property, and those who couldn't secure their freedom would be left to their fate. Everyone knew what that would probably mean."

"Death."

"Certain death. The banker offered them a way out."

"How?"

"Essentially, bribery," explained Hirsch. "Before the war, when the policy toward Jews was enforced emigration, the Nazis had imposed a 'flight tax' on Jews leaving Germany and Austria. They were stripped of their assets and left with just enough money to pay their way out. By the time Hungary was occupied, the policy had changed to the Final Solution, which meant death to all captive Jews, but Hungarian officials and even the Nazis themselves were subject to payoffs. By then there were no illusions regarding the outcome of the war and opportunism was rampant. The banker told Eva's father that he was acting on behalf of certain Nazi officials who were willing to permit prominent families to leave Hungary with assets—for a fee. Understand that the arrangement is being reported by a young woman without business experience, but it appears that Eva's father agreed to transfer their funds to a special account controlled by the banker, who in turn would arrange a transfer to his bank in Switzerland."

"Was that feasible?" I asked.

"Getting money out of the country was extraordinarily difficult for private citizens, especially Jews, but a Swiss bank with official blessing could manage. Apparently, the banker was supposed to arrange the payments and safe passage, and whatever portion wasn't needed would be held in the family's behalf. Nominee accounts were quite common in those days for what was known as Jewish 'flight capital.' "

It felt as if cold fingers were wringing my stomach like a sponge. "So, they made the deal."

"Yes, with no time to spare and no other options, they had to accept. Documents were executed and the transfer was made."

"What happened then?" asked McSorley.

"Just as the banker predicted, a few days later bank accounts were frozen and all Jewish businesses were turned over to Aryan management. Concentration and deportation of the Jews in the provinces began in earnest. The diary describes events in Budapest up to early November. Eva's family waited and waited, but they never saw the banker again. All efforts to locate him failed and, of course, they had no idea which officials might have sent him."

"What about their documents?"

"Even if they were legitimate, Eva's father was hardly in any position to complain."

"What happened to the family?"

"In late October Eva's father and brother were taken away and were never seen again. They were almost certainly used as slave labor to build fortifications. The last entry in the diary is dated November 2, which implies that Eva and whatever was left of her family were taken away at that time."

"Then they probably wound up at Auschwitz."

"That's very possible," said Hirsch. "They may have died there or on the road to the border."

"Then none of their names appear among the registered prisoners?"

"There's no way of knowing. The diary doesn't mention any names other than Eva's, which, given the content, may have been deliberate. But through process of elimination it's been established that Eva herself was not registered at Auschwitz. If she was taken there, she was gassed immediately."

It was a subdued team that left the museum. We walked down Raoul Wallenberg Place, each of us lost in thought, and wound up on a bench at the Tidal Basin. Finally Blair asked, "Well, what's next?"

"I need a whiskey," said McSorley. "Just a short one. And maybe a little food. Then we can have a meeting."

"Sounds good to me," I said.

"Where are you staying?" asked Blair.

"The Holiday Inn in Bethesda."

"I'm in Arlington. The distance is going to make this team thing awkward."

"Do you want to get a motel room?"

"Hmmm. Two guys and a motel." She winked at McSorley and said, "Sounds tempting but I've got a better suggestion. Why don't you stay at my place? It'll be more comfortable and a lot cheaper."

"We won't be imposing?" asked McSorley.

"I've got two empty bedrooms. You go pick up your things and I'll take a cab home and get stuff for dinner."

McSorley looked at me to make it unanimous. "I haven't eaten anything cooked in a kitchen in weeks," I said. "It sounds great."

Fifteen minutes later we were in the car heading for Bethesda. "Eva's Diary . . ." McSorley said softly, shaking his head.

"Right," I said.

"It's an awful story. Awful. That family waited for a rescue that never came. There are no words to describe what happened to them."

"I can think of one."

"What?"

"Betrayal."

———————————

Blair's home turned out to be a neat Cotswold cottage on a tree-shaded street in a hilly portion of Arlington. "My mother is a real-estate genius," she explained. "They stretched for this place when my dad did a tour at the Pentagon and have rented it out ever since. I'm the latest tenant. The rents cover the mortgage and now it's worth three times what they paid for it. She's been doing stuff like that since they were married. They could retire tomorrow but Dad loves the army too much to pack it in."

Dinner conversation was mostly devoted to my career in Washington. It wasn't a topic that I cared to dwell on, but apparently McSorley wanted Blair to know how important I was before my fall from grace. His professed fascination with White House and Senate doings seemed almost genuine, although I don't think she was fooled. The man was relentless.

We saved the case for dessert. Blair put a bowl of fruit on the table and refilled the wineglasses. McSorley began peeling an apple. "Let's start at step one," he said, ever methodical. "Does anyone think Martin's interest in Eva's Diary has nothing to do with the case?"

"He told the same cover story to Hirsch that he told to Jenny Castellano," I said. "Eva was part of his investigation, and that suggests a connection between her and Sonia."

"They had a lot in common," said Blair. "They lived in Budapest at the same time. Sonia was sixteen in 1944, and Eva may have been a teenager, too. The last entry in Eva's Diary was on November 2. Sonia was registered in Auschwitz on November 14. Their families could have been marched off at the same time."

"Then there's the bank part," McSorley said. "Sonia's father established an account with a Swiss bank and Eva's father did, too."

"Or tried to," I said.

"That's right, it could have been a scam." He began to cut wedges of apple and set them on a plate. "If there is a connection, what do you suppose caused Martin to discover it in the first place?"

"My guess would be the enclosure to Sonia's letter," I said.

"Something to do with Eva, then," said Blair.

"Very possible."

McSorley passed around the apple wedges and we all helped ourselves. "You know, Eva's story kinda fits with our theory."

"What theory?" asked Blair.

"We were taking some guesses on the way back from Florida," he explained. "If the case wasn't about espionage, then what was the motive? Money is usually the best guess. The idea was that somebody found something really embarrassing to the Swiss banks, and it was covered up in exchange for funds to help Senator Young. That would explain some things, including why Mrs. Young is involved."

"Well, what could be more embarrassing for the Swiss than their bankers as bag men for the Nazis?"

"Especially when the victims are double-crossed," observed McSorley. "But Eva's story isn't some big revelation, right? Hirsch said the diary was famous."

"Famous in certain circles," I replied. "But the average person doesn't know about it. Tying Eva's story to Sonia's gives it an American connection and brings it squarely within the Banking Committee's inquiry. It could have been a public relations bonanza for the committee and a disaster for the Swiss."

Blair sighed. "It all fits but it's still speculation. It doesn't make a case against Warren or anyone else above those already in custody. We need more proof."

McSorley stretched and said, "The only evidence we know about that we haven't seen is the enclosure to Sonia's letter."

I said, "Julia told me they pressed him hard for it before they killed him. Whatever it is, they wanted it bad,
but all they got for their trouble was Scripture."

"In the suicide note," Blair said.

"No, she was talking about something he said."

"He probably wrote it and said it. He was drugged."

There was a moment of silence while we ruminated
about poor Martin's fate. "You know, I never saw the
suicide note," I said. "What did the Scripture say?"

"I don't remember the exact words, but the thrust of it
was that politicians are greedy and don't care for those in
need. If you want to see it I can get a copy in the morning."

"I'm going to turn in," said McSorley. "Thanks for a
great meal and the hospitality. Today was a good day.
We're getting closer."

"Thanks to your persistence," I told him.

"I'll supply the shoe leather," he said, smiling. "You
two keep those wheels turning."

———————————

"Tell me about Constance."

She caught me off-guard. I was refilling our glasses
from the second bottle of wine, a task that required
some concentration. The question lingered while she
shifted in her chair and draped her legs over its arm. Her
sandals fell to the floor one at a time while her eyes remained on me. She was waiting. "I thought we weren't
going to talk business," I said.

"This isn't business."

"What then?"

"I'm curious."

"About her."

"About her . . . and about what happened. Am I pry-
ing?"

"It's all right."

"We can talk about something else."

"She was different."

"Different?"

"When we were married. She was different then."

"You don't have to talk about it."

"She was always smart, intuitive . . . sharp political instincts. She was great in meetings, tough but with a wicked sense of humor—cut through the bullshit, get what she needed for her senator, and leave something on the table for you. And her word was solid gold. Up there, that counts. It took her only a few years to gain a reputation. People used to seek her out—for answers, opinions, or advice. Sure, every guy wanted to bed her but she didn't have to play that game to get what she wanted."

"She sounds like quite a woman."

"She was. When we got married I was the most envied guy on the Hill, bar none."

"What position did you have then?"

"I was minority counsel to the Appropriations Committee."

"Evans told me that if you guys had won the next election you were a cinch for White House counsel, or to be one of the president's senior advisers."

"That was the plan. I went over to the Hill for the experience and to build the bridges. Everything was on track until the grand jury investigation."

"You knew what testifying would mean. It couldn't have been an easy decision."

"It wasn't a decision at all. We said from the beginning that I wasn't going to take the time-honored way out."

"What's that?"

"In Washington, the three little words are 'I don't recall.' We decided that I'd tell the truth. Constance felt as strongly as I did . . . You're surprised."

"I guess I am," she admitted.

"Afterward, we were isolated. They wouldn't fire me but that isn't the way things are done up there. It's more subtle. First you notice that no one's making eye contact, and conversations always seem to be breaking up when you walk into the room. Soon you realize that if you do hear about something, it's already happened. Then it's the weekend and you're free, just like you were the last one, and will be the next. If you've got any pride you tender your resignation and they announce that you're leaving to pursue 'new opportunities.'"

"What about Constance?"

"You can't invite one half of a married couple to dinner or a weekend getaway. And people didn't want to talk in front of her because they figured it would just get back to me. The handwriting was on the wall. We were both done for, but I think she was more angry about what happened to me than to her."

Blair stared into her glass as she swirled her wine. "This isn't what I'd imagined."

"No, I guess not." No one who'd only met the new Constance could understand why I had loved her.

"I'd like to hear the rest of it."

The rest of it. The hard part.

"For a while it looked as if we'd be leaving Washington because I was unemployable, but out of the blue comes a call from Evans. My first job in Washington was working for him when he was still in the U.S. Attorney's Office, and he was willing to make room for me in the Appellate Section at Justice. That tells you something about that guy, doesn't it? He's been on the AG's shit list ever since he put me on the payroll. Anyway, I took the job and started writing briefs."

"What happened to Constance?"

"By then Bebe was three years old. Constance had been living with the angst that lots of working mothers feel, and when she quit the Hill the chance to be with Bebe all day seemed to take the edge off her resentment. But the consequences began to take their toll. Even with cutting expenses to the bone we couldn't keep the house. Psychologically, that was big. And we went from a great social life to none, which was probably for the best because we couldn't afford to go out anyway. Every meal was in our apartment. For all practical purposes, our world had shrunk to the three of us . . . Then Bebe got sick."

"You don't have to go on," she said quietly.

Fortified by the wine, it seemed that I could. "It was as if we were being punished. Constance was on tranquilizers all the time and soon she was drinking just to sleep. She'd never been religious but started going to church with me every morning to pray. Sometimes, I'd come home from work and she'd be at the church again. At first I thought that was good, but without any faith or religious training to build on . . . she went . . . crazy. She just lost her mind. She got it in her head that the wrath of God had been brought down on our family like the plagues upon Egypt. We'd lost our careers, our home, our friends, and, finally, our daughter—'our firstborn child,' she said. She blamed everyone, but mostly she blamed me. After Bebe died we were finished. In another year she was with Warren and I was spending my first stay in the hospital . . . That's about it."

"I'm so sorry," she whispered.

"I wanted to tell you."

"The way I acted when we met—I had no idea. I feel so stupid."

I rubbed my face, getting at the dampness in my eyes. "Is there more wine?"

Blair moved her chair close and put her arm around my neck as she filled our glasses. "Philip . . ."

"What?"

"If we solve this thing . . . Constance . . ."

"Yeah . . . You want to know whether I can do it."

"I . . . no." She rested her chin on my shoulder. "I'm sure you can."

That was one of us.

23

IT WAS AFTER TEN WHEN I woke up, ten-thirty by the time I showered and shaved and entered the kitchen. Through the window I could see McSorley sitting on an Adirondack chair in the backyard, reading a newspaper. "Is she up yet?" I asked.

He chuckled and said, "Up and gone. She went for a swim and then to buy some food." He shook his head and added, "She's a heckuva girl."

"Right. Exercises, plays sports, shoots people. Last night she drank me under the table."

"Well, you wouldn't want her mad at you, but you could do worse, Philip."

"How did she look this morning, by the way?"

He smiled in response. A stupid question. "There's coffee," he said. "And she said there's aspirin on the counter."

We were at the kitchen table when she came in carrying two bags of groceries. She was wearing jeans and a black tank top, and her still-wet hair was combed straight back. "Hi," she said. "Sleep well?"

"Up at five, ran ten miles, lifted some weights. What about you?"

She took a sheet of paper out of her purse and put it on the table. "Here it is: Martin Green's last words."

Harold must have decided that stationery would give the Alta Vista a touch of class. The letterhead looked like he printed it himself: off-center lettering with a clip-art image of a log cabin. McSorley and I read it together.

To my parents and friends:

> *Forgive me, not for my actions but for all the pain I have caused. I have lived in fear of the consequences, but in these final moments I am at peace knowing I have been faithful to the principles that were instilled in me through your teachings and those of my God. I came to the capital with the idea that I might have some influence, however small, on the deliberations and actions of those positioned to relieve the suffering of multitudes in our own country and around the world. I will be condemned for taking matters into my own hands, however little I achieved, but it is the duty of each of us to do what he can, for I have seen the truth with my own eyes. Thy princes are rebellious, and companions of thieves. Every one loveth gifts, and followeth after rewards. They judge not the fatherless, neither doth the cause of the widow come unto them.*

> *God's blessings upon you all.*

> *Martin*

"Interesting, isn't it?" said Blair. "We've been over it with experts."

"I don't recognize the quote," I said. "Where's it from?"

"Isaiah, 1:23."

"Isaiah!" exclaimed McSorley. "Nation shall not lift up sword against nation, neither shall they learn war any more."

"I'm impressed," said Blair.

"Well, we heard that a lot back in '45."

"What do you make of it?" she asked.

"It looks like he didn't have much use for congressmen," replied McSorley.

Blair nodded. "And your theory seems to fit. Martin might be referring to the Banking Committee. Warren could be the prince, the son of Edward the king, and the thieves could be the Swiss bankers who stole the accounts of Holocaust victims."

"Maybe," I said.

"You don't sound very happy. It's a confirmation of your theory."

"It doesn't get us any closer to finding whatever was in that envelope. Julia said that when they tried to get it out of Martin he kept quoting Scripture. I was hoping there was something to his answer they just didn't understand."

"It could've been different Scripture," said McSorley. "For all we know it was the Lord's Prayer."

"The Prophets," I said.

"What about them?"

"Isaiah was one of the Later Prophets."

"So said our biblical scholar," replied Blair. "What about it?"

"We need to take a ride."

"Where?"

"To see a rabbi."

Rabbi Adler wasn't at his office when we arrived but his secretary called him and he showed up thirty minutes later. I introduced him to Blair and McSorley. "I saw your picture in the newspaper," said the rabbi. "I didn't know what to think."

"It's a long story," I told him, "and it has to do with Martin's case."

He was suddenly angry. "I don't believe it!" he cried. "Martin was no spy! He loved this country. He loved everyone!"

"Rabbi, we're here to find the truth. You can help."

"Anything!"

"You told me that Martin borrowed some books from you on the Later Prophets."

"Yes, I told you, themes."

"Was one of the books on Isaiah?"

"Of course."

"Could we see it?"

The rabbi went to a bookshelf and began running his finger along one row. "It's here somewhere," he muttered, then shouted, "MARILYN!"

A reply at the same volume: "WHAT?"

"I CAN'T FIND A BOOK!"

A portly woman with pearls came from the outer office, her gold carpet slippers scuffing across the linoleum floor. "Did you look?" she asked, with more than a hint of exasperation in her voice.

"Everywhere!" exclaimed the rabbi, waving his arms. "The book on Isaiah."

Marilyn brushed past him and went directly to the

books on the opposite wall, snatched a volume off the shelf, and handed it to him. She marched out muttering something inaudible.

"She moves everything," grumbled the rabbi. He looked at the cover and held it up. "Isaiah," he said.

"Passage 1:23," I said.

"Ah!" he replied. "Greedy princes!" He flipped through the pages to find the passage, then stopped and frowned. "What's this?" he said. "Who put this here? Martin?" He handed me a photograph, about four by six inches, that was stuck between the pages, held by a small piece of tape. Blair and McSorley moved in close for a look. It was of a distinguished-looking man with a full beard and moustache, wearing a double-breasted suit and a fedora not unlike McSorley's. He wasn't looking at the camera, it was more of a candid shot. I turned it over. There was a date in pencil: "2/17/55."

"Who is that?" asked the rabbi.

Blair and McSorley both shook their heads. "We'll have to investigate," I said.

"Why is this picture in my book? What does this have to do with what happened to Martin?"

"Rabbi, all I can tell you now is that this may be a clue but we don't know what it means. I can promise you, though, that we're going to find out. In the meantime, I must ask you, please, tell no one about this."

"My lips are sealed!" he declared. "Just tell me one thing: Martin was a good boy? He didn't do wrong?"

Blair stepped forward and put her arm through his. "I'll tell you something in secret, just between us."

"My lips are sealed!" repeated the rabbi.

"Martin was a good boy."

We drove back to Blair's house. McSorley was in the

passenger seat and I was in the back, staring at the photograph. "What do you make of it?" he asked over his shoulder.

"Joe, this was taken by Esther Müller."

"*What?*"

"The handwriting on the back is the same as on the photo of Sonia."

"Good Lord!" cried McSorley, shaking his head. "*That's* what Esther was holding back. She helped Sonia with her claim against the bank."

"It's coming together," said Blair. "Now all we've got to figure out is, who's the guy in the picture?"

"I already know who it is."

She pulled the car abruptly to the curb; they both turned to look at me. "Who?"

"It's Edward Young."

"What the heck . . ." whispered McSorley.

"Yeah," I said. "What the heck."

We were in the living room and Blair was staring at the photograph. "If I didn't know who it was, I would never have guessed. I don't think *anyone* would have guessed, but you knew. How?"

"That's what I was wondering," said McSorley. "Once you know you can see the resemblance but it's not obvious."

"I've seen a similar picture before," I said.

"Where?"

"Where Martin saw it: in Edward Young's office."

"How do you know that?"

"Martin had been to the palace. I saw a picture of him there with Warren and Constance. He would have gone to the oval office because it's a must-see for every visitor, and there are pictures of Edward on the wall." I tapped the photograph lying on the table. "In two or three he looks like this."

"So," said McSorley, "Martin saw a picture of Edward on the wall, then recognized him when he saw this picture in the archives."

"Actually, I think Martin saw this photograph when he was researching for the Banking Committee, but he had no way of identifying the man. The letter and enclosure would have been just a curiosity. But a couple of years later he gets invited to a party at the palace and sees a similar photograph in Edward's office. Maybe he makes the connection immediately, or maybe he's just got a hunch, but he gets his old file list from Jenny Castellano and goes back to the archives for a look. Now he knows Edward is the man in the archives photo, so he steals it."

"That all fits," said McSorley.

"Then Martin asks himself how Edward figures in this thing. He wasn't Sonia's father, he would have been too young to have a teenage daughter in 1944. And he wasn't a Swiss banker."

"Why not?"

"The letter from the U.S. embassy officer indicated that he'd checked and came up empty. But, more important, with all that's been written about Young's early years living by his wits in postwar Europe, if he'd really been a banker in Zurich don't you think *someone* would have come forward by now?"

"That leaves an option," said Blair, "a *phony* Swiss banker."

"A phony Swiss banker," I agreed. "The question is, why? Martin begins to investigate. The logical starting place is the Holocaust Museum, where the records show that Sonia was interned at Auschwitz on November 14, 1944."

"That would give him a lead," said McSorley. "That would mean she was one of that last group from Budapest."

"That's when things get really interesting. Martin had heard about Eva's Diary and he goes to Simon Hirsch for the details, or maybe just confirmation. It turns out that Eva's story and Sonia's have a lot in common: two daughters, two fathers, two supposed Swiss accounts, and their families might have been rounded up at the same time."

"And the phony banker is another fit with what happened to Eva's family," said McSorley. "It would explain why they weren't rescued. It was a scam, and the so-called banker was Edward Young."

"Which raises another question," said Blair. "What if it's *the same* story?"

"Imagine what's going through Martin's mind," I said. "He's got to be nervous as hell but he's determined to find out if the stories coincide. Eva and Sonia could have been related."

"So, the next step is Naomi Singer, the other name in the letter," said McSorley. "He checks the phone book or maybe calls the Hebrew Immigrant Aid Society, and what do you know? Naomi is still alive, and he goes to New York."

"We don't know what Naomi might have told him," I said, "but the records at the Aid Society aren't any help on Sonia's relatives, although they do reveal that Sonia was from Budapest, which is another fit with Eva's story. Then he goes to the Bureau of Vital Records, which gets him to the library, where he discovers that Sonia went off a roof around the time she sent her letter to Switzerland. He was nervous *before* he went to New York, and understanding the implications of this discovery, now he's looking for someone to confide in."

"He's too loyal to Warren to go right to the Justice Department, is that it?" asked Blair.

"Yes, he doesn't want to cause a crisis if there's some possible explanation, but the thought of going directly to Warren isn't attractive either. Warren is Edward's son, and maybe he already knows, maybe he's covering up. Martin understands the danger. So, he's in a fix: how do you balance loyalty and the need to do the right thing? It's a tough call. And then he makes his first mistake."

"He goes to Constance," said Blair. "And, sooner or later, Constance goes to Edward."

"And then it's all about gathering loose ends," added McSorley.

Blair fingered the photograph, flipping it over from front to back. "This picture would have been taken in New York. Did Sonia just run into him on the street?"

"Edward was already a public figure by 1955," I said. "She could have seen his picture in the newspaper and recognized him. However it happened, she had Esther take a photograph and sent it to Switzerland with Naomi's help. That initiated a chain of events that ended with her being thrown off a roof."

McSorley grunted. "She probably got tired of waiting for help from Switzerland and took matters into her own hands. Well, it took almost fifty years, but now we know."

"I'll bet we can prove Eva and Sonia were related," said Blair.

"I think Green already did," I said. They both looked at me. "The Hungarian embassy," I explained.

"Of course . . ." said Blair. "Birth certificates."

"That's probably what Magda Takács gave him at the Portrait Gallery. It all fits. Green's investigation was research into Sonia's background. After he came up empty in New York, the Hungarians were the logical place to turn. He probably didn't want to involve third parties but he had no choice, and with his contacts, a quiet check of vital records in Budapest would have been easy to arrange."

"Would the Hungarians involve themselves in something like this?"

"Maybe not knowingly. He probably told them it was a Holocaust project for a senator and they seized an opportunity to earn a little gratitude. I'll bet they were pretty mad when they read the newspaper."

"Meaning they wouldn't be in a hurry to do the same for us."

"We don't have to worry about that right now. You can count on it: Martin proved Sonia and Eva were related, probably sisters."

"How do you know?" asked Blair.

"Because it got him killed."

Blair studied me. "You don't look like a man ready to celebrate," she said. I shrugged. She bowed her head and began running her fingers through her hair, long strokes from her forehead to the back of her neck. "We don't have a case, do we?" she asked quietly.

"No."

McSorley was stunned. "Why no case?"

"Inference upon inference upon speculation," I replied. "Even if birth certificates prove that Sonia Denes had a sister named Eva, the jury still has to infer that it's the same Eva who wrote the diary. On a gut level you make the leap but it's not a statistical probability. I'm sure there were plenty of Evas in Budapest, just as there were plenty of characters preying on the Jews. But even if they're satisfied they still have to decide that Eva got the story right—assuming the diary goes into evidence. It's all hearsay, and the contest over its reliability is going to be a hell of a battle. If we win it, *then* the jury has to decide that Edward Young was the culprit."

"Sonia thought so."

"Sonia's not around to say what she thought."

"She's not around because she was murdered."

"The police said it was a suicide. But let's say all this goes into evidence and the jury has to infer what Sonia thought. How sure was she? What if she got it wrong? She was sixteen in 1944. She picked Edward Young out eleven years later, after living through an extraordinarily traumatic experience. On one hand you've got inferences, on the other you've got Young's own account of his whereabouts in 1944. And don't be surprised if he comes up with a few witnesses."

"That doesn't explain what happened to Martin, Naomi, and Esther," said Blair.

"And what almost happened to us," added McSorley.

"The AG already has an explanation," I said. "It was an espionage ring that went way back. The Hungarians rolled it up to avoid enormous embarrassment."

"It's different now," Blair said. "Sonia isn't part of a spy ring, she's a woman with a claim and a picture of Edward Young. Put all the pieces together and the national security angle won't play anymore. People at Justice will connect the dots just like you did."

"But I made assumptions: that Martin went to Constance and dropped a bombshell, and that Constance went to Edward. But Constance isn't going to admit anything. So, subtract the assumptions and what do you have? Unless Edward knew what Martin was up to, he had no motive to kill him or anyone else. In this room it's an easy leap. In a courtroom it's a gaping hole in your case."

"The government has taken risky cases before," said Blair.

"When it's motivated," I replied. "We're dealing with an attorney general and his cronies who, more than anything else, want this case to go away. This wouldn't just be the end of Warren's career and a political dynasty, it'll probably determine the election. Blair, I know how these people think. They're desperate, and it won't be hard to justify what they want to do."

Blair wanted to argue. "A good interrogator could get to Constance. She's got to explain Green's calls to her house. And we can place both of them near the Waldorf at the same time. How will she explain it?"

"Here's a scenario off the top of my head. Constance claims that Martin brought her a photograph and a story, and demanded something in exchange for his silence. Maybe he was acting at the behest of his Hungarian controllers, who want to seize the opportunity to get leverage on the next president. But when Constance goes to Edward he tells her the story is a fantasy. She goes back to Martin and says no deal, and furthermore, she's going to expose him and his scheme. Martin takes off, pursued by the FBI, and becomes a threat to his own people. The rest of it is the story they've already adopted: the Hungarians run for cover and cut all the connections."

"I think it's a stretch," said Blair.

"*Of course* it's a stretch. Why would the Hungarians kill old network members like Naomi and Esther? But what does it matter? Even if the AG doesn't go in the tank, the fact remains that there's a big difference between connecting dots and proving a case. You go nowhere without a confession from Constance. And let's not forget that Edward has proven very adept at dealing with potential threats."

McSorley looked grim; Blair's expression was blank. "Look," I said, "don't get me wrong, logic is on our side. A third of the people will believe us, a third will believe it's about spies, and another third will believe it's all some elaborate hoax to discredit Warren Young. But this isn't about belief, it's about *proof*. Knowing something and proving it are two different things. The same policy that applied to indicting Martin applies to indicting Edward Young: the case won't be brought unless there is evidence to carry the burden of proof."

"The Hungarians could help," said Blair. "They could prove Martin was after birth certificates."

"Their version would be seen as self-serving. The only thing they could count on is an accusation that they were meddling in presidential politics—that and pissing off an entire political party, the current administration, and maybe the next one. Trust me, they'll sit this one out. That's probably why Magda Takács was yanked out of Washington."

"Well, it might be worth a try," McSorley grumbled.

"Joe, Hungarians aside, this thing would go on forever. It'll take two years to convince Justice to prosecute."

"Young could be dead before he ever saw a courtroom," he replied.

"He'll die cloaked in the presumption of innocence," I said.

"Amen," said McSorley. "There's one thing I don't understand. If our theory is right, why didn't Edward take the problem photographs off his wall? If they link him to Sonia's claim, you'd think he'd get rid of them as soon as he was tipped off by Constance, but they were still on display when you went to the house."

"I don't know," I replied. "That's the thing with this case: every time you come up with an answer, it raises another question."

"My father took me to a concentration camp," said Blair suddenly. Her voice was flat, barely a murmur. "It was our second tour in Germany. I was fifteen years old and getting tougher to handle every day. I wanted to go back to Georgia to be with my friends. I told him the army had no business in Germany or any country but our own."

"I'll bet that made him happy."

She shook her head. "Maybe he should have seen my rebellion for what it was, but he decided that it was time I'd gotten a taste of the real world. To this day, I can't hear the phrase 'gates of hell' without thinking of Dachau."

"I never saw a concentration camp," said McSorley, "but when I was shipping home I met some guys from a unit that stumbled across one. They said that they'd never forget it."

Blair pounded the table in frustration. "Well, we did

it! Poor Martin's murder is solved. And Esther's murder. And Naomi's. And let's not forget Sonia, right? What do you think, Joe? Did the senator's daddy throw her off the roof, or did he use hired help?"

The question was never answered. We spent the evening making small talk, slowly, collectively, coming to terms with reality. The alcohol seemed to help. Things were pretty mellow by the time our senior investigator decided to call it a night.

"Well, here we are again," said Blair.

"This case is tough on the liver," I said.

"There's one avenue left. We could still do this."

"I know."

"You can do this, Philip. I know you can."

"Pour me another glass."

24

CONSTANCE DIDN'T NOTICE WHEN I approached and sat on the bench. She was on her knees with a garden spade, immersed in the task of making a hole for a planting. The look on her face was pure contentment as she sang quietly to herself. It took a moment to pick up the tune.

Skinna-ma-rink-a-dinka-dink, skinna-ma-rink-a-doo, I . . . love . . . you . . .

Bebe's favorite song. The one her mother used to sing to her at bedtime. The one I sang in the hospital. Near the end, I carried her around the room, singing that song.

I love you in the morning and in the afternoon . . .

And Bebe would open her eyes and smile, barely moving her lips to form the words. I was singing it when her eyes closed for the last time, and somehow I got it in my head that she couldn't die if we were singing her song, so I kept walking around the room in circles, carrying her and singing.

I love you in the evening, and underneath the moon . . .

The nurses tried to get me to put her down. They appealed to Constance but she was shriveled in a corner, glassy-eyed with exhaustion and pills. Then the doctor was there, and they were all talking to me, soothing me, touching me. Philip. Please, Philip, let her go.

So, skinna-ma-rink-a-dinka-dink, skinna-ma-rink-a-doo . . .

"Philip!"

"What?"

"Didn't you hear me? What are you doing here? It's only ten-thirty."

"It's beautiful, Constance. You've made it very beautiful."

"I thought you were leaving the city. Did you stay for her birthday?"

"I wouldn't miss her birthday."

"You're supposed to come in the afternoon."

"I've come to see you, Constance."

"To say good-bye?" She turned back to her task now.

"No, I came to talk about Martin."

She kept digging. "Martin?" she asked absently.

"It's time to answer for Martin, Constance."

Her head turned slowly until our eyes met. "I have no idea what you're talking about," she said evenly.

"I know what happened, the whole story."

"There's nothing to know. Martin was spying and now he's gone, dead and buried."

"Yes, he is. You left the funeral after the service but you really should have gone to the cemetery. You would have seen the look on his mother's face as we shoveled dirt on her son. Age doesn't matter when you bury your own child, did you know that? She looked just like you."

"Get out of here!" she cried.

"He's in his grave, just like Bebe."

The expression on her face changed to pure rage. "Don't you dare . . . Don't . . . you . . . *dare.*"

"You have to answer for Martin."

"I don't have to answer for anyone! You son of a bitch! You've done *everything* you can to destroy our chance to be president!" She began gathering up her garden tools.

I got off the bench and knelt next to her. "Martin wasn't sure what to do with what he'd discovered, but he trusted you. He went to you first."

"Go to hell!"

"He showed you the photograph, didn't he? He told you what it might mean. He told you what he planned to do."

"You're insane. They *never* should've released you."

"You met in New York. He explained about Naomi Singer and what happened to Sonia Denes. Had you already informed your father-in-law? Were you acting under instructions?"

"*That's it!* I'm leaving." She started to get up but I seized her wrist. "Let go of me, Philip!" She grabbed a pair of pruning shears from her basket and drew back her hand. "Let go of me," she snarled, "or I swear, *I'll kill you!*"

"Right here? In front of Bebe?"

She stared, petrified. I twisted the shears out of her hand and pulled her toward the headstone. "Tell Bebe what you did," I said.

"*Let me go!*" she screamed.

"*Tell her!*" I wrapped my arms around her and pressed her hands against the headstone. "Tell her how you murdered Martin! Tell her about those women who died because of you."

She struggled to free herself. "*You're crazy! Let me go!*"

"Bebe is watching you, Constance. She knows what you did."

She began to shake; tears streamed down her face. Then she groaned and canted forward, touching her forehead to the marble. I leaned with her, putting my lips to her ear. "Tell her, Constance," I said softly. "You can't lie to Bebe."

Her body convulsed with sobs. "I . . . I didn't . . . hurt anyone." She gasped. "I didn't want anyone to be hurt."

"Tell her, Constance. You talked to Edward."

"My baby," she whimpered.

"Tell her."

"She's gone, Philip, our baby's gone . . ."

"I know."

"We're going to see her again. You promised we'd see her again."

"We'll see her again, I promise." She pressed her lips to the headstone and sobbed. I waited another moment. "You talked to Edward," I whispered.

She gulped a deep breath, then another. "He told me it was a lie . . . a plot to get at Warren."

"When?"

"Oh, God . . ."

"*When?*"

"After New York."

"Is that when Martin told you what he found, when you met in New York?"

"He told me about a letter and Edward's picture . . .

and about a girl's diary, a story about a man who posed as a banker and stole money in Budapest. He said that Edward might be the man in the diary."

"What else?"

"He wanted the truth but he didn't want to hurt Warren. He asked if Warren might already know."

"What did you say?"

"*Oh, Philip . . .* "

"What did you say?"

"That I'd never heard such a story and I didn't believe it. He said that he thought he had a way to find out."

"Go on."

"Then he asked me not to say anything. He promised that if Edward was the man in the diary he'd let me be the one to tell Warren."

"And then you went to Edward." She bit her lip; her eyes were shut tight. "Say it: you went to see Edward."

"I couldn't wait! If it wasn't true I had to stop him before he went any further. He could start rumors that would destroy Warren's chances."

"You told Edward about Martin."

She groaned. "I told him."

"What did he say?"

"Ohhh . . . *God forgive me!*"

"What did he say? *Tell me.*"

"He laughed . . . Oh, Philip, he *laughed*! He said the whole thing was preposterous, a mistake or a plot to get at Warren. He said he spent the entire war in France and had never been to Hungary in his life. And then he said he'd look into it personally."

"And you believed him?"

She turned to look at me, wide-eyed. "I wanted to."

"Tell me what happened after New York."

"Martin called again. He wanted to talk but I didn't want to hear any more, I was . . . afraid to hear any more. I said that I was sure Edward had nothing to do with Hungary. He asked me how I knew. I said I just knew. Then he asked if I had spoken to Edward."

"What did you say?"

"I . . . I told him the truth. He became very upset. I told him . . ." Her face contorted in anguish. "Oh . . . Philip!"

"Told him what?"

"That he had nothing to worry about. It wasn't true, I was sure of it. After that, he avoided me. He was so upset. I tried to talk to him but he wouldn't speak to me. I began to wonder if there wasn't more to the story, something I hadn't been told."

"But you spoke to him the night before he disappeared, when he called your house."

She looked away, avoiding my eyes. "He was afraid. He thought he was being followed. He asked if I knew what was happening and I said no. I asked what he was going to do and he said that he had no idea. I told him, go to the police, but he wasn't listening. He said that no one would believe him."

"Go on."

"Afterward, when I heard the spy story, it all seemed to make sense. I thought that Edward was right, that Martin was involved in some kind of preposterous scheme."

"You lied to me when you came to my apartment. You said he admitted spying."

"I believed he was a spy. I wanted to believe it . . . I just wanted to protect Warren." She turned toward me again. "He's innocent, Philip!" she cried, her eyes imploring me to believe her. "He had nothing to do with this! I swear to God, *I swear on Bebe's grave,* he doesn't know anything about what Edward did."

"So, you've changed your mind about Edward." She pulled her hand free and clamped it over her mouth. I pulled it away again. "Say it!" I demanded.

"The photographs are gone. He took them down."

"The ones of him in his office," I said. Suddenly it was clear why Edward didn't take them down right away. He was bluffing Constance until he was sure they weren't going to recover the photograph that Martin had. If it was out there waiting to be found, the matching ones on Edward's wall had to disappear.

"He knows that I know, Philip. We don't talk about it, but *he knows.*"

"He's sure about you, Constance. He's sure you won't say anything."

"Ohhh," she moaned. She began to curl up, growing smaller in my arms, as if her misery was consuming her. "He killed all those people and he's sure about me."

"That's right."

I let her go and she sank against the headstone. "What's going to happen?" she whimpered.

I got up and brushed myself off. "Warren can't become president. You understand that, don't you? Edward's dream can't come true. I won't allow it."

She nodded dully. "Those poor people."

"That's right, all those people. Warren is standing on their bones. It doesn't matter what he knew or didn't know."

"Poor Warren will be ruined."

"Not if you do what I say."

"But Edward—"

"I'll deal with Edward. You're going to arrange a

meeting between us. Tell any lies you have to, but you're going to get me through the gates tomorrow and into the house. I'll call you tonight at eight o'clock. You be sure to answer the phone."

"Edward is dangerous, Philip. You have to be careful!"

"Just do what I say. Later on, when the time is right, you and Warren and I are going to have our own meeting, just the three of us. Meanwhile, you have to behave as if nothing has happened. Do you understand?" She nodded and I turned to go.

"Philip," she called.

"What?"

She was still on the ground, leaning against the tombstone for support. "I just wanted to protect Warren. I never meant to hurt anyone."

I walked down the path to the paved road used by visitors and hearses. Blair and McSorley were waiting in the car. Neither one of them said anything when I got into the backseat. My eyes met Blair's in the rearview mirror. Hers were still damp. I removed the transmitter from my jacket and unclipped the microphone. "Did you get it all?" I asked.

"It cut off after she asked you what happens now."

"I shut it off. It was just personal stuff."

"Let's go some place and talk," Blair said, starting the car.

McSorley turned and said, "I'm sorry, Philip. It's sad."

"Yeah," I said, "the whole thing is sad."

The Old Angler's Inn is an out-of-the-way Maryland spot favored by the affluent Potomac crowd and guys with engagement rings. It sits alongside the C&O canal about nine miles northwest of the city, far enough away to clear our heads and escape the melancholy of the scene at the cemetery. It was lunchtime and the weather still favored the outdoor tables.

"Well, we helped our case," said McSorley.

Blair agreed. "We can prove Edward Young knew about Martin and that he took the photographs off the wall—a stupid move, by the way. Why take them down now? We can certainly prove Esther's photograph is of him."

"Loose ends," I said. "He'd launched a scorched-earth campaign to sever all connections between him and his past—everything. The pictures were a constant reminder. They made him feel vulnerable so he got rid of them. Suspects always do stupid things. Being rich and powerful doesn't make him an exception."

"It proves guilty conscience," said Blair.

"It helps," I agreed, "but remember, he denied everything. He said it was a plot to get at him and Warren. That will be consistent with his defense. If he'd admitted his guilt, even partially, we'd be a lot better off. As it is, it's going to be a real contest."

"What kind of witness will Constance make?" asked Blair.

"Assuming she makes it to trial without having a breakdown? Who can say? She can't nail Edward without ruining Warren, too. She was contrite today, but time and massaging by Edward's lawyers could work wonders."

"We've still got the tape."

"It's going to be of limited use. The rules of evidence

in this area are complicated, but the bottom line is that she's going to have to take the stand and testify. We can use the tape to cross-examine her if she deviates from what she told me, but, like I said, the chances of her making it through this process emotionally intact aren't great."

McSorley squinted at me. "You know, I don't remember it being this hard. We'd arrest a guy, put all the witnesses on the stand, and most of the time the jury sorted things out pretty good."

"There's a difference," I said.

"What difference?"

"The difference between having the best shyster two hundred bucks can buy and having the premier legal talent in the country—and a public relations machine to boot. This isn't the postwar Bronx, Joe. This is modern Washington. We've lived through Watergate, Whitewater, and impeachment. It's not about right and wrong anymore. It's about staying on message and style points. The trial of Edward Young will be a prolonged affair that can go either way."

"I'm starting to feel just a little frustrated," Blair said.

"It's not over yet," I replied. "Constance is going to get me a meeting with Edward Young tomorrow."

They both looked at me in shock. "How?" asked Blair.

"She'll find a way, don't worry."

"What are you going to do if you see him?"

"Try to get him to incriminate himself while you record the conversation."

"He's too smart."

"Maybe, but I've got the advantage of surprise. If it

doesn't work, our case is no worse off than before. But if
it does, it can put us over the top."

"Oh boy," said McSorley, shaking his head. "Tomorrow's the end of the line."

Blair was eyeing me suspiciously. I slid my glass
across the table until it clinked against hers.

"What are we drinking to?" she asked.

"The law of gravity."

"I was expecting someone from the Justice Department.
It was supposed to be a briefing."

Edward Young looked extraordinarily calm, like a
man who's got all the bases covered. The witnesses were
dead. The links were severed. There were even new photographs on the wall: Warren taking his Senate oath; Edward and Warren flanking the president. For forty years
he'd wielded extraordinary influence and managed to
leave no footprints, only a trail of myths and rumors. He
was the silhouette behind the tinted window of a passing
limousine, the muffled voice behind closed doors. He
didn't just know what was worth knowing, he defined it.

Knowledge, indeed, was power, and at that moment I
knew him. Armed with that knowledge, facing him
across his own desk, in his own palace, filled me with a
sensation I hadn't felt in years, as if struggling to the surface after a near drowning. My eyes were clear. My lungs
were full.

"It's best if I conduct this briefing. There's been a lot
of developments."

He blinked. It wasn't my words as much as my tone.
The first indication that something was amiss. "It is my
understanding that you are no longer on the case," he

said. "You're not even with the Justice Department any-more."

"That's right, I'm not." I removed the microphone and transmitter from my jacket and laid them on his desk.

"You were going to record our conversation?" he asked, incredulous.

"That was the plan," I said.

He sneered. "I can't even imagine why you'd try such a stunt. Does Hewlett know about this?"

"No."

"I don't understand any of this but I am *not* amused. The attorney general won't be amused, either, I'll make sure of that." He stared at me, waiting, not about to end the conversation. He wanted to probe. How much did I know? Pointing at the microphone, he asked, "Why did you reveal it to me?"

"It'd be better if this conversation weren't recorded."

"Better for *you*," he said.

"You're right, better for me."

"What kind of game are you playing, Mr. Barkley?" The corners of his slit of a mouth morphed into a sneer. "Are you having another breakdown of some kind?"

"No, I'm fine. Actually, I haven't felt this good in years."

"You're wasting my time. State your report and leave." He reached for his water glass and began to drink.

"All right. This is what we've learned. If it's not ex-actly accurate, it's close. You were in Budapest in 1944 when the Nazis occupied Hungary. You posed as an agent of a Zurich bank fronting for Nazi officials willing to be bribed to let Jews out of the country. You stole a fortune from desperate families trying to escape extermination and left them to their fate. One of those families was named Denes. It had two daughters, Eva and Sonia. They were all shipped off to Auschwitz. Only Sonia survived."

"You *are* having a relapse."

"That plunder was your seed money. Maybe you invested it in the black market or maybe you didn't, but that was your start. Then you came here and multiplied your fortune."

"Pure fantasy."

"You went undetected until 1955, when Sonia saw you or your picture somewhere and recognized you, not surprising, since your image was probably burned into her brain. Imagine how she felt: the banker who betrayed her family, leaving them to unspeakable horror."

"This is beyond preposterous."

"Sonia wasn't sophisticated. She still believed her family's money went to Zurich and that she was just another victim of Swiss intransigence. She didn't realize that you weren't a banker, just a parasite."

"This is insulting. No one could believe this."

"Now you were rich and powerful, and with a different name. She was an unsophisticated refugee without resources. The prospect of the police or the courts probably never entered her mind. All she wanted to do was pursue her claim. So, she had you photographed and tried to use your picture for corroboration: 'Here is the banker that took our money.' It was pitiful, of course. Desperate, she finally confronted you, and became a threat in a way she couldn't appreciate. So, you murdered her and made it look like just another Hungarian suicide."

"Do you think I'm going to listen to any more of this?"

"Of course you will. If I stop now you won't hear all the evidence. But go ahead, say the word and I'll leave." I stared at him and waited.

He had no option. He shook his head slowly and said, "If I have to prove my innocence I might as well hear it all."

"Decades pass by and you continued to prosper. Then Martin Green found a file with a letter to Sonia from the U.S. embassy in Bern. There was a photograph enclosed. A conscientious officer had gone so far as to show the picture around. Of course, the banks didn't recognize you, but Green did. He'd seen the contemporaneous photographs that used to hang over there. By the way, what did you do with them?"

He smiled and half-turned in his chair toward the wall. "The old makes way for the new. I'm creating my own album of Warren's ascent to the presidency. The son of a refugee is going to be president."

"I wouldn't count on the Jewish vote."

"No one is going to take this seriously. A man fresh out of a mental institution, obsessed with revenge on his ex-wife and her new husband. You're pitiful, Mr. Barkley, more than this Sonia woman. The people who matter dismissed you long ago. You were fortunate to find any job in Washington, and now the attorney general has kicked you out."

"While we're on the subject of my ex-wife, do you want to hear the end of the story?"

"Is it as fantastic as the beginning?"

"Sonia's file was slim but it implied a story, and Martin already knew one just like it. It's in the diary of a girl named Eva who died in the Holocaust. He began to investigate the similarities and when the stories began to dovetail, he was in turmoil. His religious identity ran deep but so did his loyalty to Warren. In his emotional state he made a fatal mistake: he went to Constance. He admired her. He thought she might shed some light, give him some guidance. He promised that if his hunch was right he'd let her tell Warren first. Unfortunately for him, Martin thought he was talking to the old Constance. He didn't understand how she'd changed. She came directly to you and sealed his fate."

He waved a hand in disgust. "This is foolishness. Now you're engaging in pure speculation."

"No, I'm not."

"Of course you are. You didn't get this from Green."

I leaned forward. "No, I didn't get it from Green."

A second passed. His eyes widened and he swallowed hard. "No," he croaked.

"Yes." I took a small dictation machine out of my pocket and pressed the Play button.

"The photographs are gone . . . He took them down."

"The ones of him in his office."

"He knows that I know, Philip. We don't talk about it, but he knows."

"He's sure about you, Constance. He's sure you won't say anything."

"He killed all those people and he's sure about me."

"I wouldn't plan on killing her," I said. "It won't do you any good, and Warren will be very upset."

"That proves nothing. I told her the same thing I told you. It's a fantasy. You have no case against me. No evidence. The attorney general will throw you out."

"Don't be stupid. Evidence is for courts. So is the attorney general."

A full minute passed. It had been so long since Edward Young had felt any fear that he needed to reacquaint himself with the sensation that was plain on his face. He was trembling. He tried to grasp his water glass but his hand was beyond his command. He was close to keeling over. "Not a court case," he mumbled.

"That's right."

"What are you going to do?"

"I'm going to ask you a question. What do you think will happen to you if I go public with this story? More important, what will happen to Warren's chances to be president?"

An involuntary gurgling sound emitted from his throat.

"I didn't hear you."

"Wha . . . what do you want?" he sputtered.

"I'm not a mean-spirited man. I'm going to give you an opportunity—just one—to avoid the destruction of everything you've worked for, including Warren's chance to be president. You just have to do one thing." I removed a book from my breast pocket.

"What is that?" he asked, pointing.

"It's a book of Scripture." I turned to the page I marked. "I want to read you a passage, so listen closely. 'Three score and ten years are the life span of a man. Four score if he is strong.' "

He shook his head. "I don't understand."

"How old are you?"

"Eighty-five."

"You're overdue."

"What?"

"You . . . are . . . overdue."

His mouth opened. "Over . . ."

"You have until Monday. *Monday,* you understand?"

"Monday."

"That's right."

"My . . . God," he whispered.

"You have no God. But if there's a hell, there surely will be a place for you. I suggest you swallow a bottle of sleeping pills, climb into a warm bath, and open your wrists with a razor blade. Now, what's the deadline?"

He blinked.

"Answer me. What's the deadline?"

"Monday."

"That's right. You can die this weekend your way, or afterward, my way."

"How can I be sure you'll keep your word?"

"You can't. That's the nature of betrayal."

"Something went wrong with the transmitter!" cried Blair as I got into the car. "I didn't pick anything up!"

"Maybe I bumped the button."

"Oh, shit! What happened?"

"It doesn't matter, he denied everything. Let's go."

She banged the wheel with her fist. "*Dammit!*"

"I couldn't budge him."

She started the car and headed down the driveway toward the main gate. "We're going to have to go with what we've got, Philip."

"I guess so."

"Even if we don't convince anyone at Justice, the story can always leak."

"I thought you didn't like leaks."

"Shit happens."

"All right, but let's wait 'til Monday. I'd like to think about it until then."

"What's going to happen between now and Monday?"

"You never know. Maybe divine intervention."

25

THE ATTORNEY GENERAL AND HIS entourage were already waiting in Senator Young's conference room when I entered with Blair and McSorley. Sanders was there, too, and although he was surprised to see me, he just lowered his eyes and kept his mouth shut. It was The Blade, of course, who leaped from his chair to confront us.

"What the *hell* are you doing here?" he squawked, practically vibrating with rage.

"We're here as guests of Senator Young," I replied, brushing past him.

He grabbed my arm. "*Bullshit!*" he snarled, his red face inches from mine.

"There's something you need to do," I said calmly, still looking toward the table. Everyone was watching.

"What?"

I turned my head and spoke quietly into his ear. "You need to sit down, shut up, and insert your nose back in your boss's ass." Behind him, Blair covered her mouth to muffle her laughter.

The Blade hadn't recovered when Senator and Mrs.

Young entered the room from another door. Ignoring the deputy attorney general, Warren walked right up to me and seized my hand. "Thank you for coming, Philip," he said. He looked at Blair and McSorley and added, "Thank you, all. I'm in your debt. Come, please, sit down." We moved to the table and left The Blade standing in the doorway.

I took a chair across from Constance. She smiled at me the way she did years before, when we first met in another Senate conference room to haggle over some issue or another. It meant that Warren was prepared; everything would go according to the plan we agreed on two days before. Warren was truly stunned by the revelations about his father. He didn't put up a fight about the presidency. He was practically grateful to be allowed to remain a senator.

"First," Warren began, "I want to thank you all for coming in here on a Saturday. I know it's inconvenient but I have some news that I will make public on Monday and the people in this room should hear it first." He paused, gathered himself, and continued. "Three days ago, I buried my father. To many, he was a great man, a rags-to-riches story on a grand scale. I grew up believing that story, and did until a week ago."

No one moved. The AG's face had turned to stone. That introduction was enough to convey the import of what Warren was about to say.

"For reasons that will become plain, a week ago my father made a confession. I have no doubt that what he revealed will be as stunning and incomprehensible to you as it was to me. There is no easy way to begin. I'll just relate it as it happened."

Warren began in Hungary. He told it just as I explained it to him, as it would be told from Edward's point of view. At appropriate times Constance filled in her part, relating her interaction with Green and Edward, and her growing suspicion that Martin's story might be true. As told, the removal of the pictures from Edward's wall brought the matter to a head. Constance went to Warren, whom she had tried to shield from reckless assaults on his father's reputation, and told him everything that Martin had confided in her. Warren was shocked, disbelieving, but even the slightest chance that his father could have committed such monstrous crimes was reason enough to act. There was a confrontation at the palace. At first, Edward denied everything, but Warren persisted and eventually wore the old man down. Edward confessed, then pleaded with his son to keep his secret, if only to save Warren's own career. But the son refused and gave his father an ultimatum: confess his crimes to the attorney general or Warren would have no choice but to reveal them himself. Edward begged for time to make a decision, and finally decided to take his own life. Apparently, he intended to give Warren the option of concealing the truth, and in so doing, moving on with his campaign.

"For me, that is no option at all," Warren explained. "I cannot live with my father's sins sealed inside me. It would be as a cancer ravaging my very soul. Neither can I pursue his dream—our shared dream—of the presidency. I have enjoyed the fruits of the proverbial poisonous tree, and my own ignorance doesn't cleanse the taint. I cannot in good conscience aspire to higher office, instead I must rededicate myself to using my current position to make amends . . . well, *not* to make amends, because nothing within the power of any mortal could possibly compensate for my father's crimes, but to mitigate, as best I can, the harm that's been done. I will dedicate my position, my wealth, my influence, and every fiber of my being to that endeavor."

The room was dead quiet as people tried to cope with what they'd just heard. Constance reached over, took Warren's hand, and nodded encouragement. His voice trembled slightly when he said, "I also want to profess my profound sorrow over the loss of life. I didn't know any of the victims except Martin Green, a dedicated public servant and a decent, moral, wonderful man. I cannot restore his life. I will, however, restore his reputation, and do all I can to comfort his family and many friends, as well as the loved ones of all the other victims."

Warren moved around behind Blair, McSorley, and me. "Finally, I want to express my deepest gratitude to three incredible people whose lives, like Martin's, are a tribute to public service and the ideal of justice. I won't rest until their positions are restored and their reputations are burnished to their former glow."

———————————————

Afterward, we left the Capitol and for no particular reason decided to take a stroll on the Mall. The sun was shining, the air smelled clean, and the monuments and memorials seemed downright inspirational. "Washington is a heckuva place," said McSorley.

"A heckuva place," I agreed.

"You know, that was a pretty impressive speech by the senator. If Martin hadn't found Sonia's file, Warren might've been the next president."

"He probably would."

"I was just thinking," said Blair, "it's too bad the transmitter malfunctioned when you met with Edward. I would have loved to have heard that conversation."

"Me, too," said McSorley. "It must have been pretty interesting."

She'd figured it out; they both had. Are some betrayals justifiable? The answer was in a philosophy book somewhere. Someday, I just might look it up.

"I'll live with it," I said.

"And I'll help you," said Blair, slipping her arm through mine.

I glanced at McSorley. He was smiling.

The man was relentless.

EPILOGUE

Reagan National Airport:
The End of the Investigation

THE ANNOUNCEMENT OF THE FLIGHT to Phoenix broke the silence. "I gotta go now or miss my ride," said McSorley. "I sure as heck wish I had the DeSoto."

"It's waiting in your carport," said Blair, "courtesy of the FBI."

McSorley chuckled. "I hope they gassed it up."

"You could live here, you know. There's plenty to do."

He smiled. "You know what I realized? There's plenty to do pretty much everywhere you look. It's all in your state of mind. For a while I forgot that, but now I think I'm ready to take advantage of all those things to do around Phoenix. And this year I'm going to take the DeSoto to the Grand Canyon!"

She stepped forward and wrapped her arms around his neck, hugging him tight and burying her face in his collar. "This isn't good-bye, right?" she mumbled.

"Nah, you're gonna visit when the weather gets cold and we'll sit around and swap cop stories."

She wiped one of her tears off of his lapel and straightened his tie. "Should I bring anyone along?"

"Nope. I'm going to keep you to myself." He turned to me and stuck out his hand. "You can't hug me," he said, grinning. "In my day, guys didn't hug."

All I wanted to do was hug him; I was finding it hard to speak. I grabbed his hand with both of mine and pumped it while I fumbled for the right words. "Case closed," I finally blurted. "Case closed."

"Divine intervention," said Blair.

He looked at me for a moment, then put his hand on my cheek, just as my father had done so many years before, and suddenly it seemed as if all the silos were back where they belonged. "It was never a case," he said softly, then walked through the door and into the ramp.

We started to leave but Blair stopped and gave me a questioning look. I ran back. He was already at the far end, about to step into the plane.

"*What was it?*" I called.

He turned and looked back across the span, and at that moment it was as if the ramp were a bridge to another place, another era. To a *clarity* that we had somehow misplaced.

Then he answered.

"It was a quest."

ACKNOWLEDGMENTS

I am grateful to a number of people who provided information for the creation of this story. Background on the Hebrew Immigrant Aid Society was furnished by its director of overseas operations, Mark Hetfield. Archivist Gunnar Berg gave me a tour of the YIVO Institute for Jewish Research as well as facts about postwar immigration of European Jews to the United States. Doctors Melinda Gardner and Walter Goo provided information about the symptoms and treatment of psychological disorders. Archivist David Pfeiffer explained the procedures of the National Archives. My great-uncle Jules Sachson retired assistant chief of the New York Police Department and a legendary cop, educated me on certain police record-keeping procedures from the 1950s. Any errors relating to these matters are mine alone.

I have become ever more beholden to the wonderful group at HarperCollins. Carolyn Marino, my editor, helped shape the structure for this story, then provided guidance and insight as it progressed. All of her authors are lucky and know it. I have also benefited from the extraordinary support of a first-rate production team, and smart and tireless marketing and sales people who ai determined that my stories reach as wide an audience possible. In that regard, I also wish to thank publici Rosemarie Morse for all her efforts.

Once again, thanks to my agents, Peter Lampack an Loren Soeiro, for their wise counsel and encouragemen And my dear friends Pat Joinnides and Rubee Scrivan gluttons for punishment, have continued in their value role as my manuscript readers.

I am also indebted to many other people, family an friends, who have been generous in their encouragemei and support in a variety of ways. Among them are m sister, Robin Horn; in-laws Steve and Jane Motosko, Jc and Patti Corcoran, and Joan Doughty; and friends Bi and Mindi Gardner, Pat and Tom Eslinger, and Tin McGill of Mystery Books in Washington.

Last, but always first, there is the family I adore. M wife, Kerry, continues in her multitude of roles: sound ing board, local publicist, tireless promoter, and rea time editor, guiding my efforts with "uh-huhs" an "ughs," sometimes as the sentences materialize on th screen. And my children, Caitlin and Ben, provide wh every writer needs in ample doses: inspiration, perspe tive, the humility that comes with being the frequent ta get of family humor, and lots of affection to smooth o the rough spots.

From the *New York Times* bestselling author

STEPHEN HORN

comes a riveting novel of secrets, high crimes,
and treachery in the ruthless pursuit of power

LAW OF GRAVITY

"A first-rate thriller . . . [with] a power
that transcends the genre."
Washington Post Book World

"A complex tale of betrayal . . . *Law of Gravity*
opens the throttle on surprises."
Chicago Tribune

"Memorable characters, a wonderfully
labyrinthine plot, and a genuinely
surprising ending."
Booklist (*Starred Review*)

0-06-109876-0/$7.50 US/$9.99 Can.

And don't miss Stephen Horn's first
New York Times bestseller

IN HER DEFENSE

"Great fun, a legal thriller with real surprises."
Phillip Margolin

0-06-109875-2/$6.99 US/$9.99 Can.